IRON
ANGELS

BAEN BOOKS by ERIC FLINT

IRON ANGELS

ERIC FLINT &
ALISTAIR KIMBLE

A Baen Books Original

Baen Publishing Enterprises
P.O. Box 1403
Riverdale, NY 10471
www.baen.com

ISBN: 978-1-4814-8256-1

Cover art by Adam Burn

First printing, September 2017

Distributed by Simon & Schuster
1230 Avenue of the Americas
New York, NY 10020

Library of Congress Cataloging-in-Publication Data

Names: Flint, Eric, author. | Kimble, Alistair, author.
Title: Iron angels / Eric Flint and Alistair Kimble.
Description: New York, NY : Baen, [2017]
Identifiers: LCCN 2017023383 | ISBN 9781481482561 (hardcover)
Subjects: LCSH: Government investigators—Fiction. | Cults—Fiction. |
    Paranormal fiction. | BISAC: FICTION / Fantasy / Urban Life. | FICTION /
    Fantasy / Contemporary. | FICTION / Fantasy / General. | GSAFD: Suspense
    fiction. | Mystery fiction. | Fantasy fiction. | Occult fiction.
Classification: LCC PS3556.L548 I76 2017 | DDC 813/.54—dc23 LC record
available at https://lccn.loc.gov/2017023383

10 9 8 7 6 5 4 3 2 1

Pages by Joy Freeman (www.pagesbyjoy.com)
Printed in the United States of America

To Tara and Lucille

SAMYAZA WAS NOT OBLIVIOUS TO THE SWELLING CINCTURE. NO one of his nature could be, not even one who had been shrouded with a name in the hell world. But for the moment, he ignored the danger. The bordure was distant; the marges and purls of the bloating monstrosity still only cirrose. Long before the sprues could lay down their strakes and begin gyving the Nephilim within their reach, he would have phaged again. When he returned, his armature and plexus would blazon. His selve would spume; his labrum, coil into a fearsome torse.

The sprues would flichter away, searching for Nephilim without name or gender. Weak ones, unlike he.

For Samyaza was the greatest and mightiest of them all. Only Armaros neared him in size—but his irresolution made him mascle. Armaros was a mere tressure, almost beneath notice. His luster was vitreous and gyrose where Samyaza's was fusil and true.

Finally, Samyaza spotted what he had been seeking. A raddling fess that indicated a flue forming in the orle. He swept toward it, his filigree extending and his sensilla straining to detect the apertures in the weave.

The moment, now, yes! He swept through the mesh, lacing the perils with the ease of experience.

Armaros bided while the passagers grabbled the courses and flues of the orleweave. They could not be rushed, being barely more than branchers—and haggards all, of course. There was no chance of harnessing them until they were gendered and named by lorraine heralds in the hell world.

In the distance—great distance; care had to be taken—he averred Samyaza luffing the flues of passage. Envy swelled; roiled; rankled. The slive had grown monstrously great, purpure-swollen

1

and mighty. Yet so dull a sensorium! Duller, it seemed, with each maunch and lappet.

But there was no chance of reducing the pheon now. Not while he was alert and gule-braced. So Armaros returned to his creance.

For an instant, as Samyaza made the passage into the hell world, he was almost overwhelmed by the gule beyond. So much! So much! Enough power here to challenge the cincture itself and drive back its bourns, could he engulf the moictier—or even a tell fractus.

But there was risk also, greater than the dangers of the traverse between the worlds. So great was the gule, and so much of it threaded, sutured or even foamed. The cacophony was half-maddening; if he lost clear sense of the verges, he could easily lose his way—perhaps never to find the skein of return.

And there was worse still. In places—here, there, it was hard to detect surely; the sensorium beset by treachery on all sides—the gule was laced with impurities. All of those deborted estates were a source of flurry and confusion; and some were deadly. Sable and argent both.

Samyaza extended his estoile, searching for the alleluia. Difficult, so difficult! The lorraines dwelt in the most roiling guleries, for reasons unknown. There chaos, there confusion—there peril and plight. But with the tumult came the great savors also. The most purpure gule, the most increscent fleurs. Naiant and hauriant; dulia in full measure.

He sensed the heralds. Weak, their clarions, but still certain. Again, the risk had justified itself. Where there were lorraine heralds, there was sure to be the purest and most potent gule as well. Untainted; unmixed; tierce-ready; immortal-rich.

He swept down, ready—but! The heralds flared! The oblation...
Gone.
Where?
He searched, probed. But there was a great shaking of his sensorium. Vast sommes of gule were passant nearby. Neither dangerous nor ragule, though not gustace either; but so heltered! Disarray, dentilly and dancetty jumbled, everything rayonne and nebuly.

He could find nothing in this shimmery. And might lose too much of his filigree if he remained. Then—lost, adrift in the hell world! Dismay, sure to come; disaster...

Might even be possible.

He fled.

But the tumult had weakened him. The confusion and skelter vouchsafed his resolution and wauched his will.

Frantic now, he scanned and pulsed, probed and searched. His whittle swept past mound after mound of gule—but it was inert, hollow, useless. With no lorraines feak or creance, his estoile was growing helminth and addorsed.

But there! Purpure! The unmistakable fume of a saltire of the hell world!

Samyaza engulfed it. An instant for the tierce. Then, the feast.

For a moment, he wondered if the saltire felt dismay, or fear, or despair. But the moment was passing. He was the greatest of the Nephilim. He cared nothing for the girdle of lesser modes and entelechs.

Chapter 1

THE TIPS ON THE MISSING TEN-YEAR-OLD HISPANIC GIRL HAD come in within fifteen minutes of each other. One was from a man whose daughter had seen a van pull up to where her friend had been standing across the railroad tracks, and the other from a concerned woman who had seen a strange man enter an abandoned building. Crimes against children got the Federal Bureau of Investigation hopping, especially a missing child the locals asked for assistance in locating.

Z. Jasper Wilde leveled his Glock, the larger of the .40 caliber models, on the vehicle suspected in the kidnapping. The late-90s Ford Econoline van had been reported stolen yesterday, according to Jasper's East Chicago cop buddy, Pedro Hernandez. Pete was a Safe Streets Task Force officer he worked with often and now stood before the van with.

"What you think?" Pete asked. He spoke fluent English, but his Puerto Rican accent was still heavy despite decades of living way north of the island. The neighborhood in which he lived had slowly become more and more Latino over the years, thereby maintaining the accent rather than softening it.

"I think it's empty," Jasper said, "but there may be evidence."

"Call in the evidence team?"

"No time. We can handle this. Maybe later."

"It's your show."

Not really, but Jasper didn't argue. Pete was usually ready to let the Feds take the lead—and the fall—on most joint investigations. He was closer to retirement age by a lot.

From a distance of ten feet or so, Jasper could see beneath the van. There were no drips from air conditioning, but that didn't mean much. This jalopy wasn't likely to have working AC. He peered over at Pete who raised his gun in response.

Jasper nodded and approached. He reached out for the hood—warm, but from the sun, not from being run in the past two hours or so. No taps from a cooling engine.

"Unlocked doors and a drawn curtain behind the front seats."

"That mean closed or open?" Pete asked.

"Closed."

"Oh. But it can mean open?"

"I suppose, but this one is shut. That better?" Jasper shook his head. The girl could be behind the curtain. A bad guy could be hiding behind the curtain, but he doubted that. A hurt or, God forbid, dead girl could be back there. His ears grew hot, and a sheen of sweat coated his forehead. The heat and humidity were brutal today, but this was anger oozing from his pores.

Pete worked his way around to where Jasper stood, covering him as he reached for the sliding side door. The handle gave way as Jasper yanked and the door slid wide open, the door's wheel grinding against the track in a metallic glissando. The stench of cigarette smoke poured forth, overwhelming his senses—he enjoyed an occasional cigar, but the stale smell was nasty. From the amount of it, someone had smoked up a storm in there. Half a pack of cigarettes or more.

Pete dropped to a knee and flashed a light inside the darkened van. "I see nothing, my friend," he said.

Jasper peered from around the open door and into the van, keeping his weapon close. He wasn't a fan of the limited penetration technique, called a limited pen. The limited pen had the person clearing the house, car, whatever, forced into a situation where they thrust their gun hand and arm into an open area, but kept their body out. At the same time, they peeked into the space, but hopefully with one eye. The downside was that a baddie could grab the arm if the room hadn't been at least partially cleared first.

A quick peek worked better, but there was no need since Pete had flashed the light in and had taken a great look. The downside for Pete was that he had been exposed when Jasper had ripped the door open. Pete holstered his weapon.

"There's nothing," he said.

Jasper sighed. "I was afraid we'd find the girl in there."

"I was hoping we'd find the girl in there—alive, of course. Now we're back at the beginning." Pete peered inside the van. "Looks clean to me. No clothes, no obvious evidence."

"I have an evidence kit in my bucar," Jasper said. "But I don't want to waste any time. I'll check the front of the van for obvious clues or evidence left behind. Check out the back."

Pete nodded.

Jasper donned latex gloves and went through the driver and passenger sides of the van. Cigarette butts littered an overflowing ashtray.

"I'm getting lung cancer back here," Pete said.

"Yeah. It isn't any better up here," Jasper said. "The cigarettes are likely the owner's."

"Right."

"I got nothing," Jasper said, as he searched the glove compartment and console.

"Same here."

"All right. Call for some of your people to process the van, okay?"

Pete nodded. "Sure thing." He grinned. "Still having trouble with what's-his-name?"

"With Morris?" Jasper rolled his eyes. The Indianapolis Field Office Evidence Response Team Senior Team Leader was a pain in the ass, unreasonable and unyielding. Jasper's blood pressure rose every time the man popped into his thoughts or conversation. "You could say that. I got kicked off the Evidence Response Team after not showing for the last callout, even though the crime scene was in southern Indiana and would have required me to—oh, hell, let's move on to the next lead. It isn't far from here, right?" He hadn't recognized the name of the hotel, the Euclid.

"Sorry I brought it up," Pete said. "But the Euclid is close."

"Enough that someone could walk to it from here with a little girl? Or carry a little girl?"

Pete shrugged. "I guess. You know it's abandoned, right? Has been for decades."

"I do now. No wonder I've never heard of it. Call in for assistance. I don't want to leave this van here unguarded."

The sun was falling rapidly, and soon they'd be working into the night searching for the girl. It was never a good thing when a kidnapping went overnight and into another full day. Recovery was most likely to occur right off or probably not at all—and then if they did find the victim, they were usually in a field somewhere, dead.

Pete got on his radio and within two minutes a marked East Chicago Police cruiser rolled up and blocked the van. The problem with the FBI's manpower was that out in the suburbs, away from the main field offices, the help was scarce and spread out. Relying on task force officers was critical and necessary. Those were local cops like Pete, but detailed to the FBI for a specific purpose like the Safe Streets and Metro Gang Task Forces.

The uniformed officers nodded at Jasper and approached Pete. They spoke for a few minutes and Pete walked for his vehicle, an unmarked Ford Crown Victoria. Jasper dropped into his bucar, a dark gray Dodge Charger, and followed. Pete didn't go lights and sirens, since there was no use alerting anyone who was possibly holed up in the Euclid Hotel with a frightened little girl.

The Euclid was only a few blocks away on Chicago Avenue. That was a busy stretch of road, with cars and trucks moving in both directions, but from the standpoint of foot traffic it might as well be deserted. There were very few residences nearby. It was mostly an industrial area whose salad days were long gone. More than half of the buildings—machine shops, many of them, along with industrial and electrical supply houses—were now abandoned.

Pete pulled up to a crumbling curb at the corner of Chicago and Euclid, and Jasper followed. The building on the northwest corner was the hotel. The daylight, though fading, still factored into their search in a positive way. The abandoned hotel's interior would benefit from the natural light, and also expose anyone moving about the hotel proper, unless secreted in some dark room or closet. Jasper and Pete's job would be easier.

Catty-corner to the hotel was a tank farm, a large field surrounded by a tall wire fence and filled with squat white cylinders most likely filled with petroleum. That belonged to one of the petrochemical corporations in the area. Lake County, the northwestern Indiana county that butted right up against Chicago, was one of the nation's premier industrial areas. A big percentage of U.S. steel production took place within fifteen miles of where they were standing, in the huge steel mills stretched out across the southern shore of Lake Michigan.

The area also had a major petrochemical industry. Less than a mile away was a large plant producing liquid oxygen, and just a short distance from there was one of BP's biggest oil refineries. Humid, chemical-laden air invaded Jasper's nose. Even after all these years, six in his current assignment with the FBI's Merrillville Resident Agency—part of the larger FBI Indianapolis Field Office—he'd never really acclimated to the smell. It wasn't too bad in the winter, but Midwest summers weren't much less hot and humid than those of Alabama or Georgia.

Jasper trotted over to Pete's vehicle. "We know the owner of this place?"

"Can't get a hold of him," Pete said. "I had the station try."

"We try the businesses next door?"

"Closed."

Jasper sighed. "Would have been nice to get a rudimentary layout, or at least consent to enter from the owner. Let's take a look around, perhaps we'll have some legitimate reason to enter."

Pete nodded.

Jasper took in the building's front. It was a red-brick building, still in fairly good repair, and it stood two stories tall and had an entrance on the corner, as well as one about halfway down the block. An alleyway ran along the side of the hotel, separating it from another brick building.

EUCLID HOTEL was spelled out in brick above the mid-block entry. Jasper walked around the corner entrance and saw the hotel was one long building with only a slight ell. A chain link fence blocked off entry to the courtyard in front. The gate was padlocked, but in the back of the courtyard he could see a door that appeared to open onto the back alley. There was also an entrance into the hotel from the courtyard itself, but he couldn't see it very well. That door was mostly shrouded by an overgrown cluster of shrubs and trees growing out of the cracked paving of the courtyard.

The place had obviously been abandoned for a long time. Jasper walked back to the mid-block entrance. Pete popped out from the alley and motioned for Jasper. "Over here."

"I noticed from the front a courtyard with trees and shrubs obscuring another entrance into the hotel," Jasper said.

"That makes sense. Come look." Pete gestured toward a door set in the brick wall lining the alleyway.

"That a hallway or just an entrance into the courtyard, you think?" Jasper asked.

"We'll find out," Pete said. "See that handle and the wood of the door?"

"Yep, been used recently. It open or locked?"

"It's open. I tried the knob, it turns freely, and the keyhole appears to have been used. It's not gunked up at all."

"So the place isn't completely abandoned. You think the owner of the Euclid is somehow involved?"

Pete shrugged.

"Let's go," Jasper said.

He hadn't put on his Kevlar, and Pete appeared to be unencumbered as well. Jasper did have a flashlight with him, a small Surefire that'd almost burn the hair off a person's head with its focused solar-flare-like beam. Beside that and his handcuffs and Glock with extra mags, he went light. Pete had cuffs and his weapon as well.

Jasper pulled his Glock, as did Pete, and they entered the courtyard. To his surprise the door didn't creak. Once on the inside he saw the hinges had been oiled recently. He pointed at the hinges for Pete's information, who nodded in reply.

Jasper would have said that vagrants or a homeless person had set up camp in the courtyard or within the Euclid, but the well-oiled hinges and shiny keyhole suggested otherwise. He supposed the owner could have been through, but that didn't seem likely. Why wouldn't he have used one of the main entrances to gain entry rather than the alley and courtyard?

A fire lit in Jasper's belly, warming him. His ears felt like they were reddening too. He was pretty sure the girl was close by and in danger.

He didn't like the feel of the situation one bit, though. The Bureau had strict protocols in place for nearly every contingency, and preferred to enter a situation with as much intelligence as possible. But where there was an imminent threat to life, creativity and alternate solutions were often called upon. The playbook was tossed out the window with only the training and muscle memory of the agents in play. That was where experience paid off, experience and instincts. Begging forgiveness later for spontaneity and creativity was something taught him by his training agent, who had long since retired.

The shrubs and trees blocked most of the back entrance of the hotel, but for a thin path of matted grass and weeds. A broken branch was the only other sign someone else had been through here recently. They pulled aside the vegetation as they entered the path; a few feet in and they reached two concrete steps leading below to a door. A padlock hung on the loop, open and with the clasp slung back on its hinge.

Pete looked back at Jasper and nodded for him to get in position. He stacked up behind Pete against the wall and placed a hand on his shoulder so he knew he was right there and would move with him.

Pete grasped the knob and pulled. The door swung open easily and without any noise into the courtyard. Pete button-hooked left through the door, and Jasper button-hooked right into—

—inky blackness save for the cone of light from the open door.

"Damn," Jasper whispered. The hotel was eerily quiet. "You smell that?"

"Incense?" Pete whispered back.

"I think so. Mixed with a damp, musty smell like a stack of newspapers. But I can't see a thing beyond the entry."

Green tile, like that of a hospital or government building, covered the floor. A splintered door, once painted white but now hopelessly chipped and cracked, stood directly ahead. To Jasper's right was an open door where a damp, musty smell oozed up from the concrete steps descending into a cellar. Jasper clicked on his flashlight and eased the entry door shut.

"We should close that door as well," Pete said. "That one leading down to the cellar. It'd be better to clear the main and second floors first, don't you think?"

"I'm hesitant—"

But Pete had already begun moving the cellar door.

A long, slow creak echoed, followed by a crack. Jasper winced.

Pete's face screwed into one of tortuous pain, his mustache scrunched up like a caterpillar. He ceased pulling the door and gingerly released the knob. "Sorry."

Scurrying sounds like that of a small animal scrambling and scratching a wood floor to get away, sounded from below them. Other than that, the cellar remained silent and without a hint of life.

"Well, it appears we didn't disturb anything other than an animal down there," Jasper said, pointing with the barrel of the Glock.

"I bet this lead is a dead end."

"Maybe, but let's leave the cellar for now—and leave the door as it is—and clear the rest of the hotel first."

Pete nodded. "You first, I don't want to mess things up by causing a rocket."

"You mean racket?"

"Yeah, like I said, rocket."

Jasper grinned. "That door sounded more like an old car door creaking shut followed by a backfire of an old carbureted engine."

"Indeed." Pete flashed a grin, but it faded quickly.

"Yeah, let's go." Jasper edged past Pete and brought up his Glock and flashlight. He moved toward the closed door in front of them that he assumed led into the hotel proper.

Jasper's soft-soled shoes produced little sound against the entry's tile flooring. Pete wore boots that were similarly soled. Jasper took a few steps toward the closed door before them and grasped the knob.

"Wait," Pete whispered, and placed a hand on Jasper's shoulder.

"What is it?"

"You hear that?" Pete asked.

Jasper turned and aimed the flashlight away from Pete's face, but not at the steps leading down to the cellar. "I don't."

"Perhaps it's nothing, only my imagination."

"Let's hold up a second then," Jasper said, and pointed toward the cellar.

Pete nodded.

Jasper pointed at his flashlight and chopped with his hand, hoping Pete understood he was about to douse the flashlight.

Pete nodded again.

Jasper leaned against the jamb of the door leading into the cellar and killed his flashlight. They stood in darkness. Jasper strained his eyes and ears for any hint of movement or signs of other people within the abandoned hotel.

Each breath seemed to echo and fill his ears. The darkness hitting his eyes felt as if he were swimming underwater in a lake on a moonless, starless night. But slowly, a vague outline of the doorway presented itself, as did a few of the steps leading down. He turned, and saw Pete, more a shadow than a man, and Jasper's skin crawled and he shivered.

Two thumps echoed from deep under the hotel.

Jasper clicked on his Surefire flashlight and raised his Glock. "Let's go, that wasn't the building simply settling. There's someone down there."

"Should we call for backup?" Pete asked.

Jasper shook his head. "No, if that little girl is down there I don't want to waste any more time."

"I agree."

Jasper descended the steps, but at a slow and deliberate pace. At the bottom, he found the cellar likely opened left since his back was pressing against what he presumed to be the outer wall of the building. The brick wall scraped and pulled his shirt, a faded olive green T-shirt from his days in the Marine Corps. His last girlfriend had referred to the shirt as part of his lounging uniform. He loved these shirts and found they worked in quite a few situations, but never wore them into the office because the FBI preferred business-like attire. He appreciated that, and understood the general public's image of a Special Agent was that of a clean-cut man dressed in a dark suit and wearing a white shirt with a conservative tie. That worked for normal day-to-day operations, but not when doing dirty work such as dumpster diving, meeting confidential human sources in certain rough areas, and situations such as this: trying to locate a little girl who was likely kidnapped. And the local police often dressed down when working on the task forces with the bureau. FBI Special Agents often dressed according to the violations they worked, and in a smaller Resident Agency, agents wore many hats and worked many violations.

A sliver of light peered from under another door at the bottom of the steps. The gap under the door was also apparently where the incense escaped. The scent had grown stronger, but the mustiness had as well. Despite the heat of the day, the cellar's atmosphere was cold, as if the temperature was being manipulated on purpose. The difference from the main floor to just—what, ten, twelve feet down—was obvious. It felt like they were entering a walk-in freezer.

"It's cold," Pete said quietly. "Way too cold for this time of year, even in a cellar."

Jasper nodded. "See that light?" he whispered.

"*Si.*"

The light darkened, lightened, and darkened in quick succession. Something moved within. It had to be a person, since that was likely two legs. Jasper shivered again. The feel of the dark, musty old hotel was creepy and unsettling, regardless of the gun in his hand.

Jasper kept the light aimed high so the beam didn't hit the bottom of the door and cast flickers and shadows under the door. He pointed to his ear and then the door.

Pete nodded.

Jasper edged toward the door, but kept his feet back and the light aimed away. He could hear muffled voices now, the words indiscernible and unintelligible, speaking in hushed monotones.

He pulled back from the door. "Sounds like two people having a conversation behind that door—two men—but I could be mistaken."

Pete sighed. "That's one too many."

"It may not be the abductor."

"I'm betting it is—and so are you, Jasper. But if there are more than two unsubs in there this could get ugly. It could get ugly with just one person."

"True."

A shuffling noise, as if someone were being dragged, oozed from under the door. A whimper, almost like that of a dog, followed the shuffling.

A distant and weak, but distinct "no" hit Jasper's ears. That was no dog.

"We have to go in." Jasper stared at Pete, who nodded grimly, his eyes glistening in the Surefire's light.

Jasper brought the light and gun up before him and stood off to the side and nodded at Pete to open the door.

Pete reached forward, but the door flung inward with force.

Jasper and Pete jumped back.

Chapter 2

JASPER HAD HIS GLOCK AND FLASHLIGHT UP IN A READY POSI-
tion, his finger creeping toward, but remaining off the trigger.
He didn't bother glancing at Pete, as he likely had his weapon
trained on the open door.

A brown haze hung in the subdued lighting of the room,
masking its contents and whoever had flung open the door.

"This is bad," Jasper said.

"We have no choice now," Pete said.

Jasper took a deep breath. "You heard the girl's whimper,
though, right?"

"*Si.* Think that door flung open on its own?"

"Not a chance," Jasper said. "From this angle I can't see much,
but I'm pretty exposed." Part of his body was in the doorway,
but he managed to squeeze to the right of the door up against
the foundation. There was only about a foot of wall on either
side of the door, not much cover at all. He motioned for Pete to
stay back and climb a step.

"Police!" Jasper yelled. "How many people are in there and
do you have any weapons?" Depending on the mental state of
the people within and also if they felt they were out of options,
they'd likely assume the police had come in force and give up.
However, there was always a chance of a shoot-out, or even a
good old-fashioned death-by-cop scenario. None of them were
good, but the worst situation would be if they took the life of
their captive. Jasper didn't care about the abductors' health and
well-being, not one iota, but that little girl in there deserved better.

No answer.

"Police! I need one of you to come out into the open and show me your hands. And raise 'em high." Jasper waited a few more seconds. "We're here for the girl, Teresa Ramirez. Her parents are worried. We're not interested in you, only the girl." Jasper pursed his lip.

"We call in SWAT?" Pete asked.

"No. We can't wait on that. Not with the little girl in danger," Jasper said.

A muffled conversation hung in the air—two men in a hushed argument.

"I'm going to peek," Jasper whispered, "but I wish I'd brought a mirror." Safer for sure, but Jasper wasn't too concerned. Over the years, he'd developed a keen eye and ability to take in a lot of detail during a quick peek. Theoretically, it was dangerous, but he exposed only a sliver of his head for a split second during the action. The likelihood of a marksman on the other side knowing at what level he'd peek and when was very low, so being shot during a quick peek wasn't that likely. It was when they made entry that they'd be at their most vulnerable.

Jasper knelt down and popped his head in and out of the room in what took probably not even a half a second. The trick was not focusing on any one thing, but taking in the whole room in one mental image and sorting it out afterward.

"Two men in the left corner closest to us," Jasper said. "But I didn't see the girl."

The brown haze drifted through the door, the incense and musty scents battling.

"I'll go straight in, you buttonhook to the left. I saw nothing right in front of me, so I'm assuming the girl must be in the back of the room. Very little furniture, so we shouldn't have any real surprises. I also noticed what appear to be a few basins or small tubs. Hard to tell in the dim lighting."

Pete shook his head. "You got all that from a quick peek?"

"Let's go." Jasper moved with purpose into the room. "Police, hands up! Let's see 'em!"

Pete moved in gun raised at eye level on Jasper's left. "Hands up, now!"

Both of the unsubs stood. They'd been huddled in the corner. Average height, both had dark hair cut in the same manner, and remarkably similar looks. Their odd choice of clothing, however, didn't make sense—they both wore what looked like checkered shirts beneath a knee-length robe. The material was thick, like the canvas of a martial arts gi, and similarly fastened with a belt. An odd fold created a pocket of sorts in front of their stomachs. Both men stood shoulder to shoulder with their arms hanging at their sides.

"Put your hands up, fingers spread and way over your head! Come on, now," Pete said.

Jasper kept his mouth shut and eyes on the men. If either of them reached into those odd pockets he'd have no option but to shoot.

The men stepped toward the middle of the room in unison, as if they shared a hive mind.

Jasper glanced about, looking for a reason for their odd behavior, but the room was otherwise empty.

"Stop right there!" Pete said, and took a step toward them. "See this?" He waved his gun. "That means you stop when I say stop and you do what I say. We're police, and we're looking for a little girl. It's simple. Speak English? Either of you?" After a moment he added, *"Habla Español?"*

The men stared back blankly.

"You think they're on something?" Pete asked.

"This whole situation is on drugs if you ask me," Jasper said. "We need to get them under control, and fast."

The two men had paused at Pete's last command, but now they took steps sideways. They had an odd-looking way of moving. Jasper glanced over, noticing unpolished stone basins, like the sort someone might have washed clothes in, or if they'd been metal, had at a picnic filled with ice and beer. Jasper kept his Glock up and moved toward the basins. The two men halted.

"That's right," Jasper said. "What's in those basins that you're so eager to get to? Huh?"

The two men looked at each other and then at Jasper.

Pete triangulated with Jasper on the two men, weapon raised. His face was red and rivulets of sweat wended down his cheeks. The mustache riding his upper lip glistened.

"You okay?" Jasper asked.

"Just tired of this bullshit." Pete never took his eyes from the men. "You two, separate from each other slowly. You need to be two paces apart from one another. If you don't have the girl then this shouldn't be a big deal, but we heard a whimper."

"A girl's whimper," Jasper said.

"Yes," Pete said, "and if you cooperate this whole deal will go much easier for you."

Heaven forbid some hidden camera was filming this and Pete lost control or Jasper shot one of them and the two men were unarmed. Jasper shivered. It was still damned cold in this basement.

"No. Please." A little girl's voice came from the back of the room. He couldn't see her, though. Was there a closet he couldn't make out? Or another room?

"Where is she?" Jasper asked. "You two are heading for trouble. Answer me."

Pete moved for the men. "Get down. On your knees, and interlock your fingers atop your heads, and lace those fingers into your hair."

The men stared, faces blank and devoid of emotion.

"What do we do?" Pete asked.

The men continued edging for the basins. Jasper glanced in. White powder, apparently a pretty thick layer, filled the basin about halfway. Cocaine or drugs of some sort? A bath mat, glistening as if it were wet, rested before each basin. Jasper stepped away from the basins. A sick feeling overtook him. If any of them came into contact with a drug like PCP, this mess would become a lot messier and a lot more dangerous.

"What is that?" Jasper asked. "Drugs?"

Both men shook their heads.

"You two can speak, can't you?" Jasper asked.

The two men now stood roughly three feet from the basins and were still inching forward. Jasper raised his weapon.

"Stop, or I'll assume what is in those basins is a weapon of mass destruction." Perhaps that would get their attention. For all he knew, the basins' contents *were* a concoction aimed at destruction.

The men each stepped onto one of the mats with an audible squish. A clear liquid oozed between their toes, coating them and the sides of their feet.

"Don't take another step, or—"

In unison, each man hopped into a basin with both feet.

Two cones of white flame erupted, shooting up each man's body. One of them screamed. Jasper fell backward, not from a blast, but from the intense heat thrown off by the men. Pete ran forward, but about ten feet away he threw his arms up to cover his face.

"Don't!" Jasper shouted. "It's too late." He glanced up at the ceiling, scanning for scorch marks, but the flames were confined to the men. The one on the right dropped to his knees, or perhaps the lower part of his legs had been incinerated. A foul scent of seared flesh mixed with acrid smoke and sulfur smacked his nose.

Except for that one short scream, the two men hadn't cried out or shown any emotion; but then, they hadn't had any time for such. Jasper wasn't positive, but he thought he was seeing thermite at work. They'd been trained in the Marines to use thermite grenades to disable artillery. The thermite he was familiar with hadn't looked like the stuff the men had jumped into, but if he remembered right, thermite came in several different varieties.

Jasper watched as the two men glowed white, their forms barely discernible now, melting or disintegrating as the heat intensified. He was reminded of the scene toward the end of *Raiders of the Lost Ark* when the Nazis' skin and flesh melted away, exposing the skeletons beneath. Only this reaction tore these two men down to a pile of atoms in the bottom of stone basins.

He'd never witnessed such a thing before. They hadn't worked that much with thermite in the Marines, and never against humans. The sad part was that this wasn't even gruesome or gory. The two men had lit up like human sparklers.

"What the fuck?" Pete laid a hand on Jasper's shoulder, and he realized he hadn't gotten up off the ground.

"Yeah," Jasper said. "What. The. Fuck."

What was left of the two men sank into the now disintegrating basins, a shower of white-hot flame and the heat rippling the air like some twisted mirage. The white flames turned yellow and dwindled. Smoke hung in the air, acrid and mingling with incense. The smell of burning flesh and singed hair barely touched his nose. The destruction of the men had been too rapid. The flame feasted on them like some ravenous predator, disposing of the bodies within seconds.

The girl.

"Pete," Jasper said. "Teresa Ramirez. She's close by."

"There might be a trap back there."

"Yeah, I know. But we've got to look for her." Jasper squinted through swirling smoke. Was he breathing in dust from the dead men? He coughed and brought a hand to his mouth.

"You okay?" Pete asked.

"Yeah, it's nothing. Let's go." Jasper pointed with his gun hand toward the back wall.

Chapter 3

AS HE APPROACHED THE BACK, WHAT HE THOUGHT WAS THE
back wall appeared to separate, almost like one of those pictures
that used to be popular way back when—the ones where if you
stared at them in a certain way, a different sort of picture or
image would emerge. In this case, the wall was just a partition,
but it was made of the same cinder blocks as the rest of the
basement. The subdued lighting, mixed with the smoke, added
to the illusion. So did the image of human sparklers indelibly
stamped upon his mind's eye.

A five-foot gap on either end of the partition provided access
to whatever lay behind. Jasper and Pete pressed against it near
the right-side gap. The familiar pressure of Pete's hand fell on
Jasper's shoulder. He took a deep breath and poked his head
around the wall.

The quick peek revealed a rectangular room, not as large as
expected, but of the same dark gray rock comprising the rest of
the basement. In the center of the room, upon a bleached stone
slab, lay the girl, her hands and feet lashed to metal stakes punched
through the slab. The slab itself rested upon what appeared to be
a bed of smoldering coals. The room was thick with the smell
of incense.

He pulled his head back. No one else was in the room.

"She's in there," Jasper said.

Without a word, Pete moved. Before Jasper could react and
depress his weapon, he was already around the wall and through
the gap.

"So much for avoiding traps," Jasper muttered.

Jasper entered the room, gun at low ready, and scanning for any other threats. Another basin stood in the back left corner. Scorch marks crisscrossed the back wall, and the stones there had odd shapes, as if they'd been warped. Had someone else lit themselves up like a sparkler too close to that wall?

Jasper's gaze fell upon the girl. Pete was there, listening for a breath or a heartbeat. The girl's black hair lay matted to her head, a few strings plastered to her pale face. Her eyes fluttered, but she wasn't awake.

Pete lifted his head and turned toward Jasper. The East Chicago police officer looked as if he'd aged a decade in a few minutes.

"At least she's alive," Jasper said.

"Who would do such a thing?"

Jasper sighed, not out of impatience, but of weariness and agreement. "Two men who didn't want to go to jail, apparently."

The girl's knee-length skirt, at one time white but now smeared with ash and dirt and grime and soaked through with sweat, clung to her legs. Her top had once been light blue, and it too clung to the unconscious girl. No outward or obvious signs of abuse presented themselves, but depending on her memories, she could be scarred for life after this sort of ordeal.

Wailing and yelping sirens reached into the basement.

"Pete," Jasper said, but he remained focused on the little girl. "Pete," he said again with a little more force.

Pete raised his head.

"Does she appear to have any wounds?" Jasper asked.

"None that I can see."

The girl's eyes fluttered and opened. Confusion filled her eyes, which flicked back and forth as she tried moving her arms and legs.

"Shhh, it's going to be all right," Pete said, pulling out a knife and cutting her bonds.

The girl's eyes widened and her mouth opened in a large circle, but no scream issued. She sat straight up as if some puppet master had yanked her strings.

"We're police," Jasper said, displaying his badge. Most people didn't recognize the tiny gold FBI shield. Pete stepped back and displayed his large silver badge to the girl. She collapsed back onto the slab, though her chest rose and fell both rapidly and shallowly.

"Are you hurt?" Pete asked.

The girl shook her head. She opened her mouth, but then swallowed and licked her lips. "My head hurts."

"But your back and neck are okay?" Jasper asked.

The girl turned her head and gazed up at him.

"I guess that's a 'yes,'" Jasper said, and smiled. "Do you remember anything? Anything at all? Even the smallest detail or most insignificant tidbit could mean something."

"I want to go home," the little girl said.

"Soon. But a doctor will have to see you first," Pete said.

She grimaced. "Do I have to?"

Pete nodded. "Do you remember your name?"

"Teresa. Teresa Ramirez."

"Where do you live?"

She recited her address, phone number, and not only her parents' names, but also her brothers' and sisters' names. But she could not recall any details of how she ended up in the basement of the Euclid Hotel. Perhaps after she'd had some water and food in more comforting surroundings she'd remember something. Though, at this stage, it appeared as if the two men who had abducted her had been the only men involved. But, why had they killed themselves, and in such a spectacular manner? Too many questions, but they'd likely never be answered since the girl had been rescued and the perpetrators were dead by their own hands, or rather—he shook his head—by their own feet. Feet coated with whatever had drenched the mats. They'd have to get an evidence team in here, but since the girl was saved, it'd wait until tomorrow if it ever happened. Maybe the CSIs of Pete's department would get to it quicker. Honestly, he didn't want to call in Morris Chan and the FBI's ERT for this.

Pete carried the girl out of the basement as uniformed police flooded the place. The Euclid hadn't seen this much activity in decades. Hopefully, Teresa would see a victim witness specialist in a few minutes. They'd had one on standby ever since the search began. The specialist was likely racing toward the hotel or already outside.

Jasper decided on one more look around the basement for any obvious evidence. Jasper leaned over the third basin, the one he'd seen as they entered the back room of the basement, and saw that it contained the same substance as the two used by the men when they committed suicide. Or something that looked like it, at any rate.

More police entered. He told them to steer clear of the basins and the slab upon which the girl had been lashed—and the bath mats the men had stepped on. As far as he was concerned, the police could ransack the rest of the place searching for evidence, but he knew that the crimes had taken place down here, in seclusion and away from prying eyes.

His eyes went once more upon the back wall of the basement and the scorch marks there. He stepped toward the wall and ran his fingers down the stone. Rippled and charred, distorted—and surprisingly hot. He pulled back his hand. Odd. His fingers tingled. But then, his entire body was shaking a little, probably from the adrenaline.

Jasper ascended from the dungeon, trading the foul stench of the incense mixed with the thermite reaction and a hint of burnt flesh for the heavy chemical-laden air of the streets. Even in the dark, with street lamps casting their sharp light, the tank farm's big white cylinders to the southeast were easily visible. He sucked in a lungful of air, attempting to cleanse the Euclid's death smell from his lungs with a slightly less offensive odor.

During his first few years in the area, he'd worried about cancer and respiratory issues, and he'd actively sought a transfer. But one good case led to another and he'd never escaped northwestern Indiana, and now he wasn't sure he ever would. Chicago loomed, and that'd be a fairly easy transfer to pull off, but there was something about working in a smaller office and the variety of hats forced upon agents working in them that he really liked. And as time passed, he'd grown fond of the people who lived there. Well, most of them. Northern Lake County was a working-class area, a lot like the one he'd grown up in, except this area was racially mixed. But once he'd gotten used to that he'd come to like it also.

Police cruisers and unmarked cars now lined Euclid and Chicago Avenues, and in their midst was an idling ambulance. A few onlookers stood around, curious over the scene, but it was by no means a mob. There just weren't that many people who lived in the area.

"What's going on?" Jasper asked.

Pete stood with his arms crossed, leaning against the Euclid's brick wall. "Looks like your victim specialist is here, she's speaking with the girl now. You know her well?"

Jasper shook his head. "No. She transferred in a couple of months ago. She's a contract employee, not full Bureau."

Pete grinned. "She single?"

"I don't know. I don't care. Not right now. Not after what we've seen tonight." Jasper took a deep breath. "And I'm not ready, not after, well, you know. It wouldn't be fair to Shelly, even assuming she was interested herself."

"Who's Shelly?"

"The victim specialist."

"So you know her name." Pete rocked on his heels. "It's a start."

Jasper tilted his head and stared at Pete until his grin faded.

"All right. All right," Pete said, holding up his hands with the forefingers and middle fingers spread into a V. "Peace, brother. Don't get upset. Just trying to give us something else to think about, is all." He rubbed the top of his head, the short graying hair poking through his fingers. "All that shit down there, a fireworks display and that poor girl. I'm a little shook up and not afraid to admit it."

"Me too." Jasper let the words hang, and sighed. "How long's Shelly been with the girl?"

"Ten minutes, maybe?" Pete shrugged. "Ambulance is waiting. The EMTs gave her a quick once over, but they still need to take her to St. Catherine's for the usual workup."

St. Catherine Hospital was just a few minutes away. Jasper leaned against the nearest police cruiser, facing Pete and the Euclid Hotel. A block to the north, barricades came down to block Euclid, flashing their red lamps. A train was coming.

That happened so regularly that Jasper paid little attention. It was often said that Chicago was the nation's rail hub, but most of that constant freight traffic passed south of the city—and just about all of it came through the northern Lake County towns of Hammond, East Chicago, and Gary.

A line of police emerged from the alley. The one in front announced they'd cleared the building and buttoned it up for later evidence collection.

"They're calling it early, don't you think?" Jasper asked. Bureau personnel would have been more thorough during the initial examination.

"The bad guys are dead, so what else is there to do?" Pete asked.

"What if there are others out there?" Jasper spoke more loudly because the train was passing through the intersection now. It was moving slowly; not more than twenty miles an hour, but a mile-long freight train makes a lot of noise.

Pete frowned.

"Just saying." Jasper tilted his head back and gazed at the night sky. Haze and light pollution obscured all but the brightest stars and the crescent of the waning moon. "The vastness of space is out there, countless worlds, countless stars, and here we are dealing with dirtbags as if we're making some kind of difference in the grand scheme of things."

"Thought for a moment you were philosophizing, and then you said 'dirtbags.'" Pete shrugged. "If we don't deal with 'em, who will? Every one we take off the street makes things a little better."

"Yeah," Jasper said, and dropped his gaze from the murky heavens, "but they just get replaced by... That's odd."

"What?"

Jasper pointed toward the alley behind the Euclid Hotel. "That. What the hell is it?"

"Whoa."

Tendrils wafted from the alley, dark gray and silver followed by an oddly shaped body of mist strobed by the blue and red flashes of the police cruisers. A slow hiss escaped from between the buildings as if the mist was a corporeal monster. The tendrils seemed to poke and prod, as if attached to a blind person. The mist changed shape and for the briefest of moments, congealed, forming a head like that of a beast, a lion perhaps.

No. The head of a dragon with large eyes and tendril-like whiskers, dancing about as if submerged in water.

Jasper blinked. The form reminded him of Chinese-style dragons; only this thing wasn't a bunch of people in a costume tossing firecrackers. Jasper closed his eyes, hoping the image would be gone upon opening them. A negative afterimage persisted in Jasper's vision from the intense light of the men burning.

The mist dragon had to be an illusion, due to being tired and that horrid afterimage. He opened his eyes, and blinked a few times.

It was still there.

"Pete, are you seeing this?"

Silence.

"Pete?" Jasper glanced over. Pete had gone down on one knee and covered his eyes with his forearm. "You okay?" Jasper turned back for another glimpse of the mist dragon. The gurgling hiss continued, now morphing into a faint whistle, as if a distant gas line had been punctured.

The mist swirled and what had once been similar to a Chinese dragon was now a ragged cloud suspended above the Euclid Hotel.

"Could that be gas?" Jasper asked, but Pete still covered his eyes. "This some sort of religious experience, Pete? I'm not being funny."

"I—I can't explain it," Pete said. "I can't look, and I don't know why."

The raggedness of the mist smoothed and pulsed. Silver shot through the dark gray portion of the cloud like veins, a complete circulatory system. The hiss rolled into a thunderous grumble, also sounding like it was far away. The cloud solidified, once more taking the appearance of a great beast—more like a dragonfly than a dragon, now. And then it was simply gone. Gone completely, as if it had never existed.

"Where in the hell did that thing come from? It had to be some strange atmospheric condition, right?" Jasper helped Pete to his feet. "I don't smell any gas, but it certainly could have been. I mean, not all gas has an odor."

"Thing? It was a weird cloud is all," Pete said. "It's easy to see what we want to see. Believe what we want to believe." His face had gone white, even in the subdued lighting and the dwindling number of cruiser strobes flashing red and blue across the scene.

"I'm heading back to the office," Jasper said. "If I don't write this up tonight I won't get to it until Monday."

"Working tomorrow?"

"I think so. And I think we should speak with the people who phoned in the tips and then come back here during the day. That okay with you?"

"You're the boss," Pete said.

En route, Jasper updated his boss, the agent in charge of the Merrillville office, who then updated his boss, so the Special Agent in Charge of the entire Indianapolis division could appear on the news at some point with the East Chicago chief of police and claim Teresa Sanchez's recovery was a joint operation and everyone could slap each other on the back and be happy they had busted a human trafficking ring or some other nonsense they'd made up to make the public feel better and feel safer. Someone would be receiving an award for the actions Pete and he had taken earlier, but it'd likely be some muckety-muck who had nothing to do with the girl's rescue.

The Merrillville FBI office was a stand-alone building at the end of a cul-de-sac. At this time of night, it presented a half-lit face and stood deserted save for a lone person working the radio and phones. Jasper found printouts on his desk providing the biographical details of the people who had phoned in the tips on Teresa Sanchez, which would be useful for tracking them down for further questions. He entered a narrative of the events and would finalize the draft in the morning. He then went to his sparsely furnished bungalow in Hammond and collapsed on his bed.

He lived alone. No pets. No family. No wife. Lucy had left two years earlier and he hadn't seen her since. The divorce had been swift. Lucy hadn't wanted anything from him, not even a portion of his pension upon his retirement.

Jasper stared at the ceiling. Light from a streetlamp penetrated his window and in that cone of light were two men ablaze and dying in the basement of an abandoned hotel. The negative afterimage remained emblazoned, on his mind if not his retinas.

Chapter 4

SPECIAL AGENT VANCE RAVEL RUBBED HIS EYES. PORING OVER the data a few months back had been exciting, and on occasion provided some decent leads resulting in instances of anomalous activity. These past few weeks, though? Nothing. Boring. At least Sentinel, the Bureau's case management software, allowed for the use of keywords and even an RSS feed. In the old days—he chuckled—let's say, the year 2010 or so—he would have had to search manually for what he was after. Well, what he and his superior, Supervisory Special Agent Temple Black, were after.

"Hey," Temple called out.

"Yes, boss," Vance said.

"It's too late—"

"Or early, depending on how you look at it," Vance said.

Temple sighed, a sound Vance heard all too often, especially late at night when they'd both forsaken caffeine in the hopes of heading home and actually getting some sleep.

"All right, what do you need?"

"I got news of some crazy incident earlier this evening. Have you seen anything come through?"

Temple leaned close. Her soap or perfume, Vance couldn't tell the difference, was in the final throes of its effectiveness.

"Yes, and I've been sitting on it for hours now." Vance stared at the computer screen and didn't even glance in Temple's direction.

"You're becoming quite the sarcastic little human, aren't you? Tell you what," Temple said, "rather than be like that, how about finding something useful for a change?"

"How about you tell me about this crazy incident?" Vance

asked, tapping away at the keyboard, adding new search strings, and ready to add more based on Temple's information.

"There was a kidnapping out in Indiana, close to Chicago."

"Wow, that sounds so strange." Vance rolled his eyes.

"Look, I know it's late, but how about we don't turn on one another, okay?"

"Yes, boss," Vance said, and winced.

"You know how I feel about that word, right?"

"Yes, b—Temple." Vance shook his head. "Tell me more, please." But he had already begun a search for Indiana and kidnapping and before she started talking again he had it.

"—ah, here it is. Huh. This is a draft, and you know how drafts can sometimes be a little too raw and, might I add, a prank of some sort?"

"What does it say?"

Vance turned and grinned. "How does suicide by thermite sound? That strange enough for you?"

Temple pursed her lips, tapping them with her forefinger. "Not bad, anything else?"

"There is mention of a weather anomaly..."

"You mentioned thermite. Could this supposed weather simply be the remnants of the thermite's exothermic reaction?"

He glanced back and up at Temple and whistled. "I'm impressed."

"Here you go again."

"No, really, you've been listening to me."

"I do remember basic chemistry from my high-school days," she said, folding her arms. "And before you make another crack, it wasn't that long ago. Now, read that part of the report to me, that bit about the weather." She had taken to pacing behind him when they went through this exercise on at least a daily basis the past couple of days. She must be worried about her future, and perhaps that of their fledgling unit, the Scientific Anomalies Group. They'd been made fun of for the acronym, SAG, but there was nothing for it now.

"But what about the thermite? Or how the men who killed themselves with the substance looked alike?"

"Interesting. All right, you know what? I'll take the entire report. Print it out for me."

Vance sighed. "Aye, aye, Captain." He stood and saluted her, garnering a quick "pfft" from Temple. He smacked the printer, which beeped at him. "We need a new printer." He withdrew the toner cartridge and shook it.

"We need to use our funds carefully, and if this report is as good as I think it'll be, we'll be taking a trip."

The pages printed. Temple read. Vance removed his glasses, a beat up pair he kept around the office, and rubbed his eyes. Temple didn't say anything while she read, only emitting an "oh" or "hmmm" and one single gasp.

A few minutes later, Temple said, "Vance, we're heading to Indiana. You better phone the agent who drafted this and let him know. He'll bitch about getting local concurrence to travel to their AOR, but this is just a heads-up we're giving. We're not asking permission. Got it?"

"Yes, boss—uh, ma'am."

"A simple 'yes, Temple' will do." She walked off, shaking her head, but turned back before she hit the door leading to the outer office, "Go home, pack enough for a few days and get back here ASAP. We're heading out on the first available flight."

"But—"

"You can nap on the plane."

Chapter 5

BUZZING AWAKENED HIM. JASPER'S HEART THUMPED AND HE sucked in a quick breath. He glanced over at his clock, the red numbers seeming angry as they displayed four o'clock A.M. So, it wasn't the alarm buzzing.

His cell phone buzzed and rattled on the nightstand. He licked his lips and rubbed his eyes.

"Why?" he asked the ceiling, and reached for the phone. The call had to be about the girl's abduction. Probably his boss' boss. It seemed the higher one climbed in the bureaucracy, the more obtuse they became.

He hit the talk button.

"Yes?"

"Z. Jasper Wilde?" a male voice asked. There was a hint of English as a second language in the accent, but he was too tired to think about it.

"This is Wilde," he said, draping a forearm over his eyes. His friends called him Jasper, so this call could only mean more work, unless it had something to do with his ex-wife. But that wasn't likely, given the late hour.

"Ah, very good."

"Is it?"

"Yes. Your report, it—"

"Hold on. Hold on. My report? Which one?"

"Oh, of course, I'm very sorry about the early call," the man said. "You were up quite late, yes?"

"You mean the one I drafted a few hours ago now?" Jasper sat up. "Who is this?"

33

"I'm Special Agent Ravel, out of Washington, and—"

"What sort of agent? FBI? And if so, then you're calling from the District. Hoover Building or Washington Field Office. Which is it?"

These things mattered. If the man said Hoover, then he was some headquarters zombie, but if he said WFO, then this could be case-related, or a lead of some sort. But really, four in the morning? It was only five on the east coast.

"I am FBI, and calling from a secure location, an offsite if you will, but I prefer not to give away those details."

"Great, what do you want?" Jasper scratched the back of his head.

"We are flying out there. Your report contained some interesting items. We want to—"

"Whoa, whoa, whoa," Jasper said, and he felt his irritation level rising. "We? You're coming out here? Why?"

"Yes, however, I cannot talk on an open line about this. But my partner and myself will be seeing you later today."

Jasper shook his head. This was a joke. It had to be. Someone at the office—his office—had read the draft report. He just didn't understand how it was possible.

"Congratulations," Jasper said, "have a great flight."

"But—"

Jasper hung up on the agent pulling the prank on him. Someone had gotten up early and perhaps found his draft of last night's events on the printer.

But he hadn't printed it, had he? Maybe his boss had— But, no, that didn't make sense. The boss wouldn't be working on the weekend, let alone a Saturday morning during the summer. Not a chance.

He fell back on to the bed and drifted but never retreated into slumber. That ship had sailed. Finally, he got up and searched the internet for any mention of last night's rescue. But so far only a local paper had printed a bare-bones account. A story like this had a slim chance of making national news, only if the fantastic and gruesome nature of the perpetrators' deaths got out. Pretty soon the big shots at the office would be holding a press conference—but that might be put off until Monday. He didn't bother turning on the television; it was likely too soon.

The prank pushed itself forward, demanding his attention. Who at the office did impressions, and specifically who was capable of pulling off a decent Indian accent? Well, Indian or Pakistani: a person from the south Asian subcontinent.

He shook his head. His report had been fantastical in some ways, but it clearly laid out the facts, though he had mentioned the strange wispy, dragon-like fog that had appeared alongside the building, calling it a weather anomaly. The deaths were crazy, but not prank-worthy.

The timing was odd, too. Pranks usually took days or even weeks to develop. This had just happened.

He got dressed and got in his bucar, heading for the office, feeling as if he'd just been there. After getting off I-65 on U.S. Route 30, he picked up a cappuccino at a Starbucks.

He had to drive a little out of his way to do so. Northwest Indiana was not Seattle or San Francisco. You could find a few gourmet coffee places in Lake County, but you had to be willing to hunt for them. There were a couple of Starbucks in Merrillville, along with a coffee house from a smaller independent chain, one in Schererville, and one in Crown Point. The Target store on Calumet Avenue in Munster had a Starbucks inside, also. But so far as Jasper knew—and he'd looked; he was partial to cappuccinos—there were none at all in the more northerly towns in the county.

That wasn't surprising, of course. The rule-of-thumb when it came to the demographics of Lake County was that the population got whiter and more well off the farther south you went. It was only a rough rule of thumb, granted. The northernmost of all the towns in the county, Whiting, was almost all white—but it was also very working class. Dunkin' Donuts territory, not Starbucks-land.

When he pulled into the small parking lot of the Merrillville office, he saw that a few more lights were shining through the tinted windows than when he'd been there earlier. Probably support staff putting in some overtime, and more than likely, Mandy, his go-to Staff Operations Specialist when he needed information pronto. Jasper rarely entered the building before eight, and he was out in the field investigating as much as possible—an activity that was becoming a bit of a lost art in the Bureau these days due to the avalanche of administrative folderol.

He checked his work email and calendar, more out of habit

than anything else. There'd be no meetings, no mandatory virtual training or other nonsense on a Saturday morning to keep him in front of the computer and off the street today. He had a few follow-ups to yesterday's events he wanted to tackle. He gave the report he'd written last night another read, seeing nothing prankworthy, and then sent it along for approval to his supervisor. He'd seen his share of embarrassing emails pass throughout the Bureau—acrimony, incredulity, and downright hilarity contained within and forwarded on and on. A few of those unfortunate creators of the offending emails resigned, laughed out of the Bureau.

"You're in early."

Jasper jumped.

"And keyed up," Mandy said. "You realize it's Saturday, right? I mean, I have no life, but surely you have better things to do—"

"Yes, it's Saturday and you're dressed up like it's Monday." Mandy wore an ankle length gray skirt and a black blouse with a lace-like pattern on the shoulders and sleeves. "Wait, you didn't hear about last night?"

"Of course," Mandy said, ignoring the comment about her attire, "but the girl was rescued. What else is there to do?"

Mandy was young, perhaps mid-twenties, highly educated, and a hard worker, but still a little green when it came to investigations.

"There's more work to do," Jasper said. "In fact, I'm glad you're here."

"A coffee would have been nice, especially if you're attempting to talk me into helping you." Mandy folded her arms, but grinned.

"Sorry, I didn't know you'd be here."

"Didn't you?" Mandy squinted. "You didn't?" She grinned. "Okay, I'll let it slide, what do you need?"

"I'm thinking this Carlos fella is suitable for recruitment as a source. We always need someone in the local community."

"Who is he?" Mandy asked.

"He called in a tip on the missing girl."

"You're short on sources, aren't you?" Mandy winked.

"Hey, I've had a rough go of it lately. And, yes. I need a source. They grade us on how many sources we have." Jasper winked back.

"I'll whip up a quick assessment for you. May I send the particulars to your Bureau phone?"

"Sure thing, I'll be out in the field."

Jasper escaped the air-conditioned administrative confines of the FBI building and entered the air-conditioned freedom of his bucar, still safe from the sweltering August heat and oppressive humidity. He drove northwest into East Chicago and hooked up with Pete at a local diner.

Pete had willingly accepted a chance to work some overtime. Jasper was the only one not making any extra money on this. Special Agents only made overtime on extremely rare occasions, and were expected to be available at all times.

"You up for a source meet? I have Mandy, one of the SOSs at work putting together an informal source identification package for me on the Hispanic male who phoned in the tip." Jasper took a sip of coffee. The stuff brewed by the diner was decent, if not up to Starbucks standards.

Pete was still visibly shaken from the previous night. His skin seemed more ashen than tan, as if his pigment had soured overnight.

"I can't get that scene out of my mind," Pete said.

"The men going up like human sparklers?"

Pete shook his head. "No. The girl. Lashed to a stone slab. Jesus, it was like something you'd see in a horror movie."

Jasper gazed down at his half-empty cup. "They were going to kill her, for sure. It was some kind of weird sacrifice, at least that's my belief. I don't think they were going to violate her—"

"And *killing* her isn't a violation?"

"Come on, Pete, you know I didn't mean that. I'm just trying to make some sense of it."

"Yeah, I know. But the older I get the less interesting this work is becoming." Pete covered his eyes with one hand and dragged it down his face as if attempting to wipe away a layer of filth. Hernandez was older than Jasper. He was still in his fifties, but he'd been doing this sort of thing for more than thirty years now. By comparison, Jasper was a total newb with his nine or so years with the Bureau. Even if he counted his time in the Marines, he came nowhere close to Pete's experience and time dealing with monsters and staring into the face of evil.

Jasper shivered, despite the intense morning heat. Maybe the air conditioning in the diner was set too high.

"You okay?" Pete asked.

"Yeah, just thinking about how long you've dealt with the dregs, and all the shit you must have put up with over the years."

"Don't think it's all been bad. We rescued a girl, didn't we?"

Jasper laughed and sat his coffee mug down with a heavy clunk. "And here I thought I was consoling you."

"It's a long career. I'm winding down, but you've still got quite a bit of time left. This is a marathon, my friend, not a sprint."

"I'll remember that," Jasper said. "I just hope we don't have any repeats of last night, at least not for quite some time. Give me bad guy on bad guy killings, any day. Those aren't victimless crimes, but..."

"You hear yourself?" Pete asked, finally smiling. "You're beginning to sound like the news, or the ass-covering executive management we all have. Knock it off."

Jasper smiled back. "I have the information on the man who tipped us off to not only the van, but also the Euclid Hotel. I want to know how he knows so much. And speaking of the Euclid, I want to go back there and look it over again. It's still early, and I bet we can get in there before any of your CSIs or, heaven forbid, Morris and the Bureau's ERT get on scene."

"Bad news—the department isn't all that interested in evidence collection right now," Pete said. "But you still know how to process a scene, right?"

Jasper sighed. "Yeah, but I'm not even sure what we'd get out of it. I'm hesitant to use any of the ERT gear stored at the office."

Pete arched an eyebrow.

"Morris tried to get me fired."

Pete sipped his coffee.

Jasper sighed. "It isn't much of a story, really. I called him an oxygen thief and he got me kicked off the team."

"That all?" Pete shook his head. "That's nothing. But is that why you want to get to the scene early? To avoid him?"

"Personally, I don't mind being around him if there is a need, but he can't stand me."

"Gee, I can't for the life of me figure that out," Pete said. "So we'll go the hotel first?"

Jasper nodded. "I already called the potential source. He agreed to meet us this afternoon at three o'clock."

"A full day."

"C'mon. What else would you rather be doing?"

"Don't worry. I already have plans for how I'm going to spend all this overtime pay."

Chapter 6

IN THE FULL LIGHT OF DAY, THE EUCLID HOTEL LOOKED JUST like all the other abandoned buildings in the northwestern part of Indiana. Not crumbling—they were mostly made of brick and solidly built—but forlorn; the brick faded, and black lines streaking the masonry.

Crime scene tape had been placed across all the obvious entrance points. They went around to the rear, where they had entered the night before. Jasper pulled back at the sight of two East Chicago police standing guard.

"There're still people in there going over the crime scene?" Jasper asked. They stared back at him blankly.

"Guys," Pete said, appearing through the trees, weeds and bushes, "answer the man. He's not exactly one of us, but he's Bureau."

"Oh, sorry, sir," one of the policemen said to Pete. They looked so impossibly young, reminding Jasper of the young Marine guards at Quantico where the FBI Academy was housed. He'd been one of those Marines once, but had he ever looked so young and green?

"Don't call me 'sir.' Just tell us what's going on here."

"We're the ones who rescued that girl last night," Jasper said.

"Down there." Pete glanced at the ground, as if the girl had been in Hell, and perhaps she had.

Their radios clicked: *"Abandoned vehicle on Gary Avenue near Cline, possibly stolen. Requesting one unit to investigate the scene. Vehicle is an SUV parked along the south side of the road near the animal control facility. Dark-colored, late model, exact make unspecified."*

39

"Hey," Pete said, "want to check that out? It's close by."

Jasper shrugged. "Sure."

"Advise dispatch we're checking it out."

Both policemen nodded.

Jasper and Pete rolled to the scene of the abandoned SUV in their respective vehicles in less than five minutes. They passed by the tank farm and most of a nearby asphalt plant before they reached it. The SUV was on the opposite side of Gary Avenue from the asphalt plant and just before the entrance to the animal control center. The center was down a driveway, across a railroad track and behind a screen of trees and tall grass. It was barely visible from the road.

The abandoned vehicle was a dark green 2012 Chevy Equinox bearing Illinois tags, sitting off the road and well onto the shoulder. The driver's side door was open.

Jasper got out of his bucar and approached Pete's driver's side window, which was already down by the time Jasper reached the door.

"Just called in the tags," Pete said.

"Think it was stolen? Joy ride perhaps?"

"Possibly."

The radio clicked, and dispatch reported the vehicle was not stolen and the owner of the vehicle had not yet been reported missing.

"Let's check out the vehicle first," Pete said, scratching his chin. "Maybe the owner or driver got sick and wandered into the woods over there." He nodded toward the animal control facility.

Jasper didn't have high hopes for finding the owner of the vehicle nearby. He figured the vehicle had probably been stolen, just not reported yet. He and Pete approached the vehicle, each with their hands resting on their service weapons. That was somewhat unusual, but the previous night had left them both jumpy.

They peered into the vehicle and saw nothing outwardly suspicious or any sign of foul play. A sport coat lay draped across the passenger seat, folded in half lengthwise. The keys were still in the ignition. A few miscellaneous CDs were in the console along with a few pens, lip balm, a pack of tissues, and curiously, an MP3 player. The vehicle had obviously not been stolen. Neither the coat nor the MP3 player would have remained if that had been the case.

In fact, Jasper was a little surprised, given the proximity to the rougher areas not too far away, that some random passerby hadn't stopped and looted the vehicle. Gary Avenue didn't get a lot of traffic, especially on weekends. He didn't think the animal control center had anyone working today, either. The gate leading into the facility was closed. He wasn't sure if that was true of the asphalt plant, but if there was anyone over there they weren't visible outside.

Whatever had happened here, in other words, it was quite likely there'd been no witnesses—or if there were, it would have been someone driving by who didn't pay much attention to a vehicle on the side of the road. The SUV had obviously sat here for some time.

"Not stolen," Pete said.

"At least not the typical stolen vehicle," Jasper said. "But yeah, now I'm thinking this wasn't stolen. Maybe you're right, the owner or driver got sick."

Pete shrugged. "And maybe it broke down and he had a friend pick him up. There are a lot of possibilities."

Jasper sat behind the wheel and turned the ignition. The vehicle started without hesitation. "It runs nicely. Any flats?"

Pete walked around the van. "Nope."

While he checked the tires, Jasper opened the sport coat and checked the pockets. "Our friend is a busy guy," Jasper said. "Or maybe just an optimist." He tossed a pair of unopened condoms he'd found in a small inside pocket at Pete, who stepped back reflexively, allowing them to hit the ground.

"What's wrong with you?"

"They're not used."

"I don't care." Pete scrunched up his face. "What else did you get?"

"A wallet, some more lip balm, keys." Jasper opened the black faux leather wallet. "Typical credit and debit cards. A few rewards cards, all bearing the registered owner's name. There's a couple hundred in cash." He checked the slot where pictures would be kept and pulled out a driver's license. "Great photo," he said and shook his head. He handed it to Pete.

"It's like a villain from that old detective comic strip."

"Dick Tracy?"

"Yeah, that one. This guy would be rubber man or something."

"I'm surprised you know those books, Pete. Shoot, I'm surprised I know."

"I came across a stack of old papers one time, and snuck them whenever I could." Pete laughed.

Jasper had been examining the photo while they bantered. "You're right about the picture. He is sort of rubbery looking. What they call 'nondescript,' too." He frowned. "He look familiar to you, Pete?"

"Should he? The answer's no—never seen him before."

"I can't place it, but there's a familiarity there."

"He could be anyone. We've arrested how many people over the years?"

Jasper sighed. "Doesn't matter, I suppose." He tilted his head back, and ran the image through his memory. But Pete was right, they'd arrested hundreds of people and interviewed hundreds more. After a while, names and faces ran together. But this man was so average and so bland that now he stood out to Jasper.

The sun had climbed higher into the open sky, which was a dingy blue today. The morning heat threatened misery in the afternoon. Two turkey vultures appeared, their black wings forming a shallow vee as they circled a spot closer to the animal control center.

"You see that?" Jasper asked. "Something is dead or dying over at Animal Control."

"Yeah, maybe the driver is close by after all. Start looking. I'll call this in and get a squad car over here to assist. Perhaps an ambulance."

Jasper got out of the van and walked along the road, scanning the tall grass for any signs of activity and making his way toward the driveway leading into the animal control center. That would be the only way to reach the spot the vultures were circling that didn't involve fighting his way through the grass—which in some places would be over his head. The buzzing and chattering of insects filled his ears for a moment when the sounds of man disappeared briefly, reminding him of where he grew up, Tennessee, and what people referred to as the country.

Northwest Indiana was odd, that way. It was basically a heavily populated residential area, with lots of industry and commerce in the mix. Part of the great Chicago metropolis, artificially divided by the state line between Illinois and Indiana. But there were country patches scattered all through it, some of them operating farms and others just stretches of wild prairie and woodlands.

The weeds and brush gave way to the long driveway leading

to the animal control center, and he started down it. After a few yards, he came to a dirt road branching to his right. It was still a little soggy and muddy from the rain a couple of days earlier. He glanced up once more at the vultures and rather than continuing toward the animal control center went down the dirt road.

The back of his neck itched and a chill shook his body, raising the hair on his arms. Two days in a row.

A thrumming invaded the stillness that had overcome the road, as if he was nearing a nest of bees. But when he got closer he saw that it was a mass of flies, not bees, making that noise. About twenty-five feet ahead, lying in what appeared to be a puddle, was a large lump of something. At this distance, the thing was hard to make out. A dead animal of some kind, he figured. Big, but certainly not human. The shape was all wrong.

Jasper came forward slowly. After a couple of steps his hand moved reflexively to his gun's grip, his thumb on the break, ready to free the weapon from the holster.

Something wrong was up ahead. Terribly wrong.

A mound of flesh lay in a puddle of light pink, as if blood had been mixed with water and mud. Bits of white poked through the flesh—pieces of bone, clearly. A horde of insects swarmed over the mound. Jasper swallowed and took a step back, but then two forward, attempting to overcome his fear and revulsion. His heart thumped, and his chest felt hollow. Even the two men burning themselves into nothing the previous night didn't match this horror. Sure, he'd watched them die, but it had been swift and he doubted that they had suffered more than a few seconds. This, however—whatever it was—looked like a pile of uncooked, shredded meat. It was more pink than red, laced with bones, and permeated with shriveled organs.

The pulse magnified in Jasper's ears, and his vision narrowed. He leaned over, placed his hands on his knees and took a few deep breaths. He'd seen horrible crime scenes over the years, but nothing quite like this.

He didn't even understand what he was looking at. An animal? An animal killed by another animal? But if so, what kind? No animal he knew of had a shape like this. More than anything else he could think of, the bloody lump on the ground looked like a slab of halibut he'd once seen in a photograph hanging on the wall of a fishery—but it didn't really look like that, either.

A curved piece of bone caught his eye. It took a couple of seconds before his brain could make sense of what he was seeing.

That was part of a human skull. The front half of one, missing the lower jaw. The edge was sharp, as if somebody—something—had cut straight down with a huge razor, separating the facial bones—what he was looking at—from the back of the skull.

He retched, but managed not to lose his breakfast.

A female voice spoke behind him. "Agent Wilde? Zeke Wilde?"

His heart raced and he jumped, nearly falling over. He swallowed and took a deep breath, then straightened and turned around.

A smartly dressed black woman stood about twenty feet from him. She was about five and a half feet tall, maybe a little less, judging from the low heels of her shoes. Solidly built; somewhere in her early-to-mid forties. Her hair was closely cropped, and he could see a shock of white in the tight curls on both temples. Her skin was quite dark, as were her eyes. Her nose was broad and her lips were full. The navy blue suit she wore matched her looks—well-made if not flashy; sober and businesslike.

Jasper moved a little, to block her view of the remains. She placed her hands on her hips and cocked her head.

"Agent Wilde, we need to speak."

"What?" Jasper asked, nonplussed by the intrusion. "Why did you call me Zeke? No one calls me that, not even—"

"You received our phone call, did you not?" she asked. "Special Agent Ravel rang you earlier and informed you we'd be arriving today."

Jasper remembered the phone call at his home. "Oh. Right." He shook his head. "You mean that wasn't a practical joke? You're for real, then?"

"For real?" She had a rather ferocious frown. "Of course I'm for real. I'm Supervisory Special Agent Temple Black." She stepped forward and offered her hand, but stopped when she got within five feet of Jasper. She'd finally spotted what was lying on the road.

"I'm not sure, but I think that's the driver of the vehicle on the side of the road," Jasper said.

She spun away and her hands flew to her mouth.

"And yes, I'm Jasper, not Zeke. My official bureau name is Z. Jasper Wilde. Now, what are you doing here exactly?"

A man appeared behind Black, carrying a large case. This would be Agent Ravel, he assumed, the owner of what Jasper had thought was one of the guys at the office doing an Indian impression when he had received the phone call late in the night. But Ravel was obviously of south Asian ancestry. Probably a first-generation immigrant, from the trace of accent Jasper had detected.

"Agent Wilde," the man said, moving past Black. "Vance Ravel, pleased to meet—" His cheeks puffed and his free hand flew to his mouth, except he wasn't successful in tamping down his reaction. Fortunately, he was able to turn aside before he vomited. He even had the presence of mind to hold the case well away from his body, so it wouldn't get splattered.

"I kind of had the same reaction," Jasper said sympathetically, after Ravel was done and Black had brought herself under control. "Godawful-looking, isn't it? Now, will someone tell me why you're out here? Where did you come from and what are you trying to accomplish? It isn't often we get headquarters people out here on such short notice."

"We..." Temple Black took a deep breath. "We need to speak somewhere else. I can't be anywhere near that and think clearly." She nodded stiffly toward the pile of meat, blood, and bone.

"Fine," Jasper said, "but I didn't invite you over here to begin with. Did you see my partner, Pete Hernandez?"

"Is he an East Chicago cop? If so, he's up on the road talking with his buddies."

They moved away from the body and toward the driveway leading into the animal control center. Jasper helped Ravel by taking the case from him after a minor protest. The man was still obviously unsettled. "So, who are you guys?"

"Scientific Anomalies Group," Black said, staring straight ahead as if embarrassed by the name, or not wanting to go into detail.

"SAG?" Jasper asked, pronouncing it as an acronym rather than a string of initials. He couldn't help but laugh. "Really?"

Black's jaw tightened. "Look, I didn't come up with that one."

There was no point in ribbing these two agents over it any further, though. So he just said, "Never heard of it" in as neutral a tone of voice as he could manage.

"You wouldn't have," Ravel said, wiping his mouth with a handkerchief. "It's new and...ah, we don't publicize it."

"How did you find me?"

"The cops over at the Euclid Hotel told us you responded

to an abandoned vehicle over here," Black said. "We need to go back over to the hotel."

"The little girl was rescued and the investigation is over," Jasper said, but that was a lie. He just didn't want headquarters pukes stomping around the crime scene. "By me and my partner over there." They'd come within sight of Gary Avenue. He pointed toward Pete, who stood by two uniformed cops and was engaged in an animated discussion.

Black opened her mouth but Jasper held up a cautioning finger.

"Pete!" he said loudly. "You need to get over here and take a look at what I found down there. It has to be the driver." Jasper paused a moment. "I warn you, the body isn't pretty to look at."

Pete broke away from the uniformed police, and walked with purpose toward Jasper and the two headquarters people. "They said they were here looking for you," Pete said, his eyes registering Jasper's annoyance, and conveying *sorry.*

"It's okay," Jasper said. "They were just leaving."

"SAC Weber already approved this," Black said.

Jasper shot her a look he hoped would shut her up, but she went right on. "And furthermore, the assistant director—my boss—"

"Hold it right there," Jasper said. He focused on Pete. "Take a peek over there at the body. Follow the sound of the flies, you can't miss it."

Pete frowned, and walked off. Jasper turned back to the woman.

"SSA Black, we do not squabble like that in front of locals, you got me? You may be a headquarters supervisor, but in the field that doesn't mean squat. And you said Weber approved this? My Special Agent in Charge? That's a joke. He's been checked out for a year now; he'd approve anything. He's pretty much retired-in-place ever since he got the job."

Black's mouth opened again, but closed as if she'd reconsidered her choice of words.

Ravel stepped forward. "Jasper," he said, "may I call you that?"

"It's better than the alternative."

"That'd be what? Jerk?" Temple Black took another deep breath and turned her head. "I'm sorry, it's already been a long morning—"

"—and long night," both Jasper and Vance said at once. Jasper grinned. "Yeah, you called me at oh dark thirty. I didn't appreciate that."

"My apologies," Vance said. "Listen, we need to discuss what happened last night. When is a good time? We'd also really like to get into that abandoned hotel. We think there is something else going on here. Based on your preliminary report we think it's serious." He lifted the case in his hand a few inches. "There's some equipment in here… Well. We think we could be of use, let's leave it at that."

Black nodded and faced Jasper again. "We should speak with your boss, your immediate boss. This needs to get worked out, but you should finish up here first. That," she swallowed, "body was a mess and needs to be processed."

Heavy breaths came up behind them as they reached the side of the road and their line of vehicles. Pete jogged past them and signaled to the uniformed men who joined him. They then resumed their spirited conversation.

"It's about to get crowded around here," Jasper said. "I'll tell you what, if you can wait until mid-afternoon I'll take you to the Euclid Hotel. I don't think evidence recovery is going to happen until Monday at that scene, if at all, especially given this new incident." He cocked his head toward the dirt road where the mangled corpse lay in a pile. "Afterward, I'll see if we can meet with my boss. But I can't promise anything, SSA Black. It is the weekend, you know. Exhausted supervisors need their rest."

The moment he made the wisecrack he wondered if he'd gone a little too far. But Black just grinned. The expression transformed her face, turning it from something that had seemed overbearing to something good-natured and quite a bit younger. He wasn't sure, but he had a feeling that expression came more naturally to her than the one he thought of as *Supervisory Special Agent Ramrod Up Her Ass.*

"Yeah, I know how that is with some of this new breed of management," she said. "And call me Temple, would you?"

Jasper nodded. "Sure. And I'm Jasper." They'd come up onto Gary Avenue by then and he could see the entire line of vehicles parked there: a police cruiser, his bucar, Pete's Crown Vic, and two other vehicles, one a rental and the other a little farther away clearly belonged to a local.

He frowned. "You only rented one car, right?"

Temple nodded.

"Probably a reporter, then," Jasper said. A person sat in the vehicle, an off-white compact pickup, but their face was obscured by the sun visor. The pickup lurched forward and then spun in a tight turn to head back toward East Chicago proper, kicking up a dust cloud in the process.

"Damn! Too much dust to get a plate." For a moment, he was tempted to go in pursuit. But by the time he got into his vehicle, the man would be out of sight beyond a bend in the road. And once he got to the junction of Gary and Parrish, a short distance beyond, there were just too many ways he could go.

"That was a Toyota pickup with Indiana tags, I think," Temple said. "Couldn't make out a partial on the tags though, sorry."

"Well, there's an outside chance that was the person responsible for the corpse back there," Jasper said. "But that would have been pretty bold, even for a serial killer who wants to insert himself into an investigation. It was likely just a nosey citizen who got twitchy when he saw me looking at him."

"We could run a search based on the parameters of the make and model and color of the vehicle," Vance said.

"You're right," Jasper said. "I'll have Pete run it through his folks, since this homicide is likely their investigation anyway. And it's got to be a homicide, with the corpse looking like that. I can't think of any kind of accident that would do that sort of damage. Maybe in the middle of a steel mill, but out here?"

He reached out and shook their hands. "Okay, I'll meet you two at the Euclid later on? Say seventeen hundred?"

"That'll work," Temple said.

"Go take a nap or something, and please don't poke around anywhere. I don't want to have to bail you guys out of trouble."

Temple smiled. Vance nodded, his head bobbing up and down rapidly.

Chapter 7

TEMPLE AND VANCE STAYED AT THE ANIMAL CONTROL SCENE JUST long enough to see the coroner's van arrive, followed by a black SUV. A grumpy looking man with round spectacles exited the van while two women wearing cargo pants and dark blue shirts emblazoned with FBI and ERT exited the SUV and marched purposefully over to Jasper and his cop friend, Pete.

"Let's go." Temple motioned for Vance to get in their rental. She started the car but kept the air conditioning off and lowered the windows. Jasper was pointing and gesticulating like a madman as he appeared to lecture the two female Evidence Response Team members. The rental was far enough away that she couldn't make out the words, but she imagined what the man was thinking and could probably guess what he was saying. Agent Jasper Wilde was probably thinking the women loved their "chick SWAT." Bureau women didn't typically join the tactically-minded and typically knuckle-dragging group known as SWAT—Special Weapons and Tactics—but preferred the more cerebral ERT, the Evidence Response Team.

"Hey boss—"

Temple's grip on the steering wheel tightened and her head snapped toward Vance. "What?" she demanded. Then she took a deep breath and relaxed. "I'm sorry. It's just that—"

Temple nodded toward Jasper. "That annoying man out there is going to be trouble. He's already gotten under my skin and we were with him for what, five minutes?"

"I don't know, he's probably all right." Vance stared through the windshield and not at Temple. "When you were in the field didn't you resent having HQ show up?"

"HQ never showed up in the field, except for maybe meetings at the office, but—"

"Exactly."

"No, you're right," Temple conceded. "The field hates it when HQ butts in. But if he's the agent we have to deal with out here, Lord do I hope it's only for a day or two."

She swung the car around and headed for the Euclid Hotel.

"So, Temple, what's the plan? Where are we going, not our hotel, right?"

"No. It's too early, but we are going to drive by another hotel, the Euclid, and then we'll head over to Merrillville and see if we can get an early check-in."

Vance yanked his neck to the right, then the left, cupped his chin in his right hand and shoved to the right and then to the left, filling the car with pops and snaps and cracks. Temple's stomach grumbled—now she wanted some cereal, Rice Krispies.

"You done? If so, how does that plan sound to you?" Temple asked.

"I'm hungry, but yes, that sounds good."

As they drove by the Euclid, they spotted two police still watching over the abandoned hotel, so they didn't bother stopping. Temple swung into the first greasy spoon she spotted, hoping to soak up some local color, or perhaps overhear some gossip about what happened the evening before. But the place was close to empty and the few people who were in there kept to themselves, so they just ate and left.

They drove by the FBI office in Merrillville and farther down the road found their hotel. It was a decent-looking place, part of a major chain but certainly no Hilton or Marriott. She was glad Vance hadn't chosen the Express, since he'd be cracking that silly joke about knowing how to do everything since they had stayed there. Temple smiled. Vance wasn't perfect, but he was easy to work with and willing to put in crazy hours in the name of science, and that she liked.

Chapter 8

JASPER PHONED HIS BOSS, SUPERVISORY SPECIAL AGENT JOHNSON, the senior agent of the Merrillville office, requesting a meeting for around seventeen hundred. Johnson met his request with a sigh. His excuses all sounded the same—something about his kids, but Jasper read between the lines. Johnson simply didn't want to come in on a Saturday, especially when he discovered no crisis existed. After hearing about the headquarters people and the mangled body on Gary Avenue, he capitulated and promised he'd meet Jasper at the office, but that whatever this problem was better not take long.

Pete had already arrived at the diner in Hessville where they'd directed the prospective source, Carlos Ochoa, to meet them. Pete's Crown Vic was empty, and Jasper spied Pete through the window, seated alone at a booth.

Jasper found meeting contacts such as this one in a public place safer, and the odds of a successful recruitment higher. The locations for gang sources mattered, since a bad one could result in the death of the source. But with this type of person, someone who'd simply reported the whereabouts of a missing girl, the diner was a decent place to break the ice. It was well-known in the area and had been in business for years.

This particular diner was located outside of East Chicago. Hessville was one of the neighborhoods in nearby Hammond, but it was close enough that straying into another local department's jurisdiction wouldn't be an issue for Pete. They weren't actively working a case, anyway; the meeting was for informational and recruitment purposes. And meeting in the middle of the after-noon meant the three men wouldn't be hassled by the waitress to finish and get out.

The diner's exterior demanded a new paint job. The fake luster reminiscent of so many diners had tarnished, the railing was pocked with rust, and the concrete steps cracked. Often with diners like this, though, the food was a lot better than the rundown appearance. Jasper hadn't eaten here in quite a while, but as he recalled the meal had been good if not outstanding.

A middle-aged hostess greeted Jasper, but he nodded toward the dining room and she gestured for him to head on in. All neighborhood diners like this featured the same sort of smell—fried food laced with coffee followed by a tinge of sweetness.

"Glad you could make it." Pete grasped a mug with both hands, as if warming them.

"I had to call my boss."

"About those headquarters people?"

"Yep, and Mandy sent me the particulars on the man we're meeting."

"Any derogatory?"

"Minor infractions, nothing recent."

"You really need an informant, don't you?" Pete grinned.

"This is the bureau, Pete. We call them sources, or CHSs."

"Pfft. Whatever. It's an informant."

Jasper grinned. "And I always need another source."

A waitress appeared, wearing black and white attire and holding a little pad in one finely manicured hand and a pencil in the other. She had a tattoo on her neck and a spike protruding from beneath her bottom lip.

"Something to drink?"

"I don't suppose you'd be able to make a cappuccino?" Jasper asked.

"Sorry, hon," she splayed her hands, "don't do those here. But the coffee is drinkable."

"A coffee then, cream only."

"Something to eat?"

"We're waiting on someone else," Pete said, glancing past Jasper toward the entrance.

She nodded and walked off.

"Kids."

Pete grinned. "You're probably not much older, my friend. You go for her type?"

"What do you think?"

"How should I know? You don't date anyone. Just askin'," Pete said. "Ah, there he is—has to be him."

Jasper turned in his seat for a glimpse and spun back around. A short Hispanic male, glancing about nervously, stood inside the door. He wore a short-sleeved, black and white checkered button-down shirt and faded but intact jeans. On his feet were work boots, steel-toed. A factory worker most likely, but Jasper had been wrong before on his attempts at profiling. He'd been wrong about his wife, Lucy, after all. He reminded himself that there was no point in allowing his personal life and divorce to take up residence once again in his head.

"I'll go get him," Pete said.

"He can sit next to me, you think that'll work?"

"That'd be better."

The waitress returned with Jasper's coffee as Pete and the potential source, Carlos, arrived. After an awkward moment of jockeying for seats, Pete and Carlos sat across from Jasper, with Pete scooted all the way to the window.

Jasper tilted his head and Pete flashed a quick grin in return. There were always plans, and they usually never worked out the way they were drawn. The seating arrangements were less than optimal, but acceptable. Jasper believed having Pete sit across from the source better because he figured they'd do most of the talking, leaving Jasper to his coffee.

"Carlos Ochoa," the short man offered.

"Thank you for meeting us today." Jasper dumped a few drops of cream into the pitch-like coffee, as thick and viscous as ninety weight oil, and probably as tasty.

"I gave you what you needed, so why are we talking now? Am I in trouble?"

The waitress interrupted. "A drink? Some food? What'll you have?" For some reason she was frowning at Carlos.

"Water."

"That it?" She placed a hand on her hip.

"*Si.*"

"Food for you two?" Her eyebrows rose, hopeful.

"No food for me." Pete shook his head. "But I'll have a water—"

She cocked her head. "Water."

"And," Jasper said in a drawn out manner, trying to get across that he hadn't finished his sentence, "I'll have an order of wet fries, you know, fries with gravy?"

She walked off, muttering something under her breath.

"A friendly girl," Pete said.

"She isn't too bad," Carlos said.

"You know her?"

"Once a friend of mine, now more of an acquaintance. So, again, why are we here?"

Pete coughed. His hands encircled the mug, still drawing warmth despite the heat outside now in full force in mid-afternoon. "Tell us more about the missing girl, and how you knew what you knew."

"My daughter saw Teresa's kidnapping happen." Carlos stared at the tabletop. It was a dark wood-grained veneer, like the wood paneling so prevalent in the seventies, and reminded Jasper of his childhood home. "She was really scared by it."

"Explain the entire event if you're able." Pete sipped his water. Jasper relinquished the lead to Pete, happily, even if Pete sitting next to Carlos created an awkward environment for a source recruitment and debrief.

"The abduction?"

"Yes, run the scenario by us," Pete said. "We're trying to figure out if more people are involved, maybe a gang or a human trafficking ring operating under the radar."

"The stolen van belonged to a friend of a friend."

Jasper tamped down his irritation. "Go deeper, please, we need more information than you're giving us." He took a sip of the thick, bitter coffee, which turned out not to be as bad as he'd thought it would be.

"My daughter hangs around with Teresa quite a bit."

"What's your daughter's name?"

"Isabella."

"A pretty name," Jasper said.

"A pretty girl," Carlos replied. "So, they often walk together, along with a few other girls to a friend's house on the other side of the railroad tracks."

"Which tracks? At what street and near which intersection?" That was an important piece of information, since railroad tracks crisscrossed northwestern Indiana more than perhaps anywhere else in the United States. The exact location might help pinpoint where the kidnappers had operated out of, and would also provide a few more leads in the form of other eyewitnesses.

"The tracks just north of Chicago Avenue, a block west of Indianapolis Boulevard. The girls were heading north on Magoun, after leaving their friend's house a few blocks south. All of them crossed the tracks except for Teresa."

"Why? The guys in the van grab her?"

Carlos shook his head. "Not yet."

"A train, right?" Jasper asked.

"*Sí*. A train had been bearing down on them, and poor Teresa had been too afraid to cross according to my daughter. And as the train crawled past, the van pulled up right next to Teresa as if waiting to cross the tracks. My daughter said that a passing freight car blocked their view and when it passed Teresa was gone. In that moment, they must have grabbed her."

"You said, 'they.' How do you know more than one man participated in the kidnapping?"

"The news—"

"Damn it." The media had somehow gotten wind of certain details. The fact there were two men was leaked probably didn't matter, but media problems annoyed Jasper. But there was always a chance, a slim one, that this man knew more than he should. "Go on, my apologies."

The waitress dropped off the rest of their drinks and food. Jasper pushed his coffee aside in favor of plain old water to have with the fries and gravy.

Carlos took a sip of water, wiped his lips, and continued: "One of my daughter's other friends even tried to crawl beneath the slowly moving train, but the other girls pulled her back. All of the girls are so upset by this." He stared into his water.

"Any other details? Something you're leaving out?"

"Are you saying I'm purposely withholding something?" Carlos kept his eyes averted, but his clenched fist and white knuckles betrayed his anger at possibly being called a liar.

"Not at all, I'm trying to get as much information as possible." Jasper had both hands up in a placating gesture.

"I'm not sure I understand," Carlos said, finally raising his gaze. "You rescued the girl, what else is there to understand?"

Pete placed a hand on Carlos's shoulder. "What if more girls go missing because there were more than two men?"

"Of course." Carlos sipped his water, and wiped his mouth with the back of his hand. "You're right. The girls saw the van, an older make, and white. But you know this."

"We do," Jasper said. "But the details are quite a bit for a bunch of young and excited and scared girls to recite, don't you think, Carlos?" He extricated a fry from the pile and plopped it in his mouth.

"Fine." Carlos sighed. "No point in hiding this." He paused.

"Go on," Pete said. "You can tell us. You're not in trouble, unless you were in on the crime."

Carlos stiffened and made to slide from the booth.

"Hold on." Jasper wiped off his hands and motioned for Carlos to remain in the booth. "I don't think you were involved. That doesn't make any sense to me. But tell me, if the van belonged to a friend of a friend, would you really know the specifics so well?"

Carlos stared at Pete, and reluctantly eased onto the bench seat of the booth. So much for Pete building rapport.

"I drove around the area and spotted the van. I got out and felt the hood and so forth—warm metal. And the engine ticked, you know, like it was cooling off."

"So you had a woman report the activity at the hotel. A woman phoned in the hotel tip, an Hispanic woman."

"I did," Carlos said. "My wife. I told her what I'd seen and said they had to be in the abandoned hotel. I noticed the door had been used recently."

"But you didn't witness the men take the girl inside, did you?" Jasper bit into another fry, this one soaked with gravy.

Carlos shook his head. "A guess, but it was the only place that made sense."

"Fine, anything else?"

"No."

"Could we speak with your daughter at some point?" Pete asked.

"I'd prefer not, but if you must." Carlos allowed the final word to hang.

"Probably won't be necessary," Jasper said, and Pete frowned at him. "Let me ask you, would you be available to meet with us from time to time?" Jasper grabbed a couple more of the less saturated fries and stuffed them into his mouth. He hadn't realized how hungry he'd been.

"I already told you all I can about this nasty business."

"Understood, but what I mean is for other goings-on in the community. Someone with your sense of duty to the neighborhood and so willing to put yourself in harm's way, well, I'd enjoy working with you again. Would that be okay? If you need money or something, I'm sure we could—"

"No. No money." Carlos frowned, and disgust crept onto his face. "Some coffee or lunch perhaps, but no money, I can't accept money. I was simply doing my duty and helping the community. For my daughter."

"I didn't mean to insult you," Jasper said. "Again, my apologies. Can you tell us anything else about Teresa's kidnapping, and the men who died?"

Carlos shook his head.

Pete glanced at Jasper, appearing antsy to pursue a different line of questioning. Jasper raised his eyebrows and tipped his head to the side in a quick gesture.

Pete took over. "We discovered a body today—"

"In the abandoned hotel? Another man?" Carlos asked. "Not a little girl, I pray." He glanced up at the ceiling and crossed himself.

"No, nothing like that," Pete said, "but it's a strange death."

"Strange? In what way?"

"How about we just say strange, all right? The body had been mutilated."

Carlos took a sip of water. "I heard nothing about a mutilated body."

"How about a missing person? An abandoned vehicle along Gary Avenue over near the animal control center? Doesn't mean anything to you?" Pete leaned on the table with both elbows. The approach wasn't quite as effective when sitting next to a person you were questioning, even if the proximity of Pete to Carlos should have been uncomfortable. There was nothing like sitting across from someone and staring at them while leaning forward and knowing the answers to the questions posed, or at least pretending. This wasn't an interrogation, but a simple extraction of information in the furtherance of a homicide investigation—a disturbing homicide. Jasper hoped Pete wouldn't provide details, not in such a public place with food being served.

Jasper had picked up another dripping fry but he dropped it

back on the plate. The image of the pink mound with bone poking through the one-time flesh of a man overwhelmed his hunger.

Pete and Carlos hadn't noticed Jasper's action, and hopefully not the sick expression, nose kinked up replacing his attempted stoicism. In fact, Carlos's body language and attitude was that of a person who retained more information than he provided. Was he afraid to talk about the homicide because he feared the person who had perpetrated the heinous crime? He did have a family—a daughter—to protect, after all.

The clinking of silverware on plates, and clunking of glasses on table worked forward into his mind. The sounds had been there the entire time, but surfaced when the conversation chilled. Motion from the left caught in his periphery. Jasper turned and saw the waitress coming toward them. He opened his eyes wide, alerting Pete so he'd cease the current line of questions.

"You having anything else?" The waitress stood with her hip cocked to the left with a hand resting upon the ample curve.

"We're good." Jasper considered a fresh cup of coffee, but would hold out for a cappuccino at Starbucks once they finished with Carlos. The waitress slapped the check down on the table and walked off, shaking her head. "What's with her?"

"You're cops and she doesn't particularly care for me."

"That bother you?"

"Should it? I'm not doing anything wrong. She's been busted before, though, so I'm sure she has a beef with you guys."

"Pfft, not me," Jasper said. "Probably Pete, he's into hate crimes."

"Ay." Pete dropped his head into his hands.

"Kidding. Totally kidding. Sheesh." Jasper picked at the fries, just from reflex. His appetite was quite gone, for the moment. "She think you're a narc or something?"

Carlos shook his head. "No—besides, she never got into the drug scene."

"A few more questions and I'll let you get back to your weekend, okay?"

"Sure thing."

"What do you do for a living, if you don't mind me asking?"

"Metal working. You know, a machine shop and other various odds and ends."

"Like a handyman?" Jasper asked.

"Only during my off hours, fixing stuff around the neigh-borhood."

"You must hear quite a bit about what goes on around town, right?"

Carlos shrugged. "It's talking to people, being friendly. You know how it is."

Jasper did indeed. The main job of a Special Agent involved talking to people and obtaining information in the prevention of crime and in the furtherance of investigations in the hopes of locking up criminals.

"Yeah, I understand," Jasper said. "We understand." He glanced at Pete.

"The machine shop," Pete cut in, "what sort of shop is it?"

"We do specialty work. Stainless steel, mostly, and other alloys. Some of them are pretty exotic."

"You work that stuff?" Pete asked. "Impressive."

"I'm more of a helper. Sweeping, odds and ends mostly." Carlos broke eye contact briefly.

"Fair enough," Jasper said, wedging himself back into the conversation. He had the impression Carlos held back information on them, but no source ever gave up the whole enchilada during a first meeting. No need to press the man now, he'd get more information from him later. "I can contact you at the number you provided to the station?"

"Sure, that's a private number."

"Good, I was hoping I didn't need to provide a drop phone. The budget for operational items is kind of in the crapper right now."

Carlos arched an eyebrow. Perhaps Jasper shouldn't have discussed budget issues with a prospective source, but the government's financial woes were well known throughout the world.

"But if you ever needed a drop phone, that's doable. Getting one depends on the sort of information you're providing and the need to keep your identity secret."

Pete smiled, as if saying "nice recovery."

"No need. I'll be fine, but do feel free to contact me if you come up with more questions."

"Thank you," Jasper said and slid from the booth.

Carlos stood and Jasper thrust a hand out to shake. Carlos shook, hardly gripping Jasper's hand, nodded, and walked off. Jasper slid back into the booth, frowning.

"What?" Pete asked.

"His hand's not as calloused as I would have thought from a metal worker and handyman."

"So what? Maybe he wears gloves and uses hand lotion."

"Nobody in their right mind wears gloves around moving equipment. Sure as hell not machine tools. Good way to lose a hand." Jasper shrugged. "I had the impression he held back on us a bit. He knows more than he's admitting, or at least he's not admitting to how he knows so much. The waitress angle interests me—they obviously know each other fairly well."

"He said they were once friends," Pete said. "For a first meeting, I'd say Carlos acted like any other source. He did provide the information leading us right to those bastards at the hotel yesterday."

"That he did, but there's something off about the whole thing."

"A feeling you have, perhaps?"

"You're funny. No, I can't figure his mannerisms and odd answers."

"Sounded straightforward to me," Pete said.

"Hey look," Jasper said. "Out there, in the parking lot."

An off-white pickup pulled out of the lot.

"So?"

"I believe that was Carlos."

"Again, so?"

"Today at Animal Control, a pickup sped off from the scene. You didn't see it?"

"No. I was busy, remember?" Pete frowned. "What sort of pickup? Make? Tags?"

"Toyota, off-white with Indiana tags. Temple made the identification."

"But you couldn't identify the exact model, and you didn't get the tags."

"Well—"

"You know how many of those pickups are rolling around northern Indiana? Let me tell you a quick story."

"Go ahead." Jasper sighed.

Pete finished off his water and cleared his throat. "Many years ago we had a serial killer rolling around in a green station wagon, American made. This was verified by a few witnesses. How many of those could there possibly be, you ask, but when we searched the DMV records the report came back with a few hundred."

"That isn't too bad."

Pete laughed. "Yeah, but in the midst of following up on all those leads, we finally caught him, and you know what?"

"I don't know, you have me on pins and needles."

Pete waved him off. "The vehicle wasn't even an American-made station wagon, but a Mitsubishi something-or-other."

"Okay, point taken, but I'm still not convinced, it seems odd and a little too coincidental. Now let me tell you a story."

"If you must." Pete sat back and slouched in the booth.

Jasper grinned. "Not that many years ago we had what seemed an amazing source come to us—"

"Let me guess."

"Hold on," Jasper said, "allow me to finish. It turned out the amazing source was a bad guy. I remember thinking that that guy was going to be the best source ever or end up being the subject of an investigation. Sounds like Carlos to me."

"Maybe," Pete shrugged, "maybe not."

Jasper smacked the table. "If only I'd gotten the tags off the pickup fleeing from the scene I could have compared it to Carlos's DMV records."

"Well, my friend, maybe it's time for glasses."

"You two ready?" The waitress had walked up on them without either of them noticing.

"Yeah," Jasper said, and dropped a ten on the table. "Keep the change."

The waitress picked up the money and sauntered off.

The diner had grown quiet and had entered the lull before the dinner rush.

"I need to meet those agents in a bit." Jasper slid from the booth. "You're ready, right?"

Pete chuckled. "I only had water."

They exited the diner and stood near their vehicles. Pete shoved a toothpick between his lips, but then grasped it between his thumb and forefinger. "Where are you meeting your agents? You're talking about the black woman and that little Indian man?"

"Yep, those are the ones. I'm meeting them over at the hotel. They're interested in examining the scene."

"What for?" Pete asked.

Jasper released a protracted sigh and dragged his hand down his face. "They're out from headquarters, some unit I've never heard of, SAG or something. They're interested in the crime scene and the M.O. for some reason."

"You mind if I sit this one out?"

Jasper raised an eyebrow. "You're gonna leave me with those two?"

"I'd rather hang with you, but I can't go back in the hotel, or anywhere near the place." Pete glanced away from him. "And I don't know why."

"But you stared at a lump of meat, a mangled human corpse, over at Animal Control, eh? That was one of the most horrible things I've ever seen."

Pete tilted his head back, squinting against the sun. "Look," he said, dropping his gaze back on Jasper, "I can't explain. Cut me slack on this one, will you?"

Jasper rested a hand on the man's shoulder, "Sure thing. You know, it'd probably be better anyway if you aren't involved much with the headquarters folk. I'll call you if I need anything. You do the same."

"Sounds fine by me." Pete nodded and dropped into his Crown Vic.

"Hey, I won't have any problems getting into the hotel, will I?"

"I'll call over for you and tell the officers standing guard to allow you entrance."

"Great, talk to you later."

Pete waved, started the engine, and drove off.

Jasper did likewise. The afternoon sun had baked the interior of the black vehicle, but within a minute the air conditioning caught up to the heat.

By the time he reached the Euclid Hotel, the headquarters agents Temple and Vance would likely already be waiting for him. He didn't speed, though. If he got caught on the wrong side of the tracks waiting for a train to pass and the HQ zombies had to wait, so be it.

Chapter 9

UNDER THE GLARING SUN, THE EUCLID HOTEL APPEARED BENIGN. The dilapidated exterior was like the other abandoned buildings in the area, but Jasper would never view the hotel in that way again. Now that he sat parked curbside, he found it difficult to muster up any enthusiasm to enter.

Jasper squeezed the Charger's steering wheel as if he were choking the life out of the car until his fingers ached. He took a breath and realized he'd been clenching his jaw the entire time.

"Fine, I'll go in," he muttered to himself. "They're probably back there annoying the police standing guard duty."

He went around back and found two East Chicago police standing guard.

"Evening," Jasper said.

Both men straightened a bit at his approach.

"Pete called you?"

"Yes," said the man on the right.

"You see two other Bureau agents come around here? I'm supposed to—"

The man on the right held up a hand. "They're already down there, sir."

"What?"

"Yeah, they arrived fifteen minutes ago."

They must have parked around the corner. Jasper sighed. "May I enter the hotel?"

"Sure, knock yourself out. We're not even sure why we're guarding this dump."

Jasper couldn't believe Agent Black had had the nerve to enter the hotel without him. She'd overstepped her mandate. Surely

63

SAC Weber couldn't have known this would happen, that two headquarters agents would be traipsing throughout Indianapolis field office's area of responsibility. Now he couldn't wait for the meeting with his boss later on today.

"Thank you, gentlemen, if I'm not back by dawn, well, you know—"

The man on the right winked. "Copy that."

He entered through the same door Pete and he had used the previous evening. Chills coursed through him, as they had then. This time, however, someone had flicked on what appeared to be every light source still functioning in the hotel. Illuminated such as it was now, the building's years of neglect were obvious.

The heavy incense aroma from the previous evening had dissipated somewhat, but the acrid chemical odor of the thermite reaction remained as if the stench had permeated the building's old, porous bones. Jasper descended the stairs, not looking forward to his next interaction with Temple Black, despite having left her on somewhat good terms a few hours earlier near Animal Control.

He eased into the doorway at the bottom of the stairs.

"Agent Wilde held back on his reporting," a male voice said. From the accent, that had to be Vance.

"How so?" a female asked. That was Black.

"The samples I'm collecting here are quite fascinating," Vance said.

Jasper strode into the basement, the scene of the thermite suicides and the little girl's captivity. "Which samples?"

Vance and Temple jumped. Temple's lips pursed, rolled her eyes, and shook her head. "You're lucky you didn't get shot."

"By who?" Jasper placed his hands on his hips. "You? Him?" He nodded toward Vance.

"I'll have you know I'm an excellent shot." Vance frowned and kneeled before a scorch mark on the floor.

"Hey, the mark you're examining wasn't there last night," Jasper said.

"What wasn't?" Temple's brow furrowed.

"The scorch mark." Jasper walked over to where Vance kneeled and studied the black streak. "I wonder if someone else has been down here. I mean, we cleared the building last night and posted guards, but is it possible someone got in here? Another man associated with the two who offed themselves?"

"Look here," Vance said. "You see this?" His dark brown fingers traced a wavy pattern in the floor coinciding with the scorch mark.

"Strange." Jasper stood, and motioned for Vance to follow. "I noticed similar markings back there."

He moved toward the back room where the kidnapped girl had been tied to a stone slab. Vance followed and scraped the wall. Soot and dirt covered a piece of paper he held. He opened a vial, folded the paper and allowed the debris to fall in.

"What do you make of the substance you're scraping off the wall, Vance?" Temple entered the back room behind them.

Vance shrugged. "Until I can perform a detailed analysis, I can only venture a guess."

"Which is?" asked Temple.

"This isn't from the thermite reaction."

"So?"

"I'd say from the fading on the marks back here that they are older than the thermite scars in the other room as well as the identical scorch marks," Vance said.

"But what is it?" Jasper persisted. "I understand the thermite and how that'd jack up not only a person, but anything the intense heat touched. My confusion is over the odd distortions rippling throughout the wall and spots on the floor as well. What can you tell me about those?" He knelt near the stone slab where the little girl had been tied down, studying for odd marks like those appearing on the wall and the floor.

"My question exactly," Temple said.

"Patience." Vance scraped more samples from the wall, and joined Jasper by the slab. "What are you seeing here?"

"Nothing. Well, nothing but another image I'll never eradicate from my mind."

Vance raised an eyebrow.

"He's talking about the little girl," Temple said, "you know, the one we're going to go speak with? The victim?"

"Oh, of course," Vance said.

"You're gonna speak with the victim?" Jasper shot to his feet.

"Yeah, that's exactly what we're going to do. We've taken over the investigation out here, remember?"

"Now wait a minute," Jasper said, "this is Indianapolis territory, and—"

"Remember, your SAC, the one who is checked out and would say yes to anything, agreed to our presence here." Temple raised a fancy camera to her eye and began snapping photos.

"Yeah, but his concurrence didn't include taking over investigations, and what's your nexus here, anyway? We solved the case—Pete and I." Jasper's ears were red and hot. Shoot, even Lucy, his ex-wife, hadn't ever got to him this fast.

"Don't be so sure, cowboy," Temple said, continuing to take photos of the room.

Cowboy? Did she think he hailed from Oklahoma or Texas? His home was Tennessee, although he'd ditched most of the accent between his time at college, the Marines, and now the Bureau.

"Calm yourself. It isn't the end of the world. Our nexus is clear, my group investigates this sort of thing."

"What, this SAG of yours?"

"Yep. Scientific anomalies, remember?"

"Oh, I remember, but explain to me how this is an anomaly." Jasper folded his arms.

"Vance?"

The Indian man with a small potbelly resting on an otherwise spindly frame stood and pulled a notebook out of an inside jacket pocket and flipped it open. "So, you reported the thermite, which in and of itself is not out of the ordinary—"

"Excuse me? Are you serious?" Jasper's hands went to his hips.

"Completely." Hurt crept into Vance's deep brown eyes, as if Jasper had wounded him. "Now, if you'll—"

"Look, in the Marine Corps we dismantled huge chunks of machinery with the stuff. The temperatures involved in a thermite reaction are capable of taking almost anything down to parade rest. And you're saying the presence of thermite isn't out of the ordinary? I disagree."

"Wait a moment, please," Vance said. "I didn't complete my explanation and analysis. What is not ordinary is men using thermite on themselves, and also using such an interesting chemical as a means of catalyzing."

"The mats," Jasper said. "They stood on the mats, coated their feet with a liquid, and hopped into the basins."

"Yes," Vance said, "sulfuric acid. Remember, I read your report."

"How could I forget? You called me at some crazy hour to talk about it."

Vance coughed. "Now, this sort of suicide pact—"

Jasper opened his mouth, but Vance raised a hand—

"This sort of suicide pact is common with cults."

"But there were only two men, wouldn't there be more cult members crowding around for a peek?"

"A good point, but I still believe we're dealing with a group of men engaged in heinous—"

"So you're saying this wasn't some fucked-up kiddie-porn type thing, but some sort of ritual killing? A sacrifice?"

"Perhaps," Temple interjected. "We're entertaining a few theories, but we're still forming a more complete picture."

"But you figured you had enough so that your little group— your guild or whatever you call it—could roll into Indiana and take over what is essentially a crimes against children case."

"There has been more than one death," Temple said.

"Yeah, two men killed themselves. Two utterly despicable men."

"But four deaths overall," said Temple.

"What?" Jasper stepped closer to Temple—uncomfortably so for him and hopefully for her, but she stood her ground. "Are you trying to tell me the pile of meat and bones over at Animal Control is somehow related to this?"

"Possibly. Vance?"

Jasper turned his attention toward Vance, and felt Temple take a step backward.

"I found markings near the site of the uh, pile of meat and—"

"Yeah, yeah, go on. I get it."

"—uh, similar to the striations and distortions on the floor and wall here at the hotel."

Jasper dragged his hand down his face in frustration.

"But how could they possibly be connected? A cult? The mess over near Animal Control was no suicide." Jasper tried to keep the incredulity out of his voice, but failed. "The pile of meat? No way."

"No," Temple said, "but perhaps the pile of meat, as you so eloquently put it, had been witness to the cult's activities and paid the price."

"I'm sorry, but the idea that a person could mangle a body in such a way is ludicrous. Are you two about finished here? You were supposed to wait for me, remember? I was going to escort you through the crime scene—"

"Oh, I wasn't aware of any such arrangement." Temple stepped into Jasper's space now. Her glossy lips pursed and her eyebrows arched in a *go ahead, make my day* sort of way. "Remember, we've taken over the investigations."

"Wait. This one *and* the murder? The locals, the East Chicago Police, will never agree—"

"They already have." She turned her attention on Vance whose head was down studying some smudge on the floor. "How much more time do you need?"

"A few more minutes. I need to collect samples from the basins."

"Ten-four," Temple said. "Now, Jasper, tell me, has the rest of the building been checked?"

"Yes, but this is unacceptable. I can't have you two blundering all over Lake County. Don't screw around too much with this place; the Evidence Response Team is going to give this place another going over—"

"Afraid not."

"Are you *trying* to be a pain in the ass?" Out of nowhere, a chill crept up his legs and worked into the core of his body, as if emanating from deep within the earth. His shoulders shook, despite his attempt to tamp down the urge.

"Look, why do you care so much?" Temple shook her head, the tight curls wiggling. "You said yourself this was a clear case of suicide and the other a murder and they weren't connected. The girl was rescued, right? You're off the hook."

Yeah, why was he so interested in all this? Why did he care so much about the turf war? Wouldn't it be easier to simply go back to busting lowlifes? Black was right, after all. Suicides, murder, and a rescued girl. Why stay involved?

He realized it was because a part of him believed what she was saying. Both the suicides and the murder were fantastic in nature. He'd never witnessed human bodies devoured by thermite and had never seen a human corpse rearranged into a pile of meat.

Vance looked up. He'd donned thick spectacled glasses that reminded Jasper of some nutty scientist examining bugs. "Hey, this is interesting."

"What?" Jasper and Temple asked in unison.

"I can't be certain out here in the field, but a sample I took from the murder scene and another from here match. This is big, we've never seen anything like this." Vance grinned. "Once I can get the samples to a real lab, I'll go to town."

"Can you give me a hint as to what you're talking about?" Jasper asked Vance, but never took his eyes off Temple. Damn, she was good. Her eyes hadn't left his either, and he wasn't sure if she'd even blinked yet.

"You don't have to answer, Vance." Temple arched an eyebrow, as if once again relaying a *go ahead and try me* look.

"All right, I guess we'll be straightening this out over at the Merrillville office. My boss, SSA Johnson, has agreed to meet me, and he requested your presence." Temple didn't need to know he lied.

"I'll do you one better," Temple said. "Your Assistant Special Agent in Charge is going to be there as well."

"Great." Jasper hadn't ingratiated himself to ASAC Masters any more than he had the ERT leader. A minor insight hit him: perhaps the other person wasn't always the problem. A slim chance existed that on occasion he caused the problems. He laughed.

Temple's eyes widened. "What is so funny? Care to let me in?"

"Not at this moment," Jasper said. "I was simply detecting an emerging pattern, is all."

"With the investigations?"

"No. Not at all." Jasper took his eyes from Temple's. "Fine, I'll meet you over at the office. When is ASAC Masters supposedly arriving at the RA?" She'd gone above and beyond to shoehorn her little group into this investigation and then had likely gotten him in hot water. As if he needed help in the hot water department.

Temple glanced at her watch, a Tag Heuer. Perhaps this woman had some class after all.

"If we leave in fifteen minutes," she said, "that should give you plenty of time."

"Fine, I'm leaving now."

"Okay. Bye now." She fluttered her fingers, shooing him from the hotel.

He spun and made for the stairs. *What a total bitch—*

"I know what you're thinking."

He turned back. "That's good, but do I get to zap you with electricity if you're wrong?"

She laughed, the first genuine one he'd heard out of her. "That a *Ghostbusters* reference?"

"Something like that, kind of obscure I'd imagine," he said, still pissed and managing his anger poorly. "Bill Murray at the beginning when he's zapping the guy, but not the girl when they're guessing what patterns are on the cards he's holding. So, yes."

"I'm good," Temple said. "Relax, Agent Wilde, maybe you're not so bad after all."

"Yeah, maybe."

"And maybe I'll allow you to tag along."

"Too many maybes for me. See you later." He wanted to salute her with a finger, but buried his hands in his pockets like he was some little kid being run off the playground by a bully.

Chapter 10

CARLOS OCHOA'S MEETING WITH THE POLICE HAD GONE AS WELL as expected. The only problem he foresaw was the waitress, Lali. She kind of understood what he did and where he went, but wouldn't be able to provide any real details. But the police probably wouldn't bother asking her anything.

Even though today was Saturday and few of the guild members would be hanging around the machine shop, he was expected to report in after the contact with law enforcement.

He headed south and east from the diner, working his way across multiple sets of tracks. He'd been lucky so far, missing every train and hitting little traffic. Carlos drove with his windows down, enjoying the warm and sticky air mingled with the sharp scent of gasoline and slightly acrid scent of metal working. The mix of abandoned buildings standing alongside operating businesses had been the reason the guild took up residence on Summer Street, running a business called Wayland Precision.

He pulled up to the main gate, and waited. A few seconds later, the gate retracted, allowing him entrance. He drove around back and parked alongside Steve Stahlberg's extended-cab Ford pickup. He desired a vehicle as sweet as Steve's, with the heavy-duty suspension. He could practically live in the precious hunk of machinery if he had no choice. On the other side of Steve's pickup was a beater, a worn-out Ford Ranger.

"Great, she's here as well," Carlos muttered as he thumped his Toyota pickup's door shut. He had no desire to deal with Steve's daughter Penny, but no other choice existed unless he wanted to quit. Ever since her father's stroke, she'd practically taken over the day-to-day operations of Wayland Precision as well as the guild. Penny wasn't doing a bad job, but Carlos believed she influenced her old man a bit too easily, and a bit too often.

The back of the Wayland Precision building appeared much the same as the front—red brick and frosted glass windows all around. He trotted up the steps and punched his code into the keypad. A buzz sounded and he let himself in.

The building's eerie weekend stillness unnerved him a little. Only two people in the guild knew where he'd been today, meeting with the FBI and the police—and they were both here and would have plenty of questions. The machine shop itself was dark today. Steve ran a tight ship, keeping the place spotless, at least by machine shop standards. There was hardly a sliver of metal anywhere on the floor or on the machinery. It helped, of course, that they only worked with high-grade steel alloys. If they were cutting stuff like cast iron or bronze, it'd be impossible to keep the shop this clean.

Carlos walked the length of the machine shop, pushed through a swinging door into the warehouse, and descended a flight of stairs off to the side. A vegetal scent filled his nose as he proceeded deeper into the recesses of the building. Warm, damp air hung thick in the wide bench-lined corridor. Mushroom-filled boxes rested atop the benches. The public never saw any of this, only employees and guild members, who were one and the same.

"I like the Wizard of Oz," a female voice echoed from a speaker over his head. That was Penny.

A light flickered on as he approached a solid white door, its edges coated with greasy fingerprints and dirt, as if no one used the doorknob. On the other side of the peephole, he knew, Penny was staring at him.

"It's me," Carlos said—he hated this password crap she'd instituted.

"Come on," Penny said, "what's the response?"

Penny had obviously gorged herself on too many movies, probably James Bond or the old spy show, *Mission Impossible,* but this nonsense came from some Christmas movie.

"Fine." Carlos took a deep breath, and blew out the air with a sigh. "I like the Tin Man."

"Thank you," Penny said.

The door buzzed and sprung open. Carlos entered the so-called inner sanctum.

Penny grinned. "See? That wasn't so bad."

"Why do you insist on these silly spy antics?" Carlos asked. "I've never even seen the movie we're quoting."

"We're quoting *A Christmas Story*." Penny shot Carlos a reproving glare. "One of the funniest movies ever."

"What Christmas story?"

"I feel like we're Abbott and Costello here doing who's on first."

"What?" Carlos asked.

"What's on second," Steve chimed in, yanking ripped and faded overalls up.

"You people are insane." Carlos smacked his forehead. "I don't know what you're—"

Penny's face turned red, she laughed so hard.

"What?" Carlos was truly perplexed.

"Never mind. Thank you for playing, though," Penny said.

Steve grinned and rubbed his white whiskers with rough hands, like they'd been chewed on like a dog toy.

Carlos grabbed a coffee-stained mug off a shelf and filled it with water from the cooler. "Why use any lines from any movies? Gates, locked doors, and cameras aren't enough?"

"Let her have some fun," Steve said. "I don't quite understand either, but using passwords certainly doesn't hurt."

"If you two haven't noticed, people aren't beating down the door to uncover what happens in a machine shop. No one cares. Hell, I doubt if more than one percent of the people who drive by—don't nobody walk on this street—even notices we're here."

"Enough," Steve said.

"So tell us what happened." Penny grabbed another mug, dropped a bag of black tea in, and drew hot water from the cooler.

Carlos worked his way around and behind a battered old three-drawer filing cabinet, and sat in a chair resembling refugee furniture from the mid-seventies.

"They want to continue meeting with me."

"And?" Penny motioned with her hand as if trying to pull the information out of him.

"So I'm in," Carlos said, "what more do you want?"

Penny smacked the top of the filing cabinet. "You know damn well what kind of information we're seeking."

"Ease up, Penny," Steve said. "No need to get angry."

Penny rolled her eyes.

Carlos grinned. "Fine. They had plenty of questions, and for a moment I thought they had caught on to the scene over at Animal Control, but for now, they aren't sure what's going on and haven't connected the two events."

"They aren't sure, huh?" Steve rubbed his chin. "The cops or the FBI still investigating the matter?"

"I don't know," Carlos said.

Penny frowned.

"Look," Carlos folded his arms, "I couldn't ask too many questions, right? I mean, I had to kind of work with what they tossed at me. If you want my opinion, the local cop, this Pedro, isn't interested. The FBI guy did most of the asking and appears more eager to use me as an informant."

"Interesting," Steve said. "We'll keep tabs on them as best as we can to be sure they aren't getting too close."

"And you want me to continue meeting and figuring out if they're learning too much?" Carlos asked.

"Yes." Penny picked up the phone.

"It's starting up again, the demon universe leaking into ours, right?" Carlos gazed at Steve.

Steve shrugged. "Let's just call it the 'other' universe. We don't really know for sure what we're dealing with. But, yes, we think so. There've been too many horrific coincidences lately."

"Speaking of a coincidence," Carlos drummed his fingers atop the cabinet, "did we have anyone over at Animal Control today? Once the police arrived?"

Steve shook his head and glanced at Penny, who now had the phone up to her ear. She frowned. "No, not that I'm aware of," she said to Steve and Carlos, then spoke into the receiver: "Hey, John. Be here first thing in the morning. We need to be cutting stainless all day. Let Danny and Ian know also. Right." A second later she hung up.

"Our old enemy has returned, I'm afraid," Steve said. "They're up to something. The two men who died in the hotel weren't an anomaly or wannabes. No way. The Câ Tsang is back."

"Great," Penny said. "We'll be dodging the law, the Câ Tsang, and Nephilim from another world."

"Maybe Nephilim," Steve cautioned. "We don't really know what they are. We've never known."

Chapter 11

JASPER DROPPED INTO THE CHAIR OPPOSITE AGENT TEMPLE BLACK, and slumped. For some reason, someone insisted on having all the chairs in the conference room at the maximum height. He released the chair from the extreme height down to an appropriate level. Temple had kept hers at maximum height, and no doubt her feet dangled. Perhaps she needed to feel as if she were in control and wanted the height.

The conference room itself wasn't large, seating perhaps twenty people—more than enough for this little meeting. He wondered when his boss, the agent in charge of the Merrillville office, would arrive with the ASAC from the main office.

"Pssst."

Jasper glanced at Temple. "Yes?"

"How do you lower the chair?"

"The little lever on the side?" Jasper raised an eyebrow.

"I'm lifting it," Temple said, and laughed.

"Really?" Jasper shook his head, trying not to laugh at the absurdity. "When you lift the lever, plop down on the chair."

"Here goes." Temple plopped down hard, sending the chair to its bottommost position.

The conference door swung open and in walked SSA Johnson and ASAC Masters.

Jasper stood, and felt a little more loosened up at Temple's chair height shenanigans. "SSA Black, I'd like you to meet ASAC Masters and SSA Johnson."

She grinned. "Masters and Johnson, won't forget those names."

ASAC Masters sported his usual nonplussed countenance.

"Never mind," Johnson said. He obviously understood the reference, but the ASAC's obtuseness remained true to Jasper's memory. "All right, none of us wants to be here on a weekend evening."

He took a seat at the head of the table, Masters next to him. Both wore suits—a rarity for Johnson. He must be trying to impress the headquarters agent and ASAC Masters.

"No need for formality here." So Temple decided taking charge of the meeting was a strategy for success. That wasn't surprising, given the brassy nature she'd displayed during their interactions. "Jasper and I have reached an understanding."

"We have? That is how you see it?" Jasper adjusted himself in his chair.

"Yes. SAG is taking over the investigations." Temple's tone was matter-of-fact.

"Hold on." Masters ran his fingers through slicked back hair. "What is SAG?"

Jasper opened his mouth—

Temple pointed a chiding finger at him. "Scientific Anomalies Group."

"And what is this group exactly? Never heard of it." Masters glanced back and forth between Jasper and Temple.

"Neither had I, sir," Jasper said.

"We investigate matters the field won't touch and the locals ignore."

"Who runs the group? You?" Johnson asked, cutting in.

"I'm the supervisor—"

"She has one person who works with her, Special Agent Vance Ravel. He's here too," Jasper said, "but I think he's attempting to analyze a few samples they collected today."

"I'll show you." Temple stood and walked over to a dry erase board, which snapped on—surprising Jasper. "We were stood up to investigate matters of national security. Watch." She gestured at the screen and dimmed the lights.

"Huh," Jasper said, "I didn't know dry erase boards were capable of such a feat. Fascinating."

"It's a SMART Board," Temple said. "They're installed in most of the field offices."

"I don't need a presentation," Masters said. "Tell me what's going on here, but first, who do you report to?"

Temple's shoulders slumped and her head lolled backward, clearly exasperated. She took a deep breath. "Fine." She raised the lights. "I'm going to run the slideshow as I speak."

Behind Temple, slides whisked by displaying formulas and high-resolution photos of objects Jasper couldn't make heads or tails of.

"We're part of the Critical Incident Response Group," Temple continued, "you know, CIRG—"

"Yes, we're all well aware of the Division—"

Temple coughed. "We were conceived to handle counterterrorism leads believed to be nonsense. We quickly evolved beyond dull CT leads and now investigate matters falling in the cracks and outside normal FBI guidelines and protocols."

"I don't understand how the kidnapping of a child and subsequent double suicide are nonsensical or fell through the cracks," Masters said.

Perhaps the ASAC wasn't so obtuse after all, but Temple wasn't telling him the whole story, either. Jasper wanted her to keep going, because it would quickly become too fantastical for both Masters and Johnson to accept.

"The crimes are serious." Temple paced in front of the screen. "Think about their nature, though."

"But the missing girl has been found and the men are dead," Johnson said. "And the other case, a straight up homicide, has no Bureau nexus."

"A pile of meat with protruding bones doesn't strike you as extraordinary?"

"You're wasting our time—why are we even talking?" Masters asked.

"Exactly," Temple said. "My group has already been granted concurrence to operate in Indianapolis's AOR by your SAC. And your man here, Agent Wilde, seems intent on watching us, which is why we're talking. I simply can't have him hampering our investigations, especially since he doesn't believe we belong here."

"Fine," Masters said, "go about your business, but have this wrapped up by tomorrow. The SAC says yes a little too easily if you ask me. I don't want you and your group, what was it, SIG?"

"SAG, sir—"

Jasper hid a grin.

"Whatever, I don't want you ruining the relationships with the locals we've worked so hard to develop. I don't believe for a moment any of what you're investigating will make a difference to the Bureau. We're overstepping our mandate, and remember, we do not typically investigate murders and suicides." There was a pause, and he drove home one more point: "And do with this as you will, but your group sounds like another pointless headquarters initiative the field not only disdains, but despises." Masters ended the tirade red-faced.

Wow. Perhaps Masters was pissed for driving up to Merrillville on a weekend, and missing little Johnny's ballgame or something. Jasper suppressed a grin. He respected him a little more for having a pair—most executive management didn't—but he'd been hard on Temple and even though she'd tossed Jasper under the bus, he thought Masters had gone a little too far. One thing was clear, Temple believed in what she was doing. She believed in the work and the mission she'd been given by FBI HQ. She wasn't just going through the motions. Jasper had to respect that.

He cleared his throat. "Sir, I don't think Agents Black and Ravel can wrap the investigations up in a day."

"Are you for real?" Johnson asked. "All right, I've had enough of this." He spun his chair. "ASAC Masters?"

"Hold on a minute. How did HQ even find out about the investigations out here?"

"Agent Wilde's report itself," said Temple. "There were certain anomalies in the report responsible for triggering an alert. You see, Agent Ravel created a list of keywords."

Johnson cut in. "What was in the report capable of triggering the alert?"

"Oh, let's see," Temple said. "Suicide by thermite, stone slabs, possible ritual killing, cults—"

"I said nothing about a cult," Jasper protested.

"Fine, I added the cult bit, but the other evidence in the report as well as at the scene suggested cultlike activity. You get the point."

"We need Agent Wilde here assigned temporarily to this SAG thing," Johnson said.

Masters' eyes narrowed and he spread his hands, palm up. "What for?"

"Look, if it's going to take Agent Black and her assistant Ravel more than a day, I'd rather have someone from the Merrillville office tag along so those 'relationships' you mentioned don't get burned."

"Thank you, sir," Temple held up a hand, "but Agent Wilde's help won't be necessary—"

"Oh, but it is, and it's happening. If you don't like it, go back to the Hoover building with all the other zombies."

"I don't work out of the Hoover building," Temple said, a bit stiffly.

"I agree." Masters thumped the table top. "I'll square it with the SAC and make a call to the Assistant Director at CIRG. But consider yourself TDY'd to this SIG or whatever it is."

"Sir, it's SAG"—Jasper stood—"but I'd rather not—"

"Nope," Johnson said, "it's too late. I need you to watch over the HQ personnel so they don't run amok here. That's all."

"For how long?" Jasper didn't want to whine, but it must have come across like one.

"If there are more of these men out there, and these investigations are somehow linked, a Bureau nexus may exist after all. Just don't piss off the local cops, okay? Lord knows, Agent Wilde, you have a unique ability."

"Pissing people off?" Temple asked.

"Jasper knows how to push my buttons." Johnson's additions to the conversation had to be for the benefit of ASAC Masters and Agent Black.

"Anything else, sir?" Jasper stared at Masters.

Johnson glanced at Masters. "I think we're done."

"Great," Jasper said, "shall I provide updates?"

"Get through the weekend and give us a report next week."

"Roger that," Jasper said.

Masters and Johnson stood.

"Thank you," Temple said.

Both men shook their heads and walked out of the conference room.

"Well, the meeting went swimmingly," Jasper said. "Looks like you're stuck with me."

Temple had her back to him, tapping away on a keyboard near the screen, which was still flashing images. "Would you rather work applicant matters?"

"What? Hell, no. You might as well put me on permanent complaint duty, listening to all those crazy tinfoil hat people—"

Temple laughed. "Only the best and brightest, or those in

deep shit, end up with those duties. You know, Vance and I are the Bureau's tinfoil hat people." She stretched. "I'm heading back to the hotel for some sleep in a few minutes. It's been a long day and I need to recharge."

"Yeah, well, seems fitting for you two."

Temple paused a moment, said nothing, and reviewed a dozen images in seconds.

"Wait," Jasper said. "What was that?"

"Which?"

"The one with the weird-looking man."

Temple paused the display and tapped a few more keys. "This one?"

"No."

"How about now?"

"Yes. Why do you have a photo of a man that looks like that? How could you?"

"This is a photo of the man in the vehicle we saw at the homicide scene earlier today." Temple cocked her head and raised her eyebrows.

"But why include him in this display of yours?" Jasper asked.

"He was at the scene, right? And a pile of meat is not normal, or maybe you hang around meat packing plants?"

"Good one. No. But I'm thinking we're on to something. The man on the screen is about as nondescript in the same way as the two men who committed suicide. Especially if you take the dark hair off the men at the hotel."

"Interesting." Temple stood straight up and her eyes widened. "What if the men at the hotel wore toupees or something?"

"Yes, but there was no way to tell, they were ash. Man, but my brain is fried," said Jasper. "I need to go relax. Perhaps we can get Vance and analyze this tomorrow, what do you say?"

"Sure."

"I'll tell you what," Jasper said, "want to join me for a drink or two, and a bite to eat? I know a place, a dive, but the bar food is good. The clientele is interesting—and mostly harmless."

"Sounds like my kind of place," Temple said. "Let me phone Vance, though I doubt he'll join us."

Vance had already gone to sleep, so Jasper had Temple follow him in her rental to a bar he favored over in Schererville. He loved this place since they stocked a brand of whiskey that had grown on him, and served greasy bar food. They used to have live bands, but had gotten away from that ruckus in favor of a well-stocked old school jukebox and pool tables.

At least in this bar he could relax a bit and hope that Temple would as well. Another reason for choosing that bar as a venue to chill out with her was that the clientele was racially mixed, and no one was out of place. Well, Masters and Johnson in their suits perhaps, but almost anything else worked. The truth was that he was worn out, and couldn't believe the homicide at Animal Control had been earlier in the day and that the rescue of the girl and the suicides had been the previous evening.

They walked in together.

"I love dive bars," Temple said as she dragged a rickety wooden chair out from under a table and sat.

Was she being sarcastic? Jasper had a hard time distinguishing between her normal attitude and sarcasm.

"It does the trick after a long day. Spend a few minutes in here and you'll forget all your troubles."

"I bet," she said.

Even though smoking had been banned for years, the acrid stink lingered, trapped in the wood and fabric of the place, smoke mixed with beer mixed with myriad scents of people and food smells.

Jasper nodded at the lone waitress, who within a minute slid two glasses and a bottle of Stranahan's Colorado Whiskey on the table. "Thank you, Katie. And bring two of my regular snacks, please."

"So," Temple stared at the full bottle of whiskey, "you're a real hotshot around here." She picked up the bottle and studied it for a moment. "Wait a second. You're from Tennessee. Shouldn't you be having Jack Daniels or something? Whoever heard of a Colorado whiskey?" She pulled the stopper and sniffed. "Not bad, but still—"

"Give it a try. Yes, I'm from Tennessee, but that doesn't mean I can't branch out a bit. I'm not a total rube." He grinned. "Here, check the bottle. Whoever bottled the whiskey usually writes what group they were listening to while doing so—"

"Queen," Temple said. "That's a neat idea." She poured healthy amounts in their glasses, a good two fingers worth each, then took a sip and nodded appreciatively.

"Took me a while to find it, but Stranahan's is good stuff."
Jasper raised his glass and offered a toast. "SAG, there's a lot I
could say, but I won't."

Temple shook her head.

"What, not a decent toast? Fine. Here's to field agents and
HQ agents getting along," Jasper said. "Real end of the world
kind of stuff." They clinked and swigged.

"You're all right, I think," Temple said.

"Just all right, huh?"

"Too early to tell for sure, but you referenced *Ghostbusters*
for a second time today, right?"

"I watched it last week, so the quotes are still fresh. So tell
me, do you and Vance travel around the country or go OCONUS
for this SAG thing you're assigned to?"

"Not much so far, and I created the position, so I kind of
assigned myself to SAG." Temple grinned.

"I thought SAG reminded me of the *X-Files*—I mean, you're
a pariah and once had such great potential." He winked.

Temple laughed. "I'm a pariah, but from what I've read, so
are you."

"We'll make a great team—"

"Don't get any ideas, sport," Temple said. "I already have a
partner. You're only on TDY, remember?"

"Whatever, for once I'm trying to get along and play well
with others," Jasper said. "So how do you know all about me?"

"Once your report hit the servers, Vance pulled up some
stuff on you."

"Accessing personnel records isn't allowed—"

"Viewing records is permissible with valid reasons."

"And you think me filing a report about a missing child and
two suicides is a valid reason for viewing my personnel file?"

"Look, I didn't view your personnel file, so relax," Temple said.
"But—"

"But nothing. I viewed some of the cases you worked and
the writeups for some of them. You, Special Agent Wilde, have
a history of going against the wishes of your superiors."

Jasper sniffed.

"Yeah, I feel the same way," Temple said. "Being a black woman
in such a white Bureau—a white man's bureau—hasn't been easy."

"Stop a second," Jasper said. "White man's Bureau?"

"Yeah, you're the type of person I see running around playing agent." She arched one of her eyebrows.

"The Bureau can't help who applies for the special agent position. It's my fault the FBI hired me?"

"True, but are they actively recruiting minorities?"

"Aren't they? Why are we having this discussion, anyway?" Jasper asked.

"Beats me." Temple sipped the beer. "Heading down the inequality road is so easy."

"If you say so. I don't typically think about race or gender or religion or whatever gets people upset."

"Why would you? You're a white male."

"So tired of hearing what I am." Jasper sighed. "I can't win."

"At least you admit defeat." Temple smiled. "Fine, I'll lay off. My apologies, but being a black woman hasn't always been the easiest in a hard-charging historically male-dominated law enforcement agency. I did a stint in the Army, too. Enlisted."

"Wow, I'm impressed." He was, actually, a little. "Marine Corps myself. So, are we gonna get along and take care of these investigations? Bust up some crazy cult or something? Bash some skulls?" He wanted off the race subject. Jasper understood much more work had to be done in civil rights. However, as far as government agencies went, he thought the FBI did a decent job of hiring people from diverse backgrounds. Long gone were the days of hiring only white male lawyers and accountants.

Of course, he was a white male himself and honest enough to understand that had to shape his perceptions, at least to some degree. He didn't doubt the world looked different to a black woman. Sometimes a lot different.

"You drunk already?" Temple grinned. "Does thinking of the Marine Corps make you violent?"

Jasper sipped the whiskey, the color of polished leather, allowing the complex notes to linger on his tongue before the liquid slid down his throat. He took a deep breath.

"I have anger issues, but not because of the Corps."

"Oh? In the mood to share?"

He brought the glass down on the table with a thunk. "I'm surprised you don't already know." He raised an eyebrow.

"Like I said, we didn't look at your personal details, only some work product."

"Fine. And here I thought we were beginning to get along," Jasper said.

"Aren't we?"

"Okay, I've had a rough couple of years. Was married, she left."

"Kids?"

"No."

"A good thing, right?" Temple asked.

He shrugged. "I suppose kids were something I had on my mind."

"You have time still. I mean, how old are you, anyway? Twelve?"

He chuckled. "Valiant try, but I think my baby face vanished right about the time my marriage fell apart. And now I'm a pariah at work, too. Some of my coworkers love screwing with me when I show up at the office." He licked his lips and took a healthy swig of the whiskey. His eyes watered.

"You and me, both." Temple raised her glass and clanked with Jasper's. "Here's to social pariahs, may we graduate to full-on misanthropy."

"I'll drink to pariahs and misanthropy," Jasper said. "So what's your story? How did SAG come about, other than being an idea of yours?"

"Let's say I'm a favorite of the Assistant Director of CIRG."

"As in he isn't a fan of yours? I can't seem to read you, and whether or not you're being sarcastic."

"Yep, that's one of my problems."

"This is gonna be fun." Jasper grinned. "I may not be the superstar of the field office, but I'm good at my job. I'm persistent, and believe it or not, can work well with others."

Now it was Temple's turn to snort.

"Hey," Jasper said, "I need the right people around me and I'll play nice and make fast friends."

"You seem to have the right touch with the locals, an admirable quality, which means you're probably not arrogant."

"I've worked quite a few investigations with them, specifically the cop you met earlier, Pete. A good guy, but he's not into the investigations we'll be working."

"You mean the suicides and the other, uh, thing?"

"Exactly. So, with Pete abstaining, I bet his department took note and backed away from these messes, especially when you offered to take the investigations off their hands. I understand the East Chicago Police perspective; they believe nothing good could come from working those matters. It's a no-win scenario."

"Oh, yeah, a total *Kobayashi Maru* scenario."

"I see you have some Trek up in that head of yours." Jasper grinned. "But if these investigations are no-win situations, why would you want to look into them?"

He knew the answer, and in this way he and Temple were alike. He didn't believe in no-win, and discovered yet another way the failed marriage hit him hard—he'd lost. Failed. Ever since Lucy had left, he'd been picking up the pieces. Jasper filled his time with work and a bunch of meaningless hobbies designed to keep his mind going. But now, in front of this strong woman, Temple, he hoped his face showed none of the pain lingering below the surface on perpetual simmer.

"I don't believe in no-win," she said. "That's exactly why I came into the Bureau. I'm relentless when I latch on."

"My assignment to the team should be quite interesting. I hope Agent Ravel can keep up."

"Don't worry about him; he's had a year of me."

"So, during your one year, any interesting cases fall in your lap? I mean, as interesting as the incidents around here?" Jasper asked.

Temple sipped her whiskey and rolled her eyes upward in thought. "We—uh—well—yes."

Jasper laughed and clapped the glass down on the table, the whiskey sloshing.

"It's like this," she said, "we thought we had something good. We really did. So, we go out to Los Angeles."

"You can probably stop right there," Jasper said. "Good enough for me. Let me guess, a vampire or werewolf, but ended up being some Hollywood C-list semi-celebrity gone off his or her rocker, am I right?"

Temple cocked her head. "Come on, this wasn't a vampire or werewolf." She turned away, obviously attempting to shield a laugh from Jasper. Her head swiveled back. "Okay, I'm all right now."

Her eyes watered and she fought back a grin. "So we went down to Venice Beach."

Jasper snorted. "Sounds like a bad movie—I mean, quite a few oddities hang around Venice Beach, but—"

Temple stopped him with a hand, palm first aimed at his face.

"We were told something had been pulled out of the water and there were concerns, but they wouldn't tell us anything more."

"Who is they?"

"This was LAPD—the Pacific Division."

"Oh, this is getting better and better."

"Yeah, so they take us to this holding area they have over near Muscle Beach and show us this thing."

Jasper leaned forward, eager for the punch line.

Temple covered her eyes, but she didn't hide her wide smile. Her head dropped and her shoulders heaved in full laughter.

"What was it? I have to hear this now."

"It was—" Temple snorted. "Humanoid in form."

"Humanoid?"

"Yes, but a deep green." Temple pinched her nose. "Oh, Lord, the thing reeked."

"So the thing was dead, right?"

"Oh, this thing was dead all right," she said. "But I still can't believe they didn't recognize this thing was wrapped in seaweed—or if they did, they simply didn't want to deal with it."

"So, was it some sort of dead prehistoric fish thingy?" Jasper asked, and couldn't contain a chuckle.

"Did you say, thingy?" Temple's brow wrinkled, and she snorted. "Oh, not prehistoric, but old, and wrapped in seaweed. It appeared somewhat humanoid, or at least shaped like a torso. So Vance snapped on some latex gloves and peeled off the seaweed. This thing was like a mummy from the deep. For a little while we thought this was a torso of a person, but I'm still not entirely sure what the cops thought."

"Did they think they caught a monster from the ocean, like one of those Fifties science fiction flicks? Or better yet, a dead merman?"

"I wish I'd thought of the merman thing while they stood around gawking, but we weren't sure what we were going to find under all the seaweed. I braced myself as Vance peeled off layer by layer of seaweed, some of which had been wrapped around the torso for a long time. The stench confirmed the rotten vintage."

"I can imagine how awful the reek must have been," Jasper said.

"So Vance peels away the final layers, and stares, licking his lips. His head cocks to the side as if he's confused. He says, 'This is just a misshapen and unrecognizable fish, dead for ages, but sort of preserved in seaweed.' Then he slapped his gloves down on the mess and as he walks out, says, 'I'm getting some sushi, who's with me?'"

A tune played, distant, and computerized. "When the Saints Come Marching In." Temple's cell phone no doubt. That had to be one of the lousy stock ringers from the crappy phones the Bureau had entered into a seemingly endless contract.

"Hold on," she said, "this could be Agent Ravel." She fumbled with the phone— "Go." She sagged in her chair. "We'll be right there." She took a deep breath and hissed the air through her teeth.

"Problem?"

"There's been another kidnapping."

Chapter 12

THE BLACK WOMAN ALAN HAD SNATCHED FROM A DESERTED street in Gary squirmed in the back of the borrowed Chevy Astro, whining and crying, despite her ample bonding. But the khâu ignored her, just as he'd ignored Rao's caution to stay away from vans. Even though the police would likely be more sensitive to another stolen van after yesterday's failed sacrifice to the nâga, the vehicle had been easy for him to snatch. The navy blue Astro had been sitting for quite some time behind the house of his elderly grandmother's sister, Hazel. Auntie Hazel was in the hospital, so she wouldn't be missing the vehicle. He'd headed over to Gary, and specifically a section of Gary more resembling 1980s Beirut than a modern American city.

But thoughts such as those were frowned upon in the Câ Tsang. Creativity had no place among the sticks of the group. The simple act of carrying out the Tip of the Horn's orders would convey upon the sycophantic khâu a greater chance of attaining the rank of khäp, an adept.

Night snatched East Chicago as swift and certain as he'd taken the woman. Streetlights raced overhead as traffic lights turned green before him: Destiny was getting him to the meeting place with alacrity.

"Praise the nâga," he whispered.

Beneath the scents from the streets lingered the scent of a woman's perfume—his great-aunt's. The khâu pinched shut his nose, but the thought of sucking in the heavy musky stench through his mouth only disturbed his already queasy stomach. Damn the old woman for wearing such heavy perfume. The black woman he'd taken off the street reeked of fast food and sweat, which turned to the sweet smell of fear. He'd drugged her, of course, but the paralysis concoction given him by Rao had worn off quickly, and now she struggled.

The abandoned hotel was near. The police had departed hours ago, seemingly giving up their vigil. The master was livid over the incompetence of the two acolytes who'd botched the sacrifice to the unfettered glory of the nâga—who out of necessity had feasted upon the unpurified wretch of a man near the animal control facility up the road from the hotel.

This khâu volunteered to erase the failures of the other sticks, but doubt crept into his mind. What if the cops lay in wait for him? What if a trap waited for the Câ Tsang, the Iron Thorn?

But Rao would not purposely send him into the hands of the cops or worse, the FBI, would he? No. What would be the point? Glory was needed. Glory and redemption and power. The nâga expected compliant and steady Sha 'Lu once the gate opened.

Lights peeked in and out of the Astro's side mirrors. He checked the trailing vehicle's silhouette, fearing the bumps riding atop the roof, but saw none. The khâu sighed in relief, but the cold fear returned, sending a shiver down his back. An unmarked police vehicle? Or an FBI vehicle, all of which were unmarked and not always a make or model easily recognized? He wouldn't know until he reached the hotel, and what would he do if the vehicle behind him was the police? Would he keep driving or would he park and have to perform something drastic?

He released the vise grip he'd cinched down on his nose and instead white-knuckled the steering wheel. Being caught was not an option. He had no distinguishing features, no identification, and no fingerprints. The police would have no record of him either. The FBI, though, what would they have on him? Anything? No.

The sound of his own rapid breaths filled the air and he tapped the button on the armrest, sending the driver's side window down. The gushing air rushed by him, filling his nose with the scents of a town running on burnt chemicals.

He thought of the two khâu immolating themselves as an offering to the Iron Thorn, but in vain, as the nâga tore through only to find no sacrifice, no Sha 'Lu, waiting for him. The nâga rampaged through the night in search of meat to extract bjang from.

Impure kill. Impure bjang.

The khâu failed in barring these thoughts from his mind despite the repeated attempts at tamping down any free thought. The meditations failed him and the mantra fled his mind.

The light ahead at the intersection of Euclid Avenue and East Chicago Avenue signaled the end of this stage of the journey. But the light was red where all the others ushered his rush to glory and flicked green before the speeding mini-van. He glanced in his rear-view mirror. The car following him turned off—his fears unfounded after all.

Good. He'd continue on, and did not slow down for the red light before him. Two hundred feet perhaps. The light would change for a khâu of the Câ Tsang.

His foot pressed the accelerator into the floorboards and the speed shot up another five miles an hour. The red light refused to yield at fifty feet but a second later he sailed under the light—a flash of yellow appeared on the crossroad, Euclid Avenue. Excellent.

The hotel loomed on the corner. He grinned wide, feeling the creases at the corner of his eyes deepen.

He was passing through the intersection.

Lights blared into his open window. The grin disappeared. He squinted and turned his head.

Eyes widened.

Metal crumpled.

His body flew across the mini-van and his vision blackened under the impact of something giving way stubbornly to his head, now coated in warmth. A ripping noise. Now a scraping noise filled his ears.

Something was dragging him along the blacktop. The mini-van appeared undamaged from this vantage point. What had happened? Where was the black woman? Still inside, but alive? Life was necessary for the ritual and more importantly, for the nâga to achieve their true power and form. The master would be sure to end him.

Grogginess and pain filled him and he ceased moving. Whatever dragged him released his broken body.

He yelped and grabbed for his head as he rolled over.

Nothing. He got to one knee and cried out in pain once more.

The hotel. So close. The mini-van.

He stumbled for the vehicle, but sirens pierced the thick air.

So heavy was the air. He sniffed and blood tickled the back of his throat. A warm trickle dripped upon his cheek.

Accident. A vehicle had crashed into the van.

A chill overtook him and he stopped stumbling for the van. Get away from the van. Yes.

The tank farm was nearby. He could go there, or perhaps hide among the rows of houses not far from the hotel.

The khâu glanced down at his hands. Coated in a glistening substance, they shook. Blood, but in this light black rather than red, reminding him of chocolate syrup tinged with the scent of copper.

Screeching brakes and sirens filled the air and he stumbled into a run, more like a staggering drunk swaying side-to-side than an Olympic sprinter.

He dizzied, and darkness washed over his vision. His foot hit something solid and he tumbled. Cool moisture smacked his face. Blades of grass poked his head. He clenched shut his eyes.

Whoops and yelps were followed by the long agonizing wails of an ambulance. This khâu could not be caught, but movement hurt. Movement pained him.

He rolled on to his back and fought to open his eyes against the wooziness and pain forcing them shut.

Voices in the distance.

Yelling.

Doors slamming.

A long, slow hiss, like that of air releasing from a tire's valve hit him from above. A metallic scent worked its way up his nose and into his chest—so different from the acrid and burning chemical reek normally permeating the air.

His eyes shot open and he lurched, gasping for air, but none came. He sat within a cloud, flying as if upon a magic carpet and touched the other side. He'd crossed over as a mere khâu, tasting gä, true power. Yes! He was so alive now and powerful.

The khâu's face twisted—

—pain—

His jaw clenched.

—agonizing—

Eyes sealed shut.

—a faint puff of breath and the universe winked into black eternity.

Chapter 13

PULSING LIGHTS, RED AND BLUE, STRUCK THEM AS THEY DROVE upon the scene in Jasper's bucar, the Dodge Charger. He hadn't gone lights and sirens as Temple had urged, seeing no need. At this time of night, traffic was negligible in this part of town. They had rolled for the spot of the abduction in Gary, but had quickly deviated when they'd heard of the accident near the Euclid Hotel.

"Got your creds on you, I hope?" Jasper regretted asking Temple the question as soon as the words left his lips.

Her eyes bored into him. He didn't dare ask if she carried her firearm. "No need to be touchy, so many HQ types forsake their weapons—"

"I don't work in the Hoover Building, remember?"

They arrived at the hotel and Jasper parked half a block away so as not to impede the rescue work. An ambulance was already on the scene along with a couple of cop cars.

Temple immediately got out. "Let's go see what happened."

Jasper approached the nearest uniformed officer and displayed his creds. "I work with Pete."

The officer, a young Hispanic male, arched an eyebrow. "We have a few Petes running around, care to elaborate?"

"Pedro Hernandez."

"Yeah, we have one of those. What do you want?"

Temple stepped forward. "We're working a couple of sensitive investigations involving deaths, likely a murder, as well as kidnappings. Let us through."

The officer gave way and gestured for them to pass, exaggerating with a sweeping motion as if treating them like royalty.

93

"You know," Jasper said, "I do have to work with these locals. You won't be here for much longer, but this is my territory and rebuilding a bunch of bridges you apparently know how to burn down with a certain kind of flair does not sound like fun."

"Calm down, he's a big boy, he'll get by. They always do. Besides, he'll keep quiet about a woman giving him a hard time."

"If you say so."

"I do."

"That's probably the only time you'll utter those words," Jasper muttered, not thinking she could hear him.

She proved him wrong immediately. "I have excellent hearing and the words 'I do' have crossed my lips before."

"Didn't know you were married." Jasper was embarrassed and regretted the barb.

"Yes, but it's over and I don't talk about it. You of all people should understand, right? Now, let's figure this scene out before the night becomes morning. I'm tired and cranky."

"You're telling me."

Temple's head swiveled and her eyes had the *don't-push-it* stare she'd probably mastered while still in the crib.

When they got to the scene, it smacked Jasper in the face, and Temple sucked in a startled breath. A body covered in a white sheet lolled from an opening on the side of what was once a mini-van. A breeze caught the sheet, exposing for a moment the victim beneath. Jasper took in all he could—a piece of white cloth adorned her neck—a gag? Yes, a gag that had been pulled free. A thin rope, maybe twine of some sort, laced about her lifeless body, obviously cut free by the responding EMTs.

"Bound and gagged," Jasper said. "African-American."

"And now dead. You can say 'black,' by the way," Temple scowled.

"Sorry, just trying to be—"

"Yeah, I know, politically correct. But what a horrible way to go."

"Is there any other way?" Jasper shook his head in disgust. "I mean, all the deaths these past couple of days have been horrible."

Would things get worse? Could they? People were dying daily since Jasper had assisted in the rescue of Teresa at the Euclid Hotel.

They worked their way into the twisted metal littering the intersection. Two EMTs worked on one of the crash victims sprawled alongside a crushed hunk of metal, a Chevy Astro.

The other vehicle, a sedan, had suffered as much damage as the Astro, including a blown-out windshield. The person lying on the ground next to that vehicle had flown through the smashed windshield. Jasper had a hard time believing some people still refused to wear safety belts.

"Hey!" Temple called out to the nearest East Chicago cop, a young black male. He spun, searching for the word's owner. He visibly scowled as they approached. Jasper kept his face neutral.

"Civilians are supposed to be outside the perimeter." The cop turned away, expecting the encounter to be over.

"We're FBI." Temple thrust her arm forward and practically smacked the cop in the face with her credentials. He stepped back, and recovered quickly.

"So? This is an accident. Didn't realize accidents fell under the Bureau's jurisdiction." He tried to turn away again, but Temple grabbed his shoulder and prevented the action. The cop glanced at her hand and then into her eyes. He was the first to break eye contact.

"I'm not here to make trouble," she said. Despite the mollifying words, her tone made it clear that if the ECPD officer wanted trouble she'd be happy to oblige him. "But this accident is likely related to an ongoing investigation your department turned over to the Bureau."

"All right, all right," he said.

Jasper stepped forward and glanced at the cop's name tag. "Officer Jackson, I'm Agent Wilde. Jasper Wilde, I work with Pete Hernandez."

The cop's features softened. "Why didn't you say so right off? You have a question, Agent Wilde?"

"Not just yet, but I believe Agent Black here did." He glanced at her. "Temple?"

Temple shook her head. Exasperated, perhaps? "There an ID on the black woman over there? Also, how many people were involved?" She gestured at the hunk of sheet metal and plastic. "And anyone else in the van beside the woman who's now mixed in with the mini-van wreckage? The driver maybe?"

The cop's smile morphed into the deepest frown Jasper'd ever seen.

"We're not sure about the driver of the van, but the driver of the other vehicle," the cop pointed with his flashlight at the other hunk of twisted metal, "probably won't make it. That's who they're working on now. The evidence you pointed out does suggest a kidnapping, but she was deceased when we arrived on the scene."

"From the accident or other means?"

"We believe the accident killed her, and you know that's not my call," the cop said, "but what do you mean by other means?"

"May we take a peek?"

"She's already been picked over and gawked at, the poor soul."

"We insist." Temple walked around the cop.

Jasper shrugged and hoped his expression came across as apologetic. If Temple persisted in approaching every situation in her brash manner, the potential of each day feeling like a week increased.

Jasper caught up to Temple and touched her shoulder. She spun on him and her eyes smoldered with anger.

"What's wrong?"

"You don't have to be so smug," she said. "You know, every time I interact with someone you feel this need to rescue me."

"I'm not rescuing you, I'm salvaging relationships. One of the reasons I'm here is to smooth over your liaison with the locals and anyone else we meet," Jasper said. "I'm not trying to be an ass."

"You're well past trying."

"Let's not make this bad situation harder than it needs to be. How about this..." he said, and waited for her to calm herself.

"Go on."

"Okay. If we have to interact with other law enforcement agencies, I'll take the lead, please. I'll tee them up for you, but you can't come in here acting like we're the big dogs even if we are. Perpetuating what these guys already believe about the Bureau does us no good."

"All right, all right." She sighed. "Let's get this over with."

"You've been around crime scenes before, right? I mean messy, brutal scenes."

"Too many. And not all with the Bureau, I'm afraid."

"All right, just making sure."

"You don't need to protect me."

"Pfft, as if you'd ever need protecting."

Jasper edged past Temple, taking the lead and approaching the body. A breeze rippled the sheet resting on her body, allowing a glimpse, but not enough to tear away the cloth, unlike the impact responsible for tearing the life from her. Jasper's jaw clenched and the back of his head ached from the repetitive nature of the action. He loosened his jaw, working it back and forth.

"You okay?" Temple asked.

"Anger."

"Oh."

"This is senseless violence." He lifted his chin and gazed at the stars poking through the clouds. "A pointless death. I'm tired." He lowered his gaze on the rippling sheet, imagining the dead woman beneath. Who she was. If she'd been on the way to meet friends, or just coming back from a good time. He always imagined the best, even if what he witnessed most of the time was humans at their worst, but his imagination was no match for the truth laying at his feet. "Let's see if this incident is related to the other kidnapping and get this over with."

Unbidden, Temple stepped forward and whisked the sheet off the body, as if performing some sort of magic trick.

Jasper had seen many bodies during his time on the streets with the locals, as well as during his time on the Evidence Response Team. The Bureau was routinely requested by other agencies to assist with evidence recovery, since they were without peer when processing crime scenes from an administrative purity angle, not to mention the eventual testifying required.

The rumbling of running engines and chatter of police flooding the area faded into the background as Jasper concentrated on taking in all of the dead woman's features. She was a slender young black woman sporting long straightened hair with a hint of scarlet. Faded and tattered blue jeans clung to her legs, but flared out around her ankles. Her shoes were missing and she wore no socks. Her feet were scraped up and covered in dried blood. Her abductor had taken off her shoes and socks, if she'd worn any. Was this woman homeless or simply in the wrong place at the wrong time?

He knelt, careful to keep free of the glistening pavement beneath her. The back of her head had been smashed and a nasty bruise darkened her forehead. A thin line of blood had trickled from her nose, but had since ceased flowing and dried. Raw fingertips and ragged nails betrayed the struggle she'd found herself in, likely from scratching at the Astro's floor in vain.

"I can't tell if the head wounds are exclusive to the crash or perhaps from blunt force trauma from her kidnapping. The autopsy should provide more clues."

"Perhaps this death was a blessing. She was alive for the trip, or at least part of it—look at her fingers." Temple bowed her head. Her lips moved in what Jasper assumed was a prayer.

"Yeah, she fought and didn't die peacefully." Jasper's fingers clenched into fists. "Damn it. We need to find the bastard who's responsible. I don't care if this is connected to whatever *X-Files* crap you're out here peddling."

Temple stared up at him, and her face didn't betray any hurt. Jasper was glad for that. He hadn't meant to go off on her.

"I'm sorry."

"Apology accepted. Now can we move on? Unless, of course, you've deducted something else from the poor woman's corpse." Temple cocked her head.

Jasper waved over the cop who had let them through. "You guys learn anything else about the woman here?"

"From Gary. Single. I'd say wrong place, wrong time. According to the sheet she'd been busted for distribution—"

"We both know that's bullshit, don't we? A user, most likely," Jasper said.

"Likely. I think she made a habit of being with the wrong people—"

"And being in the wrong place," Jasper said. "What are we doing wrong?"

"What?" the cop asked.

"Never mind. She have any relatives, friends?"

The cop shrugged.

"How about the driver of this piece of shit?"

"No clue, but I can tell you the van is registered to a little old lady."

"Oh, yeah?"

"But she wasn't driving it. She's in the hospital at the moment."

"So, stolen then?" asked Temple.

"That's what we think at this time."

"Any relatives?"

"We're working on that," the cop said.

"Thank you, officer," Temple said, and grabbed Jasper's arm, pulling him aside.

"Thank you," Jasper said. "I was starting to lose it a bit there."

Temple covered the woman once more with the sheet.

Jasper called over to the cop.

"Will you leave him alone?" Temple chided.

"No." Funny how the roles reversed on this one. "Do you want the Bureau's Evidence Response Team to assist on this one?" he asked the cop.

The man tensed, clearly irritated. "I'm guarding the scene, that's all, so take your problem up with my so-called superiors."

Jasper grinned. "Ah, a fellow lover of management."

"You know how it is." The cop hooked his thumbs into his bat belt, and relaxed his shoulders. "Anything else or can I go back to staring off into space?"

As if on command, East Chicago Police Department's evidence people arrived at the scene. Jasper didn't bother interjecting or offering the Bureau's assistance. Maybe the locals had decided this accident wasn't related to what they were investigating or hadn't even considered the possibility. Or maybe they had reached out to SSA Johnson and the field office's ERT Senior Team leader, Morris Chan, and they had begged off or outright dismissed the request. Besides, Jasper didn't have the authority and saw no point in bothering his boss. Johnson would only react poorly if he hadn't been asked by the locals and Jasper was interrupting his off time once again.

"We need to find the driver. He must have been hurt pretty badly."

"Unless," Temple's eyes hardened, "like so many people under the influence of drugs or booze, he simply walked away unscathed." She related the tidbit a little too bitterly, but Jasper didn't intend to pry right now. Apparently they were both sporting the scars of life—one thing they had in common, at least.

"Let's poke around here a little more," Temple said. "Away from all these people, perhaps we'll find something."

They peered into the crumpled Astro mini-van. Blood had dried on the deployed air bag and dripped on and around the driver's seat. They found no personal effects save for a pack of tissues and a cross on a chain shoved in the glove box. The registration gave them the name and address of the hospitalized woman—Jasper'd follow-up on the lead later, and perhaps poke around the house for more clues.

Temple knelt on the asphalt, peering beneath the wreckage. "Over here."

"What?"

"I think he crawled out from under all this—" She wiped her hands off on her jeans and stood, gesturing to the wrecked vehicles.

One of the cops nearby swore loud enough for them to hear. "It's gonna be one of those nights. Hey, Charlie!" He pinched the bridge of his nose, and another cop ran up. "We have a disturbance. One of the houses near here is complaining of an animal attack in their backyard. Says there's a horrible racket, like something dying."

"For Christ's sake," the other cop said, "don't we have animal control around here?"

"Hey," Temple said, and the two cops turned their attention to her. "We'll take the call. You guys have a lot going on and we're getting in the way."

"Sure thing there, Agent Scully. I'm sure the complainants will be quite surprised when a couple of fibbies come by."

"I'm sure it's a real X-File case," the other cop snorted. "Little green men or something, I bet."

"Your grade school creative writing teacher must be proud," Temple said. "You jokers owe us a couple of cups of coffee for taking this off your hands."

Jasper stared at Temple, surprised at how she was interacting with these guys. At least the locals had relaxed a bit and were just having fun with her now.

"By all means. We'll even provide the pastries." One of the cops doffed his hat.

"All right, just give me the address." The cop jotted the information down, tore the page from a small notebook, and handed it to Temple. She turned and strode off toward Jasper's bucar.

Jasper shook his head and ran after her, catching up as her hand hit the door handle. "The house is close by, we can walk from here, what are you doing?"

"Grabbing some pepper spray out of my bag."

"Ah. Roger that."

"There a problem?"

"No," Jasper said. "None. Get in the car. We should have all my gear at our disposal. Flashlights, and I have an extra Kevlar vest in the trunk. I—let's go, I simply hadn't thought about grabbing extra gear. I haven't carried pepper spray in a long time. The stuff is nasty during a scuffle."

They both got in the Charger. He flipped on lights and siren for the quick jaunt.

Temple glanced over at him. "You've been in some street brawls then?"

"One or two—happens when you spend time with the great folks the locals round up and deal with on a routine basis. Pepper spray jacks up the good guys as much or more than the bad guys."

"Right. Now, which way to this address?"

"It's not far from the accident, a couple blocks south of here and a little west."

They passed the accident and the gaggle of police and medical personnel. There were now a couple of fire trucks on the scene, also. Neither of the wrecked vehicles had so much as a whiff of smoke or flame, but the Fire Department showing was standard procedure. He managed to bypass the scene and cut through the intersection and toward the address of the attack.

"You have a reason for wanting to check this out?"

"A hunch," Temple said.

"The hunch being someone's dog worrying the driver of the Astro?"

"Something like that." She smiled. "But don't you find this a little too odd?"

The other animal attack... She was right. "We're close to the area where the other attack took place," Jasper said, "the one with the pile of meat for a corpse, and this could be the same sort of thing?"

"Exactly."

He rounded the corner of Ivy Street and saw a group of people standing in front of a house. He put the Charger in park, grabbed his ASP baton and a flashlight, and exited the vehicle, heading for the group of people. Temple followed.

A wail pierced the thick, damp air.

"What in blazes?" Jasper slowed up. His skin crawled, the sound reminding him of a wounded coyote out in the desert. He'd heard them often during his time in the Marines when he'd done a stint in the Mojave Desert—one of his more forgettable duty stations, but he'd never forget that sound.

"A problem?"

"Perhaps the complaint the cops handed us is legit." Jasper trotted in the direction of the address, abandoning the leisurely pace of seconds earlier.

Chapter 14

THE WAIL SUBSIDED, BUT THE GOOSE BUMPS ON HIS ARMS REMAINED. The group of people, perhaps a half dozen, stood on the cracked sidewalk in front of the house on Ivy Street, a drab aluminum-sided number with a screen door hanging askew and a crumbling brick walkway—pretty standard for this section of town.

"Any of you the owner?"

They all shook their heads. "What's going on?" a reedy Hispanic man asked.

"We don't know yet," Temple said. "Anyone know the owner?"

"He's some crusty old white guy," the Hispanic man said. "Yabutski or something."

"A get-off-my-lawn sort of fella?" Jasper asked.

The Hispanic man smiled, revealing a bit of gold in his grill. "Yeah."

"Do me a favor, you all stay back a bit while we check this out."

"You cops or something?"

"Or something."

Jasper nearly yanked the screen door clean off and rapped on the door.

The door whisked open and he was met by a whiskery old man, peering at him with one eye squinted almost shut and wild white hair resembling a bird's nest. "And what do you want?"

"Uh, are you Mr. Yabutski? Didn't you phone in a complaint earlier?"

"Yeah," the old man said, "to the no-good cops around here. Who in the hell are you two? The mod squad or something? And it's Yablonski, goddamnit."

Jasper rolled his eyes. "You want us to check out the disturbance or what?"

"Don't you have some identification?"

Temple flipped open her credential case and thrust it in the man's face.

The old man pulled back. "Hey, what is this? I asked for the cops, not the goddamned G-men, err, G-women. Oh, never mind."

"We're FBI, and interested in a few other goings on around this area. Mind if we check out the animal attack?"

"Pfft, ain't no animal attack if you ask me."

"Then why did you phone in a complaint?"

"Because no one would have taken me seriously if I told them my real thoughts, and don't think I'm not aware you all maintain a crazy file."

Jasper grinned—the old man wasn't wrong. "Okay, so what do you believe? Take us back."

"Come inside. Come inside. Can't have all those people," he nodded toward the crowd on the sidewalk, "nosing about my business. As it is, they think I'm off my rocker. But I'm not that far gone, not yet."

The interior was about as Jasper expected—an old man's idea of freedom. Dirty dishes on a TV tray next to a recliner, and another stack on an ottoman not used as a footrest for quite some time. Thick dust covered much of the available surfaces save for the recliner. Pictures on the wall were off kilter and faded from sunlight, and cobwebs laced the room nearly as much as the drapes covered all the windows. Mustiness mingled with rotten food and body odor created a miasma making Jasper want to head for the backyard and confront the danger rather than breathe in and taste the nastiness inside.

"It's little green men," the old man blurted out. "Or a chupacabra, all those Mexicans around here, you never know."

"For crying out loud," Jasper said.

Temple sighed.

"I'm not crazy," the old man said. "You go."

"We will, but first put on your tinfoil hat, that'll help protect you from the rays of Uranus."

"I'm not crazy. There's aliens, I tell you."

"Yeah, or a chupacabra, I heard you." Jasper took a deep breath and regretted the exasperation as he'd allowed all the foulness of the air to penetrate his lungs.

"The wailing ceased as you two walked up. You gonna check it out or what?"

Jasper motioned for Temple to follow him. He flicked the back light on, a bright spotlight that could burn the hairs off the healthiest head of hair, and peered through the back door's grime-caked window. "I got nothing. Gonna open the door."

He cracked the door and listened.

"Still nothing." He crouched, lifted his left pant leg, and removed his baby Glock from the ankle holster. "You packing?"

"Already have mine out, you ready?"

Jasper stood and opened the door. He performed two quick peeks, but saw nothing along the walls on either side of the door.

"What else is out back?"

"A shed and a few lines for hanging laundry."

Temple snorted. "This guy probably only gets around to doing laundry once every couple of months."

A slurping noise got Jasper's full attention.

"Hold on, I hear something." He held a finger to his lips, but kept his focus on the backyard. He reached over and flicked off the interior lights—no point in giving whoever or whatever roamed back there a glimpse of them before necessary.

Jasper hesitated. Temple's hand found his shoulder, as if at once providing both comfort and a nudge to exit the house.

He eased open the door and took a hesitant step out, scanning the areas of danger for any movement, but saw nothing. The wood step beneath him creaked under his full weight. He winced.

The slurping ceased.

"Behind the shed," he whispered.

Temple squeezed his shoulder.

He could see a crimson haze enveloping the ramshackle shed. That was perhaps a trick of the light, but the haze was nowhere else. A strange odor—not exactly putrid, but definitely not pleasant—smacked him in the face. He imagined a dead deer on the side of the road for a few days along with a sickly sweet twist, as if someone had dumped a bottle of cheap perfume on the poor animal.

The slurping erupted into a sloshing, squishy noise.

Jasper ran for the shed, flashlight and Glock at the ready to expose and deal with whatever horror lurked.

"Wait!" Temple cried after him.

He slipped on the wet grass and slid into the front of the shed. The old man must have run his sprinklers recently, even though there hadn't been any shortage of rain over the past couple of weeks. The grass was pretty slick.

The haze congealed alongside the shed, but then disappeared behind it.

Jasper scrambled to his feet.

Temple cried out something inarticulate, halfway between a warning shout and a scream.

He glanced back at her and his body chilled. Her eyes and mouth were wide and her hands shook, causing her Glock to wave about wildly. Jasper spun back for another look at the shed and was met by what appeared to be a rather large beast—but strangely ethereal, as if occupying two worlds at once, not fully in one or the other. He shook his head, and stepped back, raising both Glock and flashlight.

The shape before him was similar to the dragon shape outside the Euclid Hotel. The beast's crimson tendrils extended from the broad snout and reached for him, groping the air, but yanked back when Jasper thrust his Glock forward. The beast's shape morphed, now resembling a giant sea creature, something prehistoric. Then, abruptly, it vanished.

"Holy shit." He hadn't smoked in years, but the habit suddenly appealed to him again. A stiff drink sounded better, though—too bad he didn't carry a flask.

"I told you," a voice said from behind him, and coughed. "See?"

"Sir, you need to get back in your house." Temple's voice trembled, all her fierceness vanished.

The door rattled.

"The old man's back inside," Temple said.

"Let's check this out." He took a step, but hesitated. Stopping now was out of the question—he was charged with protecting others—but he felt so inadequate at the moment, as if the beast stole his courage upon vanishing. He turned toward Temple. "Did you see the strange shape?"

"That depends," she replied.

"On?"

"You saw my face when you turned around, right?"

"I did," Jasper said. "We need to clear the shed. What if the animal went in there—"

"Animal, huh? More supernatural—"

"Let's discuss the particulars after we peek into the shed. That okay with you?"

"Lead the way," Temple said. "Oh, and your back is covered in a wet substance, by the way. I don't think it's water."

"Blood?" Jasper cracked the wooden shed's door, shining the flashlight in. He saw nothing, but two blind corners remained uncleared. He'd poke his head in and out.

"No," Temple said. "I wouldn't describe the substance that way. Not red, but it resembles ectoplasmic whatever—you know, *Ghostbusters*, but with a pinkish hue."

"What are you getting at?" Jasper paused before stealing a peek into the blind corners. His face crinkled as he imagined his backside covered in wet and sticky goo. The situation reminded him of the yearly blood-borne-pathogen training and the admonishment the nurse at the field office used to give: *If it's wet or sticky and not yours, don't touch it.* He shivered. Hopefully the stuff didn't seep through his clothes and touch his skin.

"My reaction, by the way, was horror at what you slid around in almost as much as the creature we're both trying real hard to not discuss."

"Oh." Jasper's face warmed, but he wasn't sure why. Should he be embarrassed if Temple admitted she too witnessed something out of the ordinary? "Tell me, what did the beast we encountered look like to you?"

Jasper heard no scurrying or rustling from within the shed, so an animal was likely out, but a person remained a possibility. He knelt, pulled the door open and poked both head and flashlight inside the shed for a second. He breathed in the scent of damp wood, like fallen trees in the woods after a rainstorm. Old sawdust, kicked this way and that, covered the floor. A wooden workbench covered with tools in varying states of disrepair ran from one blind corner to the other. A rusty old gas can and a spout were on the floor before the bench.

"Nothing inside except a bunch of junk and gardening tools." He glanced at Temple, and stood. "So, describe the thing we're not talking about? You never answered."

Temple licked her lips. "A winged beast, something out of the Bible. A—a demon or devil of some kind, since you're asking."

"A what? I have no idea what you're even talking about. Wait, don't tell me, the beast sported a cloven hoof or two—"

"Really?" Her head spun toward him and her dark eyes regained the fierceness he'd come to know and expect in the short time they'd known one another. "Mocking my opinion of what I witnessed? This is how you're going to approach the incident? You asked me what I saw and I told you."

"All right, I'm sorry, I'm tired." He held up his hands. "That shit wasn't real—I mean, how can a crimson haze attack anything?"

"Explain the substance all over your back. The goo is like something coating the floor of a butcher shop. And what if the goo is a harmful or toxic substance? I think we need to check behind the shed." Temple pushed past Jasper, flicked on her flashlight and faced the back of the shed.

Temple's chest heaved and the rate of her breathing increased, accompanied by a slight gasping sound. Her eyes widened with the same fear Jasper had seen seconds earlier.

"What?"

"It's—a person, though I'm not sure of anything beyond that," she said.

Jasper swallowed involuntarily, and a moment of intense doubt and unease passed through him. "Like what we found near the animal control facility?"

"Sort of. You better take a look for yourself."

Jasper took careful steps toward Temple and, upon reaching her, spun and flicked up his flashlight. A pile of pink and white with traces of red littered the small path behind the shed, some of the matter pressed against a weathered fence about five and half feet high.

"You think the body back here made the wailing sound?"

"I think so," Temple said. "I'm going to get Vance over here for some samples."

"But the wailing noise happened only minutes ago, how could anything—and I mean anything—do such a thorough job of turning a human into a pile of meat? It isn't like we're chasing some sort of living sausage grinder, for Christ's sake."

"What if we are?" Temple pulled on his shoulder. "Jasper, if this really is something out of the Old Testament...or Revelations..."

Jasper shrugged off her hand. "I'm taking a closer look. Call Vance if you like, but there's got to be a natural explanation for this."

He heard a click behind him and two seconds later Temple was speaking with Vance and pacing the backyard.

"What's going on back there?" the old man yelled from the back door.

"Get back inside!" Jasper yelled.

"It's my property, isn't it?"

"Yeah, but there's been a death of some sort and we're going to need to seal off the yard. In fact, we may need to search the residence."

"I'll call the police. That'll fix you Feds. Damn G-men." The back door rattled as the old man attempted a slam.

Jasper frowned at the space behind the shed. It was quite small, perhaps a few feet across. How did such a large beast fit in such a tight space? The creature he'd laid eyes on was at least the size of a horse, but the form resembled that of a sinewy dragon—an Asian-style dragon, like what had materialized before him and Pete outside the Euclid Hotel. He didn't believe in dragons, though. Even Komodo dragons were exotic to him, and this hadn't been one of those. He wished Pete were here now—why not call him, anyway? Just because Jasper was assigned to assist Temple didn't mean he shouldn't utilize all the available resources at his disposal.

He stepped back from the space and hit up Pete on his cell. The conversation was mercifully short. Pete refused, wanting nothing to do with the strange deaths and certainly didn't want to get near the Euclid. He'd already begged off responding to the accident scene, even though he'd been close by, and he'd take a lot of heat for that in the morning.

Jasper hung up, pressed the phone to his forehead, and closed his eyes. He was stalling. Admitting he faced bizarre circumstances beyond his ken was difficult.

Jasper took a deep breath, and either he'd gotten used to the scent of rotten meat, or it had dissipated. He approached the back of the shed and directed the flashlight's beam over the pile of meat and bones and skin. Under the scrutiny of the flashlight, the pile cast a greasy sheen punctuated by a bone jutting from the meat here and there. Jasper's cheeks involuntarily puffed and he swallowed down creeping bile.

A piece of cloth caught in the light. He patted himself down, searching for the cheap pen he always kept on him. The exact pocket depended entirely on the quality of his attire and the type of people he'd be dealing with on any given day. In this case he found the pen lying flat in the bottom of one of the pockets in his cargo pants. The pants were a hard habit to break, especially in warm weather when wearing a jacket of any sort was out of place and it appeared odd to do so.

He inched for the pile, avoiding any contact with the mutilated corpse of the dead person—if that's what it was—with his feet or hands. That gave him some thoughts on the matter. *Could* a man do such a thing? Probably, with the right tools, but why would someone go through this sort of trouble to mangle a corpse beyond recognition? He still didn't want to believe these incidents were anything other than a murder or some bizarre death at the hands of an animal.

He bit his lip and extended the pen toward the bit of cloth he'd noticed. But so far as he knew, there weren't any animals that killed like this. Not in North America, anyway. The pen poked the cloth and caught in a fold, allowing for some leverage to pull the piece free of the mess.

"Well," said Temple's voice from behind, startling him. He almost lost his balance.

"Holy shit." Jasper rocked back on his heels and took a few breaths, allowing the weight of his body to rest against the shed. "You scared the hell out of me."

"Sorry. I was just thinking about something I read years ago, when I was a kid."

"Okay, go on—anything to take my mind off this."

"I was fascinated by certain types of sea creatures—"

"I don't think this was caused by chicken of the sea or anything." Jasper grinned.

"You're a funny guy. Ever consider a career in comedy?" Temple paused a moment. "Anyway. Don't sea horses digest their food outside their stomach? Or maybe another sort of sea creature, starfish?"

"What? You've got to be joking."

She was back to her no-nonsense stare. "Why couldn't a land animal exist capable of the same mutilation, and we, for some reason, scared the thing off? I mean, it's possible, right?"

"I don't know." He pinched the bridge of his nose. The scent returned, mingling with the burnt odor of the petrochemical tinged air. "At this point, I'm all for calling in the locals and letting them button up this scene."

"After Vance obtains some samples, right?"

Jasper sighed. "Yeah, but you know what? I'd like to try to grab some sleep tonight, if you and your partner Vance can do without me."

"All right. He'll be here soon. But what are you doing behind the shed, anyway?"

"A piece of cloth, perhaps some identifying clothing or who knows, maybe I'll find a wallet or some identification in this mess."

"You're not thinking of picking through the pile," Temple's top lip curled upward on one side, "are you?"

"The thought crossed my mind, but maybe you're right. Vance can get in there, if his stomach holds up. Didn't he almost toss his lunch after coming face to face with the last pile of meat?"

"There was no almost—he did."

"Right." Jasper smacked and licked his lips, attempting to stave off the dryness in his mouth and was rewarded with a taste of copper, as if he'd bit his lip. "I wish Vance would just get here already."

The back door of the old man's house rattled. "Damn foreigners, so pushy."

"I'm with them." Vance stuck his Bureau credentials in the old man's face, practically crammed down his throat. Jasper couldn't tell if the tone was Vance's natural lilt, or if he used a remonstrative voice.

"He's okay!" Jasper shouted. "Please, Mister Yablonski, go back inside."

"I phoned the police," Yablonski said. "They'll be here in a few minutes."

"Excellent. I was just about to do that, thank you very much." Jasper turned away from the old man. "Vance? Whatever you're going to do, please do so with the utmost alacrity. Sleep is calling."

Vance came over to Jasper and frowned. "Sleep? That was what I was trying to do." His hair was tousled and doing a pretty good job of defying gravity in a few spots.

"Payback, my friend."

"So we're friends, now that you need something from me."

"We haven't identified the victim, but these remains resemble the mangled corpse near Animal Control," Temple said.

"An idea popped into my mind as I fell off to sleep," Vance said. "The first corpse, the mangled one, reminded me of something being digested, but on the outside, like a—"

"A sea creature," Jasper finished. "Yes, Temple thought of the same thing, but I think that's a little too far-fetched."

"Just a thought. Where is this one?" Vance asked, eyebrows raised.

"Behind the shed, but it's a tight fit, so only take what you absolutely need."

"And try to figure out who this person was. We think it may be the person who kidnapped the dead girl at the accident scene over near the Euclid Hotel," Jasper added.

Vance disappeared behind the shed. Seconds later, retching could be heard.

"Please tell me you're not contaminating the evidence with your vomit." Temple placed her hands on her hips.

"I'm—I'm fine. Almost lost my stomach's contents, but I'm good here," Vance said, "I'm fine."

"All this talk of sea creatures has given me a thought," Jasper said.

"Oh?" Temple arched an eyebrow.

"I have a buddy over a the University of Chicago, he's a biologist. Perhaps he could enlighten us a bit on this, and if he can't, I'm sure he has a roster of professors who might, and plenty of books and other research materials available. I'll call him in the morning. Maybe he'll meet with us tomorrow."

"What do you think, Vance?" Temple leaned toward the shed and shouted.

"Ugh—fine." Vance coughed. "I'm okay."

"So, yes? We'll go to the university?"

"Yes. Now please don't make me open my mouth anymore."

Vance's coughing continued throughout his examination and evidence collection. No definitive answers existed other than this mangled corpse resembled the first one, only not as pink, as if retaining more of the red in the blood.

The East Chicago police arrived and cordoned off the backyard with rolls and rolls of crime scene tape and agreed to watch over the scene until morning.

"I'm going to have to call in our Evidence Response Team, I'm afraid," Jasper said. "This is becoming too much for us to handle alone."

Temple nodded. "Fine."

"Hopefully the senior team leader won't be too much of a dick when he shows up. ASAC Masters will have to lean on him to make this happen."

"Whatever," Temple said. "We collected everything we needed from here. Right, Vance?"

When Vance emerged, his face was a shade or two more pale than when he'd gone behind the shed and his forehead sported a damp sheen. His black hair lay matted on his head, soaked with sweat.

"You brought means of preserving all the evidence you collected without a need to go back to the office?" Jasper asked.

"I did." Vance licked his lips and frowned. He must have gotten the same taste of copper Jasper received.

"Then let's go. There's plenty to do in the morning."

Chapter 15

LALI STARED AT RAO, WHO IN TURN STARED AT THE FLUORESCENT light suspended above them with its robotic hum. The light's cold flicker accentuated Rao's hard face and the deep lines there, like one of those crazy contraptions the mad scientists operated in the old horror films Lali's grandfather used to watch when she was a little girl.

Rao's mind worked at something—dreaming? If so, dreaming of what, Lali wondered. The past glories of the cult—there was no other word for the group of madmen he ruled—he hoped to restore to their supposed greatness? Or perhaps the ecstasy of crossing over to the other world he spoke of incessantly? The man had a one-track mind, all right, maybe he thought of other activities a few times daily—

Ecstasy. Rao visited his version of ecstasy on Lali often enough and with force.

"Lali."

She almost sighed, but caught herself.

"Yes, Rao."

"See the flicker?"

"I do."

"The flicker reminds me of the moment the nâga break through, stretching the plasma barrier."

"Tell me more, I seek only enlightenment." But the man's ruminations grew tiresome. She desired information to assist in deciding her next move.

"The nâga's glorious entry into our world is accompanied by a ravenous hunger for the Sha 'Lu and the lifeblood contained in the sacrifices we provide."

115

More like cattle lining up in a chute, awaiting their turn for slaughter. Lali refused to picture his description of the sacrifice in Old Testament terms, like when Abraham offered Isaac up for sacrifice to Jehovah upon the mountain.

Rao broke his reverie and turned his hard gaze upon her. She shivered, but brought it under control, hoping he had not noticed. His eyes lacked natural pigment. She never could figure the color. All black at times, but morphing into a swirling electrical storm at other times, especially when he claimed to touch another world.

Rao's eyes narrowed and his mouth twisted, the lips curving into a cruel snarl. "We need stronger khâu. The miserable lot is failing us." He struck his chest with a fist. "Failing me. One time is once too often, but a second time?" He stood before her, his sinewy arms now hanging, but both hands balled into fists.

Lali swallowed, unsure if Rao desired a discourse, but she needed to placate him if possible. His wrath took predictable turns when aimed at her. "At least the two at the Euclid did the proper thing and incinerated themselves." She nodded, as if reinforcing the khâus' failure and how none of this had to do with her. Rao had told her of their fate, but he had raged for hours on their gross negligence.

Rao closed his eyes, the lids bright red, as if kissed by preternatural fire. "Oh, but this last one, the accident near the Euclid, that failure was spectacular in its carelessness and stupidity. A car accident? In a van at the very intersection where the hotel stands? How can the police not take notice of the coincidences? The Iron Thorn demands meticulous planning and lack of selfish motives amongst the khâu. Rao," he thumped his chest, "demands this of them."

Lali stared at Rao. He cared for his glory, and his alone. Rao's fanaticism dwarfed Koresh and the Branch Davidians. But there was something real behind his claims. The man truly touched another world and had the scars and powers to prove those boasts. Demons and monsters, or fallen angels feeding on the sufferings of others? Lali wanted to find out.

"We're safe enough for now in this industrial wasteland I've conquered."

Oh, how he enjoyed speaking of himself and how intelligent and resourceful he was. Conquered? He hid in this abandoned but surprisingly sturdy building he'd purchased through a series of shell companies—at least that was how Lali understood the whole thing. The former petrochemical plant gurgled and dripped at all hours and a constant electric buzz whirred. The khâu slept downstairs in a storage room filled with bunk beds, always present and tending to Rao's needs, as well as the building's.

Tepid pools dotted the lower level. A greenish-blue film covered the still surface—a petrochemical pond, devoid of life. Like so many places on earth these days.

Rao sucked in a deep breath. "I breathed their air once, you know. The nâgas' world is dangerous and jagged, but exhilarating. I swallowed their noxious water, their version of water.

"The price I paid for that was miniscule." He studied his arms. The bands of muscle and tendons twitched in his forearms and biceps, highlighting the angry scars sheathing his arms like tattoo sleeves some people etched into their skin. Khâu cowered before him, understanding the strength coursing through him upon passing back through the aperture into the human world, but also filled them with wonder and hope. There was no doubt of his dominance over the Iron Thorn, the Câ Tsang and his place as its leader, the Tip of the Horn.

"Failure teaches, does it not?" Lali asked, keeping her tone timid and somewhat obsequious.

Rao nodded. "Yes, failure gives us new blood, perhaps a cleansing. More devoted and more important, more *intelligent* khâu who understand following my orders without question is their lifeblood." Rao stood, motionless, staring at Lali. "You, woman, have the aptitude and attitude needed for a leadership role within the organization. You will face the trials soon enough and I'll know whether you're worthy."

Rao spun away from her and leaned on the railing. Lali approached, her footfalls loud enough as to not surprise Rao. She grasped his shoulders from behind and the white-knuckled grip he had on the arms of the railing loosened.

"You're tense." She whispered into his ear, the warmth of her breath radiating back on to her face.

He shrugged her off. Rao never admitted weakness. She withdrew, and moved far enough away where he couldn't spin and strike her if he desired.

"You're not like the others; there is no worry there, woman." He didn't face her, but remained staring over the railing and down to the main area of the plant. "You don't blindly follow like the khâu. You will someday break through to the other world once my place over there is secured."

She didn't really believe him. He'd use her to gain more power, but share in the power? She doubted that. If only she could supplant him, but that would require cunning and planning, long-term goals to be sure, and all the while she'd have to endure his advances.

"Failure tenses Rao," he said. "The police and FBI search for men like those weak khâu. But Rao and you, woman, have nothing to fear."

She once again approached him. She breathed on his neck and pressed her lips there. She suppressed a shiver, fearing the touch would burn her. The man radiated unnatural heat.

"But you can't do everything yourself." Her fingertips dragged down his back.

Rao straightened and faced her, taking in her entire body. He lifted her arm and studied her tattoos, then with his other hands fondled her piercings. His face twisted, the disapproval of the markings and piercings obvious. He couldn't resist her, but would any woman have had the same effect on Rao?

"You serve the Câ Tsang." Desire sparked in his cold eyes, the only spark there. "Luckily for me, giving into my desires for your flesh is not against the tenets of the Câ Tsang."

She preempted his advance and pressed against him. Her right hand glided down his chest and slid inside the loose waistband of his pants, squeezing what she found. "The only Iron Thorn I desire rests beneath here." Rao wore no underwear, since he despised restrictive garments.

"Do not presume." He yanked her hand free of his pants. "Rao will take you when he desires. No sooner."

She touched her cheek and grinned. "Do you not desire me?"

"It is not for you to decide what Rao does and does not do. Who Rao desires. *If* he desires. You are still khâu. We seek communion with the nâga and their world. Do not forget your place."

"Of course."

"You tempt me with those wicked, half-closed eyes." He touched her cheek and dragged his fingers over her mouth. "And those lips."

Lali understood full well what she was doing with her half-asleep appearance and slightly parted lips, showing a hint of teeth and the tip of her tongue.

"You have tasks to complete before I will take you." He turned from her, and she understood why.

"Let me help you," she said. "Has something happened?"

Rao's shoulders heaved, as if he tried to stifle a laugh. She pressed against him from behind, pushing her breasts into his back.

"Do not touch Rao unless instructed to do so."

Rao didn't quite trust her, but he was close—maybe. She pulled back from him, but only a few inches.

Rao turned and faced her, taking a deep breath as he did so. "It is time you learned of the ritual. The failures of the other khâu have caused the nâga consternation and forced them to feast outside the parameters."

What did he mean? Parameters? She couldn't hide her confusion from him.

"You wear the vacant expression of the men, those pitiful khâu. Ah, but when you think for yourself you don't court disaster, unlike them." Rao shook his head. "I'll forgive your confusion, and understand I've told you more about the nâga than any of them. The last three khâu failed me. As leader of the Câ Tsang, Rao is infallible. Remember that. But you asked what was wrong, and now I've told you. Think you can help Rao?"

Lali shrugged. "Perhaps."

"The Euclid Hotel *was* the perfect place for the ritual. We risk much by continuing to use the old building."

"The police?" Lali asked.

"Yes, but the khâu, your brothers who immolated themselves, took much for granted and allowed the police—the FBI—to find them and our ritual chamber in the basement. And then the mess over near Animal Control. I don't think the authorities have put it all together yet, but we're in danger."

"Certainly not from the FBI?"

He shook his head. "Only if they move beyond their by-the-book, Boy Scout mentality, which isn't likely, given their history. The real danger, now that the police and some of the FBI people have been vocal, is the guild."

"Guild?"

"The guild. Yes. This particular branch of the guild uses Völundr's Hammer as its moniker. I have some thoughts on where they've been hiding." Rao gestured for her to take a seat.

He strolled about the metal platform high above the floor of the plant, footfalls silent under his felt soles. Night had come, and with the darkness, Rao's comfort level increased and he became more loose than during the daylight hours.

Lali remained silent, satisfied to accept his teachings, at least for the moment. Rao had no adepts, only the acolytes, the khâu, but Lali believed she was to be his one adept.

"Information you provided has assisted me greatly in my current strategy, but I have need of more information from you." He dropped his chin to his chest and stared at her. "Tell me, were you tasked with finding me? Tasked with learning about the Iron Thorn?"

"Of course not." She answered without a hint of hesitation.

"Then what is the lure? I mean, what drove you to accept my summoning?"

"You. You're fascinating." She cocked her head and tilted it forward slightly, casting what she hoped was a glint of mischief at the powerful man.

He cocked an eyebrow at her. "What draws you to the Câ Tsang?"

"To serve and learn of the nâga. Lean of the greater purpose, and seek enlightenment on the other side." A rote answer, of course, which she sort of meant . . .

"Good," he said. "But we will never achieve such if the bumbling ways of the khâu persists. You will arrange for the next sacrifice."

"But—"

"But nothing. Obey or be punished." He raised his hand high above her, as if to backhand her. "Rao needs to do something about the current group of khâu."

She winced at the thought of the coming strike, but said, "Sacrificing one or two of the khâu to the nâga would set things right through fear, would it not?"

Rao lowered his hand. Was that a smile on the man's face, a cruel smile, a sneer perhaps? "That is an idea," he said, "which I will consider. But I have another task for you."

"What will you have me do?" she asked.

"Continue with your life and your job. Pay attention to the people you meet and what they discuss. When the time is right you will be provided all you need to know of the next sacrifice."

"Yes, Rao. I seek to serve you and the Câ Tsang."

"Excellent, Eulalia. Now go."

Chapter 16

JASPER SLOUCHED IN THE PASSENGER SEAT, EYES MASKED BY sunglasses, sipping black coffee and hating every drop of the burnt liquid. He glanced at Temple.

"I have no time to baby you," she glanced back at him, "and by the way, nine A.M. is not early."

"I suppose, but bearing foul coffee did nothing to improve upon the early call." He slouched in his seat. "Where in the hell did you get this crap, anyway? And you know what?"

"I'm listening."

"You're too made-up," Jasper lifted his sunglasses, "and well, perky for this time of the morning."

"Excuse me? Made. Up?" She didn't bother looking at him, but kept her eyes on the road. "Stop your bitching and tell me which way I'm heading. This is your neck of the woods, not mine, remember? Oh, and by the way, you look like shit. Perky my rear end—never been accused of that before."

"I'm trying to sleep back here, you two mind?" Vance protested from the back seat.

"From here on I foresee a productive morning with no arguments or strife." Temple focused on the road, but Jasper sat up—

—put the passenger side window down and dumped the coffee she'd picked up for him.

"Such foul stuff," Jasper said.

"Hey!" Vance cried from the back seat.

Jasper turned and looked at Vance who wiped at his face and hair frantically.

"You ass," Vance said.

Jasper slumped and took a deep breath. "I'm sorry, Vance, really. I didn't mean to splash the nastiness on you."

"You should rush me to the burn unit—"

"See, Vance? Now that comment was funny." Jasper grinned.

"Put the window up," Temple chided. "It's like I'm driving a couple of arguing brats to school."

"Yes, mother," Jasper said, "but don't you believe in air conditioning? I'm roasting."

"Yes."

"Okay, so why aren't you using it, then?" Jasper returned to the slouched position.

"It's morning, and it's not yet sweltering. And I'm cold. And I'm driving."

"Fine, but I didn't ask you to drive."

"Yeah, but if I hadn't picked you up, it would have been lunch time before you dragged yourself to the office."

"It is the weekend still, you know. I was up even later trying to explain to my boss, Johnson, why he needed to get a team out to recover that body behind the shed. And then I received a phone call from ASAC Masters. I'm walking a tightrope with my executive management. Oh, and we're lucky my contact agreed to meet with us."

"Thanks for talking your office into assisting. Didn't you say the contact lived near the campus?"

"Well, yeah," Jasper said.

"So quit your bellyaching—you're already up and might as well get into the spirit of things," Temple said.

Jasper dialed her in as they made their way over to Chicago.

"You know, this area we're driving through, Hyde Park, is sort of known for its cultural diversity. African-Americans are known to—"

"Known to what?" Temple asked forcefully.

"Uh, live in this area? The Obamas lived here."

"And?"

"Nothing, I guess."

"Hyde Park also at one time tried to keep black people out," Temple said. "And I don't want to hear about South Shore and Farrakhan either, that's close by too, right? I'm a Christian, you know, so why would I give a damn about Farrakhan?"

"I never brought him up." Jasper shrank down in his seat.

"Spare me the lessons in black history," she said. "But it's nice to see that apparently someone has been paying attention to the Bureau's black history month."

"Wiseass, and it's African-American Appreciation Month."

"Pfft. You really have been paying attention." Temple laughed and smacked the steering wheel. "But how about this: Why don't you tell me about this guy we're meeting, this biochemist buddy of yours, before we get there. That'd be swell."

Temple grinned, knowing Jasper would be thankful for the change of topic. Why did he think she'd care about Hyde Park, anyway? Simply because she was black? That'd be like her telling him something about backwoods rednecks while traipsing around the Ozarks.

"Not much to tell," Jasper said into the window. "He wasn't exactly a buddy back then, but a professor of mine. We became friends later."

"Oh? He an older man?"

"Why," Jasper glanced over at Temple, "you have a thing for older men?"

"Oh, but she does," Vance chimed in from the back seat. "Tell him about the old guy from HQ that—"

"Vance?" Temple glared at him in the rear-view mirror. "You'd do yourself a favor if you keep that trap of yours shut."

"A pleasant start to the day," Vance said. "Donuts, some chiding, and coffee—which I received in the face I might add."

"I agree." Jasper grinned. "So, back to my old professor. He's become a friend over the years, especially since I got assigned to the Merrillville Resident Agency."

"This old coot got a name?"

"Ed White."

"Sounds like your standard crusty old white guy."

Jasper snorted, and pushed himself up. "Ed isn't all that old. Let's see, he was in his early thirties when I met him. So he'd be in his mid to late forties now."

"Oh," Temple said, realizing at once how that sounded.

"Ah ha, so you do wish he were older. How interesting," Jasper said.

Vance tapped on Jasper's seat. "Oh, that'd be so perfect."

"What?" Temple asked, annoyed.

"Black and White," Vance said. "You see? Your name is Black, and his is—"

"Yeah," Temple said, "I get it. You're a riot, now sit back and shut up."

Jasper burst out laughing.

Temple shook her head. "I'm dealing with juveniles here. Not another word until we get there, and no uncouth or childish jokes please, we're professionals." Temple glanced in the rear-view mirror. "And Vance? You're not amusing."

"All right, we're almost there," Jasper said. "Turn down this street right here and try to find a spot. It's early enough and a Sunday, so we shouldn't have too much trouble. There he is, he's waiting for us."

"Where?" Temple asked.

Jasper laughed.

Temple parked. Jasper hopped out and headed toward a middle-aged black man who was perched against a nearby fire hydrant. The man rose, smiling, and extended his hand to take Jasper's.

"Ed, how in the hell are you? Still carrying that beat-up old thermos, I see."

Inside the car, Temple spent a few seconds silently cursing herself. Without ever thinking about it, she'd just assumed a bio-chemistry professor at the University of Chicago would be white.

She got out of the car and headed toward them, Vance trailing behind her. "This is Ed, I take it," she said.

Jasper nodded. "Ed, these are my colleagues, Vance Ravel and Temple Black. And this is Edwin White, but as you can see, he is—"

"Yeah, all right," Temple said, "you got me. Ha ha."

Chapter 17

AFTER AN ABBREVIATED TOUR OF THE IMMEDIATE AREA OF THE University of Chicago, Ed ushered them into one of the empty stadium-style lecture halls he used for the lower-level science courses he taught.

"The university's changed since you stumbled through here, my friend." Ed gestured to the flat panel monitors on the wall. "Not to mention all the kids these days carry laptops, tablets, phones, you name the gadget and they'll have one."

Temple glanced about the hall. "Much different than the small school I attended."

"Things couldn't have changed *that* much since you attended college, what, a few years back?" Ed grinned.

"Really, Ed? This guy," Jasper thumbed toward his old professor, "thought women would fall for his Billy Dee Williams routine, but—"

"Hey, you're the one who invented all the Billy Dee nonsense," Ed put up his hands as if fending off an attack. "Tell me this woman doesn't look youthful."

Temple averted her eyes from Ed's and turned her head ever so slightly.

"You falling for this load of crap, Temple?" Jasper grinned.

"Well, I'd say Ed's a lot classier and more refined than some people I've been associating with lately."

"I like this lady," Ed said.

Jasper shook his head. "Ed, I hate to tell you this, but Temple is about as old as you are. Well, maybe not *quite* as old—"

"What is this, high school?" Vance dropped his bag on the lab-sized table and rustled through the contents.

Ed coughed. "This guy right here, this so-called *Special* Agent, once raised his hand during a lecture and asked—"

"Yeah, a truly painful and boring lecture," Jasper said, laughing, "I said something like, 'Hey Lando, is it true you just made a deal to keep quality education out of here forever?'"

"You believe this guy?" Ed chuckled, deep and good-natured.

"I don't—oh, I get it, Billy Dee, Lando from *Empire Strikes Back*," Temple said. "What did you do?"

"I answered him like Lando, and even got the line correct." Ed smiled broadly.

"Hey guys?" Vance peered at them from behind his bag of whatever, a gigantic grin on his face. "Let's talk science."

Temple, Jasper, and Ed laughed long and hard.

"What?" Vance looked at each of them in turn and held up a sample he'd taken from one of the scenes they'd visited.

"Forget it. Ed, I'm gonna sober this up a bit—we're investigating a few disturbing matters with bizarre occurrences we'd like to run by you."

Ed's brow furrowed. He clunked the metal thermos down on the table and pulled a pair of glasses from the breast pocket of his dress shirt. Ed ignored Jasper and peered over octagonal framed glasses at Vance. "You seem eager to discuss science, at least."

Ed reached for the sample and peered at the liquid within the vial. "Light pink in color, nonviscous in appearance. What am I looking at here?"

"Well," Vance said, "this was the only liquid found at a crime scene, the remains of a human. I also found—"

Ed turned to Jasper. "You didn't mention anything about human remains. Was this a murder?"

"We can't figure out what is happening," Jasper said. "It's beyond my understanding."

"Perhaps you should start from the beginning. Provide me some perspective." Ed spread his arms wide, palms up.

They briefed the entire affair to Ed, told him what they'd witnessed and everything they'd found so far.

The lecture hall was still and devoid of any sound. Ed sat, an intense expression on his face. Finally, after a long pause, he spoke. "I'm not sure I'm following the part with the haze and the dragon and these, what did you call them?"

"She called them demons," Jasper said. "I'm not sure that part of this equation is even real. Did we imagine fantastic creatures? Or perhaps the mist congealed in such a way—"

"No. I don't think so," Temple said. "You obviously aren't familiar with certain books of the Bible."

"I *have* read the Bible, you know." Jasper folded his arms.

"This is fire and brimstone stuff. I can't help but think we need to pay attention and not dismiss a possible Biblical origin of these ... creatures, if the word 'demon' bothers you too much."

"I'm not disputing any of your religious beliefs. But too many other factors exist. You're acting like this is the start of the End Times, for crying out loud."

"And why not? God promised not to send another flood, but—"

"Yes, yes. I'm familiar with *that* part of Genesis," Jasper said.

"But he didn't make a covenant *not* to send forth demons and therefore pave the way for the second coming of Christ, did he?"

Jasper threw his arms up.

"I'm not sure I understand why the Bureau is getting involved in this," Ed interrupted, peering over his glasses. "I didn't think you investigated murders, unless they involved something like national security."

"Oh, allow me to explain," Jasper said. "Temple and Vance are assigned to SAG." He let the acronym hang—

"SAG? Like Screen Actors—"

"All right," Temple said. "I can't help the acronym. SAG wasn't my first choice but people at headquarters have zero imagination. SAG stands for Scientific Anomalies Group. And by the way, Jasper is assigned to us now as well, and I am his supervisor—"

"Temporarily assigned," Jasper added.

Ed rotated the vial in his fingers. "Vance, if what you told me is correct, well—this would be the discovery of a lifetime. You're talking alien life, alien elements. I can't even imagine how such chemistry could exist on our world."

"It could if supernatural forces were involved," Temple said.

"You mean divine intervention?" Jasper shook his head. "And why would God send some terrible creature, one resembling a Chinese-style dragon, down here to digest people outside its body? Can you explain that?"

"I didn't say anything about divine intervention," Temple replied.

Ed flipped through a textbook lying on the table. "All right, are any of the materials you've shown me here classified information?"

"No. I haven't made any of this classified," Temple said. "So far, this is a criminal investigation, not national security."

"In my mind," Jasper said, "our discussions have no choice but go down the path of weaponization."

"I don't think so," Vance and Ed said at the same time then regarded one another, as if in unspoken respect.

"I'm no scientist, but if Temple asserts divine—or satanic, whatever—intervention in the daily lives of people and Vance asserts alien elements? Well, I'm afraid the government, and specifically the military, would say otherwise. Almost everything has weapon potential."

Temple smacked the table. "That is the whole reason I'm not classifying anything right now. I want to keep all talk of aliens off the radar."

Jasper pursed his lips. "Damn. I hadn't thought of that angle. Good call, Temple. Withholding information from headquarters, since they typically stick their noses in places they shouldn't." He laughed.

"What's so funny?"

"Oh, nothing really, only that you're headquarters, right? And SAG is sticking its nose in fieldwork. But you sure aren't like them; you're not even close to resembling standard HQ bureaucrats."

"Gee, thanks for the compliment," Vance said, "I think."

Jasper shook his head. "We're letting speculation get too far ahead of us. As of now, mangled bodies are our only concrete evidence."

"I wish I'd seen the specimens in person," Ed said.

"Specimens? I'm not so sure." Jasper made a face. "It's one thing to view bodies and speak of bodies in a clinical manner, but on a crime scene, when they're bloody and mangled, well—"

"Yes," Temple added, "when confronted with the brutality of man directly, it's sobering."

"Horrific, I'm sure, but you didn't witness the acts." Ed peered at them from over his glasses. "Don't get me wrong, I'm not trying to diminish or downplay any of what you've all been through."

"I witnessed two men incinerate themselves by way of thermite."

Ed winced. "Sorry. Nasty stuff. I can't imagine a human

being making a conscious decision to end their life in such a horrible manner."

"Me, either." Jasper's shoulders twitched, as if suppressing a shiver.

"All right. Let's discuss what we actually have here." Vance spread a line of photos on the table. "This is what the bodies looked like."

Ed leaned over the photographs and picked up a magnifying glass. After perhaps a minute of examining the images, he said: "If I didn't know better, and without getting overly technical, I'd say this was an attempt to digest food outside the body."

"My thought as well," Vance said.

"But what kind of creature is capable of such destruction?" Temple demanded. "Certainly no land animal I've ever heard of."

"Man, for one, though I don't want to believe a man or men performed such heinous acts," Jasper said. "But we talked about a few possibilities last night, while stomping around the old man's backyard. You mentioned a sea creature, didn't you, Temple?"

"Close enough." Ed kept his head down, continuing his examination of the photographs. "Certain types of starfish are known to extend their stomachs outside their bodies."

"I'm not a biologist. Not by any stretch, but are there any land animals capable of this?" Temple asked.

"Fungi are saprobrionts and engage in extracellular digestion. But this is odd and combined with the samples you provided and from all you've told me, well, the lack of foreign digestion enzymes precludes an entire line of reasoning and type of animal. However, the evidence does suggest an animal that savages its prey."

Temple stood straighter, leaning back a little from the photographs. "But we never saw an animal."

"It has to be an animal," Jasper said. "There is no other explanation."

"I disagree," Vance said. "I found material suggesting an alien world."

"Are you saying we're being invaded by aliens from another world?" Jasper asked. "Look, aren't we getting carried away? Innocent people died at the hands of what we believe are a cult operating in the area."

"What, all of a sudden you're buying into the cult idea?" Temple asked. "Seriously?"

"After the van last night and the proximity to the Euclid Hotel, linking the kidnapping with the first one, the little girl, yeah, I am. Look," Jasper said, "I'm accepting the initial theories you proposed when we first met. As I was saying, we have insanely carried-out suicides, kidnapped people—one living and one dead, and two other dead bodies, both human, but mangled beyond recognition. And we're worrying about aliens and demons? Am I the crazy one here? How about we focus on reality; what lies within the realm of possibility on earth?"

"Relax, folks." Ed placed a hand on Temple's shoulder, and she didn't flinch or attempt to pull away. "Jasper's got a point, but how about this: we ask another type of expert around here, an astrophysicist. Also, I'm gonna suggest Vance stick around. We should take all of the material you've gathered and run some more conclusive tests in my lab."

"An astrophysicist? Why?"

"Vance said that some of the material he collected points beyond our world, and should be examined, no? I'm not discounting anything at this point," Ed said. "But, and this is my opinion as a non-law-enforcement type, you all should be on the street trying to find the cult members. Makes me not want to leave Chicago. You Indiana folks are just plain weird."

"I'm not *from* Indiana," Jasper said. "But going out and catching bad guys is exactly what I'd like to do, and we have other leads to follow up on."

Ed grinned. "Now you're sounding like some TV cop show."

"I'd be impressed if you somehow came up with answers as fast as they do on all the crime scene investigation shows on TV," Jasper said.

"I thought the FBI crime lab was world class. Why not use them rather than me then, wise guy?" Ed removed his glasses.

"Come on, really? They're good, but if you need an answer now, not so much."

"So true," Temple added.

"Indeed," Vance said, "why do you think Temple brought me on to her team?"

"You and I both know, my friend." She winked at Vance. "This was not only my last chance, but yours."

That was so true, also. They'd both been misfits—well, Vance was. For her part, Temple had pissed off all the wrong folks along the way, even though her case work had been outstanding over the years. Hers was a permanent exile to headquarters. Vance still had a shot at a normal career, whatever that was in the modern day Bureau.

"I've missed quite a few things, I think." Ed twirled his glasses. "Does the plan work for you?"

"Yes, let's ask this physicist of yours, but how about later? We'll leave Vance here with you."

"This'll likely take most of the day," Ed said. "How about you guys come back this evening, we'll chat and grab some drinks?"

Jasper grinned; glad the topic of drinks came up. "Hey Billy."

"Will you please stop with the Lando crap?" Despite the harsh-sounding warning, Ed was all smiles—Temple could tell he loved this sort of banter and doubted any of his professor and scientist buddies acted like this around him.

"You know, speaking of drinks," Jasper said, "I hear there are two rules to having a good time."

Vance was looking confused again.

Temple rolled her eyes. "Jasper thinks he's a real comedian with all these Billy Dee Williams jokes. You probably don't remember those beer commercials Billy Dee did back in the day, Vance. It isn't that funny, so don't worry about it."

"What?" protested Jasper. "Come on, that was a pretty good joke. Even Lando thought so."

Temple smiled. "Me, I think Ed is more attractive than Lando Calrissian, just the way he is—and I'm guessing, and really going out on a limb here, way more intelligent."

"Why, thank you." Ed stood taller, beaming.

"Though, I'm not sure how much given your choice of friends." Temple rolled her head, aiming her gaze at Jasper.

Chapter 18

"I LIKE HIM, THIS PROFESSOR FRIEND OF YOURS."

The smile hadn't left Temple's face ever since they'd departed the university, leaving Vance behind with Edwin White. Temple was happy to meet Ed, but what could possibly come of it, what with her being exiled to the Washington, D.C. area and Ed out here in Chicago? Unless she swung a transfer to the Chicago field office someday, after all the people she pissed off retired from the Bureau. Yeah, right. Once more Temple was getting ahead of herself. And Jasper sure as the Lord above made little green apples wasn't playing matchmaker. There was no way he'd want her steaming in on his buddy, Ed. Call her old-fashioned, but she wasn't down with long-distance or internet-based relationships.

"He's a doctor, no kidding, but he's not all that braggadocious. Oh," Jasper said, "you're gonna wanna hit the exit here and then straight on down Indianapolis Boulevard. We're gonna have to meet up with the source I told you about, Carlos."

"Let's back the conversation up a bit. I need to apologize," Temple said.

"For?"

"Not what you think." She reached over and turned on the air conditioning. "I was a bitch early this morning and not at all cold—temperature-wise," she added, glancing at him. "But don't get on my bad side."

A stream of steady clunks rocked the rental car.

"Great roads you have in this neck of the woods," Temple said.

"They're constantly repairing," Jasper said. "But with such heavy daily traffic and rough winters, keeping the roads in navigable condition is nearly impossible. I think the roads on the Indiana side are much worse than Chicago's."

"I'm guessing a lot of trucks go along with all the industry in a relatively confined area," Temple said. "Right?"

"Yes. There's no question this area benefits greatly from industry, but it is or was no friend to the roadways or the ecosystem. This is mostly steel country, and still is—although a lot of jobs in the steel industry have been lost."

"Plants moved overseas?"

"No, automation mostly. A lot of the secondary industries got hurt worse. That's why you see so many abandoned buildings and plants in this part of Indiana."

"Where are we headed?" Temple finally asked, happy to change the topic to the task at hand. "You don't want to hit your rez first and change before we meet the source?"

"What? No. What I'm wearing will work for the purposes of this meeting."

"If you say so." Temple glanced sideways at him and pursed her lips.

"It's fine for a diner."

"I suppose," Temple said. Jeans and an old olive green T-shirt, likely left over from Jasper's Marine Corps days, were unacceptable in her version of the Bureau, and certainly in Hoover's Bureau of the past. Of course, in Hoover's Bureau, Temple would never have been a Special Agent. Not simply because of her skin color, but also because of her gender. Despite all that, the Bureau enjoyed a reputation built on Hoover's ideals—and one of those was agents looking professional. Suits. Clean cut, that sort of thing.

"So anyway," Jasper continued, "I want to do a daylight drive-by of a few areas before we meet with Carlos. The diner has decent food, but don't ask for a cappuccino. We're going out of the way, but unless we get caught on the wrong side of a long train, we'll be fine."

"No worries there." Temple was pursing her lips again.

"What?"

"You're a former Marine—"

"Not former. Once a Marine, always a Marine."

"Yeah right, so you're a former marine and you sip cappuccinos? You expected one from a diner?"

"Whatever," Jasper said. "Turn down this road, I think we

can do two things—speak with the old woman whose van was stolen, she's at St. Catherine Hospital, and why not pass by the Euclid Hotel and the house we visited last night?"

"You're thinking it's odd so much is happening in such a confined area, aren't you? See? You're predisposed to working SAG type leads." Temple grinned.

"It's logical for any type of investigation. For instance, the animal control place would make sense if the attacks were easily explained, but the fact that the mangled bodies were found near the Euclid Hotel is too coincidental."

"Okay, but I'm not sure what we're looking for."

After a minute of following his directions, Temple said, "Wow, this route seems circuitous. Have you ever worked counterintelligence?"

"No, not really. Not beyond helping out some of the other squads when necessary, why?"

"If I didn't know better, I'd say you're performing a surveillance detection route."

"Maybe I am. This route wouldn't exactly be the one most people take to where we're going, and I wanted to ascertain if any interested parties tailed us, but what I said a few minutes ago still applies."

"Since you brought up the subject, anyone following us?"

"I don't think so. I didn't want to tell you the plan simply because you might have driven differently. You're not upset, are you?"

"Do I look upset to you?"

"To be honest, I have a hard time reading you." Jasper sighed. "Not that my expertise ever rested in reading women, obviously, based on my ex-wife Lucy."

"Something tells me you're being a little too hard on yourself. It takes two to tango, you know? We all have relationships go pear-shaped on us."

"See all those train tracks on your right?" Jasper nodded out the window. "We're on Chicago Avenue now, cutting across East Chicago."

"Train tracks, so what?"

"Yes, but look at the sheer number all lined up. More rail runs through northwestern Indiana than almost anywhere else in the United States."

"Again, so what?"

"I'm thinking if I'm part of a cult, we hide in this area, what with all the noise, trains, and industry. The exact location of these events is niggling at me—why are so many strange things happening in or around the Euclid Hotel? There are plenty of train tracks around, but the hotel overlooks a fairly busy intersection with residences not far off. There are better, more deserted places in the area, and even more in the next city over, Gary, where anything goes."

"Hiding in plain sight, most likely," Temple said. "And in an abandoned building no one cares about and no one visits."

Jasper shrugged. "Let's drive through and see if any ideas shake loose. Perhaps we'll have some questions for Carlos when we meet him at the diner."

At least plenty of green remained in this part of the state. Industry hadn't destroyed all the plant life—and there must be plenty of animals roaming about despite the large number of people and dangerous surroundings.

At Jasper's direction Temple headed down Elm Street, toward St. Catherine Hospital.

"The building looks old," Temple said.

"I think it was built in the Twenties. I'm a big fan of that time period," Jasper said.

Temple's eyes widened. "You? Really?"

"Yeah. The area needed a hospital because of the heavy industrial focus and number of workers in the East Chicago area. The exterior has changed over the years, but the original spirit of the building has been preserved by keeping the brick and the original arches resting in the middle of the main entrance. They've increased the size of the hospital substantially over the years."

"Come on," Temple said. "That sounded as if you recited it from a book or some Wikipedia entry."

"All right, you got me," Jasper said, and held up his hands. "While I am a fan of the Roaring Twenties, the truth was that I had an investigation once that led me to this very hospital and I asked a lot of questions."

"You have a good memory," Temple said.

"That might be the only thing that got me through college." Temple laughed.

Jasper approached the reception area and smiled at the youngish woman behind the glass.

"May I help you?" Her voice and demeanor were pleasant.

Jasper displayed his FBI credentials and badge, pressing them against the window.

"I'm Special Agent Jasper Wilde, and this is my partner, Temple Black."

"Oh." Her chair glided back, as if Jasper had informed her he'd contracted a horrible communicable disease. "What—what can I do for you?" She swallowed. "How can I be of assistance?"

"A stolen vehicle involved in an accident last night," Jasper withdrew his credentials, "is registered to a patient of yours, a Mrs. Hazel Thomas. We learned she'd been hospitalized recently."

"Of course," the young woman said, "I'll check for you. Though, I'm somewhat taken aback."

"Why is that?" Temple asked, stepping forward, eyebrow cocked.

"Don't FBI agents wear suits? Black ones? You know, white shirts, ties, and a hat? What are those called?"

"Fedoras?"

"Yes, fedoras." The young woman tapped away at a keyboard, the light of the monitor reflecting in her eyes.

"Told you," Temple said. "You look like a bum."

"Why are you interested in a stolen vehicle?" asked the receptionist. "That seems, well, I'm not sure how to put it, small potatoes for the FBI."

"There's more to the investigation, Miss," Jasper said. "Much more, but I'm not really at liberty to discuss the details. But I can assure you, the hospital is in no danger."

The young lady nodded. "Well, she is here. Go to the second floor and visit the nurse's station. I'll inform them you're on your way."

"Thank you."

A nurse on the second floor escorted them to the old woman's room. Two beds stood side by side, one of which was empty, while the other held Hazel Thomas, frail and withered.

"Had to be my lazy nephew who took my minivan," she croaked. If dust had flown from her mouth, Temple would not have been surprised. She did, however, remind Temple of her own grandmother, even if this woman was white. The thought warmed her heart.

"How can you be sure?" Jasper stood at the side of the bed. "And what is his name?"

"Alan Smith, lazy little bastard," she said. "And you know, he came right out and asked me if he could borrow the van for a while. I told him no, I needed my minivan to get around. Then I fell that very night."

Temple stood beside Jasper and leaned over. "Oh?" Temple placed on a hand on her arm.

The old woman patted her hand. "Breaking a hip at my age would likely be the end for me. Thought I was going to die." She licked, then smacked her lips, but they remained cracked and dry save for a bit of thick white moisture tucked into the corners.

"You think he did something to cause your admittance here?" Temple asked.

"Not sure. Awfully coincidental, don't you think?"

"He ever hang around with questionable or undesirable types?" Temple squeezed her arm gently.

"Like attracts like. Oh, who am I kidding? He was, pardon my language, a shit magnet."

Temple snorted and covered her mouth. She glanced at Jasper, whose eyes had widened.

The old woman chuckled. "That boy never done good by anyone. He lived in his mother's, my sister's, basement all the way up until last year. One day he comes home and says he's moving out. My sister had always coddled him—"

"Where did he go?"

"He never moved out. My sister died before he could get his carcass out of her house."

"Ah. What was the cause of death, if you don't mind me asking?"

"She broke not only her neck, but just about everything in a fall. Going down into the basement of all things to get him up for work."

"How do you know?"

"I was there."

"So, no foul play then?"

"Not unless you count the fact he lived in his mother's basement, a grown man, lazy and not getting up for his so-called job."

"Which was?"

"What, his job? Hell if I know. Tell me, what happened to my van and where is that no good bastard?"

Temple released two cheeks full of air through parted lips.

"Your van is totaled and we're not entirely sure where your nephew is." Temple didn't want to get into the gory details of the pile of meat that quite likely had been her "bastard" nephew.

"Serve him right if he'd been thrown from the van and broke his neck." The woman's eyes watered and her cracked lips trembled. "My sister didn't deserve a lousy son like him."

"Of course not," Temple kept her hand on her arm. "Did you ever meet any of his associates?"

"Pfft. Associates." She certainly recovered from her sadness in an instant. "You make him sound like some kind of businessman or attorney. Ha. Alan hung around with a bunch of degenerates."

"But can you describe any of them?"

"Odd looking. Ridiculous looking." She looked up and to the right, and pursed her dry lips, deep vertical lines carved above her top lip like the ground splitting under the strain of an earthquake. "Their appearance—too similar, like they were all part of some weird rock group. Damn kids."

"Similar?" Jasper cocked his head slightly.

"Generic, that the right word?" The old woman's cloudy eyes gazed up at him.

"No distinguishing features—"

"Pale and plain. Their heads were all shaped the same way and their faces cut in the same manner." She shivered noticeably beneath the blankets and the hand atop Temple's trembled.

"You don't mean cut by a knife or blade—"

"Oh, heavens no," she said. "Like their heads, their faces were angled, yes, angled the same way. Sunken cheeks and bald."

"Alan was bald or he shaved his head?" Jasper asked.

"He must have shaved; that boy had the most beautiful head of hair. People do the darndest things to themselves these days, it's beyond my understanding."

Temple squeezed her gently. "There are many things about all of this we still don't understand ourselves. But you've been a big help. You have anything you'd like to add or ask, Agent Wilde?"

Jasper's eyes narrowed and he bit his lower lip.

"Do me a favor," the old woman said. "Would you hold the cup to my lips? I'm so thirsty."

Jasper reached for the cup.

"No. Her," the old woman said.

Jasper shrugged and stepped back.

Temple held the cup to Hazel's lips, leaning close. The old woman whispered in Temple's ear.

Temple straightened and sat the cup on the bedside table.

"Let's go," Temple said. "Don't we have another stop before we're supposed to meet your source?"

Once back in the car, Temple sat for a moment in silence, as did Jasper, but she knew what was coming:

"What was the whispering all about?" Jasper turned to Temple.

Temple drummed the steering wheel. "You wouldn't believe it if I told you."

"Go ahead. Try me."

"It's nothing really, just took me by surprise."

"You seemed a little gruff after she whispered in your ear."

Temple made a face. "Apparently, Alan hates negroes."

"What?"

"Direct quote."

"Well, I'm sure we can put the quote in the category of hated—past tense. We're pretty sure the pile of meat behind the shed was Alan, right?" Jasper asked.

"That explains the dead black woman at the accident scene—or at least why he chose to kidnap a black woman," Temple said. "Hey, I think a search of Alan's house would do us good, perhaps tell us more about him, perhaps he left something useful behind. You think Pete could score a search warrant?"

"Maybe, I'll ask him later on."

"All right, let's go. Point me in the right direction."

Jasper directed her over to Euclid, then south, but just before East Chicago Avenue an excruciatingly slow train impeded their progress.

"Look familiar?"

"A little," Temple said.

"We're near the Euclid Hotel. We have a few minutes before this thing crawls past, how about we go over what we know for certain." Jasper faced her. "Sound good?"

"Sure. You start."

"We have the first kidnapping—"

"How do we know the cult didn't kidnap and sacrifice before?" Temple asked.

"Good point, the basement, the stone slab, and the wall appeared used, as if they'd performed rituals below the hotel before."

"Right."

The train clacked, and eased to a stop.

"I hate when they do this. We definitely have time to sort through things." Jasper rubbed his chin. "They kidnapped a girl. Me and Pete thwarted the sacrifice and they offed themselves in a bizarre manner. When you and Vance examined the basement, he found what appeared to be an alien element."

"Alien as in foreign. You don't think he meant from an actual alien, do you?" Temple had one eyebrow raised.

"Well, I took his comment as alien, little green men kind of alien, even if I don't believe in them, but you on the other hand, you think we have demons flying about like evil harbingers of an unknown apocalypse—"

"You make my beliefs sound infantile," Temple said. "I think the demon angle makes a lot of sense."

"All right, moving on—and I'm not dismissing you or your luna—"

Temple poked him.

"Kidding. Totally kidding."

"Go on."

The train's boxcars in front of them, labeled Santa Fe, edged forward and squealed and screeched once again as they halted. Temple put the windows down and turned off the car.

"Aw, come on," Jasper said, "and I'm not just talking about the behemoth of a train—I'm talking about why turn the air off? It's sweltering out."

"Being bitchy again, the malady comes and goes. As you were saying before the train stopped?"

Jasper sighed. "Vance found foreign material amidst the detritus, both human and otherwise, in the basement. Next up: we find a mangled corpse near Animal Control."

"Don't forget the vehicle racing away from Animal Control yesterday," Temple said.

"Oh yeah, we're still figuring the vehicle out, aren't we? The plates came back as belonging to a rental company. Figuring out who rented the vehicle is a matter of liaison with the rental company. And the victim of the first mauling near Animal Control appears to be circumstance."

"Yes," Temple said. "Wrong place, wrong time. Blah, blah, blah."

"And later another kidnapping, but this time the driver of the vehicle, and possible cult member, was snatched and subsequently mauled in the crotchety old man's backyard. Anything else?"

Jasper stared at the car's headliner, his face blank—and was he keeping something from her?

"You forgot one or two items there, chief."

"Such as?"

Temple started the engine, rolled up the windows, and hit the air.

"Bitchiness subsided?" Jasper grinned.

She put her hand back on the keys. "Don't make me."

"All right. All right. What did I forget?"

"For starters, you forgot the absence of blood the mangled bodies displayed. A pinkish substance coated them. Not to mention the strange animallike haze materializing, or perhaps a demon like the one you're raking me over the coals over."

He swallowed, and took a deep breath.

"What else?" Temple asked. "You're withholding something from me."

"Wow. My ex, Lucy, used to accuse me of not telling her everything all the time."

"Did you withhold?" She raised an eyebrow. "Wouldn't be the first time a male agent used the title to score pretty young things."

"You're not quoting Michael Jackson, are you?"

"What if I were? And you know what you're doing? You're evading both questions now."

"Damn it."

"I have to say," Temple said, "your casual blasphemies aren't attractive. Maybe that's your problem. You toss around a sacrilegious attitude like confetti."

"Yeah, I'm a regular Rip Taylor, but enough about me, let's talk about you."

"Nice confetti reference, but no. Let's get back on point here," Temple said. "We have work to do."

A squeal got their attention.

"Was that the train?"

"Don't think so." They both bobbed back and forth attempting to peek between the cars, to the other side of the tracks.

Jasper's cell went off, generic beeps. "Ah, saved by the phone."

Temple rolled her eyes.

"This is Wilde."

Temple imagined he loved saying that when he picked up the phone.

"Right, thank you very much. I'll have to think on that a bit. Hold on, I'll put Temple on."

"What is it?" Temple asked.

"Tomorrow we'll be attending a few autopsies," Jasper rubbed the bridge of his nose, "but there are problems."

"Like what?"

"Well, they may not have the resources or forensic abilities to provide us with any answers, well, useful ones at least." Jasper shrugged, and passed her his cell. "Here, speak with Vance."

"What's going on?" Temple asked Vance. "Fine... You know what to do... Uh huh... Great. That will work just fine then... Thank you." She handed the cell back to Jasper.

"What did you have Vance take care of?" Jasper raised an eyebrow.

"I asked him to secure assistance, nothing big."

"Right. Anyway. I'm going to have to inform my boss, you know. Hopefully he doesn't make a big deal about the autopsies."

"Do what you have to do, Agent Wilde." She looked him in the eye and said, "Now, back to my questions you thought you had escaped—"

A sick rumble followed a high-pitched whine, like an engine winding down after being revved hit them. Had to be one of those rice burner motorcycles with an overly large tailpipe. Temple hated those things.

"I think we're a little jumpy is all," Temple said. "Look, the train's moving again, but I'm not letting you off the hook, so to speak. Spill it."

"Fine. You know why Pete isn't working with us on this? He's spooked."

"What? I don't understand."

The loosely spaced clacking picked up in speed and the train rattled by, car after car and the end was in sight.

"The Asian-style dragon appeared the night of the first kidnapping. After we'd rescued the girl."

"In the basement?"

"No. We'd pretty much buttoned the place up and we're standing curbside outside the Euclid when Pete and I both see a giant mist. I perceived the haze as an Asian dragon, but when I turned, Pete had collapsed to his knees. The encounter, the vision, was religious to him, and you're approaching this as he did."

"Oh my," Temple said. "You witnessed a demon *outside* the hotel."

"So?"

"Well," Temple said, "and this is a theory, of course, what if the demon went looking for food?"

"What if it did?" Jasper asked. His eyes and demeanor told her he understood where she was headed with this line of thought, but wanted her explanation, from her lips.

"You found the first pile of dead human near Animal Control, not far from the Euclid Hotel. The mauling took place sometime during the night, right?"

"As far as we can tell. Vance's assessment too, right?"

"Yes," Temple said. "So, this thing went and found the guy in the SUV on the side of the road, and carried him over to Animal Control."

"How? What I saw was mist or gas or haze or something."

"What makes you think I have the answers? I'm just tossing ideas out."

The train passed and the gate rose, granting them passage across the tracks.

"The Euclid Hotel's just up ahead. Animal Control, as well as the old codger's residence, is nearby. Park after you get through the intersection and we'll walk back."

Traffic had piled up behind them while they waited on the train. Temple pulled over in front of a small house with a meager, rough-looking front yard.

"Don't worry, we'll get to the hotel," she said. "Wait, that sounded bad. We'll get to the scene."

"I didn't take offense, besides, you're acting like you have warm feelings toward my friend Lando at the university."

"He ever get cross with you on account of the ribbing?"

"You kidding? He eats it up. No doubt." After a pause, he added: "If you're wondering, he's not married. Used to be, but he got divorced...what's it been? About four years ago, now."

Temple felt a little edgy, partly because she wasn't certain yet of her own interest in Ed White and partly because Jasper could be more astute than she expected. "We should move on, get off this topic. I just met the man, you know?"

"We're running out of time," Jasper glanced at his watch. "We should meet Carlos over at the diner. I think we dallied too long. Maybe we'll have another shot at the hotel after the meeting."

Chapter 19

TEMPLE STOPPED, PLACED HER HANDS ON HER HIPS, AND STARED at the diner. "This is gonna be outstanding."

"Don't let the charming facade fool you, this place has great food. Just don't expect any frou-frou coffee-type drinks here."

"Wouldn't dream of fancy here," Temple said. "This is a diner. Plain old coffee, or milk shakes, or soda." She licked her lips. "I love diners."

Jasper held the door for Temple and followed after her. A hostess walked up—no, she was the waitress from his previous time here, he'd recognize her piercings and tattoos anywhere.

"Hello again," Jasper said.

"You're with Carlos," she said. "Right?"

Temple glanced at Jasper in disbelief. Bad tradecraft for sure— but how many agents changed venues for every single meeting? This wasn't an espionage investigation.

"This way. He's already here."

The waitress seated them—Temple slid in, Jasper sat next to her and made the introductions.

"Where is Pedro?"

"Pete isn't coming, so Special Agent Black will be sitting in on these for the time being."

"You some kind of replacement?"

"Something like that, but I'm pretty sure Pete can't be replaced so easily."

"Eh," Carlos said, playing with the fork in front of him on the table. "He's kind of a sell-out."

"Watch it," Jasper said. "What's wrong with you today, anyway? You seemed friendlier during our last meet."

"Trouble at work."

"Oh?"

"I'm not trusted with stuff as much as I should be."

"What do you do?" Temple asked.

"Machine shop. Cutting metal, that sort of thing. Handyman on the side."

"Carlos called in the tips on the first kidnapping," Jasper said to Temple, "which was why we met and why we're talking now."

The waitress came up and spread her hands, a pencil in one hand and a small notepad in the other. "Well?"

"Water for me," Carlos said.

"Figures," the waitress said with a derisive snort.

"Quit with the wise remarks for once, Lali," Carlos said.

"You two know each other?" Temple asked.

"Yeah, Carlos here is a real treat. A stand-up guy," the waitress said.

"All right," Jasper said, attempting to interrupt the mutual love festival, "I'll have a cheeseburger and fries."

"What to drink?"

"Just water."

The waitress didn't bother writing down the order. She looked at Temple. "You?"

"Water, please."

"That all?"

"Give me a second." Temple flipped the menu over. "Chicken Caesar salad, light on the dressing."

"Nope."

"Excuse me?"

"Dressing's already mixed in. So—nope."

"Whatever." Temple handed back to menu. "I can live with it."

The waitress stomped off.

"What in the Lord's name is her attitude all about?" Temple asked.

"She's loco. Messed up in the head." Carlos pointed at his head and twirled his finger. "Bad upbringing, bad relationships, whatever. If I cared enough, I'd attempt to figure her out, but she falls in the I-don't-give-a-damn category."

"You seem to be in a less than chipper mood today, so we'll make this quick," Jasper said.

"Sure. What do you need from me?" Carlos raised his eyebrows.

"I didn't have anything to ask you, not until last night. You heard what happened?"

"The accident? Yeah, how could I not hear about it? Some serious twisted metal."

"And twisted up people," Temple said. "You hear anything about the kidnapping last night?"

"Why would I?"

"Cut the crap," Jasper said. "There's no need to play coy like this. I'm not—we're not—accusing you of anything. Did you hear anything? Do you think last night's kidnapping relates in any way to the kidnapping of the little girl—"

"Teresa, remember?" Carlos filled in the blank, an empowering ploy by Jasper, making Carlos feel like he'd done something good, which he had.

"Yeah, the little girl you had a hand in saving, Carlos."

A glass of water clunked down in front of Jasper. "Yeah, he's a real American hero, this one," the waitress said.

Jasper glanced up at her. She'd worn makeup the last time he'd seen her, but now she'd applied thick layers. Not thick enough, though, to cover a few marks on her face, as if someone hit her recently.

"You okay?" Jasper asked the waitress, who clunked down two more glasses of water, and stared at him.

"All the sudden you care about some waitress at a greasy spoon?"

Jasper shrugged. "Have it your way."

"I will," she said, "and that's the way I like, uh huh, I like it. Uh huh, uh huh." She sashayed off.

"That girl is a certified fuh-reak," Temple said.

Jasper couldn't take the mystery any longer. "Seriously, Carlos, what's the story with the waitress? What's her name? Where does she live?"

"Who cares? I thought you wanted information about the accident and the driver of the van. The kidnapping."

"Wait, you know the driver of the van?"

"The crazy girl's name is Eulalia, but she goes by Lali."

"Okay, Lali. Wonderful. But what can you tell me about the driver of the van?" Jasper sipped his water.

"The rumor going around says a chupacabra ate him, drank his blood."

Jasper felt one corner of his mouth creep upward, but Carlos wasn't laughing and no hint of a joke rested in his eyes.

"A chupacabra," Temple said. "Up here in Indiana? Doesn't seem likely."

"Who would have thought those Chinese fish would be loose in our waterways destroying the native species here in the United States?"

"Touché," said Temple, nodding in acknowledgement of his point.

"So, a chupacabra ate the driver," Jasper said. "Why?"

"Wrong place, wrong time I suppose."

"Come on. A chupacabra, a blood-drinking cryptid. But I thought the blood came from livestock?" Temple leaned forward, resting her elbows on the table.

"A what? A crypt?" Carlos's eyes and mouth crinkled, confused. "Word gets out. The old man who lives in the house, the one where the chupacabra did its thing, came out after you left and told the group all about the mess in his backyard, and how a mangled body lay back there drained of all its blood."

The old man shouldn't have been talking to anyone, but stopping people from flapping their gums always proved difficult. What were they going to do to him anyway? He wasn't impeding the investigation. The concern here was if Carlos was hiding something else—he didn't seem to want to provide any details about the driver.

"You think your BFF, what's her name, Lali, would know anything about the driver?"

"She probably hooked up with that freak, you know, they're pretty much cut from the same freaky cloth," Carlos said.

A plate slid in front of Jasper. The heat of the cheeseburger and fries rose up, as did the very pleasant scent. The diner had a limited menu, but what they did, they did well.

"So I'm a bit freaky," the waitress said, "who isn't?"

"How do you keep appearing out of nowhere?" Jasper asked. "Delivering food and joining the conversation—a private conversation."

"Secret talent."

"You know the driver of the van that crashed last night? Or anything about the kidnapping?" Temple asked.

"Or anything about a chupacabra?" Jasper added and took a sip of his water.

"A what? Chipacabra?" The waitress's eyebrows knit together. "What the hell are you talking about? Something that steals all the tortilla chips?"

Jasper nearly spit the water out of his mouth. Temple's smile expanded beyond the boundaries of the hand covering her mouth.

"Ay." Carlos covered his face and shook his head.

Jasper wiped the corner of his eye and took another bite of the cheeseburger.

"Anything else?" the waitress asked.

Temple eyed her Caesar salad and held up a hand.

"Something wrong?" The waitress put a hand on her hip.

Temple's smile vanished. "You didn't answer *my* questions. The driver? Kidnapping?"

"Ran into the driver once, if it's the guy everyone's talking about." She put the pencil eraser first between her red lips, thick and a little pouty, holding it for a minute as her gaze roamed. She shook the pencil at them like a wand. "Can't say I know who was kidnapped, but I ran into the driver at a party once. Can't remember his name, though, if I ever knew it at all." She shrugged.

"If you think of the name, let us know," Jasper said.

"Sure thing." She walked off and attended another table.

"Anything you care to add?" Temple asked.

"That's probably where I know the driver from—"

"Where from?"

"Like Lali said, probably some party."

They ate in silence for a few minutes and Jasper made quick work of his cheeseburger and French fries. Temple picked at her Caesar salad. Carlos sucked down his water and jammed a toothpick between his teeth.

"I gotta get going. Sorry I couldn't be much of a help today." Carlos slid from the booth, half-saluted them and exited the building.

"Odd," Temple said, "but then, the entire meeting was not how I remembered source meetings."

Lali appeared out of nowhere with an expectant look on her face.

"We're fine," Jasper said, "oh, you want to take your salad to go, Temple?"

"No, I'm good."

"So sorry to see little Carlos go so soon." Lali dropped the check on the table.

"You know him? Date him? Anything him?" Jasper asked.

"Date him?" Lali turned her head and cocked an eyebrow. "Hate's much more accurate."

"You a jilted lover maybe?"

"Heh. I'm the jilter, not the jiltee." She bumped Jasper's shoulder with her hip and strolled off.

"Somehow I can see that," Jasper said, watching the waitress and her swaying hips, "despite the bruise and marks she's covering with the shit ton of makeup."

"Ah, you noticed," Temple said, reaching for the check.

"You're paying? But Carlos is a local CHS."

"You're temporarily assigned to SAG, remember? This meal will come out of our budget, and we've managed to secure quite a nice little war chest for this fiscal year." Temple paid with cash and took the second copy of the check.

"Care to head back to the Euclid? Have a look around?"

"Sure, let me pick at the salad for another minute," Temple said.

Jasper polished off his water.

"Ready?"

They both slid from the booth and exited the diner. Lali leaned on the counter, and each time Jasper stole a peek, she was still watching them, all the way to their vehicles.

Chapter 20

THEY ROLLED UP ON THE TRAFFIC LIGHT ACROSS FROM THE
Euclid Hotel around three in the afternoon. The intersection,
teeming with police, firefighters, and EMTs the night before, stood
eerily quiet for a weekend day. The mayhem and destruction and
death were thoroughly erased, as if the kidnapping, accident, and
pointless deaths had never occurred.

Jasper shivered despite the heat of the day—and the hotbox
Temple created out of the rental vehicle. They waited for the
light to change.

"Hard to believe."

"Yeah, not so much as a piece of glass out here. Hey, you
think your Evidence Response Team descended on the old man's
residence this morning?"

"They're probably at the scene now. But they'll be by the
numbers and not extrapolate, I'm sure." Bile crept into the back
of Jasper's mouth just thinking about the Senior Team Leader of
the ERT program for the Indianapolis Field Office, Special Agent
Morris Chan. Jasper swallowed, but the sour taste lingered. "Got
any breath mints on you?"

"No, but I bet the woman in the hospital, Hazel, had Certs
or LifeSavers."

"Wow, your grandmother did that too?" Jasper grinned.

"All the smokers did." She laughed. "I have some gum if you're
so inclined." She rustled in her bag with one hand, but kept her
eyes on the road. "Here."

The light turned green after what had seemed an interminable
amount of time.

151

"Once you're through the intersection," Jasper stifled a shudder as they crossed over the spot of the accident, "flip a U-turn and pull up to the side of the hotel."

"Ten-four."

Temple swung around and Jasper peered at the alleyway behind the hotel as she drove past—the same alley he'd seen the haze resembling an Asian-style dragon.

"Hey, I think Carlos's truck is parked behind the Euclid—an off-white Toyota pickup. Pull up a little more and park."

"You sure?"

"Yeah, pretty sure." Jasper frowned and propped his chin up with his fist as he rested his elbow on the armrest. "I wonder what he's doing here."

"I think learning more about Carlos should be on our list," Temple said. "The same goes for that Eulalia chick from the diner."

"Agreed." Jasper rubbed his chin. "I remember saying the same thing to Pete during the first meeting with Carlos."

"What should we do? Go in? See what he's after? Confront him?"

"I was hoping to get out of this hot box and walk around the perimeter of the hotel, but now I don't—"

The nose of Carlos's truck poked from the alleyway.

"Get down," Jasper said. "Let's hope this rent-a-car is generic enough that he didn't notice it at the diner."

They both ducked. Temple had pulled almost to the intersection—not far from the alleyway, but far enough that Carlos might not think anything of the vehicle.

"I wonder what he was doing here, anyway." Temple asked. "You think the hotel's still buttoned up, crime scene tape, and so forth?"

"Beats me."

The sound and smell of ragged exhaust poured into the rental car. Carlos had pulled up next to them—hopefully waiting for the light at the intersection. Neither of them dared poke their heads up. For a moment, Jasper wondered why they cared so much, but if Carlos had anything to do with the mysterious cult, it'd be better to not alert him to their presence.

"We can come back to the hotel later," Jasper said softly. "We need to follow Carlos."

"But what if he left a signal or a mark or something?"

"Sounds like spycraft to me, and we're not after spies, are we?" Jasper raised an eyebrow.

"It's called tradecraft—but why can't anyone use signals? Gangs do, right? How is graffiti any different than a spy leaving a chalk mark on a telephone pole?"

"I see your point."

The truck's rumble deepened and for a moment grew louder, but trailed off.

They both sat up.

"He's westbound on East Chicago Avenue, I bet, uh, turned right—"

"I'm aware of which way west is." Temple frowned and started the engine.

"You never know," Jasper said, "so many people have no idea about the points of a compass. Anyway, we can always come back here. Let's see what he's up to."

"All right."

They followed Carlos, which was simple when he stayed on major roads and other vehicles provided cover between his pickup and themselves. But after a quarter mile or so he made a southbound turn on Huish Drive.

"Interesting," Jasper said. "He isn't heading home. Staying on East Chicago Avenue for a while would have been a safe bet. Okay, this road turns into Kennedy Avenue down here."

"Maybe he's going to his place of employment." Temple glanced at Jasper.

"Maybe. It's a weekend, but ... maybe his shop is working overtime. If he gets on the interstate, following will be easy."

But Carlos didn't. Instead he went under the interstate and looped around to head west on Michigan Street and then south on Indianapolis.

"There are quite a few shops—not department stores—"

"Yeah, I understand—I didn't think we'd find a Nordstrom's over here." Temple rolled her eyes.

"Sorry. Don't have to bite my head off."

"I won't, if you stop acting like I'm some dizzy broad," Temple said.

"Fine. I'll try. I'll try to try."

"You may be right; his employment might be over here. It's kind of a mini-industrial area."

They had taken a few turns with Carlos where no other vehicles offered cover, and now approached a wide band of railroad tracks with an approaching train.

Carlos's Toyota pickup belched a black glob of smoke and he accelerated over the tracks before the arms came down.

"Damn. He must have spotted us."

"Or he rushed to beat the train?" A bit of hope crept into the sentence as Temple finished.

"I hope you're good at reacquiring after losing the eye," Jasper said.

"Maybe you worked some spy stuff in the past after all." Temple turned and raised an eyebrow at him.

"Once or twice. Interesting stuff, but slow."

"Counterintelligence isn't for everyone."

"Well, I say we head down to Summer Street. We can roll through the parking lots of a few businesses over there. With luck, we'll spot him."

"If not," Temple said, "we can always head back to the Euclid."

"Roger that."

Mercifully, the train passed in short order. They hit Summer Street and Jasper directed her westbound.

"Up here, turn right at the next street, I'm not sure of the name."

Temple laughed as they approached. "Hump Road."

"And people say men are crude." Jasper grinned. "Stop thinking about Ed." He leaned away, expecting a poke, but received her disapproving stare.

They crawled past the first building, all brick, but with thick, smoked-glass windows and unlike some of the other businesses nearby, still in business. A fence surrounded the property so one couldn't drive on to the complex, but the front of the building remained accessible by walking right up and ringing the front bell.

A row of vehicles populated a parking lot behind the building.

"Holy shit," Jasper said.

Temple glared at him.

"Fine: why, I'll be a monkey's uncle! That better?" He pumped his eyebrows up and down.

"A little."

"And besides, you made a hump joke!"

Temple's mouth twitched, an almost smile.

"Anyway," Jasper said, "I can't believe we found him—the Toyota parked in back is Carlos's. Keep rolling up this road and we'll pause before turning around—looks like Hump Road dead ends anyway."

Temple swung the car around at the end of the road. Buildings resembling hangars lined the road. Some appeared empty and dilapidated, while others were dilapidated but still in use.

"What should we do?" Temple asked.

"I don't know, what do you think?" She'd been allowing him to make a lot of decisions today, and he wondered if this was her way of apologizing or making him feel like he was part of the Scientific Anomalies Group.

"All right." Temple drummed the steering wheel. "What are the odds he's part of a cult whose members commit suicide at the first sign of cops?"

"I'd say low."

"And what are the odds he'd phone in the tip on the kidnapped girl if he were part of this cult—which, by the way, we haven't proven exists yet?"

"Pretty low." Jasper chuckled. "Thank you for the bit about the phantom cult. I thought you made up your mind on the cult's existence."

"I think the cult's real. It fits. Demons, cults, ritual suicide. We even have a working name for them now, the Phantom Cult—I like it."

"All right." Jasper suppressed a laugh. "I'm not sold, but I suppose one of us should be a skeptic, right?"

"Sure," Temple said.

"So, if this goes sideways on us, I'm not wearing any body armor, my Kevlar's baking in the trunk of my bucar, and I doubt you're wearing any."

"Let's hope this doesn't get ugly on us and let's hope Carlos isn't a bad guy." Temple smiled. "We've all done stupid things over the course of our careers, what's one more?"

"Yeah, unless this time is the last stupid thing we do. You know what? I'm gonna call us in with the Merrillville office's switchboard, so they know where we're at."

Jasper would have called in on his bu-radio, but again, it was installed in his bucar, so he used the smartphone. Boy, he wished he'd talked Temple into taking his car rather than the rental, but he'd been so out of it this morning.

"All right, we're set."

A metal sign attached to two metal poles jammed into the ground identified the business as Wayland Precision. No witty tag line, only the name of the business with a blacksmith's hammer beneath. Spartan, but word of mouth and reputation rather than advertising likely brought them business.

Crabgrass littered the patchy strip in front of the red brick building. A cracked sidewalk and brick steps led to an imposing metal door, which wouldn't have been out of place in Fort Knox.

"The door must weigh a ton." Jasper pointed. "They expecting to repel an assault or outlast a siege?"

"Maybe they're a bunch of doomsday types—"

They ascended the steps and the tiny porch provided a respite from the pummeling waves of heat.

"Oh, there's a doorbell and intercom, exciting." Jasper jammed the button; a buzzer inside the building was loud enough to elicit a wince from both him and Temple.

"Makes sense for a machine shop, eh?"

They stood for a few minutes and still no one answered the door.

"All right, I'll give the intercom a whirl."

He reached for the button, but the speaker rattled: *"Yes?"*

Jasper pressed the button: "I'm Special Agent Jasper Wilde with the Federal Bureau of Investigation. I'm here with my partner, Temple Black. We'd like to speak with someone."

A long pause.

"What is this about?"

"Carlos Ochoa, He works for you. His Toyota is parked out back. No one is in trouble."

Longer pause.

"Yes, Carlos is an employee of Wayland Precision. What is this about?"

Jasper pinched the bridge of his nose. "A few questions regarding some kidnappings, is all. We need to speak with him." Jasper hoped for Carlos's sake his employer was not part of some criminal enterprise—which was why he didn't reveal Carlos was an FBI source. The Bureau protected the identities of sources, but in this case, they needed to get to the bottom of Carlos's activities and motivations. Jasper would only reveal Carlos's role if necessary.

"Give us a minute. We're in the shop; someone will be up to greet you."

Jasper took a step to one side of the door and Temple did the same on the other side. Standing in front of the door was not tactically sound, even with a door capable of repelling a medieval battering ram. He cursed himself for wearing the baby Glock on his ankle today, or his hand would have been at his hip poised to draw.

Temple's hand retreated to her hip.

At least one of them was in a better position, more tactically prepared.

Latches and locks clunked and turned from the other side before the door creaked open a bit.

"Hello?" a female voice asked.

Jasper leaned to the left and Temple took a step to her right. He waved his credentials and displayed his badge. Temple did the same.

"We're with the FBI—"

"So you said." A solidly built blonde woman stepped into the light. She wore not a hint of makeup on her strong Nordic features. The only fitting description of her was as if Freyja herself came to life—if his memory of Norse mythology was still any good.

Jasper's tongue was suddenly incapable of producing words.

Temple shook her head ever so slightly, and stepped forward. "I'm Agent Black, and this is Agent Wilde."

"What can I help you with?" The woman who answered the door didn't offer her hand.

"We need to speak with Carlos Ochoa," Temple said.

The woman looked at Jasper. Whose contribution was "Uh..."

Temple smiled slightly. "What he means is," she said, "we have a few questions for Carlos and his recollection of a crime."

"Yes." Jasper managed. "We need to speak with him, Miss—"

"Penny Stahlberg," the young woman said.

"Are you the receptionist?" asked Temple. "Is there someone else we should speak with?"

Penny's eyes darkened as if ready to swing a hammer or hurl lightning bolts.

"No, I'm pretty much your point of contact," Penny said. "I'm part owner of Wayland Precision."

"May we come in?" Temple leaned forward.

Penny gestured for them to enter.

"You said Carlos wasn't in any trouble." Penny offered them a bench in the dimly lit reception area. "Oh, pardon the atmosphere; we don't receive many people here at the shop."

"No, uh, Ms. Stahlberg," Jasper said.

"You can call me Penny."

"No, Penny," Jasper said, "Carlos isn't in trouble. He may have information on the recent kidnappings. I'm sure you're aware of them?"

"Oh yes, horrible. I can't imagine investigating such matters. Care for some water? It's boiling outside."

"No thank you," Temple said. "May we speak with Carlos?"

"I'll send him up." Penny moved for another solidly built door sporting a combo lock, where a sequence of numbers are pressed and a switch is turned, opening the lock.

"May we have a tour of your building?" Temple asked.

"It's a machine shop—not much to see, really."

"I'd be interested." Jasper couldn't believe how much of an ass he was making of himself.

"I'm sure." Temple poked him in the ribs.

"How about another time?" Penny said, "We're quite busy today."

"On a weekend? Your business must do okay. What exactly do you do here?" Temple fired away with the questions and remained standing, as if displaying her dominance over the Norse goddess denying them entrance to the temple.

Jasper shook his head. What in the hell was wrong with him, he hadn't felt this way since, well, since Lucy way back in the day when they'd first met. Not a good omen, but also not anything to put much stock in.

"Like I said," Penny's stance faltered, "we're busy, and—"

The intercom crackled. "Show our guests in." That was a man's voice; not Carlos's, but an older one, projecting gravitas.

"You heard the man," Penny said.

"And who would that be?" Temple asked.

"Steve Stahlberg," Penny said. Jasper wondered if that was her husband and suddenly he was crestfallen. But—

"My father," she explained. "We own and operate Wayland Precision together."

"You can relax." Temple glanced over her shoulder at Jasper and pursed her lips, as if calling him out over his ribbing of her earlier regarding his friend, Ed White.

Jasper's ears radiated heat. Embarrassing.

Penny bit her lip, trying not to smile, and turned away.

Damn it.

"This way." Penny punched the code into the keypad and pulled open the door.

They descended a long flight of stairs upon stepping through the door. A vegetal scent filled the air.

"I thought you ran a machine shop." Jasper glanced about, attempting to locate the source of the odd scent.

"We have some strange hobbies," Penny said.

"Such as?" Temple wasn't even trying to hide her skepticism.

"You'll see," Penny said. "For one thing, we like growing mushrooms down here."

"For what? Extra mushrooms on your pizza?" Temple's tone came right to the edge of outright sarcasm.

"Don't mind her." Jasper said to the Norse goddess. "You must have a good reason, I mean, other than loving fungi."

Temple shook her head, and yes, he continued making a fool of himself.

"I'll let my father speak with you on the finer points," Penny offered.

"But we're here to speak with Carlos," Temple said.

"I'm sure that can be arranged."

Penny said the last line as if Carlos was indisposed, or a prisoner locked away in a dungeon.

The group descended into a damp cool. A substance, not slick, but slimy, coated the surface of each step, and Jasper was relieved when they reached the bottom.

The hallway glowed unnaturally under the current lighting conditions—was the light blue? Violet? Penny flipped a switch and good old incandescent bulbs flared to life, providing a harsh yellowish-white light.

"Better?" Penny smiled disarmingly.

A bench lined the hallway on one side, but acted as more of a planter. Mushrooms in varying states of growth and maturity filled the box, planted in the blackest soil. A few of the mushrooms attained gargantuan proportions.

A strange feeling crept into Jasper's gut and he tensed up.

"What is it?" Temple whispered into his ear.

"Nothing, at least I hope it's nothing."

"There's nothing to worry about," Penny said.

Jasper winced. He'd never had a soft whisper.

A door opened at the opposite end of the hallway; a figure blocked the light coming from the other side.

"Bring them along, Penny." The gruff voice echoed down the hallway.

"Don't mind him," Penny said.

"Who? Your father? Steve, right?" Jasper asked. Why did he feel as if he were meeting a girlfriend's father for the first time? He shook his head.

"Yes. I'm sure we can clear all this up." Penny swung her gaze around on him and smiled.

"Calm down there, Romeo," Temple whispered in Jasper's ear. Penny didn't react.

"Here we go." Penny stepped through the door past her father, who immediately blocked the entrance.

"So, you're FBI, eh?" Steve folded thick arms across a broad chest. He was an imposing man with an equally imposing beard and head of hair. The silver locks fell across one side of his face, which was interesting since the uncovered side appeared as if it'd been terribly scalded—apparently he didn't care and perhaps wore it as a badge or show of defiance. Regardless of the burn mark or port wine stain, Steve's appearance resembled the same mythological Norse stock as Penny.

"Yes, sir," Jasper said, and introduced himself and Temple.

"Steve Stahlberg, proprietor of Wayland Precision."

"Nice sign out front," Jasper said. "Noticed Thor's hammer under the name."

Steve grinned and glanced at Penny, who stood directly behind him. "See? I told you someone would notice."

"May we come in?" Temple asked. "I have to admit, I'm not overly fond of the pungent smell out here in the hallway."

"I'm afraid it won't be much better in here," Steve said, "but please, come in." He stepped aside, granting them entrance. "The main office is down here, away from the metal working upstairs. One of the few places we can speak at a normal level and not go deaf."

A few aquariums dotted the office, but they were all dim at the moment, and Jasper couldn't make out what sort of fish lived in them. Typical office furniture filled the room: filing cabinets, desks, conference table, a few computers, and other accouterments one would expect.

A chair squeaked, and Carlos stepped out of the shadows near the back of the office, as if he'd been hiding.

"What can we help you with today, officers?" Steve leaned against a filing cabinet, which emitted a screech as it slid an inch or two on the tile flooring.

"Special Agents," Temple said.

"Carlos may have information on the accident and kidnappings. May we speak with him alone?" Jasper asked.

"Nah, let's just chat all together here, sound good?" Steve stated, more than asked.

"If Carlos agrees," Temple said.

Carlos stepped forward and nodded. "We can talk about anything you like in front of them."

"All right, general question here," Jasper said. "Why are you growing all those mushrooms? It's odd."

"Let's say we're a tad superstitious," Steve said.

"I thought I'd heard it all," Temple said. "I mean, all the random acts people practice because they think it'll bring them luck or ward off evil spirits."

Steve shrugged. "You going to ask anything relevant? If not, I'll show you out."

"Hold on," Jasper said. "We're part of a special unit within the FBI—"

Temple held up a hand, stopping Jasper. He hadn't realized how proprietary she was regarding SAG. "Yes, I head up an investigative unit called the Scientific Anomalies Group. We have reason to believe there is something going on in the area involving a cult. We've also found traces of an element a scientist attached to SAG has never seen before."

Temple paused. Steve, Penny, and Carlos didn't flinch or blink.

Temple continued, "This element is foreign to our world. My agent thinks it's alien, from another universe. I think it may be demonic in origin."

Penny's eyes flicked toward Steve. Her father chuckled. "Aliens or devils, huh?" He scratched at his beard. "You're serious?"

Temple nodded.

Carlos stepped forward, appearing eager to get this impromptu meeting over.

"Ah," Jasper said, "tell us, Carlos, what were you doing at the Euclid Hotel earlier?"

Steve and Penny shot each other indecipherable glances.

"I wasn't—"

"Save it, we saw you there. Awfully suspicious behavior." Jasper raised his eyebrows. "Wouldn't you agree? And you never glimpsed us following you?"

"What? No."

Jasper focused on Carlos, staring him down. "So, why were you at the Euclid Hotel?"

Penny spoke up. "He was at the hotel under my orders."

"But what could you possibly want with the Euclid Hotel?"

"Is parking behind a hotel against the law? I frequent a nearby auto parts store, and I'd rather park in the alley." Carlos seemed proud of himself for that bit of lying.

Temple sighed. "We're not your enemy. We're trying to stop a bunch of senseless murders—"

"And suicides," Jasper added.

"All right. How about this," Temple said, "do you know anything about mangled bodies and strange figures made of mist or haze?"

Steve and Penny glanced at one another again—clearly aware of what Temple said, and clearly hiding something.

Jasper decided to take a different tack. He walked toward and pointed at the aquariums. "What sort of fish do you have in the tanks?"

"Not fish. Sea squirts."

"Salt water tanks, huh?" Jasper bent over and peered inside. "So, you grow mushrooms and have a bunch of sea squirts. This is truly an eclectic machine shop."

"We spend a lot of time here," Penny said, "and we each have our little diversions."

"Okay, back to business," Jasper said, and moved away from the aquariums. "What sort of metal work do you perform here?"

"We specialize in stainless steel and exotic alloys."

"Ah, okay. I see." But Jasper didn't, really. His familiarity with machining was passing and, in any event, quite a few years back.

One of his cousins in Tennessee had owned a small machine shop, but he and Jasper had never been close.

He stood near a desk and glanced at the papers littering the surface. Temple spoke up—good, a distraction while he stole a few furtive glances.

"Ever deal with thermite?" Temple asked.

"No." Steve, Penny, and Carlos all answered at once.

Jasper scanned the desktop: a few papers with Wayland Precision on the letterhead, a notebook, a ledger, and poking from the corner of another notebook, a symbol. No, a hammer, and arcing atop the hammer the words: Völundr's Hammer.

"Find anything interesting, Agent Wilde?" Penny asked.

"You can call me Jasper. Sorry, I was intrigued by the hammer on this piece of paper." He tapped the paper in question.

"Oh, that," she said, waving as if the paper were a trifle. "I considered renaming the company Völundr's Hammer at one time, but Wayland Precision was my father's brainchild, so we let the name be."

"This may be a silly question, but why Wayland Precision?" Jasper glanced at Steve, Carlos, and settled on Penny. "I mean, no one named Wayland works here, right? Does Wayland mean something to you?" He turned his attention back to Steve.

"It's an old blacksmith thing, from Northern Europe—a fairly common tale, that of Wayland the Smith. Do you have any other questions for Carlos? We're busy, and running a business, you know."

"Of course," Temple said, "but I'm not sure I understand why Carlos was at the Euclid."

Carlos started: "I told you—"

"By my direction," Penny repeated. "And that's all I'm going to say for now."

"You're going to leave it at that? Do you have anything you can tell us that will aid our investigation? We're trying to prevent any further kidnappings and deaths."

Steve, Penny, and Carlos remained silent.

"May I contact you again?" Jasper asked, hopeful Penny would say yes, but Steve stiffened.

"If we learn anything, we'll reach out to you. Do you have business cards?"

Temple and Jasper handed them each one of their cards.

"You can call me at any time," Temple said, and glared at Jasper, stopping him from saying the same to Penny.

They were promptly escorted from the building and back in the oppressive heat.

"Well, that was different. I'm not sure what to make of them." Temple squinted and shielded her eyes.

"We got some info from them, and a bunch of weird hobbies. We need to put all this together and see what we can come up with."

Temple's phone erupted into "When the Saints Come Marching In." "Ah, that'd be Vance. Hopefully they've come up with something on their end."

Gravel crunched, the sound of tires rolling over loose rocks and pebbles. They'd almost rounded the building to where Temple had parked on Hump Street, but both of them stopped and gazed behind them.

A deep blue compact car sped off, but in the opposite direction, up Summer Street. A Yaris, perhaps? Jasper squinted.

"Think the car is related?"

Temple shrugged and answered her cell. "Hold on one moment, Vance."

"Eh. Probably not," Jasper said. "Maybe I'm paranoid after our bizarre encounter among the toadstools."

"No, you're in a daze after drooling all over Princess Toadstool."

Jasper grinned. "Good one."

Chapter 21

"WHERE HAVE YOU BEEN?" RAO FLIPPED UP HIS SLEEVE AND twisted his wrist over, examining a gleaming band. He wore the face of his watch on the underside of his wrist.

Lali's fascination with the man had begun a few months ago. He lacked distinguishing features, but the man's oddness remained with her—shaved head, bleached eyebrows, and face dull and smooth. At first, she'd thought the man plastered his face with an off-white powder.

The mushy-faced man was curious over her relationship with the young Hispanic man, Carlos.

She'd dated Carlos, but they'd broken up after he decided he wanted to work things out with his wife. He still insisted on coming around the diner afterward, but to what end? Taunting her? Tormenting her? Carlos was lucky she'd never dumped hot coffee in his lap. But the bastard only ordered water.

"I summoned you well over an hour ago," said Rao harshly. "If this is how you respond to Rao's commands, perhaps you need another lesson."

Lali's hand twitched, but she resisted the urge to touch her cheek where he'd slapped her earlier. He'd roughed her up a bit, but she didn't hate it when Rao did so—she was biding her time.

"Are you listening to me?" Rao stood a few inches from her, invading her personal space, which he'd taken from her over and over the past few weeks in so many ways. The man had an insatiable appetite.

"I am listening, Rao."

He raised an open hand, but she grabbed his wrist. "Wait! Please. I have information."

His hand remained open and raised, but she squeezed harder.

"You know the consequences of such insolence." He ripped his arm from her grip. "Rao does not tolerate such."

The odd man had invited her to a party, telling her the experience would be unlike anything she ever witnessed. She agreed and he picked her up at the diner after her shift ended. He drove what she called a child molester van—the cargo type with no windows down the sides. She went along willingly with the strange man, not thinking much about the van. She never turned down a good party, and she could take care of herself if push came to shove. Even now, she carried with her a small pistol.

An abandoned hotel, the Euclid Hotel—and like the van, she didn't give it much thought. Not until she figured out the fate they'd planned for her: sacrifice. Rao spied on her from an area beyond the basement—behind not a wall, but a divider of sorts. Rao stepped through, draped in white robes with crimson gashes running diagonally across the chest. He mesmerized her when he approached, his supplicants melting away into the shadows.

"What is this news of yours?" Rao's harsh tone snapped her from the reverie and back into the present.

"I may have located something of interest. A company named Wayland Precision."

"And?" Rao stepped back. "Why does Wayland Precision matter?"

She suppressed a laugh—the mighty Rao, obtuse? And people always misjudged her based on her piercings and tattoos, not to mention the way she wore her makeup and hair. For a Latina woman raised by good God-fearing Catholics, she was as far out there as Pluto to most people who crossed paths with her.

"Carlos visited Wayland after he met with the police." She put a hand on her hip. "Met with the FBI, to be exact—they didn't try too hard to conceal their conversation, either."

"Now, this is fascinating, but how do you know they were at Wayland Precision. Did they mention it during the conversation?" Rao folded his arms and stepped back a little.

"No, I followed them."

"What? You *what*?" His voice cracked as the pitch and volume increased. "You followed FBI agents to what may be the hiding place of Völundr's Hammer?"

Lali stepped back. Her heel caught something, sending her tumbling backward, and sprawling on the metal flooring.

Rao stood over her, hands balled into fists. "You remained hidden, right? Assure me both the FBI and the guild remain ignorant of where your allegiances lie and your role in Câ Tsang."

She swallowed, and for the first time since she'd met Rao, no, the second time, she feared for her life—the first being the night of her sacrifice. But the sacrifice had never happened. Rao took Lali as his own, saving her life and indebting her. But had Rao really saved her life? He'd been the one who ordered the kidnapping and sacrifice in the first place.

"The FBI agents were too busy following Carlos. So it was a simple matter, remaining hidden."

"You are overly confident," Rao said. "You'd better pray they were unaware of you. We need another sacrifice before we can stop caring if anyone finds us. Finds me."

His fists unclenched and his breathing slowed.

"I'm not going to punish you, at least not in a way anyone will see." He bent over and yanked her to her feet. The sudden show of force exhilarated her—a taste of the power from beyond? The nâga and what their world had to offer those of the Câ Tsang? "We'll discuss the next course of action once you're fully one with Rao, the Tip of the Horn, leader of the Iron Thorn."

Rao popped the buttons of her blouse as well as the button on her jeans. He tore the clothes from her and stepped out of his robe. He wore a chain with either a horn or thorn dangling from the links. Rings adorned every finger, including thumbs. He discarded the watch, also.

He scooped her into his arms, carried her up another flight of stairs, his bare feet thudding the metal. Upon their entry to his sleeping platform in the abandoned plant, a red light flicked on, casting an eerie glow upon everything.

She'd been up here many times in the past few weeks, but he'd never been this angry with her.

Rao tossed her on his bed as if she were nothing, like a backpack or something. He was very strong, much stronger than you'd expect of a man of average size.

He stood over her once again, and pointed toward a carved headboard, the images nearly impossible to make out other than they represented some kind of orgy taking place in a hellish nightmare. She pushed herself upright and scurried for the head-board. Rao approached and tied her wrists to thick wooden rings protruding from the orgiastic scene.

Given her Catholic upbringing and repeated viewings of *The Exorcist* while growing up, she wouldn't have been surprised if Rao sported hooves or spewed pea soup.

It was exhilarating.

Rao took her with force and rougher than was his usual way. The bastard never protected himself during sex, and he forbade her to use birth control, but Lali always protected herself without him knowing.

Once he'd finished, he paced the room, his naked body glistening against the red light, lending the entire scene a sordid, no—debauched—appearance. He kept her tied up as he paced, and beneath her, a wet spot like one of the Great Lakes welled. What if everything about Rao was now affected by the other world, that of the nâga? Would she contract some sort of disease or give birth to some demon baby? No. She used birth control, the pill, and if worse came to worst, she'd toss herself down some stairs. She'd never give birth to this man's child, and certainly no half-nâga hybrid...

"We'll find out more about this Wayland Precision, Völundr's Hammer, whatever they name themselves. If they are truly the guild and are indeed lurking here, they must be dismantled."

She remained silent—interrupting him while her arms and legs were bound was foolish.

"We need to sacrifice the leader of Völundr's Hammer. Yes. You will lead this for me. But first, we need to deal with the FBI agents. Now tell me, who are these people?"

Lali related all she knew of them from what she'd overheard at the diner—which had been fairly substantial.

"Rao is pleased. Very pleased." He paced, his bare feet padding against the metal platform.

At least the bed was comfortable, though her arms were falling asleep now and her wrists ached, not to mention her insides.

"Will you accept the following plan," Rao paused, "no matter what it entails?"

She nodded.

"No matter what you'll have to do or sacrifice?"

She nodded.

"I need your oath." He leapt on the bed and straddled her naked body. "Speak."

"Yes, I swear to you, Rao, and pledge loyalty and devotion to the Câ Tsang." She desired power, and a glimpse of the fantastic, a taste of the fantastic.

"Manage to do what I set forth and you'll be promoted to the rank of an adept—a khäp." Rao beamed. "You begin tonight."

Rao took her again.

Chapter 22

TEMPLE HAD NEVER ATTENDED AN AUTOPSY. SHE'D SEEN QUITE a few dead people over the years, and not in the *Sixth Sense* sort of way, though she wouldn't have been surprised to witness souls loosed upon the world—and why not? She'd witnessed otherworldly events, Biblical by her reckoning. Certainly an autopsy wouldn't, *couldn't*, be more vomit-inducing than the mangled bodies she'd seen the past couple of days.

Jasper had pointed her to the Lake County Coroner's office, part of a larger local government facility. Though they handled routine autopsies at this facility, when presented with a difficult case, such as the bodies they'd come across the past couple of days, they often had the autopsies performed elsewhere. After Jasper explained this to Temple she had Vance track down a medical examiner to assist them.

"You guys, I mean SAG, often contract out for stuff like this?" Jasper asked.

"Stuff like this?" Temple snorted. "There has never been stuff like this."

"You know what I mean. You have a list or something you go off?"

"No. But the Chicago Field Office used this doc before. Vance called an agent he knew there who recommended her."

As Temple pulled up to the building, Jasper swore.

"What? You despise the look of these buildings as well?" They were all ugly in that late Sixties and early Seventies way. Clearly governmental offices.

"No," Jasper said. "Although you're right. These buildings couldn't look more drab."

Temple laughed.

"But no, the problem is that right there." He pointed at a black SUV with tinted windows which completely obscured its occupant, or occupants.

"Is there something I should know?" She raised an eyebrow.

"Yeah, unless someone borrowed his bucar, that's the no-talent clown who currently takes up space as the senior team leader for FBI Indianapolis's Evidence Response Team."

"Let me guess, you two don't get along."

"Not even a little."

"And why am I in utter shock at this discovery?" Temple grinned.

"Ha. Ha. Trust me," Jasper said, "this man isn't here because he wants to be here. He must have gotten up quite early to get here, since he had to come up here from the Indianapolis area. That's at least a two-hour drive, more usually two and a half. Let's just hope he brought along someone I can stomach."

"You mean there is that special someone in the Bureau that you can stand? Anyone?"

Jasper turned toward her and scowled, but that sly grin and sparkle his eyes often held returned. "Yeah, I'm a pain in the ass for sure. Now, I'm going to try not to start anything with him, but he's a prickly bastard. He should get it over with and call it a career," he said, then added in a mumble, "such as it was."

"This should be interesting," Temple said.

"Yeah."

With that they entered the building and soon came face to face with the "no-talent clown," whose name was as of yet unknown to Temple. He was a Special Agent, appearing to be on the verge of the mandatory retirement age of fifty-seven, and likely Pacific Islander in his origins. He had a tired face, droopy and without humor. He wore khakis and a navy blue shirt adorned with an Indianapolis FBI Evidence Response Team patch. If he packed a firearm, he must have hidden it on his ankle. The fact he didn't wear a fanny pack with the gun tucked away inside surprised her: He was definitely that type. In short, he looked like a pain in the backside.

"Who's this?" the clown asked, chubby arms folded.

Jasper cocked his head.

"Ah, yes," the clown said, "the headquarters puke."

Temple grinned and Jasper remained silent, though she could sense his temptation to say something.

"Something amusing?"

"No, not really."

Jasper shot her a look, as if saying, *see*?

"Hi, I'm Temple Black." She extended her right hand, which the man stared at and pursed his lips. Wet things, those lips of his, and unnaturally red, as if Temple and Jasper had interrupted his sucking on a cherry-flavored ice pop.

"Yeah," he said, giving her hand a quick, limp shake. "Can we get this over with? I've been ordered by higher pay grades to be here for this debacle. You know, this should have been shipped elsewhere, or better yet, not been anything at all, since I've received the prelims and I don't think we're going to get anything out of this."

"Whatever you say, Morris." Jasper took a deep breath and continued. "Look, these are unusual deaths, Morris, and while I'm sure you have some Little League game to attend or some other father of the year type thing to do, this is important."

Temple raised an eyebrow and looked at Jasper.

Morris rolled his eye and a sigh escaped from the man's lips, a sigh that held the pent-up aggressions and stress of a man resigned to the life he had built for himself.

"You have anyone else tagging along?" Jasper asked in a more conciliatory tone.

"Nope," Morris said, "you can do the photo log. I'll take the photos, that's the only way they'll get done properly. You do remember how to do a photo log, I presume?"

"Uh, yeah."

"And she can be a witness in case there is any evidence that needs collecting, though from what I've heard, there won't be much."

"We shall see," Jasper said, and with that, the three of them entered the stark building.

Antiseptic, but not fresh smelling, not by a long shot. Temple's jaw was clenched; the back of her skull ached. She released the tension by moving her jaw around, as if she were trying to pop her ears during a rough flight.

"Hey, you okay?" Jasper touched her shoulder.

"Not sure yet. You never know what will set a person off." Jasper removed his hand and shrugged. "That's true enough."

"The smell is giving me a headache," she admitted.

Morris chuckled. "That chemical scent? Soon you'll be thinking back on this fondly."

A man wearing light blue scrubs and a white apron paid them no mind as he arranged the instruments resting on a tray. He had a Nordic look to him, which was confirmed by his nametag, Janssen. The man and the setting reminded Temple of a torture room with tile and metal and running water in *The Girl with the Dragon Tattoo*. A sink was positioned at the end of an angled table of stainless steel, not unlike her food prep table back in Arlington, Virginia. The thought wrinkled her nose. She'd never see the shiny surface the same way again. Scales hung near the table, much like the type found in a produce aisle. There were also scales resting on a shelf, like the sort a deli counter would employ. Ladles? Like a kitchen. Her stomach turned. She swallowed a retch creeping up her esophagus.

"Here." Jasper thrust two pieces of flimsy blue material at her which she could see through.

"What are these?"

"Booties."

She examined them. "And what good will these do me? I mean, they're see-through."

"Just put them on," Jasper said. "It's not like you're wearing open-toed shoes."

She mock-saluted Jasper and slipped them on over her shoes—not her junkiest shoes, either, although they were indeed expendable if need be. Would give her a reason to buy another pair of nicer shoes if fluids of some sort were to get through the flimsy barrier Jasper had provided.

"You want some Tyvek?" Jasper raised an eyebrow.

"No, I think I'll be fine," she said. "It's not like they'll be flinging stuff all over the room, right? And that stuff ramps up the sweat factor."

"That depends," another voice said, female, commanding in timbre. The woman who entered the room was the same height as Temple, but sporting a reddish tan and freckles up and down her sinewy arms. "You never know what may get flung about if I really dive in. Hi, I'm Doctor Irene Lewis."

Temple smiled. "Doctor Lewis, so glad you made it, I was beginning to worry. Special Agent Temple Black."

"Agent Ravel got me out of a function I'd been dreading," said Doctor Lewis. "So, thank you all for the bailout."

"Doctor Lewis, from what I understand," Temple aimed her words at Jasper and Morris, "is a top-notch medical examiner."

"A regular Quincy, eh?" Jasper asked.

"Uh, yeah, good one, I love being compared to man on-the-verge-of-old-age," Doctor Lewis said. "I'm a real forensic pathologist, unlike Quincy. And you are?" She raised an eyebrow at Jasper.

"Special Agent Jasper Wilde," Temple cut in.

"The emphasis on special?"

"I don't like this woman," Jasper said.

"This woman would be 'Doctor' to you." The woman shook his hand, squeezed, and followed it up with a wink. "All right, you can call me Irene."

"Whoa, that's my gun hand there Doc." Jasper flexed his fingers and turned to Temple.

"You sure you didn't mistakenly hire a mixed martial artist from the Ultimate Fighting Championship?"

"Are you through?" Morris leaned against a wall, the Nikon D700 camera typical of ERT hanging around his neck. "Can we get this show on the road?"

Jasper jerked his head toward him. "Oh, and the ultra-friendly guy over there is Special Agent Morris Chan."

Doctor Lewis's mouth opened and shut, keeping whatever barb on the tip of her tongue for herself. Jasper slipped a mask over his face, attempting to hide the broad smile. "You know what, Doc? I think I like you after all."

"I'm still evaluating all of you, but how about we discuss your needs. From what I understand there are multiple autopsies, but at least one will be different from the others?"

Temple explained the situation to Irene with an occasional interjection by Jasper. Morris kept quiet, a good sign.

The assistant, Janssen, apparently knew the doctor, or at least acted as if he did and found none of the banter unusual. He didn't even crack a smile, but continued prepping the room.

Irene went about her business, too, arranging the instruments on the tray in the way she preferred. She gave the area a once over while Jasper and Morris prepped the necessary paperwork and obtained the names and signatures of everyone present.

They agreed on performing the first autopsy on the woman

who had been kidnapped and presumably tossed from the minivan in the accident near the Euclid Hotel.

"Temple," Jasper said, "feel free to observe, but you don't have to stand back. If you want a closeup look, come forward. You should also be watching for possible evidence or things we overlooked while Morris takes photos and I do the log, okay?"

Temple nodded.

"Also, I'll be using you to assist with the evidence we collect, clothing, and any pocket trash if there is any."

Janssen wheeled in the first of the three bodies. The remains were in a black body bag atop the rolling cart. How would the others be brought in? Temple wondered. Large plastic buckets, like the ones Home Depot sold?

Janssen positioned the rolling cart next to the stainless autopsy table. Morris moved in and took a photo of the bag and the seal on the zipper, calling out to Jasper what he wanted annotated on the photo log.

Irene cut the seal. Jasper flipped a page on the clipboard and, Temple guessed, noted the time.

Morris took more photos once the bag was unzipped and called those out to Jasper, who was already writing in the log.

Irene and Janssen grabbed hold of the body and removed the poor woman from the body bag and rested her on the table. The doctor took extra care to position her head on a rubber block of some sort. She spoke softly into a small recorder, low enough that Temple couldn't make out the words. The smell hadn't gotten any worse, but it certainly hadn't gotten better.

"The decomp is minimal," Irene said, addressing the group, "but that's expected based on when the accident occurred. She's in bad shape, tossed around quite a bit from the looks of her wounds." Irene examined the woman's exterior while Morris snapped photos and Jasper wrote in the log.

"Her fingernails and hands in general display signs of struggle and scratching at a surface."

"Anything under the nails?" Jasper asked.

The doctor nodded and the assistant handed her a small jar. They proceeded to cut the nails and deposited them in the jar.

"Might as well get the prints right now, okay, Doc?" Jasper asked. "Oh, and the swabs?"

"Sure."

"Temple," Jasper said. "Would you like to do the honors?"

"Not really," Temple said. "But what's this about swabs?"

"For DNA mainly," Jasper said. "A mouth swab, and uh—"

"Vaginal and anal," Irene interjected. "Helps with identifying potential subjects in cases of sexual abuse."

"Right." Jasper coughed. "Morris?"

Morris cocked his head. "She's all yours."

"Fine, I'll do it," Jasper said. "You sure I won't screw it up?"

"Be my guest."

Jasper put the clipboard down and proceeded to fingerprint the woman. They then swabbed and deposited the results in evidence packaging.

The woman had not a piece of identification on her at the scene, and not a single piece of jewelry adorned her body. Odd? Temple wasn't sure. The men didn't seem to think much of the lack of jewelry, but tucked the fact away. The identification may have been taken by the dead driver and then destroyed by the monster.

Temple scrunched her eyes as the autopsy proceeded and the woman's clothes were removed. More photos and more logging. Irene practically whispered into her recorder, but Morris and Jasper asked no questions as they proceeded.

"All right," Irene said, after examining her from head to toe. "Her external wounds are consistent with being tossed around in a moving vehicle as well as being ejected from a vehicle. Her entire head is crisscrossed with lacerations as well as contusions. But I doubt that is what you're interested in, Agents Black and Wilde." Irene stared at Temple, eyebrows raised and dark eyes wide behind her safety goggles.

"Uh, we—" Temple began—

—and Jasper finished, "with this autopsy, we're interested in any trace evidence that may assist in identifying people other than her kidnapper—well, we're assuming she was a victim of kidnapping. Also, was she drugged? That sort of thing."

The woman's autopsy provided very little in terms of evidence, but any blood test results would take time—not weeks, but possibly more time than the investigation and the crazy events handed them. Temple, though not normally squeamish, closed her eyes for most of the internal examination, spreading her eyelids on occasion for a glimpse, and regretting those glimpses. No one seemed to be paying her any mind, thankfully. Morris and Jasper kept taking photos and logging all through the opening of the woman's chest cavity and skull, through the weighing of her organs. All the while, the faucet's steady flow, ringing metallic against the bottom of the sink, never ceased. And where did all that human detritus sloughing down the table and into the sink end up? The sewer system? A special holding tank of some sort?

"Temple, see those brown paper bags?" Jasper pointed. "Those bags are going to be used for her clothing and personal effects. What I need you to do is label each one to coincide with the articles spread out on the table there. Once we're done with the photos, I'll help you."

Temple went about labeling the brown paper bags, which were larger than grocery store versions, and perhaps a little thicker, but the brown color was the same.

Jasper and Morris finished the photos and moved to assist with the evidence.

"I assume you're taking custody of the clothing and so forth, Jasper?" Morris asked.

"Of course, wouldn't want you to be too involved. What does executive management expect of me, anyway?" Jasper raised an eyebrow.

"To simply ensure you're not going off the deep end with all this nonsense. So far, I haven't seen anything noteworthy. This woman obviously died from the car accident," Morris said.

"The next two are going to be the interesting ones," Temple said. "I promise you that."

Irene and the assistant handed over the packages containing the DNA samples to Jasper.

"We're taking the old body bag as evidence, in case we have trace evidence in there. Okay, Doc?"

Irene shrugged. "Fine by me."

Jensen grabbed a black garbage bag and stuffed it inside the woman's now empty torso.

"What in the Lord's name was that? That garbage bag?" Temple asked.

"The organs," Irene said casually, as she removed her gloves.

"Oh," Temple said, "just like a—"

"Yep," Irene nodded, "a Thanksgiving Day turkey."

"Ah," Temple said.

Janssen proceeded to button up the body, replacing the section of skull they'd removed and sewing up all the torso. Temple found the process difficult to fathom and even more difficult to accept. A woman had been alive minding her own business and now had she not only been kidnapped and tossed around in a van before dying in a horrible wreck, but had her body desecrated by strangers who knew nothing about her.

"This is a wonderful argument for cremation," Jasper said, "don't you think?"

"But if you have a viewing before cremation, guess what happens?" Morris added, breaking the silence he'd kept for much of the autopsy. "The mortician embalms and does all sorts of wonderful things to you."

"Great," Temple said.

"But you won't know anyway, you'll be dead," Morris said.

"Maybe I would know," Temple said. "You don't know what happens when you die. You have some insider knowledge, Morris?" This man was indeed annoying, even though he hadn't said a whole lot.

"All right," Jasper said, "how about we move on, eh?"

Irene had conferred with Janssen and the assistant wheeled the body out.

The autopsy had been both horrible and fascinating. If the autopsy helped them catch the cult then she might feel a little better about it, but not much. Yet the process amazed her, how Irene and Janssen had turned the woman inside out and somehow made her look almost human again by the end.

"By the way," Morris said, "I'm not witnessing anything on the evidence."

"Whatever." Jasper wrote on the bags, and handed a black marker to Temple. "Please initial next to your name on each of the evidence bags."

Ten minutes had passed and the squeak of wheels pricked Temple's ears. Another black body bag, another dead body—this one though would be one of the mangled bodies. She winced and scrunched up her nose.

"And what can you tell me about this one?" Irene asked, picking new latex gloves from an overstuffed box.

"I think we'll let you take a gander before we say anything about the body itself," Jasper said. "But I will say this is the first body we found."

Jasper grabbed one side of the body bag while the assistant grabbed the other and both lifted. The bag sagged in the middle as the contents shifted. Irene's eyes widened, then narrowed in suspicion.

Morris moved in for a photo of the seal on the bag and stepped back.

"I think you're going to have to dump this one out on the table, Doc," Jasper said.

"What?" Irene unzipped the bag and flinched. "What in the—"

"Holy hell," Janssen gasped. He'd been wordless for much of the proceedings, but the outburst was understandable.

Temple recoiled, not from the sight, since she didn't have a good view, though a vivid picture had imprinted upon her mind from having seen this body before. No, it was the smell that got to her. Human decomp—once encountered, one never forgot. Not meat gone bad, or roadkill sitting in the sun for a day or two, not even if the stinkiest rotten cheese were mixed with dead animal could it attain the putridness of a human body in decomposition.

She closed her eyes and swallowed. She had impregnated her mask with a menthol substance not unlike Vicks, but nothing other than a fully enclosed full face mask combined with a bio-hazard suit would be able to block the stench.

Jasper's eyes squinted and Morris went behind a wall and cursed and retched.

"That's pretty bad," Irene said. "And uh, yeah... let's roll this over and dump the remains on the table. Care to keep this body bag, too?"

"I'm afraid so," Jasper said.

Irene and Janssen each grabbed an end and twisted, but the bag sagged. Jasper dropped his clipboard on the counter and shoved the middle of the bag. His right hand pushed against what must have been a bone while his left hand disappeared into the black bag, plunging into soft tissue of some sort on the other side of the bag. The contents spilled onto the autopsy table.

"This is like a whole animal that went through a meat grinder or something," Irene said. "What in the hell happened?"

"We don't know."

"Where did this happen?"

"Over by the animal control facility on Gary Avenue, East Chicago," Temple said.

"You think an animal did this?"

"Something did, it's not like spontaneous combustion," Jasper said.

"Nice one, but I'm serious," Irene said.

"You wouldn't believe us if we told you our opinions on the matter, especially her," Jasper hitched his thumb at Temple.

"Hey, my explanation is just as plausible." Temple folded her arms.

"Let's hear it," Irene said.

"Tell us what you think, Doc," Jasper said. "Come on."

Irene went to work, but Morris hadn't emerged from behind the wall.

"I take it you're done, Morris?" Even though Jasper's face was mostly hidden behind his mask, those eyes of his twinkled with mischief. Temple found herself thawing quite a bit toward the smart aleck agent.

Morris coughed and cursed and gagged and cursed from behind the wall.

"I'll take that as a 'yes.'" Jasper joined Morris behind the wall and emerged with the camera and handed Temple the photo log. "You've been promoted to photo logger. It's pretty self-explanatory. I'll call out what I'm photographing and the distance, that sort of thing. You'll get it in no time. If you miss anything I can go back and fill it in later," he explained. "It's one of the benefits of digital photography." The Bureau had sometime after 2005 allowed digital to replace good old film, if Temple remembered correctly.

"I miss anything, Doc?" Jasper asked.

"Not a thing," Irene replied, "I'm still trying to figure out where to start." Irene shrugged and dove in. She spoke into her handheld recorder often, and whenever Jasper ducked in for photographs under the cold glare of the fluorescent light overhead.

The initial waves of stench had subsided, but they still lingered. Temple decided she had no choice but to remain in the room despite the growing need to use the restroom.

"What do you think so far, Doc?" Jasper finally asked, and Temple was glad, since she didn't want to interrupt, but her curiosity attained an all-time peak.

"The clear substance and lack of blood is disturbing, and if I didn't know better," Irene said, "I'd say all the red blood cells had been eradicated."

"Or siphoned off?" Temple asked.

"You're not suggesting some sort of vampire, are you?" Irene said, and both she and the assistant stared at Temple.

"Of course not."

"All right, then—"

"But are there any creatures inhabiting our planet that could do such a thing?" Temple asked.

Irene's shoulders dropped and her head cocked. "You're not suggesting aliens now, are you?"

"I'm not suggesting anything right now, only looking for an explanation."

"Last thing I need is for some crazy *X-Files*-type nonsense," Irene huffed.

"That's what she works, Doc," Jasper said. "You do know what SAG stands for, right?"

"Who? SAG? Like the actors organization? I knew this was some sort of Hollywood garbage."

Jasper laughed. "No, it's the Scientific Anomalies Group."

"Oh, great, so this *is X-Files*? Where is the hidden camera?"

Morris emerged from behind the wall, apparently over his gagging and cursing fit which had lasted a good ten minutes. "That's what I said, Doc."

"No one asked you, Morris," Jasper said. "Anyway, this is real shit, Doc."

"I know it's a pile of meat and bones that was once human, but how in the hell did this happen?"

"We don't know," Temple said. "We've seen strange things the past couple of days. What we do know is that we have a group of men running around kidnapping people."

"And they did this?"

"We don't think so," Jasper said. "I saw two men commit suicide by thermite."

"Thermite? Nasty stuff. How did they do such a thing?"

"They stepped in an activator and simply hopped into stone basins filled with the rest of the ingredients for thermite. They went up like a Fourth of July display. We did rescue the little girl they'd kidnapped, though. At least we have that." Jasper's eyes darkened.

"That woman I autopsied was a victim of one of those kidnappings, too, right? What do you suppose their fate would be, these kidnap victims?"

"I'm thinking that body you have in front of you, or should I say pile of meat and bones, would have been their fate," Temple said.

"So the kidnappers aren't the ones doing this?" Irene asked.

"Not directly, but because of them this happens," Jasper said. "All right, I'm going to level with you."

"It's about time."

Jasper took a deep breath, but Temple jumped in. "We saw something move toward the next body you're going to look at, and he's in the same state as the body you're examining right now."

"Something moved toward," Irene said, considering.

"The lighting was dark at the scene, but a wispy form congealed into what can only be described as an Asian-style dragon."

Irene yanked her mask down, exasperated. "Excuse me?"

"You know," Jasper said, "like the type you see during, I don't know, Chinese New Year or something, with a bunch of dudes chucking firecrackers, only this wasn't a bunch of guys in a dragon costume."

"There has to be a reasonable explanation," Irene said, then paused. "Let me tell you a quick story. Okay? Right, so one of my early autopsies featured a body that sat up a bit and then promptly laid back down."

Temple's eyes widened.

"And there is an explanation beyond the fantastic here," Irene said.

"Electrical impulses?"

"That happens, but may cause twitching and other things," Irene said, "No, this was from a build-up of gases. Nothing more, nothing less. Not that those things don't freak you out at first, but really? For what you're speaking of? There *has* to be a reasonable explanation." She replaced the mask.

"That would freak me out, no doubt," Temple said, "And I agree, there must be an explanation, whether it seems reasonable or not. And now I'm going to have to ask you to sign a nondisclosure agreement. We can't afford to have the press or anyone else for that matter speaking about this."

Irene laughed. "As if I'd ever say anything about this nonsense! I have a reputation to uphold."

Morris sucked in a huge breath and gagged. Apparently he'd been about to start laughing, but the smell had gotten to him again. He finally regained control, and said, "I'll sign the nondisclosure as well, but you can bet I'm going to tell Masters and Johnson that you're all off your rockers."

"What do the sex people have to do with this?" Irene asked, genuinely confused.

Temple laughed and Jasper joined her. After they had settled down, Jasper let the doctor in on the joke.

"Any personal effects at all in these remains?" Temple asked.

"None as far as I can tell, but there are remnants of clothing." Irene picked through the remains, producing a strip of cloth here and a shirt button there. A piece of glass followed, presumably from a pair of eyeglasses. "A curious lack of metal, too. Can't explain any of this. But most baffling to me still is the lack of red blood cells."

"Like a severe iron deficiency?" Jasper ventured.

Irene chuckled. "Yeah, a *fatal* case of iron deficiency. I think this is a piece of liver here. It's hard to tell, of course, but it's washed out, and if I could find the heart in here, I bet it'd be just as pale and any blood within would be only a tad more pink. The liquid we're seeing is mostly plasma, that is, blood without the red blood cells. I wonder if any white cells survived. We're taking samples, of course. Many, many, samples."

"Will you be able to test them on your own, Irene?" Temple asked. "I mean, I don't want any old lab performing these tests."

Irene sighed. "I suppose I could find—"

"We'll take them, Doc," Jasper said. "I have a friend who works at a university who'll do us the honors."

Irene paused. "You have to forward me the results, though. I'd be interested in what exactly remained in the blood."

"And we'll take some tissue samples. I see some marks over here, can't make them out, though." Irene leaned forward.

"I'll need a photo of whatever it is you're looking at," Jasper said. "And if you could somehow bag that section for us, that'd be great."

"Oh sure, I'll just get you people a doggy bag, eh?"

"What about the bones?" Temple asked, ignoring the doctor's attempt at humor. Any other time she would have found the woman entertaining.

"What about them?"

"Do they appear normal? I mean, are they brittle or been broken and had the uh—"

"What? Marrow sucked out?" Irene asked. "Let's see, there are plenty of broken bones; in fact, I think every bone in this person's body was broken. I don't see anything out of the ordinary beyond that. Let me rephrase—this entire glistening pile of meat and bones is out of the ordinary."

Janssen nodded vigorously.

"We'll get some marrow and why not take a small bone while you're at it?" Irene suggested.

"That'd be great," Temple said.

"I was kidding about the bone."

"Oh. You don't see a reason to take one?"

"Not really. I mean, if you're testing for alien materials, and by that I mean, foreign substances not normally found in a human body, you'll find them in the blood or the tissue samples. Maybe even in the DNA, if we're really going to get crazy here and buy in to the *X-Files* nonsense."

Irene collected samples, weighed pieces of organs, but wasn't able to come up with a way any of this mess could happen to a human body. A woodchipper wouldn't have done this, or even falling into a set of giant gears. Maybe the complete mangling of the body, but the clear liquid? The plasma? Irene had no explanations for them.

"Hey, Doc," Jasper said, "are there any means available that separate red blood cells from blood?"

"From the plasma? Yes. There are a few ways, even using magnets, but for an entire body? That would require quite a bit of work and is certainly not done out in the field."

"So, hypothetically speaking of course," Jasper said, "if a group of madmen—"

"A cult?" Morris laughed.

"Yeah, a cult. If a cult took a body to a—"

"Secret lair?" Morris laughed again.

"Yeah, a secret lair in an extinct volcano, Morris," Jasper said. "They took the body and had the red blood cells removed, that would be possible?"

"If they had someone trained and had the right equipment, sure. But look at the state of this body." Irene folded her arms.

"They could have mangled the bodies afterward, though, right?" Jasper said.

"Maybe."

"It's a remote possibility," Temple interjected, "but I doubt it. Why go through all that effort when those sick bastards could simply torch the remains with thermite?"

"She has you there," Irene said.

"You're sounding like you're beginning to believe this cosmic crap, Doc," Morris said.

"Not really, I'm just trying to keep an open mind. The Bureau is paying me for my services, after all."

They tidied up the area and moved on to the next autopsy. The final body, that of the cultist, Alan Smith, wasn't quite as mangled, but the pile of meat and bones still didn't resemble a human other than the somewhat intact skull with loose skin.

"This one," Irene said after examining the remains for a few minutes, "hasn't had all the red blood cells eradicated. This one has a lot more of, shall I say, 'normal' blood?"

"We may have interrupted the attack."

"Attack?" Irene shook her head. "You're still not telling me everything, and how am I supposed to conduct this autopsy without the facts?"

"We responded to a disturbance not far from where the woman," Temple said, but Jasper interjected—

"The woman who died in the car crash, the first autopsy you performed—"

"Yes, the first autopsy," Temple said. "But this body we found behind a shed and were confronted by what appeared to be a large creature—"

"An animal of some sort," Jasper said, but winced.

Temple sighed. "The creature disappeared."

"Oh, come on," Irene said. "You expect me to believe there are animals on this planet that cannot only drain red blood cells from other animals, but also disappear? I can see maybe camouflaging itself, but—"

Now that was a creepy thought, and one Temple hadn't considered. What if the dragon had been there all along, watching them? Sizing them up, or waiting for them to leave so it could finish the job it had begun on the cultist's remains?

"We think it flew away," Jasper said.

"Fine, flew away then." Temple rolled her eyes.

"So, a giant flying creature did this. Uh huh."

"Look, Doc," Morris said, "just perform the autopsy so we can finish with this charade."

"Big word there, Morris," Jasper said.

"Shut up, Zeke. Next you'll be saying it was a pterodactyl."

"Another big word, but we don't know each other well enough for you to call me the Z word," Jasper said. "Anyway, please continue, Doc. We're really just looking for abnormalities, beyond the obvious, of course."

Irene resumed the examination.

"One other thing," Temple said.

Irene paused and looked at Temple. "You want me to do this or not?"

"Another agent, a scientific type," Temple said, "former FBI laboratory body, snagged samples at the scene."

"What? And now you're telling me this body was tampered with before even the coroner arrived on scene?"

"Uh, yes," Jasper said.

"You really fucked up this time." Morris whistled.

"And what do you care? You don't want anything to do with this, but I suppose you're going to run off to your buddies, ASAC Masters and—"

"Oh, calm down," Morris said. "You're signing for everything, and since none of this was an official ERT search, I don't much care other than that it better not ruin any more of my free time."

"Are you all done?" Irene asked. "I have something interesting here."

Morris and Jasper ceased their bickering and along with Temple stared at Irene in anticipation.

"So, there are some pieces of this man, muscle in particular, that have a charred quality, as if seared or severely burned—but only for a moment. Like a cauterization, but not quite."

"What would do that?" Temple asked.

"Who in the hell knows? But more interestingly..." Irene lifted the skull from the pile. Skin sloughed off, like chicken boiled too long, and the eyes appeared to have been plucked free. The mouth hung open, lips thin and the tongue protruded, bleached and strangely desiccated. "This man has had extensive work done on his teeth, and recently."

"What's the relevance?" Jasper asked.

"There are temporary crowns here, as if the man had a bunch of cavities taken care of at once, but opted for better crowns. I see at least one porcelain crown in here..." She poked at the ruined mouth of the ruined skull.

"Perhaps his aunt would know the dentist he used," Jasper said.

"Between his house and the dentist we may be able to crack this thing," Temple said.

"You two are like a Hardy Boys and Nancy Drew television episode," Morris said, "Bravo." He clapped, the plastic smatter of his latex gloves funnier than the man had intended, but Temple didn't laugh.

"Oh, shut up," Temple and Jasper said at the same time, eliciting a chuckle from Irene.

The rest of the autopsy revealed little of value. They arranged for the mangled bodies to be stored for the duration of the investigation, but allowed the dead woman's body to be released to her next of kin. Temple considered interviewing the next of kin, but the better lead was the mangled body of Alan Smith—the search of his house and a possible interview of his dentist, if he or she could be located. Perhaps they'd have time to run by the hospital and speak with Alan's aunt about the dentist.

Chapter 23

JASPER AND TEMPLE DROVE TO THE UNIVERSITY OF CHICAGO, which was located near the lake in the Hyde Park neighborhood, about seven miles south of the city's downtown. Despite being across a state line, it was actually quite close to northwest Indiana—no more than a half hour's drive from Jasper's condo in Hammond.

Vance's phone call had been urgent, canceling their plans to swing by the hospital and speak with Alan Smith's aunt once again. Temple's excitement upon hanging up hadn't puzzled Jasper, but he didn't know yet if the excitement was caused by Vance's evidence or the prospect of seeing Ed White again. Probably both.

Jasper couldn't remember the last time he'd run around this much in one day. Temple's energy and constitution apparently allowed her to operate at full steam nonstop, all day. Was she hiding Red Bulls somewhere? His eyelids were drooping and his entire body wilted under the heat. But despite the heat, he had her stop at a Starbucks along the way for a dry cappuccino. And damn if it hadn't hit the spot, despite her oven of a car baking under the August sun.

"You look like a flower left in the sun too long there, kid." Ed greeted them as they entered the building, smiling widely. "But you, Temple, you look like you're ready for a photo shoot."

Temple rolled her eyes. But Jasper was certain by now that she enjoyed Ed's attention.

"What do you have for us, Ed?"

"We've been chatting with a friend of mine, a physicist." Ed glanced back at them as he opened a door into one of the

189

university's big buildings. "He's enjoying the speculative angle Vance's been chatting away about. That little guy is all right, where'd you find him? He should be doing research for a university, or a Department of Energy lab."

Ed led them through pleasantly cool hallways. Jasper felt a second or third wind coming on. But, boy, he'd still sleep like a baby tonight.

"Vance is a misfit, sort of like me," Temple said.

"Looks like you found yourself another one," Ed nodded at Jasper. "He's king of the misfits over at the Bureau. You should hear him talk about his executive management and all the nitwit decisions they make or, most of the time, don't make."

Temple grinned. "So we do have something in common after all."

They reached a nice-sized office brimming with books and walls plastered with papers and white boards filled with equations.

Ed looked around. "Now, where'd they get off to? They were just here a few minutes ago."

A few seconds later, laughter filled the narrow hallway leading to the office. In walked Vance with a rather tall and chiseled man with black hair and dark eyes. They both held coffee cups and wore smiles.

"Thank you, Temple, for leaving me behind," Vance said. "I enjoyed catching up with my own—"

Temple's head cocked.

"Kind. Scientists, I mean."

"Mmm hmm." A smile crept onto Temple's lips.

Ed introduced them to Doctor Greg Clark, an astrophysicist. Jasper had to suppress a smile himself. Clark was the picture image of a scientist taken from some old black and white film. The kind with titles like *It Came from Beyond Space.*

Doctor Clark extended his hand. "Pleased to meet you. Ignore the lab coat, it's just old habit. Call me Greg."

Greg now placed the hand on Vance's shoulder. "This man is a genius."

"Please, enlighten us," Temple said.

"Greg, tell us your theory—we've already been down the road with Jasper and Temple here on the religious aspects as well as some of the biological ones." Ed gestured for Temple to sit, which she wasted no time in doing, and he plopped down next to her.

Jasper leaned against a wall covered in paper. Startled, he pulled away.

"Don't mind that, you're not ruining anything," Greg said. "I'm kind of a pack rat." He eased into a creaky chair behind a desk supporting piles of random debris and littered with pencils—some broken in half and others with their erasers worn or chewed off. "All right. When Vance described the foreign matter, and without getting too down in the weeds here, I proposed the possibility of brane cosmology."

"Brain? As in the lump we all have in here?" Jasper tapped his head.

"No, brane as in membrane."

"Doesn't help," Temple said.

"Imagine two universes—"

"I have a hard enough time imagining one universe," Temple said, beating Jasper.

Greg leaned back in his chair, fingers steepled. "How to explain this..."

"Imagine there are a multitude of universes and two of them happened to collide—or just brush against and slightly interpenetrate each other," Vance said.

"Still not getting it and what this has to do with all these weird events." Jasper shifted his weight from one leg to the other.

"I can't think of any other way to describe this," Greg grabbed two random objects off his desk. "Imagine these two objects are balls of Play-Doh, of different colors. So we have red and blue Play-Doh, giant balls of the stuff and they're slowly coming together." He brought the two objects closer to each other in illustration. "Then—"

"Why are they coming together in the first place?" Temple asked.

"Could be a million reasons," Vance said.

"Give me just one, then."

"They're attracted to one another, sort of like Temple and Lando over here?" Jasper thumbed toward the pair sitting on the sofa.

Vance snickered. Jasper hadn't known a snicker hid within the little man.

Temple glared at Jasper and slid one inch from Ed.

"That'll work," Greg said. "The universes are drawn to each other based on some property—what it might be doesn't matter at the moment."

"But it might if we wanted to stop them, right?"

"Yes, Jasper, but you're getting ahead of the explanation," Vance chided. "Continue, Greg."

"Right, so the balls of Play-Doh touch one another and you get some of the red mixing into the blue and vice versa. You understand?"

"I think so," Temple said.

"Two universes," Jasper said, "seem so hard to imagine. How is it possible, I mean, how could one part of another universe touch ours, and of all the possible places, touch northwestern Indiana? How does this fit into our recent problems?"

Greg held up a finger. "Why can't space bend and twist? The universes may touch and interpenetrate in areas we'll never know of."

"And not on this planet, but somewhere else in another part of our galaxy," Temple said.

"Why not an entirely different galaxy?" Vance shrugged. "Anything is possible."

"Hold up a second." Jasper held up a hand. "I'm as skeptical as they come, but what are the odds? Temple believes we have Satanic creatures roaming around. I'm inclined to think they're more likely to be aliens—if they exist at all. So how does this fit?"

Ed sort of rolled off the sofa and took a sheet of paper off of Greg's confusing desk. "This," he tapped the paper, "is a preliminary report on some of the samples, and I can't find any sort of match with known substances."

He now picked up a vial full of a deep red liquid, that had also been on Greg's desk. "Keeping in mind that problems may exist with the tests themselves and we're not getting accurate results. But if the test results are accurate, this might be from somewhere other than earth. But we're far from the craziest thing." He glanced at Greg. "Were you finished with the brane talk?"

Greg gestured for Ed to continue.

"Wait," Temple said. "Everyone here realizes, and I hope you brought NDAs with you, Vance—"

Vance opened his case and rifled through a ream of paper. "I have them right here."

"Ah, I wondered why we hadn't seen any of those yet," Greg said. "I do my fair share of consulting for think tanks and other entities, if you follow."

"What are we talking about?" Ed asked.

"Non-disclosure agreements," Jasper said, "which means you can't go about bragging to your dates what you're helping the Bureau with, got it?"

"Hey, I'm not privy to what y'all are doing with the investigations, but I will say this." Ed rubbed his face, and continued, "If some bad shit's entering our world, shouldn't the military be apprised?"

Greg sat up. "He raises a good point."

"Do either of you two understand which agency is responsible for the national security of the United States, domestically?" Temple's gaze darted between the two.

"Uh, the President?" Ed shrugged.

"Yeah, right. No. Try again."

"Department of Homeland Security?" Ed grinned.

"Now you're just being a pain in the ass," Jasper said. "Come on."

"This is a national security issue, which falls under the FBI's jurisdiction, which is part of the Department of Justice. Homeland Security? Exactly what have they secured? And don't get me started on TSA—they don't even try messing with us." Temple took a deep breath.

"You two need to sign these NDAs and not speak about any part of this investigation to anyone other than the people in this room, okay? We don't need a bunch of bulls breaking up the china shop we set up. It's bad enough the local FBI office thrust this guy on us." Temple jabbed a thumb at Jasper.

"It could have been worse for all of us, I suppose," Jasper said. "There are a few knuckle draggers in the office who would have driven you crazy by now."

Ed and Greg both signed the NDAs with little fuss and promised solemnly they wouldn't discuss any of this outside of those present.

"Now, Ed, you were going to relate something else about a sample before I cut you off?" Temple asked.

"Oh, yes. The craziest part of all this is the other sample taken from the mutilated bodies. This liquid," Ed picked up another vial, "is blood."

"What? How? It's almost clear, it's kind of a pale yellow, like straw maybe," Jasper said, thinking back to his days on the farm and all the hay they'd baled.

"It's blood, but missing one important component." Ed's

eyebrows shot up and down one time, an old tic Jasper had noticed whenever Ed made a point he wanted to punctuate.

"Are you pausing for effect, Ed?" Jasper folded his arms.

Ed stared at the vial. "This blood is missing, to put it quite simply, all of its red blood cells."

"You're saying this is human blood, drained of all its red blood cells." Jasper's tone was flat and one of disbelief. "You know, the medical examiner determined the same during the autopsies earlier this morning. Next you're going to say some jacked-up vampire—"

"No, a chupacabra." Ed said the words, but a smile crept on to his face.

"A goddamned chupacabra—"

Temple glared at Jasper.

"Ed, you can't be—wait, did Vance put you up to this? What a funny guy."

"But seriously," Jasper said, "tell me this isn't some vampire thing, please. I'm sick of vampires and zombies on TV and books. It's all nonsense."

"But you're okay with aliens, huh? And the demons Temple's tossing about."

"No. I'm not." Jasper's ire rose. "I think we're dealing with a group of assholes running around as part of some bullshit cult, hurting innocent people."

"That was certainly frank." Greg rocked back and forth on his squeaky chair. "A cult, huh? A cult devoted to brane cosmology, but they aren't aware of the scientific points, only the fantastical version where the other side leaks over into ours and we're leaking into the other side."

"How is that different from Temple believing in demons rather than the scientific explanation?" Jasper arched an eyebrow.

"I want to smack you when you do that," Temple said.

"What?" Jasper spread his hands.

"You smirk with your eyebrow, yeah, like that!" She pointed at his face. "What you don't understand, farm boy, is that the two aren't mutually exclusive—God and demons and science can all coexist."

Jasper took a deep breath and blew it out. "Okay, fine. I can't argue with logic that abstract—but I can tell you this. I'm still betting on the Kool-Aid drinking asshole cult."

"Hypothetically," Temple asked, "what would a creature from another universe look like? How would such a creature live in our universe? If they come from a completely different universe, everything about them—their biology, chemistry, you name it—would be different. They might—they probably must—be made of different elements altogether, right?"

Ed shrugged. "What do you think, Greg? Vance?"

Greg's eyes scrunched shut; he stretched his arms up over his head and yawned. Vance adopted a thousand-yard stare.

"Wow, a regular brain trust." Jasper grinned. "You three are like those see-no-evil monkey guys."

Temple snickered. "See-no-evil monkey guys, a new name for the scientific triumvirate."

Greg frowned. "They could appear as anything your imagination might conjure. They might live on hemoglobin, or have an affinity for iron, that make sense?" He glanced at Ed, who shrugged.

"Maybe they can't live in our universe at all," Vance added.

"I'm gonna go with that one," Jasper said. "You watch. After all this, the cult of assholes will be the culprit."

Temple's eyes lost their fire and appeared to succumb to Jasper's opinion, but he suspected she merely lost her energy—finally.

Ed coughed again. "I'll end with this, because it's getting late, and we're all tired, but here it is," he paused, as if lecturing to a room full of students, "No creature I'm aware of is capable of filtering blood in this manner, and also, combined with the way the bodies were mutilated, it's unlike anything I've ever seen or heard or read about."

The office was silent for ten seconds, but felt like ten minutes.

Ed broke the silence with a single, forceful clap. "Now, who wants some food and some drink?"

Chapter 24

WAYLAND PRECISION WENT DARK ONCE A BLONDE WOMAN, AND later an older, grizzled man, departed. Only two lights remained on—both outside, one out front and one in the back.

Lali decided against using khâu for this part of the plan. Rao would brook no failure now, there had been too many disasters. Rao would never admit to it, but Lali felt his power waning, and his desire to touch the other side, cross over and absorb the powers provided by the nâga, increasing.

She'd ditched her car, a beat-up Yaris, down Summer a ways, and mostly out of sight near a copse of trees. Few cars or trucks traveled down this road after eight in the evening, so she'd crept toward the building with ease, and without fear of being seen by chance. The closer she crept to the building, the more the hot August night smothered her. The clouds pressed down as if sealing her at this location on Summer Street.

A nearby building provided cover for her as she'd watched the building, waiting for the people within to leave. The burnt odor dissipated, or she'd grown accustomed to the ever-present acridness, but her mouth fouled and coated her tongue. She'd considered bailing out, but gathering information on Wayland Precision and the people working there was important. Rao needed a sacrifice, and in turn, Lali would benefit from the sacrifice—Rao had promised.

The low-cut grass at the front of the building pricked her bare feet. She loved walking around without shoes and socks, but the dryness created needles out of the grass, and she winced with each step. The light around back flared out.

197

Luck? No. Motion sensors likely controlled the lights.

No one walked the streets in this area, and no headlights poked through in either direction. No residences, either. She scaled the chain link fence, the thin metal clinking and rattling. Snipping the metal would have been easier, but she hadn't thought to bring a bolt cutter or heavy metal snips.

Lali approached the back steps slowly and swiveling her head at every little noise. The light remained dark. Rather than use the steps, she opted for the concrete ramp leading up the side. Hopefully movement up the ramp wouldn't trigger the motion sensor, and she'd escape detection.

She took a few steps, nothing happened. No alarms, no lights.

"Hmm. The break-in might be easier than I thought."

Another step.

She smiled.

Another—

A light blared, projecting into the parking lot.

"Shit."

She padded up the ramp and dug a ring of keys from her bag. Dumb luck, this part. When she'd dated Carlos, she'd made copies of all of his keys. She hadn't known then she'd be using them to break into Wayland, if in fact, any of these keys worked. The first key she tried slid into the lock, but didn't budge the cylinder.

The yellow light blared, but she hoped it'd go out after a few minutes—if she kept movements to a minimum and only worked keys with the lock, and did not move her body or arms too much. How sensitive were motion sensors, anyway? She'd chosen flat black tights and a thin black jacket for the entry. Her hair was already black and she'd even painted her toenails and fingernails black, but she wasn't Goth, not by any stretch. An image of her younger brother playing one of his silly video games flashed in her mind—Lali's attire and actions like one of the women in the current batch of stealth games and urban fantasy novels.

She poked key after key into the door. Her hands shook from excitement and nervousness, which didn't help with the last few keys. Her eyes darted back and forth almost involuntarily, futilely scanning for headlights. None of the keys worked in the door. None. Zero. Good thing she didn't break her arm patting herself on the back over copying Carlos's keys.

A rusted box protruded from the brick wall. She tugged open the tiny door, revealing a keypad. So, did the lock on the big door function or did an electronic system control the entire building? Circumventing alarms and electronic security systems was beyond her.

Lali sighed.

She dug into her bag and withdrew a leather case containing a lock pick set. During the wild days of her youth, she'd made a hobby of picking locks. Nothing major. Nothing serious like safes or bank vaults, but padlocks and a few doors. Easy stuff, but her lock-picking days were in high school, long past, and her skills had eroded. At least the floodlight meant she wouldn't have to risk chipping her teeth from jamming a small flashlight in her mouth. The first pick eased into the cylinder—

A mechanized rattle, like a gate being pulled by a chain, echoed off the buildings behind Wayland Precision.

Her center of gravity lowered in response. The second pick slipped from her fingers, clinking against the cement.

Was the gate Wayland's? From her position, the building obscured the gate situated near the front of the building on the western side.

Lali slid from the ramp, her tights and jacket hissing and scraping against the concrete. She crouched inside a deep shadow, and waited.

The rattling ceased a few seconds later, but no vehicle appeared in the lot adjacent to her hiding spot next to the entry ramp. After a few minutes, the floodlight above the rear entrance clicked off, the bulb's red glow lingered a moment before fading. Good. Her eyes adjusted, but painfully slowly. She closed her eyes and waited—hoping another option would present itself.

She scanned the darkness and found that no one had entered Wayland's yard, but instead a building on the western side. Fluorescent lights flickered on in the building, obscured by trees and overgrown bushes.

Lali turned and faced the ramp. She reached up, but a window at the base of the building caught her eye—a window likely leading to the basement. Breaking the window would not be a big deal—not compared with the destruction she'd render once inside Wayland. She grinned.

The grass behind Wayland, what little grass grew, remained

damp and quite a bit longer than its front yard counterparts. She slid along the slick grass, back against the wall until her fingers found the edge of the window. She puffed a little laugh—the window was open a smidge. For all the security, someone forgot to close and lock the window.

Lali tucked the lock pick kit back into her satchel and lifted the window. She'd be able to squeeze through, but she removed her jacket, laying it near the open window.

She leaned inside the window frame for a quick look.

Darkness. Complete. No flashing red lights signaling some sort of electronic equipment. No hum. Nothing. They must also turn off the air-conditioning at night, for she didn't hear any unit outside causing a racket.

Lali reached for her flashlight and flicked it on once she'd thrust her hand into the opening. The thought of her hand wading into the strange darkness creeped her out a little.

Smell. The scent within the building wrinkled her nose. It wasn't unpleasant, but a little off, like some sort of metallic garden salad.

She swept the cone of light back and forth, and took in a large office area, filled with filing cabinets, desks, chairs, tables, paper, and—aquariums. Inside a supposed machine shop? Strange people.

Entry didn't prove difficult. She slid inside and grabbed her jacket as she eased to the floor. Tile.

Her heart rate blipped up a notch and her hands jittered. Adrenaline. She closed her eyes and took a few deep breaths. Inside enemy territory, and so far, nothing bad happened. No one saw her.

She focused on the desk nearest the entry point and studied the contents. Papers. A lot of papers. A ledger. A few notebooks. A woman's handwriting on almost all of the letters on the desk. She opened the ledger—a bunch of numbers. Nothing. She flipped through the notebooks. Formulas and equations, but nothing noteworthy, and in her opinion, nothing Rao might desire. Ah, but this was something—

A stack of paper with the name Völundr's Hammer with a hammer drawn beneath. A log of their activity. Stainless steel of various grades featured prominently in the most recent entries. She tucked the stack inside her satchel.

Penny Stahlberg. Steve Stahlberg.

A husband and wife team? Mother and son? Father and daughter? Brother and sister?

She twitched her wrist and the flashlight's beam found a photo, an eight by ten labeled Wayland Precision and the current year underneath. Her eyes found Carlos in the photo, and her heart clenched inside her chest. Why did she still have feelings for the lying, cheating asshole? He was married, and had a kid. Lali fell for him and his lies. Dirt bag.

The blonde woman and grizzly man in the photo must be the Stahlbergs, and likely father and daughter, unless they had one of those, the phrase escaped her—fall-summer romance? A December—oh who cared? All the others in the photo were typical for the area—though predominantly white. The photo joined the papers she'd already shoved into the satchel.

The Câ Tsang had just gained a new batch of targets.

The other desk must have been the old man's, Steve's. A stack of bills rested there, but little else other than a nasty coffee mug with an image of a hammer and an anvil on the side. Boy, were these people single-minded. She peeked into the envelopes. A different address—Steve's home address. She opened another— Penny's home address. The other correspondences were all either Steve's or Penny's. She searched for payroll information—payroll would contain all the data she'd need. She poked around the third desk, but found little of use. The filing cabinets gave up the payroll information—all of their personal identifying information, actually. The perpetual smile on her face since entering widened. They, she and Rao, could seriously fuck with these people, with the information she'd obtained.

She bit down on her desire to pat herself on her back.

The air moved within the office, and she realized how hot and close the basement was, but the air moved, why? Had someone entered the building? A silent alarm had triggered and one of the employees had entered, and would find her. No. A ridiculous notion—paranoia.

The odd scent returned, breaking her from thoughts of discovery. Metal and vegetal. She strode over to the aquariums. No fish. Coral? A sea thingy—an anemone? A cucumber? Whatever.

Before moving on to phase two of Rao's plan, she'd poke around a little more.

A door barred her exit from the office. The knob wouldn't turn, locked from the other side? Not too safe, really.

She picked a lighter from her satchel and turned back for

the stacks of papers on the first desk. Rao wanted the building vandalized, well, more than vandalized, burned to the ground. But she entertained a different notion. Even if she paid the price by enduring the man's twisted desires, she wouldn't burn the building, not yet. Why be obvious when screwing with the people and torturing them presented itself? Burning the building would only send the Völundr's Hammer guild into a rage.

No doubt Rao would desire Penny for sacrifice, but what if he desired Penny in other ways rather than sacrifice, the way he did Lali? Rao would never want a sworn enemy like that for a concubine, but would he force himself on her? She pushed the thought from her mind. The truth was, she didn't really care either way. She only sought the power Rao promised, not Rao himself. She'd spent her whole life feeling powerless, and she was sick and tired of it.

For Lali, Carlos should suffer. She'd feel no guilt over his torture and sacrifice. What if she could talk Rao into sacrificing him to the nâga and allow her to touch the other side? Ambitious thinking. Dangerous thinking if Rao became angered over her decision.

One more circuit around the room revealed nothing of value. The strange scent remained unanswered. She shrugged and tossed her jacket and satchel through the open window, and glanced back one more time to make sure she'd left nothing behind. She pulled herself up and through.

The spotlight above the rear entrance remained off, and the night sky twinkled through wispy low-lying clouds. She stole into the black alongside the building, scaled the fence, and saw not a person or vehicle on the way to hers. Success. Of course, Steve and Penny would notice the missing items, which would cause them worry. Let them be paranoid, and perhaps they'd blame someone from within, Carlos perhaps.

Lali sat in her car for a few minutes watching the darkness— even the fluorescent light in the next building over was no longer on. She hadn't heard the gate rattle, but it had likely happened during her time inside, down in the basement.

A half hour passed. A few cars drove down the road, but no one stopped at Wayland Precision. Not a single vehicle even slowed down or so much as tapped their brakes as they passed the building. She started her engine and drove off, back to her apartment per Rao's instructions, in case someone followed after her break-in.

Chapter 25

A PHONE CALL ROBBED JASPER OF SLEEP ONCE AGAIN. SINCE driving with his eyes practically glued shut wasn't at all safe, he took a shower before leaving. But that wasn't really much help. He'd stayed out very late the night before with Temple and Ed, eating and—mostly—drinking. Wisely, Vance and Greg had begged off.

Temple had dropped him off only a few hours ago, and now he was on his way to pick her up at the hotel in his bucar.

Damn.

He flipped the air conditioning on max and reached for the large black coffee he'd picked up at Starbucks as they opened. He needed the caffeine desperately. His tongue tingled after the scalding liquid burned all the way down his throat.

He reached for the sunglasses compartment built into the Charger's overhead but discovered it was empty. He'd probably left them at home, since he hadn't used the bucar yesterday and been off his typical routine when Temple picked him up, rather than the other way around.

He took another sip of coffee. The fog in his brain—no, the sandbag filling the entire cavity—eased up a bit. What made him think he'd achieve a full night of sleep, anyway? Any night out with Ed White usually ended the same way, with at least one of them hugging the commode and both of them with hangovers.

More coffee.

He popped open a bottle and dumped a couple of ibuprofen down his gullet.

✧   ✧   ✧

The impetus that had dragged him out of bed at the literal crack of dawn was a frantic phone call from Carlos. *"Come to Wayland Precision. This is serious. I think I know who did it."*

Jasper asked the obvious questions, like "Head to Wayland right now?" "Who did what?" "Anyone hurt?" But Carlos didn't provide details, only broad strokes. With Jasper awakened from an alcohol-soaked sleep, he'd probably missed half of what Carlos told him anyway.

He rolled up to the hotel and found Temple sitting on the curb with her head down, resting on her arms, which in turn rested on her knees. Her head came up as he stopped the car. She too squinted the squint of someone fighting a long night and no sleep.

Jasper reached over and flung the passenger's side door open. "How does it feel?"

"Excuse me?" Her lips looked dry.

Jasper laughed. "Seeing you like this makes it all worth it."

"What are you talking about?" She slumped into the seat and slammed the door.

A bell dinged. Dinged. Dinged.

"Fasten your seat belt, please," Jasper said, "unless you love hearing the car complain. The dinging won't stop; believe me, I know."

She wrestled with the shoulder strap and fumbled with the clasp for a few seconds while the car kept bitching.

"A lovely morning." Jasper glanced over at Temple, who stared at him with slitted eyes. Did he notice a hint of murder lingering in her gaze? "Oh, relax. I'm just giving you a hard time. You know, payback for you dragging me out of a restful slumber yesterday?"

"Whatever. Hey, you didn't get me a coffee?"

"Nope."

"At least I got you some coff—"

"I wouldn't call that stuff coffee."

"Stop somewhere, please," she said. "And turn down the air." She hugged herself.

"You know, this is the first time since I met you that you look uncomfortable and out of sorts."

She glared.

"But don't get me wrong, you still managed to pull yourself together."

She was still glaring. Jasper smiled and reached for his coffee. "I'll stop somewhere for you, but I'm not turning down the air. My car. My rules."

He related what he'd learned, and stopped off so Temple could grab a coffee and something to eat. Temple had left Vance behind—he'd go to the FBI office and put together what they'd learned so far and wait for the rest of the reports to come in, which would include the medical examiner's.

They drove in silence the rest of the way, with Temple huddled and pushed into the seat as deeply as possible, sipping coffee with both hands wrapped around the cup.

The early time of day allowed them to reach Wayland Precision in short order. Two burly men stood out front. They could have been Penny's brothers, or at least somehow related to the Stahlbergs.

One of the men directed them to the gate on the west side of the building. The chain links rattled and the wheels squeaked as the gate retracted. Jasper drove to the parking lot at the rear of the building. Standing there, looking pissed off, were Steve and Penny, while Carlos nervously paced. A group of people, presumably employees, were gathered around the rear entrance and on the concrete ramp leading up to the same rear entrance.

Jasper took a deep breath and put the Charger in park. He finished his coffee and stepped out of the car. Temple followed.

The air had cooled a bit during the course of the night. Although the sun was now over the horizon, the summer heat hadn't yet hit.

Everything around Jasper seemed amplified—the din of the Wayland folks' conversation, the gravel crunching under his and Temple's feet as they walked, the rumble of a train passing nearby, even Temple sipping her coffee. If only the aspirin and the caffeine would fully kick in and provide a respite.

Carlos broke from the group and reached Jasper before he got too close to Steve and Penny.

"What's going on?" Temple asked.

The young Hispanic man turned his head. "I lied to you about a few things, and I think she's come back to bite me, bite everyone in the ass."

Jasper stopped walking.

"What did you lie about?"

"Remember the waitress?"

"Yeah, so what? What does she have to—hold on. Are you saying you *did* date the waitress? Aren't you married? You told me you were married, right? Yeah, when you phoned in the tip regarding the kidnapped girl."

"Wait a second," Temple broke into the conversation. "You're saying the waitress is involved with the break-in? The kidnappings and the murders, and the—"

"I—I'm not sure." Carlos stammered.

Penny strode with purpose toward them, but Steve remained behind. She pushed Carlos aside. "He tell you what happened yet? He tell you about how stupid he was? Is. Will continue to be?"

Carlos shrank, as if he'd lost a few inches of height.

Jasper held up his hands and Temple took a step toward Penny.

"Back off," Penny stared down Temple. That was quite a feat. Jasper was impressed.

"We're here to help." Jasper moved in between the two women, both with hands on their hips. "Tell us what happened, please."

"Wayland Precision was broken into last night." Penny glanced back at Carlos. "You don't need to be a part of this conversation." Carlos skulked off. Steve waved him over to his group at the rear entrance.

"Do you suspect him?" Temple asked.

"We're not sure," Penny said. "He's the one who found we'd been broken into, and then he informed us he thinks he knows who did the breaking and entering."

"Wouldn't that be a little in your face?" Jasper asked. "And then for him to stay around and admit it to you all?"

Penny sighed. "I don't know what to think."

"Show us what happened."

Steve glared from his perch at the rear entrance.

"What's his deal?" Temple nodded at Steve.

"He doesn't want your help, and I'm not sure you *can* be of much help."

"Why?"

"Never mind for now." Penny gestured at a window near the base of the building. "The window leads into the basement, directly into our office, and was left open."

"By who?"

"My father and I never open those windows, but we were the last ones out of the building. We should've noticed."

"Let me guess, Carlos."

Penny grimaced. "Yes."

"But that doesn't necessarily mean he was complicit."

"Anything stolen or vandalized?" Temple asked.

"Stolen, yes. Nothing vandalized."

"How does Carlos know who did this? I mean, he somehow figured out the perpetrator was the waitress, Eulalia," Temple said. "Is this a revenge thing, to get back at him for having an affair with her while he was married?"

"Let me show you a few things." Penny took them up the ramp toward Steve and pointed at a metal object resting on the concrete.

Jasper kneeled and examined the object without touching it. "A lock pick, well, part of a lock picking set. What, the pick's engraved with her name?"

"The lock pick didn't give her away," Penny said. "We found something in the office—mistakenly left behind, I'm sure."

Steve came over. Jasper gazed up at the big man, who stood there arms folded and appearing impossibly broad across the chest, like an angered Norse god ready to pummel the nearest mortal.

"We are not asking for your help," Steve said. "We can handle this ourselves."

"But there's been a break-in, and Carlos stated you were all in danger. Why does he think that?"

Penny's mouth parted, but Steve placed a hand on her shoulder and her lips sealed.

"Come on." Jasper stood. "We're not the bad guys here. I want to help. Agent Black wants to help. We have resources at our disposal, we—"

"Our group has dealt with this sort of menace before." Steve's face reddened, nearly matching the port wine birthmark adorning the entire side of his face.

"What does any of that statement mean? Your *group*?" Jasper glanced at the small crowd of men gathered nearby. "I thought they were your employees. And what's this about a menace?"

Steve folded his arms again and leaned against the brick wall.

"Follow me." Penny opened the back door.

"Penny," Steve said, "don't."

"Father, I'm sorry, but we should ask their opinion on a few items. Maybe we're not dealing with what you believe is happening and Carlos's fling is simply coming back to haunt him." Steve sighed and turned away.

"Leave the lock pick on the ground," Jasper said. "Any other evidence out here?"

"We can tell where Lali walked across the grass and where she went over the fence." Penny guided them into the building and led them down into the office.

The vegetal and metal scents flooded Jasper's nose, and the tangy film coated his tongue.

"I wish I understood why you grew mushrooms in a place like this," Jasper said. "You all seem eccentric, but this is just plain weird."

Temple remained quiet; perhaps the lack of sleep doused her natural combativeness.

Penny, too, said not another word until they entered the office. "Lali never got past this door, right here. All the security in the world doesn't make up for lack of attention to detail—like the simple act of shutting a blasted window."

"True enough." Jasper thought about her comment, lack of attention to detail. "Was your father in the military? Navy or Marines perhaps? I'm a Marine, myself."

"Navy," Penny said, "but not my father—I served. Enlisted, too."

"You must have been young," Jasper said.

"I served for one tour, four years, and got out." She shrugged. "I couldn't imagine a full twenty years of alternating sea and shore duty every couple of years. If I'd stayed in I'd have over ten years active duty already."

How old did that make her, then? If she'd gone in at eighteen then she'd only be around thirty right now, right?

He needed to stop thinking this way. He was too damaged by his divorce from Lucy to even consider jumping into the pool again.

"Yep, understandable," Jasper said. "I resigned my commission, so I'm a free man. There are times I miss the structure and camaraderie, though."

"Let's talk about the office here." Temple cut in—sensing his need for a rescue attempt. He appreciated that. There were times when he and Temple acted like real partners. They were coming more often, too.

"She stole a lot of our personal information," Penny said, "as well as photos and some more—I don't know how to put this—secret information."

"May we go inside?" Temple asked.

Penny flipped on the lights. "Over there, footprints. Smallish, like a woman's."

Jasper squinted.

"They're hard to see, but they're there. Especially near the window where she entered. Let's go in, just be aware of where you're stepping."

"I'm still puzzled how Carlos figured out Lali did all of this, and how did he arrive at the conclusion she acted alone?"

"Good point," Penny said, "but I only found one set of footprints inside and outside. Now, someone may have waited in a car for her—which is possible if what my father believes is actually true."

"Which would be what?"

"Let's stay on how we're certain Lali acted alone, okay?" Jasper asked.

Temple frowned at him.

Jasper cocked his head slightly and widened his eyes, attempting to get Temple to play along. If they stayed partnered up long enough, most of their interactions when working a case or interviewing people would work themselves out and they'd communicate nonverbally and would simply understand how the other person would handle any given situation. They'd also both acquire a sense of when to jump in and when to stay the hell out of the way. Overall, though, as new partners they weren't doing too poorly.

He turned his attention to the office. Other than the footprints, it appeared to be in the same condition as when Jasper visited the day before. Even the footprints were faint: traces of dirt and grass barely shaped like feet were noticeable on the floor beneath the window.

"So, how do we know this was Lali?" He felt as if he asked the same question over and over again and Penny avoided the explanation.

Penny pointed at a piece of paper on the floor—a scrap of paper, hot pink in color and torn from a sticky note.

"Well, Carlos recognized the handwriting on the note, and furthermore—"

"What, he's an expert on handwriting analysis, now?" Temple's hands were once again planted on her hips. Her interactions with people so far—too standoffish at times, too aggressive at others—led Jasper to believe her experience conducting witness interviews lagged behind his.

Penny laughed. "No, her name is on the note."

"Oh." Temple looked a little embarrassed. "Sorry, didn't mean for this to get contentious."

"What does the note say?" Jasper asked. "Anything on the other side? We might as well examine the note if Carlos already touched the paper. Besides, I don't think your father is going to want to call in an evidence team or the police on this, am I right?"

"Yes," Penny said. "But he doesn't have the final word on any decisions around here."

"No? I thought he—"

"Wayland's a joint operation, and as he gets older, more and more of the business is delegated to me. Including the...ah..." Her voice trailed off.

"Uh huh," Jasper said. *Including the what?* But he let that go for the moment. "Before we get to the other activities, what does the note say?"

"Nothing important, a note from her job at the diner."

"Well, I'd say this pretty much seals Lali's participation, but you—or your father—think the break-in involves something deeper?"

"My father will be upset if I share with you. I need you to promise not to mention any of what I tell or show you to anyone outside, got it? No one."

Penny's gaze fixed on Jasper for a few seconds, then Temple. Seeing the resistance in their expressions, she shook her head. "Look, I don't expect you to keep anything illegal to yourselves. But this isn't...it's just...well, hard to explain."

"Just tell us all you can," Jasper said, "but understand, we've seen some jacked-up stuff the past couple of days not easily explained. Not through investigation, and not through traditional science, though we've made some inquiries. Can you explain mangled bodies with clear liquid dripping from them rather than blood? Or mists appearing like dragons?"

"Yes, I can. There is a cult—"

"The kidnappers, I'm guessing?" Jasper asked.

Penny nodded. "Carlos watched a few of the suspected cultists, but we weren't sure they'd moved into the area. They're called the Câ Tsang."

"The Kah Sang?" Temple raised an eyebrow and glanced at Jasper, then back at Penny. "What does the name mean? Where are they from?"

"It means 'Iron Thorn.' They originated in Bhutan. We're not entirely certain of when they were established, but they've been around longer than our group."

Jasper snapped his fingers. "The papers I saw here last time, Völundr's Hammer, right?"

"Yes. Wayland Precision is a cover—a real business, of course, that usually turns a profit every year—but its main purpose is still to be a cover for the guild. The name Wayland is based on the old myth of Wayland the Smith."

Jasper grinned and looked at Temple. "See? I told you all of this was the work of some asshole cult. Didn't we make a bet on this?" He nudged Temple.

She held up a finger. "Not so fast. What is the cult's purpose? And what makes your guild willing and able to fight them?"

"They seek demonic power from—let's call it the hell world. Or just 'the other world.' The reason we can fight them is . . . well, we've been doing it for a very long time and we have a lot of experience. Unlike the Câ Tsang, the guilds of the Blacksmith aren't monolithic in nature and they're all quite different in their origin. Ours originated in Scandinavia."

"Originated—how long ago?" asked Temple.

Penny hesitated. "We're not actually sure. Several centuries."

"And you're saying this Kah Sang cult has been around even *longer*?"

Penny nodded.

"How many are we talking about here?" Jasper asked.

"Members or cults?"

Jasper and Temple looked at each other. "You're saying there's more than one cult, too?" asked Temple. "I thought you said there was only one."

"No. What I meant was that the various Blacksmith guilds generally cooperate with each other, but the cults don't. The relations between them are hostile. To the point of being deadly, more often than not, when they clash with each other."

Jasper thought he finally understood how Alice felt, when she fell into the rabbit hole. "And...just how many cults are we talking about?"

"Here in this area? Just the Câ Tsang. So far as we know, they're the only Nephilim cult operating in the United States. Well...east of the Mississippi, anyway. We occasionally hear rumors about things happening in California, but..." She waved her hand. "You know how it is with California. There's always *something* weird happening out there."

He grabbed onto the one new item in what she'd said. "Nefillin? What's that?"

Temple was now squinting at Penny. "She didn't say 'Nefillin,' she said 'Nephilim.' They're mentioned in the Bible a few times. Usually as giants of some kind, if I remember right. But I don't really know much about them."

"No one does," said Penny. "The truth is, we don't really know if they have any connection at all to the Nephilim of the Bible. We've just been using that term for them out of tradition—and no one remembers anymore when the tradition started." She shrugged. "People have been arguing about them for several thousand years. The original theory was that they were the offspring of fallen angels and human women. Not Lucifer and his crowd but a different bunch. Later, most theologians thought they were illegitimate offspring from the line of Seth. The most detailed depictions of them come from the Book of Enoch, but that's not recognized as canonical by any church except the Ethiopian and Eritrean Orthodox churches."

Jasper stared at her, as if Penny had suddenly starting speaking in tongues. Temple's expression was skeptical. "And you know about the theology of churches in northeast Africa...how?" she asked. "Meaning no offense, but you don't *look* Ethiopian."

Penny chuckled. "I know about them for the same reason any guild member does. The oldest of the Blacksmith guilds come out of Africa. Blacksmithing was a sacred vocation in that part of the world. They were followers of Ogun, originally. He's reputed to be the Yoruba *orisha* who's worshipped as the god of iron all over West Africa—although he goes under a lot of different names: Gu for the Dahomey and West African vodoun cultures, Ogu in northern Nigeria. From there, it spread across the world, especially to the New World. In Santería, Ogun is syncretized with St. Peter. In Haitian vodou he's blended with St. James the Greater and known as Santiago Matamoros. That means 'St. James the Moorslayer,' which the Islamic guilds find a little irritating."

Now Temple was staring at Penny as if she were speaking in tongues. The coowner of Wayland Precision grinned mirthlessly. "Oh, I could go on, trust me. Guilds in the Muslim world have their own traditions and beliefs. They don't think Nephilim are fallen angels, as most Western guilds believe. They think they're a type of djinn. The Câ Tsang cultists, on the other hand, think they're a type of nâga, likely based on their origins in Bhutan. In the Hindu tradition, nâgas are—"

"Serpent deities," Jasper filled in. Seeing the respect at his erudition in Temple's eyes, he saw no point in explaining that his knowledge came from role-playing games, not scholarship.

Penny pursed her lips. "I can't say much more, really. I'm bound by the rules of the guild."

Jasper decided not to push that, at least for the moment. Thankfully, Temple seemed inclined to let him lead the questioning. "The cult is the only concrete piece we have to this puzzle," Jasper said. "We need to be pursuing them. What makes you think Lali is involved with them?"

"A hunch?" Penny shrugged. "Why would she steal all of our personal information and information on the guild? And she also took a photo picturing all the people currently working here."

"That's still not anything definitive," Jasper said. "There's a lot of work to be done to prove any link to a cult with what happened here." The air inside the office moved, bringing metallic and vegetal scents, renewing them in his nose and mouth. "So, the mushrooms and the fish tanks, what role do they play with all the cult and guild stuff you've been filling us in on?"

"We have old diaries handed down from the inception of our guild hundreds of years ago listing mushrooms and some sea creatures capable of repelling monsters from beyond, like the Nephilim. Whether those old legends are true or not..." She shrugged. "Who knows? But we figure it's worth a try."

"Everyone has superstitions, athletes for one. FBI agents, too." Jasper hoped he didn't come across as simply placating someone with a few screws loose.

"What we're dealing with here is real. You saw the mangled bodies," Penny said. "But I can't say anything more on the topic. I wish I could, but I'm bound by the guild's laws."

"Understood. We have our own rules we must abide."

"Penny," a voice boomed from the hallway outside the office. "I believe your friends have heard enough." Steve entered the room, hobbling from a leg or hip injury. Jasper meant to ask Penny how her father's injury came about.

"I see you staring at this," he patted his leg. "Old war injury."

Penny tilted her head and pursed her lips. "You weren't in any wars, father. Remember? I'm the veteran in the family?"

"I meant war as in metal working and the hazards of the machine shop." Steve winked. He certainly had dialed down the hostility he'd exuded earlier. It occurred to Jasper that the conflict between father and daughter might have been staged, and that Steve had his own reasons for wanting the FBI drawn in.

Stahlberg eased himself into a chair. "So, Penny has provided you some information, which means you'll be running back to your little FBI building and running a bunch of checks. I'm also sure you've run us through your databases, and—"

"Actually, we haven't had time." Jasper rubbed the back of his head and walked toward the office door. "Been too busy investigating a couple of strange murders you're not likely connected with—"

"Hold on—"

"So you are connected to them?" Temple asked, realizing what Jasper was doing—perhaps they were further along the partner path than he'd realized. His back was turned to them now, but he smiled, and then hid the smile as he spun back around.

"Of course, we're not responsible!" Steve said, his expression angry. "But—"

"But what?" Jasper took a step toward Steve. "If you've withheld information that could have saved lives, even of those jackasses who committed suicide in the basement of the Euclid Hotel, you're partially responsible. Omission is almost as good as lying in my book."

Steve's face reddened and Penny stepped between her father and Jasper. "We aren't the bad guys either."

"No? Then why aren't you more forthcoming?" Temple demanded. "Carlos was at the Euclid. Carlos reported the first kidnapping. Carlos dated the person who broke in here. And you suspect the person who broke in here, Lali, is also part of a cult. What else aren't you telling us? What if more people die?"

Jasper motioned for Temple to follow him. "We have enough to work with, let's just hope no one else gets hurt."

Penny frowned and Steve's mouth hung open. His face lost a little life and his beard drooped a little more.

Temple handed Penny a business card. "Call me any time of day if you have anything else to report. And I mean *anything* relevant to these deaths and suicides."

Before he went through the threshold, Jasper craned his neck. "Oh, one more thing—" He paused a moment, realizing how Columbo he sounded, but continued anyway. "Don't go near the Euclid, and leave Lali to us."

Neither Penny nor Steve offered to escort them out, so they climbed the stairs and emerged into bright sunlight. Carlos was nowhere to be seen and his vehicle was gone from the parking lot. Jasper was going to tell him the same thing he'd told his bosses—to stay away from Lali and the Euclid.

"That went well," Temple said.

"At least we have quite a bit to research today," Jasper said as they walked toward his Charger. "I'm not confident Lali is connected with those idiots who fried themselves, though. Or the kidnappings. Her piece in this puzzle still doesn't fit very well with any of the others."

"I think we have a day of sifting through data ahead of us." Temple dropped into the Charger.

Jasper opened the door, receiving a wave of heat.

"I'm turning the air on, full blast," he said.

"No arguments here."

Chapter 26

THE FBI BUILDING IN MERRILLVILLE BUZZED WITH ACTIVITY, which was not unusual for a Monday morning.

Jasper set up Temple and a lost-looking Vance—who said he waited outside for the past hour—in a small meeting room capable of providing video conferences and contained a couple of FBINET computers, as well as two unclassified internet computers.

They'd agreed to each tackle portions of the information they'd received over the past couple of days. Vance would handle all the scientific evidence they'd already gathered, as well as a few of the unclassifiables like the mushrooms and sea creatures at Wayland Precision. Temple's job was to research Völundr's Hammer, Câ Tsang, Bhutan, and any and all customs and religious information. Jasper's task was to run FBI database checks on all the names, addresses, and vehicles they'd come across and see if any tied to other investigations. He'd build a list of contacts and leads for them to follow and marry up his information with Temple's and Vance's later on. They'd agreed on meeting around lunchtime in the conference room.

He took a deep breath and, with a cup of coffee, eased into his cubicle. What a horrible invention, these cubicles. He'd heard stories of the old days, where bullpens were groups of four desks shoved together with all four agents sharing a phone sitting in the middle. Back in those days, agents dictated their casework and sent the tapes to the steno pool—not anymore. Each and every agent was responsible for typing their work into the computer. Not a big deal, he supposed, but the administrative burden tied him to a desk more often than he liked. Even though he worked mainly with the locals, he still had FBI rules and regulations to follow. Cubicles isolated people, and with agents spending more and more time in the office, shouldn't they be face to face? Be forced to interact? A Special Agent's job involved talking to people, recruiting human sources and working investigations, maybe one day prosecuting someone, or preventing another catastrophe like 9/11.

His eyes closed. Drifting off would have been easy, so instead he rocked forward and grabbed his coffee.

The desk phone rang, loud and obnoxious—he nearly jumped out of his skin and spilled his coffee. Some joker changed the ringtone on him. Gee, what a fantastic practical joke. The agent in the next cube snickered.

"Very funny, Poindexter."

"I told you not to call me that, Zeke," the voice on the other side of the wall said, and Poindexter's receiver slammed into the cradle.

"Yeah? Well, stopping screwing with my stuff, Poindexter." How childish, like he was in grade school all over again. Special Agent Dexter was a wormy fellow with thick, black-rimmed glasses and a pinched face above which he wore his black hair slicked back. All he was missing was a bow tie, worn with a short sleeved button-down shirt with suspenders.

"Whatever, Zeke, you're a loser and you know it."

Jasper closed his eyes again, and counted to ten. Hard to believe they were all on the same side. He didn't understand why Dexter hated him so much. His devastating good looks? He grinned and opened his eyes. His superior intellect? He laughed. Right.

He got up and stood behind Dexter. "What is your problem with me?"

Dexter spun around in his chair, his top lip curled up, exposing his top row of teeth. He kind of resembled a dorkier version of Buddy Holly, if possible. Dexter didn't say anything.

"Well, Buddy...?"

"I'm not your buddy," Dexter said.

"That's not what I mean, Buddy. You know, as in Buddy Holly?"

"Who?"

"Never mind," Jasper said. "What is your fascination with screwing with my shit?"

"Oh," he held up his hands and waved them, "you gonna go all Marine Corps on me? Code red?"

Jasper squinted. "What in the hell are you talking about?"

"Forget it."

"Whatever. If you ever grow up, someday you'll tell me what I've done wrong." Jasper walked back to his cubicle and plopped down in his chair. He sensed Dexter giving him the finger through the wall.

His phone blared again.

"Damn you, Poindexter, I said stop!" Jasper picked up his phone and slammed the receiver down as hard as he could.

A loud chuckle came over the wall from Dexter's side, every bit as annoying as the loud ringer. He reached for the phone to take care of the ringer right now.

The intercom speakers overhead crackled. "Jasper Wilde, please call extension 1002. Jasper Wilde, please call extension—"

"Great," Jasper said. "You're an asshole, Buddy Poindexter. You jackass."

"Such foul language today. Seems like the front office wants to have a word with you, I hear they want to flush your lousy attitude down the toilet."

Jasper took a deep breath and dialed the phone. His boss's secretary, Jack, answered, and told him SSA Johnson wanted to see him immediately.

Jasper breezed into Johnson's office and into the glares of both Masters and Johnson.

"A problem, Special Agent Wilde?" ASAC Masters stood, straightened his shirt and gestured for Jasper to take a seat.

Masters reseated himself behind Johnson's desk, with Johnson standing next to him. Odd. But Masters was his boss and he'd obviously relinquished the seat of power to him. Of course, Masters had his own office, but at the main office in Indianapolis.

"No, sir." Jasper automatically retreated to his military days when confronted with Bureau management and when he thought he was in trouble.

"Excellent. Well, you'll be pleased to know we're pulling you back from your temporary duty assignment with this so-called Scientific Anomalies Group," Masters said with a smug grin.

Jasper frowned. "Why?"

"We thought you'd be happy. We're kicking the headquarters people out of our AOR and back to wherever they came from,"

Johnson said. "I've been on the phone all morning with SSA Black's superior back east, you know, the assistant director of the Critical Incident Response Group?"

"Oh? Why?"

"Look," Masters spread his hands, pivoting on his elbows resting on the desk, "ever since she—"

"SSA Black," Johnson interrupted.

Masters shot him a look—"she came into town, one disaster after another cropped up, plus she hasn't been making any friends." His walruslike countenance worked into a fit of jiggling folds.

"She doesn't make friends—what a weak argument. I don't have time for nonsense. I have work to do. People may be dying or be in danger right now as we speak." Jasper's temper was starting to flare. Too bad Dexter had already raised his blood pressure this morning. Mixed with lack of sleep, Jasper knew he was volatile.

"There is no argument. It's a decision. End of story, you're off SAG. You better watch yourself, Wilde." ASAC Masters jabbed a chubby finger in his direction.

"But what about the SAC? You said SAC Weber wanted me on SAG, since he was friends with the AD, you know, Temple's supervisor back east?"

"Yes, but the SAC left the division last night," Masters sat back and folded his meaty arms. "The director tasked him with handling some mess out in Albuquerque. I'm in charge until Weber returns—the acting Special Agent in Charge."

"Your mom must be so proud." Jasper regretted the words the instant they crossed his lips.

Master's face reddened, as did Johnson's, his direct supervisor. "You want to be written up? A letter of censure for insubordination?" Sweat erupted from the man's giant face pores.

"Not really, but does it matter in the end? Look, why not give me a few days on the bricks while you're at it? You'll only be shooting yourself in the foot when all this cult stuff blows up. You'll be the laughingstock of the Bureau. They'll make you step down, or worse, send you somewhere horrible to hide your sorry ass."

Masters shot to his feet. "Are you—why, I—"

Johnson stepped in. "Sir? Let me have a few minutes with Wilde."

"I won't be spoken to like this." Masters shook.

"Sir, please. Stay here, we'll go somewhere else. Give me a few minutes with Wilde." Johnson spun Jasper around and pushed him toward the door.

Jasper was surprised Johnson remained this calm. His boss escorted him to a little used office down the hall and shut the door behind them and pointed at a chair.

"Sit down."

Jasper sat, not saying a word.

"Are you out of your mind?" Johnson glared at him, hands on his hips. "Why can't you simply play by the rules? You do your own thing all the time playing around with the locals and all their crap. We're sending you back out with the locals and now you're trying to piss away this miserable career of yours?"

"You're upset because you've never had the balls—nerves—to say all that yourself. You don't like Masters any more than I do."

"That isn't the point, jackass. He's gonna make sure you get some time on the bricks, you realize that, right?"

"So? Like I said, he'll only be hurting himself." Jasper believed everything he said, but a touch of doubt lingered in his mind as to whether the system would work to his favor in the end.

Johnson's hands flew to his head, grasping at his now tousled hair.

"If he wants to get me OPR'd, it'll take a while. Hopefully by then all of this crazy shit going on up here will have been taken care of." The last thing any agent in the Bureau needed was the Office of Professional Responsibility investigating them.

"Oh, my God," Johnson said. "Are you really buying into all the hokey crap Temple Black's been slinging?"

Jasper stared at him, and kept staring until his boss cracked.

"You are buying into her shit. I can't believe this."

"Boss." Jasper finally caved in and decided to be reasonable. "Look. We're putting together everything we have so far. Give me the rest of today, will you? I'm asking you for a onetime favor."

"Apologize."

"I'm sorry."

"Not to me," Johnson said. "Are you kidding? Apologize to ASAC Masters."

"Oh, God, really?" Jasper drummed his knee and swung his head back and forth. "Damn it. Come on, Steve."

Johnson's eyebrows shot up, wrinkling his forehead.

"Fine."

"Good. We'll let him cool off a bit. Now, tell me why you're into these investigations all of the sudden."

"We gathered evidence of a cult in the area perpetrating the kidnappings. They're also responsible for the accident two nights ago now. The one at Euclid and East Chicago—right near the same hotel where the first kidnapping victim was found and those two jackoffs offed themselves."

"How eloquent." Johnson rested his ample ass on the corner of the desk, folded his arms, and loomed over Jasper.

"The best I could do on the spot, sorry."

"You're something, Wilde. You really are."

"Well?"

"I do wish I had the balls to say the things you said, but I have kids and a wife, and—oh, hell. I'm sorry, Jasper. I didn't mean it like that."

Jasper sighed. "Yeah, fine. But you're right, I don't have anyone, only myself, and if I fuck *my* career up, so what? I hear you. So, you gonna give me the time I need?"

"You gonna apologize to the dim bulb waiting in my office?"

"I didn't know you had it in you, boss. But since you put it like that, fine, I will, but only to smooth this rough patch over so I can get on with my work."

"All right, but don't expect any resources from the office, and until this is over, you're a headquarters guy. Let's go." Johnson left the office.

Jasper took a deep breath. Then took a few more before getting up and finally facing Masters.

Chapter 27

"WHERE WERE YOU?" TEMPLE ASKED AS JASPER PLOPPED INTO his chair.

"Getting my ass chewed on."

"Sounds lovely."

"The tried yanking me from SAG, pull me back to working the mean streets." Jasper chuckled. "Hey, is Poindexter over there?"

"Who is that?" Temple asked.

"You see a Buddy Holly looking jerk in the next cube over?"

Temple leaned to her right and popped her head back into Jasper's cube. "No."

"Okay, good. He doesn't care for me much and I'd rather he not be around for this part." Jasper leaned back in his chair.

"I thought you'd jump at the chance of being pulled off of this," Temple said. "And then you wouldn't have to deal with me."

"Heh. You wish." Jasper grinned. "I've a vested interest in this case now."

"What, Penny?"

"No. Well, yes, I suppose that, too. But this case has merit despite how crazy it all sounds. God help us—Nephilim, who might be bad angels or devils or djinn or take your pick. But we also have honest-to-goodness humans doing bad shit, and we're going to put them away."

Jasper rocked forward and rifled through the stack of papers on his desk. "So, while the ASAC cleaned out my ears, or should I say, acting special agent in charge, some of my records checks came back."

"That bad, huh?" Temple's eyes held genuine concern for him. "The ass chewing?"

"I'm flattered," Jasper said. "I said a few bad things and almost got myself some time off. I could use some, but what would I do with it?"

"Wow, you're kind of rambling. Been sipping away at cappuccinos all morning?"

"Yes. But Poindexter pestered me, and then I bent over and spread my cheeks wide for the ass reaming. Despite all the issues, I'm actually in a pretty decent mood. I won for the time being and I'm being allowed to continue fighting the asshole cult with you."

"There is more to it, I'm afraid," Temple said.

"You and Vance already come up with something? I haven't even been given the chance to do much here. I was called to the principal's office almost as soon as I sat down. How about we keep to the plan and meet for lunch?"

"How about you come to the conference room and work there? That way we can bounce things off each other. I still have some open source checks to run, anyway." Temple nodded. "Sound good?"

"Actually, yes. If Poindexter comes back I'm liable to get sidetracked by his stupid pranks."

The conference room table once sported a polished wood surface, but now binders, papers, pens, and pencils littered the surface, along with Vance's bag of tricks and a rack of vials, and what appeared to be a rather large scientific calculator.

"You guys are serious," Jasper said.

"Yeah, we don't fool around, mister." Vance glanced at him from behind goggles.

"This isn't a laboratory, you know. My boss is going to be pissed if he sees this. Well, no more than he already is, I primed him up for you guys." Jasper approached the table and glanced at some of the papers near the top of a stack.

"Before I go through the records checks I requested, what do you have for me? Anything that might inform what I do?"

"I got results from the medical examiner." Vance pulled off a pair of latex gloves and rifled through a stack of paper. "Here they are."

"Okay, and?" Jasper leaned forward.

"These reports were hastily written," Vance said.

"I prodded Doctor Lewis to finish up her reports." Temple shrugged.

"Excellent," Jasper felt his impatience growing. "So what's in them?" He glanced at Temple, who smiled knowingly.

"Right." Vance fumbled with the reports. "Doctor Lewis also found materials foreign to what is typically found on earth."

"That was a quick turnaround on the lab results, huh?"

"Your friend Ed White and myself ran all the tests and shared with Doctor Lewis. She independently examined the lab results and we all arrived at the same conclusion."

"But the doc is not saying it's from some alien life-form or devils, correct?" Jasper leaned on the table. "She say what the cause of death was on the first mangled corpse? The one we found near Animal Control?"

"They aren't sure. Inconclusive."

"Did Irene speculate?" Temple asked.

"Irene?" Vance frowned, confused.

"The medical examiner, Doctor Lewis," Jasper said.

"Oh, right. Some. But not like us."

"Oh, of that I'm quite certain."

Temple's phone rang and she stepped to the other side of the conference room and plugged her free ear with a finger.

"I may be a scientist," Vance said, "but Bhutan rests on the borders of India and China and therefore has a foot in both countries when it comes to culture."

"What's your point?" Jasper asked.

"I'm just saying, don't be so quick to dismiss Temple's beliefs, or even those of the guild you two visited. Science and the so-called fantastic are compatible."

"Fine, I'll give it a shot." But Jasper wasn't convinced. Everything they'd seen so far still could be easily explained as a group of assholes running around causing trouble. Coupled with odd atmospheric conditions—extremely odd conditions.

Vance tilted his head. "Really? Anyway, I've also run tests on the residue left behind by the suicide twins from the Euclid." He picked up a vial. "This guy right here had small traces of alien material mixed in, but the other did not."

"What does that mean?"

"Could mean a few things, I suppose. One theory holds the sample is contaminated, and the other being he was exposed to an alien or Nephilim before, in a prior ceremony. An even more remote possibility is the other universe—remember the brane cosmology theory posited by Doctor Greg?"

"Doctor Greg?" Jasper laughed.

Vance grinned. "Yes."

"You have a man crush on that guy?"

"No, okay, maybe. But not a full-blown bromance." Vance shook his head. "And certainly not like Temple's—"

Jasper turned his attention to Temple for a moment and listened to her conversation with Ed.

"Yes, thank you very much, Ed. I'll let Vance know." She noticed Jasper staring at her. "Yes, Ed. I think so. Uh huh."

"Hey, tell Lando I said hi, okay? And keep a Colt cold for me." He chuckled.

Temple frowned. "Ed? Jasper says hi." A pause. "Yeah, he mentioned him and beer."

Jasper snapped his fingers. "Damn. Ed's catching on a little too quickly."

Temple tucked her phone in her back pocket.

"What did that old rogue have to say?" Jasper asked, happy with himself for giving Ed a little shit.

Temple ignored Jasper and turned to Vance. "Ed has reconsidered his ideas on the, uh, extra—"

"Extracellular digestion?" Vance raised an eyebrow.

"Yes. That. Well, he hasn't abandoned the idea, but believes the mangled bodies are a result of foreign matter unable to efficiently extract iron from the blood."

"What does that mean?" Jasper asked. "Foreign matter? And don't say Nephilim."

"And why not?" Temple's head bobbed back and forth. She held up a finger. "Don't."

"For crying out loud, Temple. Do you really believe in all this otherworldly shit?" Jasper yanked a chair out from under the conference table and sat.

Temple's mouth opened, but Vance spoke: "Nothing on earth could extract only the iron content and leave a body in such a state. How would a cult achieve such a thing?"

"So, the mangled bodies are directly connected with the cult now? I thought the kidnap victims were directly connected to the cult," Jasper said.

"Yes, but the foreign material I found at the Euclid—where we found no mangled bodies, only suicides and what looked like a sacrifice in the past—was also present on the mangled bodies, and don't forget, one of the suicides. I think it's clear." Vance nodded.

"Fine. I concede. Now let me think for a few minutes." Jasper took his stack of records and sat in front of one of the FBINET computers in the room. "What do you want for lunch?" He asked after a minute. "I'm starving."

He phoned up some delivery from a nearby sandwich shop, and while they waited, each of them worked on their own part of the project.

Jasper's part was not all that difficult. In fact, a Staff Operations Specialist he'd co-opted, Mandy, ran all the name checks and cross-referenced the information with both open and closed investigations and provided him with a link chart. He examined the results and determined there were no links between the cult members and the victims. A few closed and active investigations were listed and represented on the chart. He scanned them, and transferred what he deemed as pertinent to a small notepad he carried around. Many Agents still carried around pen and paper, but some of the real young ones stored everything in an electronic format. He also jotted down a few names associated with those investigations for further look up if needed. Even the records on Steve, Penny, and Carlos were sparse—and there were no mentions of Câ Tsang or Völundr's Hammer in any FBI database. Wayland Precision, however, did have a hit, but from an old white-collar case that had gone nowhere involving some sort of fraud, but the allegation was unfounded.

Lunch arrived and Jasper retrieved it from reception—they'd never allow a delivery person access to the innards of the FBI building, and especially not unescorted. Jasper plopped the bag down and slid bottled waters to Temple and Vance.

"Shall we discuss over lunch what we've come up with so far?" Temple asked. "Or are you still looking over all those records?"

"I'm good to go. These charts have some possibilities, but nothing earth-shattering," Jasper said. "I'm going to have Mandy, the SOS who put all this together, do a little more digging on a few of these other names."

"Sounds good," Temple said. "I'll offer up what I've done, since we've sort of heard from Vance already."

Jasper ripped into his sandwich, a nice roast beef with mayo on the most amazing soft hoagie roll. "Go," he said, mouth full of bread and beef,

"I researched Bhutan a bit, and some of the religions there. I'd say, this cult, the Câ Tsang, originated as an offshoot of an old religion named *Bön*, but they broke free a long, long time ago."

Jasper laughed, still chewing. "Let me guess, in a galaxy, far—"

"All right, wise ass. Great one. Moving on—and Jasper? Don't talk with your mouth full of food."

"Yes, Mom."

"So anyway," she continued, "the cult's origins may be sha-manistic, which may explain the sacrificial rituals we've seen. Oh, and get this," she unwrapped her sandwich, "ever see the flag of Bhutan?"

Jasper shook his head, but Vance appeared to know what she was going to say.

"Their flag has an Asian style dragon on a field of gold and red. The country is nestled in the Himalayas, between India and China."

"Fascinating," Jasper said. "Tell me more—"

"And Bhutan? The precise etymology isn't clear, but I came across some information what else the country's been called: *Druk Yul.* And you know what that means?" Temple asked. "Didn't think so. Land of the thunder dragon."

"So a few guys are running around worshipping dragons." Jasper took another bite of the sandwich.

"This fits. I will bet you anything Penny and Steve know a hell of a lot more about the Câ Tsang than they're letting on." Temple opened her bottled water and drank half the bottle in one tilt.

"Impressive. But Penny and Steve aren't likely to give us anything anytime soon, remember? We kind of pissed them off when we walked out."

"What I'm fascinated by," Temple said, "is how a guild based on Northern European myths and stories ever became mortal enemies with one from the Himalayas. Don't you find that odd?"

"A little," Vance said. "But remember, not too long ago, Mongols made their way across Asia and almost conquered Europe."

"I wouldn't say 'almost' conquered," Jasper said.

"I would." Vance bit into a sandwich comprised entirely of vegetables.

Jasper wrinkled his nose. "All right, how do we use any of what we learned to our advantage moving forward?"

Vance edged forward in his seat. "Oh, I forgot something—you provided me with an odd list of things earlier   sea squirts and mushrooms at Wayland Precision."

"Do they have anything in common?"

"I don't think so," Vance said.

Jasper threw up his hands. "Then why bring it up?"

"In case you were wondering."

"Oh, boy. It's probably like Penny said, old superstitions—they were used to ward off Nephilim or some nonsense." Jasper finished his sandwich and gulped the water.

Temple started picking at her sandwich.

"But I asked Ed about it, you know, him being the biochem guy," Vance said.

"And?"

"He didn't know either, but would think about the possible connections."

"Vance? How about you only give pertinent information from now on, and without any prodding. Okay?"

"Look, I can't help how I think and process information. Get used to it." Vance ripped at his sandwich like a dog, biting down on it from the side of his mouth.

Temple tapped away at her phone.

"Texting Ed?" Jasper grinned.

"No. Trying to look up something." She frowned. "Forget it, wanted to see if I could figure out the mushroom thing." She slid her phone across the table, disgusted.

"All right, so do we have much else to discuss right now?" Jasper asked. "I say we put in a couple more hours and pull together what we have into one cohesive report—"

"You weren't planning on uploading our findings into the system," Temple asked, "were you?"

Jasper held up his hands. "I was leaving that up to you, this is ultimately your show, right?"

"I tend to keep things out of the system until it makes sense to put information in. The last thing we need is executive management poking their noses into our business."

"Agreed. I had enough of executive management today, but I'm going to have to show my direct supervisor something, or they may pull me off the TDY."

"At the moment, aren't I your direct supervisor?" Temple grinned.

"Technically, yes."

"No, I understand," Temple said. "You have to come back to this office and work with these people at some point, and the last thing you want to do is burn bridges."

"Too late, I'm afraid." Jasper dragged his hand down his face.

"Yeah, Vance and I know nothing about burning bridges, don't we?" Temple's eyes twinkled.

"Let's knock this out so I can go home and get some rest," Jasper said. "I think you two could use some as well."

Chapter 28

JASPER STARED AT THE CEILING. SLEEP EVADED HIM DESPITE HIS weariness.

His work phone buzzed. Even the phone's vibrate setting proved too loud for him right now. His ears rang a bit, nothing too bad, but enough for him to think about it from time to time. The Marine Corps played a role in the irritating malady.

He reached over and snatched the phone—didn't recognize the number—and tossed the phone back on the nightstand.

The condo's air kicked off, but the heat remained, as if roasting him in a pan inside an oven. He licked his lips and rolled over. The bed cradled him and the aches melted from his body, but—

Too quiet. Too hot.

Buzz.

Damn phone.

He sighed and answered.

"Yes?"

"It's Carlos—his truck."

"Who is this?" Jasper's mind raced. "Penny?"

"Yes. I'm not sure what to do next. Carlos's truck was found alongside a road."

Her voice quavered. Did they discover his mangled corpse? Jasper's heart raced. He sat up. "Okay. Slow down. How did you find this out?"

"The East Chicago Police phoned his wife, and she phoned me."

"Let me call my friend Pete." Jasper turned on his lamp. Nothing. Bulb burned out. "Penny? Pete is a partner of mine from the PD. Okay? May I call you back on this number?"

"*Yes.*"

Jasper glanced at his television—the red light denoting the TV was off wasn't illuminated. No power, which explained no air conditioning and the ovenlike conditions.

"Okay, Penny. Sit tight. I'll see if I can get some answers."

"*Okay, Agent Wilde. Thank you.*" Penny's voice regained some of the strength of their previous interactions.

A long sigh, like a window sliding open, caught his attention. He never opened his windows during the summer—too damn hot, even at night.

"I've got to go. I'll reach out to you later." He hung up and rolled off his bed, grabbing his baby Glock off his nightstand.

A board creaked in the hallway.

He fought to keep his breathing under control and stepped carefully, avoiding the hardwood floor and remaining on the rug poking out from beneath the bed. The rug would take him near the bedroom door, which he kept closed and locked. For a brief moment, he entertained the daft idea Lucy had come home, but he doused the notion as fast as it entered his mind. He wasn't even sure he wanted Lucy back any longer.

So, definitely not Lucy, and Temple didn't have a key. He never gave anyone else a key.

In the complete silence, he cursed himself for shutting and locking the bedroom door—if he unlocked or opened the door whoever roamed about his place would hear.

He stepped toward the door, one foot on the hardwood and the other on the rug. His fingers reached for the lock.

A crack split the silence in two. The bedroom door splintered at the jamb and flew open.

Jasper shielded his face without thinking.

An unseen force hit him hard in the midsection, sending him backward on his bed.

He gasped for air and in the dark saw a man standing at the foot of the bed. An unremarkable man with a shaved head and generic features. The man smiled. Movement behind the man caught Jasper's eye—another person. So, at least two people were in the condo.

The man held a finger to his lips—as if Jasper would simply obey and be quiet. They planned on kidnapping Jasper.

Jasper rolled off the bed once more and raised his weapon. "Not another step. Hear me?"

The man's smile disappeared, replaced with a contemplative look. "Hands up! Now!"

His would-be kidnapper stood his ground and didn't obey, keeping his hands flat against his sides.

Another man appeared in the doorway behind the first. Metal clanked against the floor—the implement they used for entering his room, no doubt.

"Raise your hands and get down on your knees."

The man grinned and took a step toward him.

"Stop right there." These freaks were itching to get shot.

A blow from the side knocked Jasper down. His Glock slid under the bed.

"Fuck."

Another man—a third one—grabbed Jasper's arm, but exerted no control and leaned awkwardly over him. The man obviously lacked training in hand-to-hand fighting. Jasper stood rather easily since his elbow remained free, and broke the man's grip on his wrist. Something pricked Jasper's shoulder. In response, he back-fisted the man on the bridge of the nose. The man stumbled back, dropped a syringe and held his nose—by doing so, also covered his eyes. Jasper found his footing, rotated his hips, and followed with a side blade kick, sending the man into the wall and on his ass.

Jasper spun his attention back to the man who'd knocked him onto the bed. A crowbar lay on the ground behind the man. The first man resembled one of the men who had incinerated themselves at the Euclid, and acted just as oddly.

The man's face appeared puzzled, as if he didn't understand how his cohort ended up slumped against the wall, moaning.

Jasper moved for the man, figuring his ineptness matched the other one's, but someone else lurked about, he was sure.

But the men were amateurs, and Jasper took another step. The closest man backed up, toward the door, as if luring him through.

Jasper dropped to the floor and reached under the bed for his Glock. His fingers gripped the handle and he pulled the gun from under the bed and jumped to his feet.

The man was gone. Jasper's gaze darted about the room. Crumpled man down against the wall. Check. Movement beyond the bedroom door? None.

A banging from below caught his attention. One of the neighbors on the floor below poked a broom into the ceiling. If this kept up they'd be knocking on his door soon and calling the cops. Either way the situation at the moment wasn't too bad. The would-be kidnappers had screwed up big time. At least one of them was going to jail tonight.

"Show me your hands." Jasper raised his Glock, keeping the weapon depressed slightly, his eyes above the night sights.

Crickets.

More banging from below. He stomped on the floor.

He glanced to his right and back on the door again—the man he'd kicked sagged against the wall.

Jasper moved for the doorframe. He moved diagonally left on the doorway so as to keep an eye on the man inside the bedroom and also scan as much as he could of the living room on the other side of his door. The downside was the small hallway connecting his bedroom with the living room. But no one moved within the funnel. His diagonal view only provided a slice of the living room.

"Step to where I can see you. Now!" he yelled down the hallway. "That means into view of the hallway, you dumb fucks."

And yet more banging from below—louder and with more force. Boy, his neighbors were gonna have dents in their ceiling.

Now, if these clowns carried firearms, kidnapping him at gunpoint would make sense. But these men weren't the brightest bulbs apparently.

A door slammed.

Jasper hesitated for a moment, torn between going after the rest of his assailants or staying in the room to make sure the one he'd captured didn't escape. But it didn't take him long to choose the first option. Maybe he'd get lucky and the man against the wall wouldn't recover quickly enough to escape.

"Screw it." Jasper abandoned all caution and ran down the hallway, his bare feet slapping the floor. He only wore shorts to bed, but at least it was hot inside and outside.

As he crossed the threshold from hallway to living room he glanced about frantically searching for his attackers. The front door stood half-open.

He glanced into the kitchen as he ran by, and reached the open front door in another second. The streetlamps glowed; swarms of insects flittered about the light, providing the only movement in the parking lot. Where did the men get to already?

Rustling and a thump came from behind him—his bedroom. A slam, like a window hitting the top of the frame made him wince. Another thump, more distant, followed.

A car started and tires squealed, drawing his attention back down to the parking lot. From the right, a man, favoring his left leg, raced for the car as it neared the parking lot's exit.

"Stop!" Jasper yelled, but understood the futility.

The car's brake lights lit and the tires locked up, as if they'd stopped for his command, but he knew better. He stood on the walkway of his second floor condo and squinted at the license plate—none, removed from the car. The third man glanced up at Jasper as he opened the car door and disappeared inside. They took off in the mid-sized sedan, but no details stood out, and the color, in this light, was impossible to determine.

Power. Did they simply hit a circuit breaker or had they done worse? Jasper checked the box—the breakers were in place. He grabbed a flashlight and checked the outside—the bastards cut the power at the meter. He sighed.

He trotted back inside and made for the bedroom. His toe caught a solid hunk of metal on the floor, and he fell forward. He squeezed his foot. His eyes welled and he sucked in air, hissing.

"Fuck!"

They'd left the crowbar. As his pain softened and his toe stopped throbbing, he thought over their entry tactics. He examined the front door and found where they pried it open. They must have been quiet, or happened to open the door when his phone buzzed.

He grabbed his cell phone and sat on the edge of his bed. Sleep was never going to be a part of his life any time soon. Not until this case was over, at least. He stared at the phone.

Call Pete? Maybe. No. His old pal didn't want any part of this business.

Call his boss, Johnson? Absolutely not.

Temple? Yes.

He hit a button on the phone and remembered Penny called him right before the attack. Shit. She said Carlos was missing— well, she said his truck was found alongside the road.

He dialed Pete—his old partner wasn't thrilled, but confirmed for him through the department they had indeed found Carlos's vehicle. He also reported no mangled corpses discovered in the vicinity. Pete asked what was wrong, but Jasper insisted all was fine.

Next, he phoned Temple and explained the situation. She was on her way over.

He dialed Penny and told her Pete's information, and assured her the matter was being looked into, but didn't tell her about his attack.

Finally, his finger rested on his boss's number. He debated how the interaction would go, but decided against telling his boss anything. Sure, strange men broke into his residence, but other than bruises on both sides and some property damage, what would he tell Johnson? Cult members tried kidnapping him probably for a sacrifice to space creatures from another universe? No. ASAC Masters would kick Temple out of Indiana and transfer Jasper to closed files where he couldn't hurt anyone.

But—if they found out he hid the attack from them, he'd be in more trouble. The investigation needed to be worked to conclusion—by him, by SAG. The locals would never look at something like this so fantastic. They'd just call the Bureau for help since this was, in their mind, a messy situation, both figuratively and literally, and easily handed over to the FBI.

"I'm buying into all of this, aren't I?" Jasper asked into the darkness. He'd slid off the edge and leaned against the side of the bed. "I can't believe I'm falling for—"

"Falling for what?" a female voice asked. His skin prickled. Temple. He released a breath he didn't realize he'd taken.

"Well?"

"Thank goodness you're here." Jasper got to his feet.

"What in the hell happened here? And your power is off, by the way," she said.

"No, really?"

"All right, wiseass. Calm down. I'm here to help, okay?"

"I'm sorry. Rough night." Jasper placed his Glock on the nightstand and tossed his phone on the bed. "What a mess."

He gave her the blow by blow of the incident.

She whistled.

"Yeah, and the guy whose ass I kicked into the wall will probably sue me." Jasper laughed. "Be my luck. Oh, and I didn't breathe a single word of this to my boss yet. If ASAC Masters finds out, it'll end poorly for me, and likely get you kicked out of Indianapolis's AOR."

A siren blared in the distance.

"Shit. You call the cops?" Jasper walked to his bedroom window and peered out.

"Nope."

"My neighbors, I bet. They were hitting their ceiling with a broom of something." He glanced at the windowsill; a few drops of blood smeared the wood. "Blood."

"Yours?"

"No, the guy who is hurting right now. He went out the window here when I pursued his buddies."

The siren cut through the dense air. Boy, his neighbors would have a lot to discuss with the cops in a few seconds. He leaned out of the window, but from this angle, the parking lot was only partially visible. A dark, unmarked cruiser pulled up curbside near the front entrance of the building. A dashboard light strobed as did the wigwags in the grill.

Thumping and pounding filled his apartment.

"Here we go," Jasper said. "You might want to have your creds in your raised hands when we open the door."

"Right." Temple's eyes were wide and worried. "You've had this happen before? Blue on blue?"

"No, but I've been on the other end, when we've dropped in on some corrupt law enforcement."

Jasper pulled out his creds and Temple followed suit.

The pounding continued.

"Jasper," a voice yelled from the other side of the door.

The voice was familiar, though muffled.

"It's Pete. Open the damn door."

Jasper sighed. "My old partner, you met him near Animal Control."

"Oh, right. I remember."

He opened the door and Pete's face was drained of its color.

"You okay?" Jasper asked.

"I was worried about you, my friend. Ever since the night outside the Euclid, when we both, well," he glanced down at the ground, "you know what we saw."

"Pete, I appreciate the concern, I do, but—"

"What did you two see, again?" Temple stepped forward.

Pete glanced at her, and his shoulders and head jolted, as if he didn't noticed her. "We—I can't." He crossed himself and pulled a crucifix on a silver chain from inside his shirt, and pressed the metal to his lips.

"A religious experience for you as well."

Pete remained silent.

"Pete, why are you here, really?"

"On the phone, you sounded shook up a bit, as if you'd been in a fight. Or I thought someone was holding you against your will."

"They tried. Here, come in." Jasper gestured for him to enter.

"Ever hear of lights?" Pete's head swiveled has he took in the apartment.

"They cut the power. And they left behind a crowbar—" Jasper pointed at the hunk of metal on the floor.

Pete frowned. "Serious, these people. They try to kill you?"

"No. I think I was to be a kidnap victim. Sacrificed or tortured perhaps."

Pete crossed himself again.

"When did you become so into the church again?" Jasper asked.

"What we witnessed the other night, you know, the haze outside the Euclid after we rescued the little girl..." Pete looked at the floor again, and licked his lips. "It forced me to rethink certain parts of my life."

Jasper patted him on the shoulder. "Need a drink?"

Pete laughed. "And here I headed over to rescue you."

"I do need your help—"

"Anything," Pete said. "Anything within reason." He smiled.

Jasper grinned. "Please keep the attack on the down-low."

"Not reporting stuff to your management again, eh?"

Temple grinned, as did Jasper, and finally Pete smiled broadly.

More sirens blared in the distance.

Jasper raised an eyebrow at Pete.

"Not me. This isn't even my jurisdiction, this ritzy area you live in."

"There will be no hiding this from my management, not if the neighbors have anything to add, and if the media gets wind of an attack involving an FBI agent in his own home, the whole affair may be sunk."

"Leave it to me," Pete said. "I'll smooth the mess over with the local police."

Chapter 29

LALI WATCHED AS RAO LINED UP THE THREE KHÂU SENT TO DEAL with the FBI agent she'd met at the diner, this Z. Jasper Wilde. Lali understood the consequences of kidnapping a federal officer and the attention it would draw, but if he disappeared permanently, and with no trace, how long would the investigation last?

The three khâu stood chained together on a metal platform across a gap from Rao, shivering. Soaked robes clung to their bodies, dripping ice cold water which Rao called down on them from above with a flourish. Magic to these idiots, clever, but Lali had spied Rao's use of existing mechanics and plumbing inside the petrochemical plant.

The sniveling and groveling fools had failed Rao, which only made Lali look better. Rao was clear that locating competent people to join a cause such as the Câ Tsang proved difficult at best, for if they entertained independent thought, endless questions would pour forth from them.

Lali had separated herself from the khâu, proving her worth and securing a place beside Rao. He glanced at her and smiled, a twinkle shot from those dead black eyes. He saw through her ambition, there was no doubt about that, but she had no doubt that although he'd attempt to cull her ambition she'd be able to handle it.

"You three. You failed—how is this so, when a single woman," Rao gestured at Lali, "managed to not only gather intelligence in the furtherance of the Iron Thorn's cause, but also provided a sacrifice worthy of calling down the mighty nâga, and in doing so, granting me access to the power of their world. Eulalia has risen to adept while you three are—"

Rao wrapped his fingers around a heavy, linked chain and yanked down hard. A pulley above whistled and creaked, and the chain rattled.

Below Rao, in the gap separating him from the khâu and Lali, a crimson sheet rose.

Lali smiled.

"Eulalia," Rao waved her over, summoning her to his side. "You belong with Rao, at his side, not with those," he sneered, "khâu."

Lali's head dipped. A sign of obedience and reverence; an act, but necessary. Her move from the platform of shame to Rao's platform of radiance took only a few seconds as she glided across the walkway, her booted feet barely making a sound against the metal.

None of the khâu reacted to his words, and showed no anger as Lali ascended and joined Rao.

"Behold," Rao said, "the Sha 'Lu lashed to the platform, the sacrifice upon which the greatest of all nâga will feast, extracting the precious honey and granting access to a place both wonderful and terrible, but full of power."

The crimson sheet rose, the edges falling in as the silk broke the surface of the slab beneath, appearing as a giant handkerchief hanging limp between pinching fingers. Beneath, a man struggled against his bonds on an immense metal slab.

"Perfect." Rao reached for Lali's hand and intertwined his fingers with hers. She suppressed a shiver as the man's power arced through her.

A blindfold covered the sacrifice's eyes, and another cloth gagged him. A spare swath of cloth, a loincloth, lay across the man's hips. Rao's jaw clenched—he understood all too well that the man down there, Carlos, had been her lover. Lali tried not to think on that too much, and while Carlos had treated her poorly, did he deserve sacrifice? Such a horrible death? Well, maybe. Carlos threatened her and threatened the Câ Tsang—but more importantly, he could be an impediment to her continued rise and eventual assumption of Rao's power.

"This evening, once we've retrieved our other target, all will be well." Rao fixed his gaze on Lali. "Well with us, but also the nâga. Two sacrifices mean two may enter the other world beyond the membrane." He grinned, but wasted no time in flattening that same grin and turning his attention back to the khâu and the wriggling sacrifice upon the slab.

When would Rao deal with the khâu? After the sacrifice? Of course, they were needed for the security of the building and the protection of the sacrifice.

"We have one more task to perform!" Rao thundered. "One more blow to deal Völundr's Hammer before evening arrives."

Chapter 30

JASPER WOKE AS DAWN LIT HIS ROOM TO THE PLEASANT SCENT of coffee wafting under his nose.

"The power, it's still out?" he asked, still groggy from the rotten night's sleep—two hours. Maybe.

"Yeah, open your eyes. This is a dry cappuccino from your favorite place. You take your frou-frou drink dry, right?"

He opened his eyes, and smiled. Temple stood over him, wafting the scent of the cappuccino onto his face.

Temple had remained at his place overnight, sprawled out on the couch in his living room. Pete made good on his promise, soothing the neighbors as well as ironing out problems with the local police who arrived not long after Jasper's old partner.

Temple thrust the cup at him. "I'm not gonna hold onto this much longer, and I doubt you want it in your lap. I've heard coffee drinks are much better entering through the mouth rather than absorption through the skin."

"Okay. Okay." He sat up, and cradled the cup, taking a cautious, exploratory sip, closing his eyes as he did so, and smiling. Divine.

"We should check out the waitress's apartment, don't you think?" Temple wasted no time getting down to business. "Vance is on his way to the office and ready to handle anything we toss at him. You ready?"

"Whoa, whoa, whoa, hold up there." Jasper held the cup to his lips. "You're making my head spin—shaking the cobwebs from my head takes some time."

"That another weak attempt at a *Ghostbusters* quote?" Temple grinned.

"What?" Jasper sat hunched, cradling his cappuccino. "Unintentional movie quoting, for once. My brain's not yet up to speed." He sipped and Temple stared at him in silence.

He ran the facts through his head: the cult needed another victim for sacrifice. Had they taken Carlos or had the waitress, Lali, done something to him? Had they run off together? Or had Carlos fallen victim to the same creature responsible for mangling the two bodies they found? Then there was the attack on him last night, when the cultists broke into his condo—they obviously wanted to kidnap him as well. If they had been sent there to kill him, the fight might have gone south on him. He took a deep breath and sipped the cappuccino.

"Ah, this is so good. Thank you. Thank you. Thank you."

Temple smiled. "Okay, you done thinking things over?"

"Pretty much." Jasper spun and dangled his legs off the bed and stood. "We should go to Lali's, and check her place out. I'm guessing we're not worrying ourselves over obtaining a warrant?"

"You think your buddy Pete could help and get one from the local magistrate?"

"I don't want to implicate Pete any more than I already have. Let's just go knock on her door," Jasper said. "Who knows, maybe something will happen while we're there." He grinned. "And then I think we should check the area where Carlos's vehicle was found, and I sincerely hope we don't find Carlos, mangled." He placed the cup on his dresser. "I need to grab a quick shower."

"Me too." Temple frowned.

"I have an extra bathroom. You're welcome to it." Jasper pointed down the hall.

"Tell you what," Temple said, "my hotel isn't far. Meet me there in thirty minutes and pick me up."

"Roger."

Jasper phoned Penny on his way to pick up Temple at her hotel, but she did not answer.

He yawned and his eyes watered. The cranked-up air hit his eyes, not helping the situation. Sunglasses. His mind churned, slowly catching up. At least the air wouldn't irritate his eyes now.

Jasper tried Penny again. Still no answer, and a full voicemail box. He called his office and asked for Vance. A few seconds later, Vance provided the phone number for Wayland Precision. No answer there either. He tried again. Nothing.

"Screw it."

Temple stood at the hotel's entrance. At least she looked put together and ready to tackle whatever they came up against.

They didn't say much during the ride to Lali's apartment. Jasper's mind turned the events over and over, searching for answers, but none came. He glanced at Temple and read the same kind of wheels turning in her expression.

At least Temple wasn't attacked—though he bet Temple could handle herself with aplomb in stressful scenarios. His attackers were amateur fighters and amateur kidnappers. Despite jamming him with a needle, they failed, never getting the drug into his system. Too bad they weren't as inept when they kidnapped the little girl, and the poor woman who'd died in the car wreck.

His ears heated as his anger rose.

"Yeah," Temple said, "me too."

Good. They were on the same page.

They arrived at Lali's apartment complex, a rundown, faded group of buildings. Tiny balconies jutted from each apartment, some filled with junk, others with grills, still others with laundry, and a few with big crates for housing animals—dogs, presumably. They performed a quick pass through the parking lots and around the perimeter before committing to entering the building. No Toyota Yaris registered under Lali's name was in the lot or parked along the adjacent streets. The other vehicles ranged from rusted out jalopies to late model luxury vehicles.

Jasper and Temple next glanced at the rows of mailboxes—slips of paper with names scratched upon them and others blank, save the unit number. Eulalia Cordova appeared on apartment number 314's slip. They didn't recognize any of the other names on the mailboxes.

They crossed paths with a few people on the way up, taking the stairs when the elevator didn't answer the button press. Most of them were likely heading off to work or school, and mostly younger—close to Lali's early to mid-twenties.

Bright lights lined the third floor hallway, calling attention to the drab and worn carpet. Stains and dirty fingerprints marred the walls. Jasper put his ear to the door: nothing. He rang the

bell, and Temple moved off to one side, as did he. No answer.
He rang again and pounded on the door.

Nothing.

Jasper shrugged. "Any ideas?" He scratched his head. "Lali's
life may be in danger, or she's hurt, or ignoring us. We could—"

The door next to Lali's creaked open and a head poked out.

"She ain't in there," a raggedy looking woman said, her hair
dark and wild and eyes angry. She yanked her head back inside
her apartment.

Jasper rushed for her door and jammed his foot in the opening. He winced in anticipation of a slam; instead, the woman
opened the door further and took a step back into her apartment,
away from Jasper.

"I'm not going to harm you." He reached for his credentials.
The woman cringed, as if expecting a weapon. He showed her
his creds. "We're with the FBI." He waved Temple over. "Mind
answering a few questions regarding your next door neighbor?"

The woman's red eyes stared back at him, still distrustful but
softening. She placed a hand atop her head and shook her hair.

"I'm sorry if we woke you," Jasper said. "I empathize, completely."

"He does." Temple stood behind him.

"What do you want with Lali?" The woman yawned wide;
dark fillings lined her bottom row of teeth.

"We'll get to that," Jasper said. "I'm Special Agent Jasper
Wilde, and this is Special Agent Temple Black. We're investigating a disappearance."

"She ain't disappeared," the woman said.

Jasper pinched the bridge of his nose.

"May we come in for a few minutes?" Temple stepped forward.

The woman nodded, the loose curls on top of her head waving.

"And what is your name, miss?" Temple asked.

The woman, clad in a thin gray T-shirt and flimsy shorts, swept
a pile of clothes off a worn sofa and motioned for them to sit.

"Joy," the woman practically spat the name out. "Was Joy
Banks, till the bastard left me. Guess I'm still Joy Banks, but I'm
going by my maiden name now, and—"

"Thank you, Joy." Jasper didn't really care about this woman's
story, but he tried tamping down his lack of interest. They had
a missing person to find.

Temple coughed, sensing his edginess, and once again took over. Jasper sat on the couch, and brushed off a layer of crumbs that hid under the clothes pile. Temple sat as well, but on the edge of the couch.

Temple wiggled on the couch, clearly uncomfortable. "So, what can you tell us about your neighbor?"

Joy walked with a marked bow toward her kitchen. "Need some coffee first." Dark veins writhed along the length of her bony legs.

Jasper tried not to stare, and instead took in the rest of the apartment. Not as dirty as many of the places he found himself, but not spotless and able to withstand a military white-glove inspection either. Tattered furniture and worn rugs adorned the place. A few dishes littered the countertop. A bookshelf stood on a wall next to him—filled with children's books. His eyes narrowed. Jasper peered over the backside of the sofa and found a chest full of toys.

A kid cried—a young kid, a toddler perhaps. The crying hit an unexpected nerve. Jasper had always wanted a family, and now, with Lucy gone, would have to start over. Hopefully he'd get a second chance.

Okay, Mister whatever-his-first-name-was Banks had apparently left this woman in a bad way. Jasper's patience returned and his heart softened. He hated this part of the job—seeing not only the worst of humanity, but also the effects the worst perpetrated on their victims. The real story here presented a thinly veiled mystery, and putting together the puzzle wasn't too difficult. No one ever truly understands what transpires between two people in a relationship, or a family and all their secrets. Joy might be a total bitch, and Mister Banks an asshole. But they'd brought a kid into the world—a crying kid with no father around the house. Jasper tightened his jaw.

Joy sighed. "Sorry 'bout that." She finished prepping her coffee. "I'll tell you all about Lali, just please give me a minute." She coughed and walked off down a small hall and disappeared.

"Wow," Jasper said to Temple. "This sort of thing always gets to me. When we zing in and out of a place during a standard arrest you try not to notice. But when we're forced to take a breath and interact, slow down and see how people live, well—"

"Yeah, I know."

Temple handled this odd situation better than he thought, but she likely lacked the same amount of time on the street working drugs and violent crimes with the local police department. On the other hand, Temple didn't share much about her past, her childhood, and the obstacles she faced. Even in today's Bureau, strong females were often viewed negatively, and when you added her race on top of that—Jasper didn't doubt for a moment that she'd had a tough road.

Joy returned with a small child propped on a bony hip. "Don't mind Robbie, though he's as whiny as his old man, but he'll be okay." She smiled, and Jasper was relieved the woman had all her teeth—which meant quite a few different things, all positive from where he sat. She couldn't have been all that old, but life hadn't been kind to her. Her appearance was that of a woman in her forties, thought she was likely to be only in her late twenties or early thirties. Of course, they hadn't caught her at her best, either.

Jasper took a deep breath. He wondered why this hit him so hard. Exhaustion. Being attacked. Seeing horrible things. Yeah, those took a toll on him.

Temple stood. "Need any help?"

"Nah, I got it." She sat Robbie in a booster seat and shoved the chair forward at a banged-up dining room table. "Now, this Lali—she keeps interesting company. Strange fellows coming in and out lately, and at all hours."

"By lately, what do you mean? And can you describe the strange men?" Temple stepped toward the kitchen. "There anyone else in the apartment, by the way? Beside you and little Robbie?"

"Nope. Just us. Me and Robbie," she said and smiled. "Get you anything? Have to fix him some breakfast before I take him to daycare."

"We'll get out of your way soon," Temple said. "Mind telling us a little more about Lali's visitors? The odd ones?"

Joy held a carton of milk, poised to pour, but paused. "She had some odd ones around the past couple of days. They're all kind of plain looking. Odd. And I hate to say this, since I have a cousin going through it, but they all looked like they'd been stricken with some disease, like a cancer. Leukemia or something. Shaved heads, pasty skin. Sickly. But not the other guy—he used to come around quite a bit."

"Oh? What did he look like?" Temple asked.

The other guy may have been the cult leader. It made sense—leaders hardly ever practice what they preach. Now they were getting somewhere.

"The guy used to come around quite a bit, I don't know, a month or two ago. It all runs together after a while."

Joy's demeanor warmed and Jasper smiled. For the first time he thought her existence not as bleak as he first imagined. Her life still couldn't be easy.

Temple moved over to where Robbie sat at the table. Robbie's crying had ceased almost the second Joy had picked him up. He was well behaved, and waiting patiently for his breakfast. Temple smiled at the little guy and fussed over him—he giggled and waved his arms and kicked his legs about.

"The other guy, he was Hispanic. Not a bad-looking fella, but he wore a wedding band. I noticed it one night when I was taking trash out. He came down the hallway and as he approached Lali's door, he pulled the gold band off his finger. He didn't see me right off, but his eyes told me he knew I'd seen him take off the ring, and he stared at the floor."

The description might be of Carlos. Too bad Jasper didn't have a photo of him. "I'm going to make a quick call, okay?" He dialed the office.

Temple frowned at him. He gave her the "trust me" look. She shrugged.

Joy didn't seem to care. She carried a bowl of cereal and a plate of fruit over to little Robbie. She sat down and helped her son eat. She pushed a sippy cup filled with some sort of juice toward Robbie.

The receptionist at the FBI building answered Jasper's call. He asked to be transferred to the radio room. Harry answered, the man usually manning radio and Jasper had him run Carlos's driver license information and send a photo to his smart phone. The photo was only a couple of years old, but unmistakably Carlos.

Temple had been talking to Joy, but he had no idea of the current topic.

"Joy," Jasper got up off the sofa and approached the dining room table. "Is this the man who used to come by here? And when was the last time you saw him?" He flipped his phone around for Joy to get a good look.

"Yep." She didn't hesitate. "That's him."

"Carlos," Jasper said to Temple, who sighed.

Joy looked up, her eyes flicking back and forth, thinking. "He came around a lot, and the last time I saw him was yesterday. They were fighting over there," she tilted her head toward Lali's apartment, "something fierce."

"Could you make any of it out?" Temple asked.

"No, I just wanted them to be quiet is all. The last thing I want is for Robbie to be exposed to shouting. He'd heard that enough already."

"Fair enough. Do you have any idea what happened?" Jasper asked. "I mean, after the fight? Did they make up, did he storm off?"

"He left, and a few minutes later, she followed." Joy spooned cereal into Robbie's mouth. "The oddest thing about it, though, were the blank-like men, I mean—the strange-looking men."

"What about them? You're talking about the same plain, pasty-looking men, right?"

Joy nodded. "You're being such a good boy." She wiped Robbie's mouth. "Yes. From out this window right here, I saw two of those men follow Carlos."

"What kind of vehicle?" Temple asked.

"I'm not good describing cars or knowing makes and models. Lord knows I should be though—all my father did in his spare time was collect old cars, fix up or not fix up old cars. He dreamt of old cars."

Jasper understood. He'd grown up in a rural area, and loved fixing up classic cars simply because his father loved classic cars. But he hadn't touched a car to fix or restore in a long time, not since his pre-Marine Corps days.

"Not a mini-van, then."

Joy shook her head. "No, a four-door car; dark colored. One of the taillights was out. But that's all I recall."

"That's a big help. Huge." Jasper smiled. "Is there anything else? Anything that may help us find Lali? We need to speak with her. But if you see her, don't say anything. I take it you're not exactly on friendly terms with her."

"At first she was fine, but then she went downhill fast. She took college courses, but her classes went by the wayside when she started seeing this Carlos fella and began hanging around with those freaks." Joy shivered. "But I can't think of anything else right now. She works at a restaurant and keeps odd hours."

"We're aware of her job at the restaurant," Jasper said. "If I have any further questions, may I come back and talk to you?"

Joy's face turned, suddenly worried. She glanced at Temple.

"What he means," Temple said, "is if *we* could come back and ask you a few questions."

Joy relaxed. "Okay, but try not to make your visit so early? Evenings are better."

Silently, Jasper cursed himself. Why was he so blind to certain reactions? He intended to come back here and speak with her again, but under the pretense that she was a confidential source. He would open her up as a real source once back at the office. He wanted to give her money for the information she provided this morning. Some sources refused money—and for different reasons, pride being one of them. Many sources didn't want the money as if it was some sort of charity. He thought Joy would accept money, especially if Temple paid her for the information.

Temple's phone rang.

Joy kept her head down and fed Robbie.

"Excuse me," Temple walked into the hallway outside the apartment, leaving Jasper in a somewhat awkward position.

"I'm sorry we barged in on you here," Jasper said.

"It's okay, we had to be getting up anyways." She handed Robbie the sippy cup and he smiled as he brought it to his mouth.

Temple returned seconds later.

"Joy, thank you so much for the information," Temple said. "But please keep this between us." She turned to Jasper. "We have to go. Now."

Chapter 31

WAYLAND PRECISION DIDN'T LOOK RIGHT, AS TEMPLE AND JASPER approached it. Wisps of black smoke came into focus, rising from blown-out windows. Two fire trucks poked into view as they passed in front of the building. Temple had refrained from explaining anything beyond saying there was an incident at Wayland Precision.

Jasper punched the Charger's accelerator and winged through the open gate and into the parking lot behind the building. An ambulance sat near the rear entrance.

A group of people milled about, not looking all that worried— except Penny. She was easy to pick out of a crowd, as tall as she was and with her bright hair. She leaned, face pale and distraught, up against one of the parked trucks. But at least she didn't look hurt. When Temple hadn't said anything, he'd assumed the worst.

They both exited the Charger and went up to Penny.

"The bastards took my father." Penny's voice trembled. Her hair hung limp, covering most of her face as she dropped her chin.

"Penny, please tell us what happened." Temple said.

"It had to be an industrial accident of some kind," Penny said, "although I can't for the life of me figure out what could have happened. Machine shops are full of machine tools and whatever steel alloys they're working on. There's nothing to burn or blow up."

"Not that, Penny," Temple said. "Steve. What happened to your father? Did they abduct him from here?"

"Yes, early this morning."

"You know what time?"

"Father arrived early, and opened up. He said he wanted to examine all of the evidence so far and determine our next course of action against the Câ Tsang and the Nephilim entering our world. He'd finally decided he wanted to assist you with the investigation.

"Steve's been kidnapped, then?" Jasper folded his arms.

"That has to be what happened."

Penny raised her head and wiped the hair from her face, revealing red and swollen eyes. "But the fire department—now, the police too—are starting to make noises about arson. They're saying something about insurance money and suggesting my father is the culprit, wanting to collect on some policy that as far as I know doesn't even exist—and I'm the one who handles the company's books."

"There's no way he'd do such a thing," Jasper said. "Not with what you've told us about the, uh, you know."

"Yeah." Penny sniffled, but regained some of her poise. The anger and grief, however, simmered below the surface, ready to go off like a geyser. Jasper understood those feelings.

"How much damage was done inside?" Temple asked. "And were any clues left behind pointing us to where they may have taken him?"

A few firemen loped by, heading back to their trucks. EMTs remained in the ambulance. Apparently, no one had been hurt and the firemen hadn't found anyone inside the building. No one paid them any attention.

Penny grimaced and turned her head. "Damn it. I wish my father would have given in earlier."

"Given in?"

"It took me a while, but I finally talked him into it." She shrugged. "I don't like the idea of working with you, myself, but the world has just gotten too complex for guilds like ours to be able to operate completely out of sight of the official authorities, the way we could for centuries. I think we need to establish liaison with some branch of government, and you guys look like our best bet. So I wanted to bring you Feds in to help us out, even though both my father and I understand how government assistance typically turns out, right? Eventually, if not the CIA or NSA, certainly the DOD would get their hands on the information and attempt to weaponize the material from the other world."

Jasper blinked and shook his head. He'd thought Völundr's Hammer leanings were more religious, like Temple's.

"Well, it seems we need you now," Penny said. "But we need an understanding, and promises from you."

"Oh? You mean finding your father and Carlos and rescuing them isn't enough?" Temple arched an eyebrow.

"No, I'm sorry, it isn't." Penny wiped her nose with the back of her hand. "We need an agreement. I think you're both reasonable people, but that doesn't mean the people above you in the food chain are. This," she spread her arms, "is a secret thing. The guild has had many incarnations over the years, and to this day, offshoots exist throughout the world. We're all sworn to battle the Câ Tsang and other Nephilist cults." She licked her lips. "Help us eradicate them and send the evil back to where it belongs. If any other three-letter agency gets wind, or the military, or heaven forbid another government, this will get out of hand. The entire world might become at risk."

"That's some speech there, and the second time you mentioned government agencies and military. Automatically that makes me a little suspicious," Jasper said.

Penny looked at Jasper. "Makes *you* suspicious? This back and forth we've had with the cults over the past *centuries* has been difficult. But in the highly surveillance conscious world in which we find ourselves living, and all the gadgets and hoo-ha, well, keeping the fight with the cults hidden from the government—not just ours, *any* government—only got worse. The Câ Tsang or any of the cults would be hard to stop with the power of the other world behind them, granted. But something tells me whatever power lies on the other side would also become dangerous if in the clutches of—no offense—government folks like you."

Temple laughed. "Would it make you feel better if we signed a nondisclosure agreement? Or we arrange a pact with you? How would you be sure we'd keep it anyway? Relax a little, will you? Whatever we do directly with you will only be known by my Scientific Anomalies Group. Who'd believe us in the first place? Do you know how crazy talk of another world and aliens sounds—or demons, take your pick?"

Temple's words brought home a reality to Jasper that he hadn't thought much about. They might find and arrest the cult members, but she was right that portions of the investigation would remain unsolvable and/or unanswerable. He'd have to be satisfied with that, and so would Temple. The objective now, however, was finding Carlos and Steve. If the pattern—what little pattern they had to work on—was accurate, they had until evening before any sacrifices would be made. It was still late morning, but time ticked away, and despite proof of the cult's bumbling, they couldn't take the chance they'd bumble some more.

Jasper cut in: "We want to find your father, and we want to find Carlos as well, but what exactly would you have us do? We can't just be partially in. We, SAG, need to be full in—not the FBI as a whole, at least not for now, only SAG. You want us to help but you're also afraid of people like us, figurin' the big bad government will swoop in and steal some of this phantom power I've yet to lay eyes on. Make up your mind." He stared at Penny.

"Seems at this stage I have no choice. My father's life is in danger, as is Carlos's—though I'm still not sure he didn't have something to do with all of this." Penny gestured at the smoldering building.

"Any clues as to where they took Steve?" Temple asked. "And you're sure they kidnapped him?"

"Had to be." Penny folded her arms. "Unless he caught the bastards messing with our place here and gave chase when they ran. He'd do that sort of thing. But he would have called me by now. So, he must have been taken. His truck is still here, for one thing."

"That's a fair assessment and we don't have much else to go on. Is there somewhere we can speak in private? If we're going to work together, there are some events we need to brief you on—stuff we've learned."

Penny directed them to another building set off from the main part of Wayland—a storage building. They briefed her and she in turn provided what she could. They had no idea where to start looking other than where Carlos's vehicle was found and back to the Euclid Hotel, the site of the first rescue. Would the cult be so stupid as to keep using the same place for the sacrifices? Quite . . . Possibly.

Jasper and Temple, now back in the Charger, dodged the fire trucks angling to get out of the parking lot. Two policemen came out of the building, frowning at them; one raised his hand as if telling them to hold on a second. Jasper ignored him, and as they left the parking lot, saw Penny approaching them—hopefully diffusing the situation with the locals.

"Back to the Euclid," Jasper said. "I'm getting tired of that place. Maybe we should look into having it demolished after all this is over."

Temple grinned, but her expression morphed to worry.

"What?"

"Time is not on our side," she said, holding up her watch. "We spent a great deal of time at Lali's apartment, well, at her neighbor's apartment, and we've been here an hour. It's already one in the afternoon."

"Oh, hell," Jasper said. "We never even tried to get into Lali's apartment—we got distracted speaking with the neighbor and responded to the phone call to head to Wayland. What if there is something inside Lali's place that would direct us to Carlos and Steve?"

"Let's get Vance—he's not doing any good over at the FBI building at this point." Temple pursed her lips.

"But he can't go into the Euclid alone—What if the cult is there? He'd be out of his depth, don't you think?" Jasper glanced over at Temple and then back on the road. Traffic picked up, but since they weren't in Chicago, their biggest problem would be avoiding the constant movement of trains.

"Good point. So, you're saying we should go to Lali's apartment and break in if need be?" Temple raised an eyebrow.

"Yes."

"Fine by me."

Jasper and Temple took careful steps down the hallway leading to Lali's apartment. The light in the hall appeared dimmer than before, and the carpet—worn and threadbare—only somewhat masked their approach. Even though they figured she wouldn't be home, why take any chances?

They crept past Joy's door, hearing no sounds coming from within, and reached Lali's apartment.

The door was cracked open.

Jasper put a finger on his lips, pointed at himself, and then at the opposite side of the door. Temple nodded. He drew his Glock and Temple pulled hers from beneath her jacket, keeping the weapon depressed as Jasper crossed over. He positioned himself where if he pushed the door open a bit more, he'd get a better idea of what waited. He cursed himself for not having a little mirror with him—one with a telescoping arm for a better glimpse within.

This was bad.

He pointed at his ear, at Temple, and at the door.

She shook her head. Hopefully she understood he wanted her to listen for movement within.

He pushed the door open a few more inches. The hinges cracked, but at least the sound wasn't an agonizingly long squeak.

Nothing. His view of the apartment opened up a bit—sparse from what he ascertained with a mere six inches of opening. He pushed the door all the way open.

No rustling noises. No movement. No creaking floor boards.

"Anything from your viewpoint?" Jasper figured the game was up now anyway if someone waited inside.

Temple kept her Glock depressed, but ready to bring up to eye level if needed. Her head moved side to side and her chin elevated glimpsing a different angle of the apartment's insides. "Appears empty from my perspective."

Jasper cleared his throat. "FBI, anyone inside?" He repeated the phrase three more times, louder with each utterance. To his surprise no one from other apartments on the floor poked their heads out as Joy did earlier.

"All right," Jasper said. "Nothing over here either, and if a bad guy's inside, they aren't coming out. We'll button hook in. I'll go right, you go left."

"Ten-four."

He held up three fingers and folded them down one by one.

They hooked in, Jasper first, Temple following.

The apartment appeared empty, a little too empty, as if she planned on moving out soon or had never really moved in. A small dining table littered with stacks of letters, and two worn chairs pushed up against it stood near a wall close to the kitchen. A love seat and a smallish television on a stand—an old television—looked lonely in the living room, without the company of a coffee table, bookcases, side tables, and lamps. Only a chintzy chandelier hanging above the dining table and harsh fluorescents in the kitchen provided light.

"Didn't even know you could still get these, or that they'd

still function if you did." Jasper patted the top of the old television, a twenty-five incher if it was lucky.

"Huh?"

"The old CRT over here."

"Not everyone is rolling in government cheese like you." Temple didn't bother turning to address him, but he saw the smile on her face anyway.

"I've got nothing," Jasper said. "I'm going to check the kitchen. Then we'll hit the bathroom and bedroom."

"Ten-four. I'll keep an eye on the bedroom and bathroom doors."

Jasper searched the kitchen, finding nothing but a tray of takeout food.

They cleared the bedroom and bathroom. No one hid under the bed, in the closet, or in the bathtub. They retreated back to the dining area.

He worked through the possibilities, but drew no concrete conclusions.

"What do you think, Temple?"

She was shuffling through the papers on the table. "Okay. Another odd situation, which doesn't make much sense at all."

"Agreed."

"But if Lali is one of the perpetrators, why would her door be cracked open?"

"That's exactly what I've been wondering."

Temple tossed letter after letter aside into another stack, and took a few of the others, forming yet a third stack. "Possibility number one: Steve came here after discovering what happened at Wayland."

"We would have just missed him, right? I mean, Wayland isn't far from here."

"Yeah, I'm not keen on that one myself, which is why I put it out there first," Temple said. "Two: Lali isn't involved with the cult, but after being observed with Carlos, was targeted by and kidnapped by the cult—yeah," she didn't even wait for Jasper's response, "I'm not buying that one either."

"I'm going to check the closets, keep going." Jasper opened the closet near the front door they cleared earlier, but didn't search for clues. A few jackets, a hoodie, some gloves, a few pairs of boots and shoes, nothing too crazy.

"Three: Lali is involved with the cult, but forgot something and came back. Maybe she saw us coming—you know, your car rolling through the parking lot by chance, and ran out of the building before we got up here."

"That one sounds reasonable. Gonna check the bedroom closet." Jasper strolled into the bedroom and ripped open the closet, one of those flimsy French door deals on a track that wouldn't last a minute with a kid around. "Keep going. If you have any other ideas, I'll hear you."

The air was off, and the building seemed eerily quiet, especially for one where you'd expect a lot of people not working or if they worked, kept odd hours.

"Hmm," Temple said. "Okay, four: She was robbed by someone else during the time we left and returned."

Jasper laughed. "I bet they made off with all the fine silver and priceless jewelry."

"Yeah, good one."

"You finding anything in the bedroom?" Temple asked from dining area. "I've run out of ideas."

"Still poking around." He shuffled through the clothes and then the long shelf running above the hanging clothes. There was a laptop up there. He pulled the computer off the shelf, and flipped open the screen, which lit up. An Apple laptop—he never used one, but the display prompted for a password.

He tried a few random passwords, like Lali's name, her street name with apartment number, but none of them worked. Another option appeared offering help to remember the password.

Bingo.

The prompt for the forgotten password offered: SACK OF LYING SHIT.

"Oh my God, how stupid and simple." Also an odd phrasing, he thought.

He typed in Carlos. The password section shook—wrong answer. What? He pulled out his smartphone and studied Carlos's photo and biographical data. Okay. He typed in Carlos followed by his birth year. Another wrong guess. What would Lali have chosen?

"You okay?" Temple came into the room, no longer trying to be silent.

"Yeah, but I can't figure out this password." He showed her the laptop.

"Trying to crack a password? Good luck." Temple sighed. "We don't have much time."

"Yeah, but the laptop is offering a hint."

"Oh?"

"The hint is: sack of lying shit."

"That's an interesting way of putting it, don't you think? I mean, wouldn't we say, lying sack of shit?" Temple frowned. "She obviously means Carlos, right?"

"Yeah, but as for the phrase, it probably has something to do with speaking Spanish as well as English?"

"You're probably right."

"I tried Carlos as the passphrase—didn't work. I also tried his name followed by his birth year."

"How about his full name?"

"Ah." Jasper typed in Carlos's full name, and the screen unlocked.

During his search, Jasper hadn't found any modems or routers, so Lali's lack of Internet connection didn't surprise him. She must use free Internet at places like Starbucks. But, if she used the built-in email, it would be saved on her computer. He clicked an envelope on the bottom of the screen, but it prompted for setup. Damn.

Next, he clicked the photo gallery—the first photo interested him greatly. "Ah. Here is option number five: Lali is involved with the cult—intimately involved, I'd say. What do you make of this?"

The photo was of a sleeping man, sprawled out on top of rumpled sheets. The view was narrow, not providing many clues, but appeared to be a large industrial building. The bed rested on a raised platform of some sort, but the angle of the photo precluded exact details of the location.

"Looks to me like some sort of weird S&M thing. See the bindings here and here?" Temple pointed at loops attached to the headboard—an extremely odd headboard depicting what could only be described as scenes of debauchery. "You think she ties him up or the other way around?"

"If only there were any clues as to the location." Jasper handed the laptop to Temple. "I'd bet a year's salary this is the place they took Steve and Carlos. This is the Câ Tsang's club house where they hang out and sharpen their knives and lower their IQs."

"Has my vote as well." Temple squinted at the screen. "Any

other photos in here?" Temple clicked on the track pad and slid her fingers across the surface.

"You're an old pro at the Apple stuff, huh?"

"We use these in SAG for field work. All the typical Bureau paperwork and databases still require PCs with Windows."

"Here's a thought," Jasper said. "What if Lali is the leader of the Câ Tsang?"

Temple grimaced. "I don't think so. Look at this guy closer." She flipped back to the original photo. "He has markings on the back of his arms—tattoos I guess. I'd say tribal, but I'm no expert in such things."

"Asian characters—"

"That's a pretty broad statement," Temple stared at the screen.

"Remember what we learned from Penny? Weren't their origins in Bhutan? The cult's origins? That would account for the odd characters. You think these characters stand for words or they're simply random symbols?"

"If this is the cult leader on the bed here, the characters mean something." She squinted again. "Here, these are odd marks on his back and on his legs where the sheets cover his calves."

"Mind if I?" He reached for the laptop, which Temple relinquished.

"Let's take this into the dining area. I have a few letters of hers I want to go through."

They moved to the dining room, and Jasper wondered for the first time what they'd say if caught by someone or questioned. But he dismissed any worry immediately—people were in danger, the door was open and Lali's expectation of privacy at this stage was nil. Hopefully, nothing to do with this investigation would ever find its way to court anyway.

He set the laptop down on the dining room table and pulled out a chair. Temple continued scanning the letters and papers now littering one half of the table.

"The marks on his body appear to be raised scars, what are they called—"

"Keloids?"

"Yeah, like rippled and wavy scars. Odd." Jasper frowned. "They aren't large, but they definitely exist. Some more angry red than others."

"Maybe some are older."

"Could be."

"If they're into rough sex," Temple glanced up from the paper she focused on, "which it appears they are, the scars may be the result of some bondage thingy?"

Jasper laughed. "Bondage thingy?"

"Yeah," Temple grinned. "Bondage thingy—not my sort of thingy, but hey, they're bizarro consenting adults, right?"

"You know," Jasper said. "Was it you I was with when Lali's makeup appeared thick and overdone? You know, when she slathered the makeup on to hide bruises and marks on her face?"

"Yep, and it fits now. So the marks weren't necessarily abuse if this adds up like we think."

Jasper scrolled through the photos in the laptop. "Here she is with Carlos, so their relationship is confirmed."

"Nothing perverted?"

"Thankfully, no. A shot of them with their heads together, smiling. They don't have the appearance of a real couple to me. But what do I know—I couldn't hold on to my wife, and everyone—friends and family—thought we were the perfect pair, everyone except my mother."

"Yeah, it's always the case. Couples have a private life no one has knowledge of, and taken separately, they're probably both great people, but put them together and sometimes the mix isn't always peanut butter and chocolate."

"And who is recycling jokes and sayings now?" Jasper smiled.

"At least it isn't *Ghostbusters* or *Star Wars* references. But, really, think about relationships—how many of your friends appear to be happily married and when you're in public they act perfect and never quarrel?"

"True. Only your closest and dearest friends ever confide unhappiness, and even then, don't want to be viewed as failures. I'm learning a lot about myself, here." Jasper never admitted to failure, and didn't want to appear foolish, but in the end, when Lucy left, he had no choice but to come clean to his parents and family and friends. "Okay, let's change the subject. Too depressing—I think you've jaded me toward all the poor saps pretending to be happy."

"I'm sure happily married people, or people in perfectly normal relationships of one kind or another exist." Temple held up an envelope. "Here we go. A credit card statement. I bet she pays for her gas with the credit card, as well as quite a few other items. Perhaps we'll figure out a pattern and get in the general vicinity of wherever the S&M photo was taken."

"Excellent."

Lali's spending habits, indeed, showed a pattern. She owed quite a bit on her credit card—a little more and she'd max this piece of plastic out. Where she bought her gas was consistent enough, and in a commercial area with few industrial buildings, so no luck there. She stopped at the same fast food joints and shopped at the same places for food.

Temple pulled out two more statements from the previous months for the same credit card account and put them all side by side. "This is better than waiting on a subpoena for the records or doing a trash cover—"

"Yeah, and picking up thrown out mail covered in gravy or slop or worse." His face scrunched up recalling some of his dumpster diving attempts. Rotten food, baby diapers, hair clippings, dental waste, and at times, all of them combined, creating a miasma of muck—all in the furtherance of investigations now deleted from his memory.

Temple flattened out the statements, offering them both a better view. "Here," her finger traced a line down the statement. He hadn't noticed before, but her nails were finely manicured—not too long, though—and with not a chip on the polish. The woman had such a forceful personality that it was easy to overlook the fact that she was also quite elegant.

Jasper glanced at the statements.

"Here, she started going to a shop, the Far East Night Bazaar—"

"Makes sense so far."

"The shop must be an Asian food, herb, or supply store. Her trips there began a few weeks ago. But since the first time on last month's statement, she goes there two times a week like clockwork. Where is the Bazaar located?"

Jasper pulled up the web browser on his phone. "The store's oddly placed, not what I'd expect, but near a heavy industrial areas. They sell exotic and rare herbs and medicinal remedies. Maybe I should have been quoting *Big Trouble in Little China* all this time."

"Too late now," Temple said, "but Chinese herbal medicine, huh?"

"Yes, Chinese herbal medicine is listed. Any other obvious entries on her statement?"

"An influx of cash within the past couple of week—deposits larger than she receives from the waitressing job."

"Selling drugs? You think this cult thing is just a cover for a drug operation?" Jasper didn't think that was true, but he still held out hope this wasn't supernatural or fantastical in nature.

Temple shot him her *Really?* face.

"Yeah, taking a shot, that's all."

"Something Joy said popped into my head." Temple kept her gaze on the statements. "She said Lali was hanging around with some creeps—"

"She didn't quite put it like that, but yeah." Jasper smiled.

"What if some of the cult lived here, in the building? We should check on this building, it isn't large, only a few floors. While we're at it, the owner—we need to find out who owns this dump."

"We shouldn't go to the building manager, though. I have a feeling he or she wouldn't be compelled to keep their mouth shut. I'd be afraid of them being in on whatever all this is or having loose lips."

"You have someone you trust back at the office to run all the checks on the apartment building for us?" Temple scooped up the statements.

"I do, the same person who helped run all of the initial stuff we'd found. I'll give Mandy a call and tell her exactly what we need. You're not taking those, are you?" Jasper raised his chin at Temple, meaning the credit card statements.

She turned sheepish for a second. "Bad idea?"

"Probably. But here's an idea. Put them on the table, spread out like before."

Temple did so, but seemed confused. Jasper stepped forward and pulled out his phone. Temple smiled, and nodded. "Got ya."

Jasper took close-up photos of the documents with his Bureau issued smartphone. "There, now we didn't take anything we shouldn't have. Anything else in here, you think?"

"You perused her laptop's browser history?"

"Yeah, but the history was wiped clean. Nothing, just like the email. And I didn't find any other photos we'd care about. Let's button this place up and get going. You can drive while I call in what we need to the office, okay?" Jasper tossed the Charger's keys to Temple.

Chapter 32

WATCHING SAMYAZA ENTER THE FISSURE, ARMAROS DECIDED THIS was his chance. He'd been observing Samyaza closely for some time, and knew that the *pheon* had had little success in his recent forays into the hell world. He had taken too many chances, too often. His sensorium was duller than ever, his labrum ragged at the edges.

Samyaza disappeared.

Now.

Armaros followed him into the fissure.

Chapter 33

BY THE TIME JASPER AND TEMPLE ROLLED UP TO THE EUCLID
Hotel, the afternoon was half over. And so far they'd found no
sign of where Carlos and Steve could have been taken, and still
didn't understand Lali's role in the affair. There were no other
vehicles present and no signs that anyone was inside the hotel.
But if anyone was in the basement they'd never know until they
descended the steps and poked their heads in.

Vance pulled up behind them on Euclid Avenue in Temple's
rental car. She'd called him as they left the apartment building
and told him to bring all the testing and evidence collecting
gear he'd brought to Indiana. Jasper had phoned in his request
to Mandy, the Staff Operation's Specialist. She would gather as
much information as she could on the apartment building and the
residents. Jasper assumed she'd run open source as well as all the
FBI, state and local, as well as paid subscription databases—Dun
and Bradstreet, Lexis Nexus, and Acurint—and whatever else she
could get her hands on. Hopefully she'd do a quick compile and
get Jasper the results as soon as possible.

A bit to Jasper's surprise, Ed White was with Vance, brandish-
ing his thermos. Having Ed in the rental car was technically a
violation of Bureau policy since a rental was considered a Bucar.
But, oh well, who cared about Bureau policy—it wasn't like they
were breaking any laws, and this was important.

"What are you doing here?" he asked, after Ed got into the
rear seat of the car.

"I came down here to see you, actually." That sentence from
Ed struck Jasper as a bit shifty. He'd be willing to bet Ed had

been a lot more interested in seeing Temple than him. But he let it pass.

"Okay, why?"

"Just had some ideas I wanted to kick around." He pointed with his thumb at Vance, sitting next to him. "When I got to the FBI office, he was just leaving, so I hitched a ride with him."

Which meant he'd left his car parked in the FBI's parking area, which was not exactly what you'd call public parking. Oh, well. Jasper figured that was maybe the eighty-seventh thing he'd get chewed out for by his bosses. Lot of transgressions—way bigger ones—were lined up ahead of it.

He glanced back at the object in Ed's hand. "That your security blanket there, Linus?" Jasper grinned.

"Ha, ha." Ed pointed the dinged up hunk of metal at Jasper. "You better watch yourself, young man, or you'll get a whooping from your elder. What's worse, you won't get any of the Starbucks coffee in here."

Jasper slapped Ed on the back. "You know I love you."

Vance coughed. "We've come up with something which may or may not be something." Vance carried his kit, which dipped his body to one side noticeably. He waited a second, but realized he should just keep speaking. "Right. So, we found a commonality, well, Ed did"—he nodded toward the biologist standing next to him—"regarding the mushrooms and sea squirts. I added in the high-speed steel component and what we found was that all of them have vanadium in common."

Jasper frowned. "What is vanadium? And why do we care?" He started for the entrance located in the courtyard of the abandoned hotel. Temple followed.

"Hey, wait," Vance said, following him. "This may be important. Vanadium is a metal used to make some steel alloys. One of them is what they call high-speed steel, which machinists use to cut other metals. But mushrooms and sea squirts contain high concentrations of the metal also, either as a toxin or an aid to producing enzymes."

"I'm still not seeing why this would be important," Temple said.

Jasper paused before entering the building. "Okay, so Wayland Precision works specialty steel alloys and also tends mushrooms and sea squirts. They obviously discovered the connection—" The light bulb went off in Jasper's head. He laughed. "Of course. Penny told us herself."

Temple's eyes acknowledged she remembered as well.

"You were right, Vance," said Temple. "But I don't think any of the other parties in this, neither Völundr's Hammer nor the Câ Tsang, are aware of exactly why any of this works. At least with the guilds, it seems obvious that a lot of their knowledge doesn't amount to much more than lore passed down by tradition. Which doesn't mean a lot of it isn't true."

"So, the vanadium works against whatever alien or other-worldly creatures they think they're fighting against or helping, depending on the viewpoint?" asked Jasper. "This brane..."

"Cosmology," Vance supplied.

"Brane cosmology," Jasper said, "suggests another universe is leaking into ours and perhaps alien life is finding a way through. They're apparently drawn by iron in some forms and...repelled by vanadium, I assume."

"Presumably, given that Wayland seems to use vanadium to ward off...whatever these things are," Vance said.

Temple shook her head. "I still say they're Satanic in origin."

Ed twisted the beat up thermos in his hands. "You two are arguing about this as if it's an either/or proposition. They're either demons from Hell or aliens from another universe. But they could be both, you know."

The FBI agents stared at him. Ed smiled and spread his hands, the thermos spinning atop his right hand. "Hey, I'm not a theologian—although I know some and I'll point out that there at least two theological seminaries associated with the University of Chicago so it's not as if we can't get expert advice if we want it. But even a layman like me understands that unless you belong to one of the literalist denominations"—he broke off, glancing at Temple. "Uh...do you?"

"Depends on what you mean by 'literalist,'" she said.

"I mean by the term the belief that every word in the Bible is literally true. No ifs, ands, or buts—the Bible, as written, is inerrant. And never mind whether we're talking about the original Aramaic or the Greek Septuagint or the King James English version." He waved his hand. "To a fundamentalist, that's piddly stuff."

Temple was almost scowling. "That's *not* what 'fundamentalism' really means. But...never mind. No, my church is not literalist." The scowl shifted to a slight smile. "We don't even have a problem with evolution." The scowl came back. "We got no truck with abortion, though."

Ed tucked the thermos under his arm and looked a bit relieved. More than a bit, actually. Jasper knew that Ed, like himself, had a basically agnostic attitude on matters of religion. He could probably get along well enough with a woman who was a devout Christian, so long as she wasn't somebody who thought the Earth was really only six thousand years old—which meant she didn't believe in any science at all, certainly not the one he'd devoted his life to.

"Okay, good," he said. "The point is that unless you're a literalist you can't claim to really understand how God shaped the universe—or how many he created. Maybe this 'other world' is both alien *and* demonic. Who knows by what means the Almighty chose to let Satan manifest himself and his minions? Maybe he let the devils have their own universe—or forced them to take one He made for them and adapt to it, whether they liked it or not."

The three FBI agents were staring at him again. Then Jasper sighed. "Look. We know there is a cult and we know there is another—well, not cult—but guild that opposes them. So the two groups hate each other, but does that necessarily mean there are aliens—or devils, whatever—running around mincing people up or putting them through sausage grinders? Why couldn't a group of demented and fucked-up assholes do the same thing? Hell, if I'm in a cult and my leader tells me to stop eating mushrooms and stay away from sea squirts—not that I'd even know how to find a sea squirt; sushi bars, maybe?—I'd damn well stay away from them because I was told to and I'm a mindless freak who needs guidance from some charismatic clown claiming he's a guru or grand poo-bah, or—" Jasper broke off his rant and took a breath. "Oh, fuck it. Let's go in and look for evidence. At this point, I'll go with the flow."

"It's about time." Temple laughed and entered the building.

Jasper followed, while Vance and Ed brought up the rear. Electricity had been restored to the building for some reason and they descended the stairs to the basement with caution.

The door at the bottom of the stairs was wide open, but a strip of crime scene tape ran diagonally from top to bottom, covering the entrance. Jasper yanked the yellow tape down.

An acrid scent filled the air, but not as strong as when the two men had committed suicide. This acrid scent had a stale quality—like someone had shot a gun off and the cordite had lingered in the still air indefinitely. The overhead lights had the look of those old filament-style bulbs that had come back in fashion the past few years; they cast a yellow pall on the walls and stone floor. For a moment, old horror flicks ran through his head. Jasper half-expected to see a giant table surrounded by Tesla coils arcing blue while a mad scientist wearing a head mirror flipped a knife switch, completing a circuit and bringing a horrible creature back to life.

"You okay?" Temple asked.

"This place still creeps me out," Jasper said. "I didn't think we'd actually find Penny or Carlos here, did you?"

Temple shook her head. "If we had, we wouldn't have entered the way we all did."

Jasper sniffed. "You're right. Does this place look any different from last time?"

"Not so far," Temple said. "But you spent more time in here than we did I'm guessing. How about you, Vance? Noticing anything different?"

"The smell," Vance's nose wrinkled, "not sure how—"

"Like a gun discharged down here." Jasper arched an eyebrow at Vance.

"Something like that."

"I'm going to check the back area where Pete and I found the girl and the—" Jasper's phone rang.

Vance snapped his fingers. "I know what's missing."

"Hold that thought." Jasper answered his phone. Mandy, the SOS from the office, had dug up quite a bit of information for them. He put her on speaker for Vance and Temple. Mandy gave the rundown:

She explained that Lali's apartment building, the Euclid Hotel, and a bunch of other apartment complexes and rundown hotels were all owned by the same umbrella company, which had also acquired property within the past year where an abandoned petrochemical plant stood. Mandy hadn't had time to run the occupants of the apartment building, but concentrated instead on the properties and the owner. The person listed as the registrant of the company was Perwocko Banyang—almost certainly a made-up name. Mandy sent a photo of the man in question to Jasper's cell phone. A decent enough looking man: He had beige skin, very close-cropped hair and was on the muscular side—kind of like the poor man's Vin Diesel—and could pass as almost any ethnicity.

"Anything you have right now?" Jasper asked Mandy.

She provided the man's biographical information as well as all the pertinent addresses he was involved with, to include a home address. He thanked her and said he'd check in with her later, but she informed him she'd be leaving for the day shortly. Damn. Jasper relayed the data to the group.

"That was interesting," Temple said. "And informative. So we were kind of on the right track, but who would have thought the owner of this dump here would be the guy we're searching for now?"

"Seems logical he's our man, but we don't yet have definitive proof." Jasper sucked in a deep breath, and blew out slowly. "The photo on Lali's laptop doesn't exactly match up with the one on my phone."

"Yeah, but this is lining up for us, don't you think? What we really need to do is run through the rest of this place and then I'd say we hit the last property your SOS mentioned, the old petrochemical plant." Temple was nodding as if to prod everyone else into her line of thinking.

But Jasper didn't need the prod, because he thought the same way. At this stage, heading to the man's home address seemed futile. A sacrifice, or sacrifices, would more than likely be held in a place like this, or somewhere remote like an abandoned petrochemical plant.

"Why do you think they didn't use the petrochemical plant to begin with?" Jasper asked.

"The plant wasn't ready? Or as suitable as the hotel?" Temple glanced around, as if not believing she called the hotel suitable for anything other than demolition.

"What if we're missing something? Something big?" Jasper shrugged. "Just a thought. Vance, what were you going to say before my phone rang?"

"I know what is different about this place," Vance said.

Jasper walked toward the back area where they'd found the little girl lashed to a stone slab. Temple stayed behind, as did Ed White.

"The stone basins are—"

"Missing," Jasper said as he rounded the dividing wall. "So is the stone slab that used to be back here, the one Teresa was lashed to."

"They were here, the cult members, they took the basins—"

"As well as the slab." Jasper studied the area where the slab had been, but didn't see any new blood spatters, only a blank space where the slab once rested. He had examined the wall, marked with striations and odd ripples as if a strong force had distorted the stone.

Strange.

"You okay back there?" Temple yelled to him.

"Yeah, just thinking. They must have taken the slab to their new place of sacrifice." Jasper yelled back.

"We're going to check the rest of the building real quick, then we can jet," Temple said. "Okay?"

"Roger."

Jasper ran his fingers down the wall along the ripples and striations—warm and pulsing, or was that his imagination? The parts of the wall without the marks remained cool and smooth, not puckered like—

Puckered.

The man in the photo. His scars. They were angry red and puckered, resembling the marks on this wall—but they'd been on his skin.

"Holy shit."

The wall before Jasper rippled under his touch. He yanked his hand from the wall, but some of the stone stuck, stretching. His eyes widened. Searing pain suffused his right hand and forearm.

His eyes scrunched, and he hissed in air through his teeth.

Jasper staggered backwards and bumped into the dividing wall behind him. The elastic rock stringing from the wall to his fingers snapped back into place. His hand throbbed. He dared not glance at his hand for fear of the damage it might have suffered.

"Temple! Vance!" Jasper yelled as loud as possible.

They'd only been gone a minute.

The stone wall swirled and bulged. A red glow penetrated the stone, and intense heat smacked him in the face. Pain flared back to life in his hand. He slid against the wall, groping for the edge, but not taking his eyes off the stretching and bulging foundation wall.

The time arrived for his universe to explode. All he believed unreal became real with each inch he crept down the wall. The new reality he hadn't wanted to accept would be in his face in a second if he didn't retreat faster.

"Jasper!" Temple's voice called from the other side of the wall.

"Don't come back in here!" Jasper responded, but not as loudly as he'd hoped.

Temple's head appeared in his periphery—she extended her arm. He released the grip his left hand had on his right arm and reached for Temple's. Their fingers intertwined and she pulled him to her around the backside of the dividing wall.

"What is that?" Temple's words were forced and her breath ragged.

"I think we're about to meet one of these Nephilim."

Chapter 34

A HUM REVERBERATED THROUGH THE DIVIDING WALL—NOW A wall separating Jasper, Temple, Vance, and Ed from whatever had spilled through the rippling and pulsing foundation wall.

"I can't believe this," Vance whispered. "Why don't we do something?"

"Like what?" Temple's eyes were wide. She drew her Glock, pointing the gun straight up at the ceiling—but she kept her finger off the trigger.

"Get out of here maybe?" Vance's eyes were also wide. "I love science, but not this much."

"Yeah, I agree," Ed said. "All I have is a goddamned thermos for a weapon."

"Let me see the hand you're hiding from me." Temple touched Jasper's shoulder.

Jasper drew his Glock with his left hand across his body. He probably shot pretty well with his left—all agents were required to do some one-handed shooting exactly for situations like this. Well, not exactly like this one, where demons straight out of the Bible attacked you, but for times when your strong hand was injured.

He extended his right hand for Temple's examination.

She sucked in her breath. "Sorry," she said. "So red."

"I bet. What else is wrong with my bloody stump?"

Temple smiled despite the crazy situation. "All right, let's not get overly dramatic."

"Hey, didn't Luke Skywalker have a bloody stump in *Empire*?" Ed said.

Temple shot him another look, this one with raised eyebrows and wrinkled forehead.

"Good one," Jasper said, and chuckled. "Guess I had that coming. Give me the bad news: Bleeding? Missing any digits? Do I have to pick my fingers off the wall over there?" Jasper tried making light of the injury.

"You're afraid, aren't you?" Temple asked.

"Of?"

She cocked her head. "If you lost your hand, you'd be done as an agent."

"Shut up." Jasper's brow lowered so much it nearly obscured his eyes.

"All right, I'm sorry. You have what appears to be some lines and ripples on your hand. They'll likely scar," Temple's voice carried an apologetic tone.

"Ripples and scars marred the wall. You know who else had those types of wounds?" Jasper asked.

"The man in the photo," Temple said. "The man who we think owns this hotel and all the other buildings and property."

The wall they leaned against warmed, and the reverberations grew louder. Jasper worked his way down the opposite side of the wall from the corner they'd turned and peeked at the wall from a low vantage point. Then, quickly pulled back. Apparently no obvious dangers poked through the now elastic foundation wall—a membrane?

Temple poked her head around again—and up the other side, Jasper did the same. The stones of the foundation warped and bulged and pulsed. Red morphed into crimson and retreated back to red and then orange. The motion mesmerized Temple.

Despite the realization that danger was close, she could not stop staring at the warping wall.

Jasper's jaw dropped.

What had he seen? Temple wished Jasper was positioned a little better, like on the left side where she was. His position on the right side of the wall made raising his gun with his left hand difficult without exposing more of his body. He dropped to the ground, his right elbow absorbing the shock—she didn't notice a flinch and heard not a peep from him—then rolled onto his right shoulder, obviously clearing a way for a shot with his left hand if needed.

The wall split; not as a simple vertical split, but more like a random pattern of squiggles. Red light oozed from the splits.

"Temple, get back!" Jasper yelled, barely audible over the din of the pulsing.

Ed retreated, as did Vance with his kit, both toward the basement entrance, but Temple remained fixed at the other end of the dividing wall, the red glow lighting her face. She raised her Glock and her finger moved toward the trigger.

A burst of light followed the ooze, and a head coalesced, emerging from the split as if being born from a supernatural being.

"What are you saying?" Jasper yelled, "I can't hear you."

Temple shook her head. "Nothing. Sorry." She'd been muttering a prayer without even realizing what she was doing. She kept her gun pointed at the birthing and whatever fought through.

"Vance! Ed!" Jasper yelled. "Either of you happen to have mushrooms on you? Maybe a sea squirt in a pocket?"

"Are you shitting me?" Temple cried out. "You're cracking jokes now? What's next, another *Ghostbusters* joke, something about"—the pulsing ebbed for a moment—"the power being shut off for the containment grid and spirits running loose?" She winced.

"Hadn't thought of that," Jasper said. "Good one."

Temple couldn't even look at him right now, she was transfixed on what was coming, something large—

The beast's head waggled and pushed from the cracks in the wall. Before them was exactly what Jasper had described and she'd so far had only seen a glimpse: the form of the Asian dragon, long and sinewy and mostly red.

"Wasn't what you described hazy? And then the one in the old man's backyard was much the same?" Temple asked.

"This one is different," Jasper said. "This one is more solid, more concrete."

Tendrils shot forth from the head, bright red with black tips, reaching for something as if to grab on and pull the dragon figure through the cracks. What appeared to be two arms struggled through and rested on the floor, sending cracks shooting toward the dividing wall. Temple glanced up at the ceiling.

"We need to get out of here." Jasper turned back to Temple.

Her entire body shook, and the gun in her hand wobbled, but she firmed up her grip and her finger eased on to the trigger.

"Don't!" Jasper yelled over the renewed noise, now more than a din, a roar as more of the beast fought through the membrane. "This whole building is likely to cave in on us. Get out!"

Temple was focused on the beast, however, and her eyes scrunched—a problem she'd always had when she was about to pull the trigger—anticipating the noise and recoil.

The beast, or dragon, or alien, or Nephilim—whatever it was—spotted Temple. The tendrils protruding from its snout changed direction and reached for her.

Temple's head cleared and her eyes fixed on Jasper, who appeared energized, like unseen powers coursed through him. He raised his Glock, and with his weak side hand, his left, squeezed the trigger over and over until he'd emptied his entire magazine and Temple noticed his slide lock back. He switched out the magazines without a hitch, sheer habit, but wasted no more rounds on the creature, since they'd had no visible effect. His forty caliber rounds may have punctured the membrane, and sailed into another world, another universe—if Ed and Vance were right.

Temple remained behind the dividing wall, but hadn't made for the door. Abandoning Jasper was not an option.

Vance, accompanied by Ed, had crept back into the room and in an act of stupidity or audacity—probably both—snapped away on a camera he'd pulled from his bag. Vance couldn't have snapped any photos of the monster itself, however, since it was still on the other side of the dividing wall.

The head of the creature released a long hiss, and rammed through the dividing wall, which quivered and waved like air in the intense heat of the desert. The stone wall, rather than crumbling, absorbed the creature and remained standing as the sinewy form passed through the stone. Was the thing chasing after Temple?

Vance's camera flashed—the monster paused, then shot forward like a missile, ignoring Ed, who, for his part, stumbled back and fell on the floor.

The camera fell from Vance's hands. His eyes widened, his mouth went slack and his body went limp. He dropped to the ground. The monster streaked into the room. Half of the crimson-orange body remained behind the dividing wall, while the other half filled a good portion of the main part of the basement.

Vance cried out. His hands flew to his side and he writhed on the basement's stone floor. Half-rising, Ed picked up a loose piece of debris from the floor—a stone, maybe, or a cement-encrusted chuck of pipe—and threw it at the monster. He missed—not that Temple believed the actions would have made any difference if he hadn't.

The Nephilim ignored the biologist. It floated, its body compressing and expanding above Vance. The tendrils, and legs or arms, reached for the small man writhing on the stone.

Temple felt helpless, but regained her composure, stood tall, and raised her weapon once more. Maybe taking a chance at distracting the creature from Vance—whose eyes were sealed shut, his face scrunched—would work.

Jasper dropped to the ground and despite his right hand, crawled for Vance, trying to stay beneath the hovering creature's body—a pulsing and heaving shape.

The monster was going to do to Vance what it or something like it had done to the two mangled bodies.

A loud cry came from the basement door.

Through the haze, a lithe figure emerged. Penny.

She stood tall and ferocious, wearing a brown leather jacket and dark jeans. Penny wielded a hammer, its handle as long as a sledgehammer but with a somewhat smaller head. Temple had never seen it before but she recognized the design—it was the same as the hammer symbol that Wayland Precision used for their logo. The hammer gleamed red, reflecting the monster's own colors. Penny appeared taller than she had at Wayland Precision, and a lot more intimidating.

The creature's tendrils and limbs recoiled. The immense body compressed, the head and limbs retreating inside the ball the rest had become.

Penny charged and, taking a wide and furious homerun swing, let loose on the Nephilim. Temple half-expected to see the red ball propel off the hammer and shoot through the ceiling, as hard as she'd struck the monster. Instead, the ball the Nephilim had become loosened to the shape of the Asian dragon they'd witnessed and become accustomed to.

Penny allowed the momentum of the hammer swing to twirl her around and as the hammer reached its apex, she snapped her hips around and brought the hammer down through the arc, and up, slamming into the monster's snout. The blow dispersed the creature's head, but didn't destroy it.

The creature gathered into itself again and shot up, hitting the ceiling, and disappeared.

"Oh, hell," Jasper said. "That thing is gonna get loose."

"Gonna?" Temple's eyes widened. "It's already gone."

Chapter 35

JASPER SCANNED THE CEILING, LOCKING THE SIGHTS OF HIS GLOCK with his gaze: nothing unusual and no structural damage. He peeked behind the dividing wall, where the Nephilim had forced through the stone. Ripples and striations glowed red like a network of exposed veins against the stone wall. The membrane hardened and the stone of the foundation became solid even as he watched. Had the other universe come into their own? Was an alien now loose on earth?

He took a few deep breaths and faced his friends.

Friends. Of course, Ed, and yeah, Temple and Vance were his friends, and Penny saved them all with her father's hammer. Unreal.

Vance cried out.

Jasper ran over to the little man, but Temple had already dropped to her knees at his side. Ed was there also, hugging his friggin' thermos.

All Jasper saw of Penny was her backside as she bolted through the basement door and stomped up the stairs, presumably searching for the fleeing Nephilim.

"He needs an ambulance," Temple said. "Now." She removed Vance's hands from his left side and recoiled.

Jasper's eyes widened and his stomach roiled.

Vance's body sagged, suddenly unconscious, but he still breathed. His white button-down shirt and undershirt were shredded. His left side oozed pinkish fluid, the muscle and skin there were like ground-up raw meat.

Heavy footfalls pounded above them; a crash and splintering

wood followed, and then a squeal and screech. The building shuddered.

"How in the—" Ed said, but didn't finish the question.

Temple and Jasper fixed their stares on the ceiling.

"Lord, I hope the ceiling holds," Temple said. Her eyes were wide, but not fearful.

Strange odors filled the room. During the incident, Jasper hadn't noticed them. He couldn't put his finger on the smell, a mess consisting of copper traces mixed with cordite mixed with ozone and rotten air. The copper was likely the scent of blood and the cordite from him discharging his weapon.

"Jasper," Temple pushed his shoulder, "call an ambulance, now. You know, nine one one? I'm attempting to tend to Vance."

He snapped from his reverie and dialed immediately.

After a brief conversation, he put the phone away. "They're on the way," Jasper said.

Vance's body shivered and convulsed. That was hard to watch.

Stomps echoed into the basement and Penny appeared a few seconds later, hammer lowered.

"The damned thing fled. I caught the Nephilim hiding up above and smacked it with a little earthly hell. Didn't like my hammer one bit." Penny smiled, but her gaze dropped to Vance, and her face soured. "Poor little guy. That's a nasty wound, there."

Temple glared at her. Penny's face reddened.

"Sorry." Penny shrunk in size from Temple's withering glare.

"He doesn't need to hear things like that," Temple said. "He may understand, you know, and it wouldn't help him. Not at all."

Ed and Temple kneeled on the stone floor in silence over Vance, but unable to help the injured man. Penny stood tall once again, keeping watch and guarding them. Jasper got up and walked over to her.

"Your hammer—" Jasper studied the weapon. The gleaming head had a large striking surface. "You forge that? Or is it an heirloom?"

Remote sirens wailed, and would be at the hotel in a minute to treat Vance.

"We have an heirloom hammer, goes back for generations. Does a fine job, too. But this one," Penny smiled and patted the handle, "my father crafted himself. The head is entirely made up of high-speed steel."

"What exactly *is* high-speed steel?"

"It's an alloy. Outside of iron, the main elements are tungsten, molybdenum and vanadium."

Jasper nodded. "That fits with what we've been debating."

Penny's head tilted.

"The debate was on the mushrooms and sea creatures—"

"Sea squirts," Temple said.

"Right," Jasper said, "and now this hammer. They're all ways of repelling or fighting Nephilim, right?"

"The Nephilim react differently to different types of steel," Penny confirmed. "Iron doesn't seem to interest them, but steel attracts them mightily. That's why when you encounter them in our world it's almost always in a place with a high concentration of steel. Stainless steel, however, seems to confuse them, disorient them. That's why we work it so much in our shop. It acts as a shield, essentially."

She gave her hammer—the head of it, rather—a fond glance. "High-speed steel is what hurts them, though. It's the only thing we know that does."

Penny looked back at Jasper. "So we have you believing Nephilim exist. Good."

"How could I not believe after what I've just witnessed here?" Jasper dropped his gaze to Vance. "And his wounds are real—you don't have to be Thomas shoving a hand in Christ's side. Vance's wounds are real and he would have been a pile of meat if not for you, Penny."

Vance's body convulsed. Ed held him down, preventing any further aggravation of the wound.

"He's so cold." Temple pressed a hand against Vance's forehead.

The haze, a byproduct of discharging a Glock at and through the Nephilim, began to dissipate. Jasper reached in and felt Vance's neck for a pulse. It was weak and distant.

"I'll head upstairs and guide the EMTs down here." Penny spun and ran off. Ed trailed after her. The biologist's expression was strained. He was unaccustomed to violence and feeling the effects, obviously. He'd held up quite well, though.

The EMTs soon arrived with a litter and went to work on Vance. Jasper and Temple answered their rapid-fire questions as best as they could without revealing the true nature of the injuries Vance suffered. Jasper kept his right hand hidden as much as possible, since it didn't hurt. In fact, he felt an unexpected surge of strength course through him. But his hand, and how red it was, would likely draw comment.

They hovered as the EMTs prepped Vance, moved him to the litter, and strapped him down. Their faces were grave, and as they lifted the litter, one of them shook his head slightly.

Temple kicked the wall, and a moment later, followed them upstairs, as did Jasper and Penny.

"Are any of you coming with us?" one of the EMTs asked as they slid the litter into the ambulance.

"I'll come," Ed said. "You'll either have to let me ride in the ambulance or dig the keys to Vance's car out of his pockets."

"We can't," Jasper said, "we're in the middle of a sensitive investigation, but here," he extended a business card, "please call me if you need one of us, or if Vance's condition changes at all."

Temple thrust a business card on the EMTs as well.

"If we're not reachable, call the Merrillville FBI office," Jasper said. "They'll find a way to reach us."

"He may not have much time," one of the EMTs said.

Temple's face filled with horror, and Jasper understood she believed all of what occurred was her fault. She took a step toward the ambulance's back door, retreated, and repeated the motion again, the conflict within her regarding Vance and the investigation obvious. Ed came over to her and said something very softly. Probably something on the order of "you take care of what you have to do and I'll look out for Vance." She nodded and turned away.

"What's wrong with him," Jasper asked, "other than the wound to his side?"

The EMT shrugged. "He's in shock and may have an infection coursing through his body—I've never seen this before, it's odd."

Jasper bit his lip and wanted to tell them the truth, but they'd laugh and probably call the local psychiatric hospital.

"Look, someone from the hospital will call you," one of the EMTs promised.

"And I'll keep in touch," Ed added, holding up his cell phone.

The ambulance's lights lit up as did the siren, and the vehicle sped off.

Temple covered her eyes, her shoulders convulsing. Penny draped an arm over her shoulder. Jasper wondered if he'd ever see the little man again. He'd come to respect Vance's scientific and unfettered mind, as well as his enthusiasm for the work.

The sky darkened, as if hastening the sun's descent, but enough afternoon remained to rescue Steve and Carlos. Was there a deadline for the sacrifices? The thought sparked them into action, and they worked faster putting the pieces together. Right now, Steve's and Carlos's lives might be ending at the hands of the sick Câ Tsang people, or the Nephilim he'd witnessed breaking through the membrane and savaging Vance.

Jasper's phone buzzed; he glanced at the screen: his boss, Johnson. Now what? He ignored the call. The phone buzzed again. He didn't answer.

"We need to get going," Jasper said. "Penny, thank goodness you showed up here. We wouldn't have lived."

Penny tilted her head in acknowledgement. For someone whose father was missing and had her business trashed, she appeared calm—but maybe she was in a state of denial. Maybe she figured her father, Steve, was tough, and they'd still find Steve and Carlos alive.

Temple snapped out of her trance—watching the ambulance as long as she could. "We have information that may lead us to your father."

Penny's eyes softened and watered. "Let's go, then. I'll follow you, and on the way, I'm calling for backup from some of my employees—all of them are guild members. Give me the address."

"No argument from me," Jasper said, and Temple shrugged, as if saying, do whatever you want.

Once in the Charger, Temple reclined the passenger seat and draped her arm over her forehead.

Jasper's phone buzzed.

"Damn it. My boss won't leave me alone," Jasper said. Temple remained silent.

This buzz wasn't a phone call, but a text: CALL ME!

A few seconds later, another one followed: NOW!

And then a few seconds after: YOUR JOB DEPENDS ON IT!

"Fuck." Jasper smacked the steering wheel. "Management's function seems to be getting in the way of real work."

"Call him, he won't stop until you do," said Temple.

"I'm about to pull over, get out of the car, and throw this stupid phone on the asphalt as hard as I can."

"Great idea," Temple's voice remained flat.

"Fine, I'll call Johnson. I won't be surprised if ASAC Masters is behind this somehow."

"You'll never know until you call."

Jasper dialed and took a few calming breaths.

Before he could even say "hello," Johnson lit into him:

"What in the hell are you doing?"

"What do you mean?" Jasper bit down on his anger and typical wiseass retort.

"Are you kidding? You were attacked at your apartment and didn't report the incident. Instead you try to have your friend, Pedro, a local cop, cover it up. Guess what? It didn't work."

"Really? You think?"

A long silence. In the old days, this would have been the time Johnson yanked a flask from his drawer and took a healthy pull of whisky.

"Don't push it. This only gets worse. A few minutes ago I received a phone call from the hospital—"

Shit.

"—and I'm told an agent of mine is in the hospital and in critical condition. When they tell me the name—Vance Ravel—I don't even know who in the hell that is. And then it dawns on me—he's part of this HQ group of yours, and—"

Jasper held the phone away from his ear for a few seconds.

"—Agent Wilde, get your wiseass into the office right now, we have much to discuss." The heat of his boss's anger screamed through the phone, as if Johnson's red face and hot temper transcended the normal means of heat transference.

"Doesn't seem like there's anything left to discuss."

"Wow, you're really pushing it, aren't you?" Temple popped her seat upright, coming back to life a little.

Jasper grinned. He actually enjoyed the exchange with Johnson more than he figured, given the circumstances.

"You're purposely causing problems in our AOR, and circumventing established Bureau procedures. Get in here now!"

"I'm sorry, but last I checked I was on TDY to SAG, so you're not the boss of me." Jasper suppressed a chuckle.

Temple's eyes widened, then she laughed. "Did you really just say that? You're not the boss of me? Wow."

"Remember the time on the bricks ASAC Masters and I promised?"

"Boy, you're really posing some tough questions, Johnson. Sorry, I don't care right now. I'm busy saving some lives, but what would you know about real work, you pencil-pushing desk jockey?" He shut off his phone and tossed it into the back seat. "Well, so much for my sterling career in Federal law enforcement, huh?"

"As true as your comments were, well—" Temple covered her eyes and propped an elbow against the doorframe. "I'm not sure even my boss can rescue you from the grave you dug for yourself just now."

"Whatever. I'll deal with them after we rescue Steve and Carlos. I swear, Vance better make it, or I'm a nudge away from going all vigilante."

"I'm gonna start calling you Bronson."

Jasper grinned. "Nicely played." His grip on the steering wheel eased.

Chapter 36

JASPER GLANCED IN HIS REAR-VIEW MIRROR AND SAW THE LIGHTS of Steve's truck lit up, with Penny behind the wheel. The sky had darkened drastically and the sun had all but disappeared behind low-lying clouds, projecting a suffocating green pall over them.

The air had cooled drastically also. It was as if the opening of the portal—the elastic membrane between worlds, whatever the hell it was—at the Euclid had sucked the heat from this world into whatever was on the other side. He half-expected a plague—locusts smashing the windshield, or frogs falling from the sky. He shivered.

"You okay?" Temple's hand touched his arm.

"Yeah, well, I think so." Jasper licked his lips. "Actually, no. This is bleak. Do we have any chance of getting to Steve and Carlos in time? And if we do reach them, what about the cult? There could be a hundred of them waiting at the petrochemical plant we're headed to. I'm not even mentioning the Nephilim in the room."

Temple smiled. "You know how to maintain your sense of humor, at least."

"There's always that, though I'm not sure my boss appreciates my jocularity at the moment. He'll likely send people searching for me, shoot, he may already know where we're heading if he got to Mandy." He shivered again. "Are you cold?"

Temple shook her head. "No, now I'm warm, but then, I doubt you and I will ever agree on the temperature."

Jasper pulled his right hand off the steering wheel and made a fist.

"Your hand. It's reddish purple, almost like the sky is right now. Does that hurt?" She reached for his hand, but he held it close to his body.

"No, it doesn't hurt, not even a tingle or pins and needles like I've been sitting on it. It's a weird sensation, though."

"Want me to drive?"

"I'm okay, I can still wiggle my fingers and all that—my grip isn't weak, quite the contrary." Jasper glanced at Temple. "I feel as if I could rip the steering wheel off or crush something with my hand."

"Oh. That's interesting. I'm sure Vance would—"

"Yeah," Jasper said, "hopefully he'll get the chance."

The abandoned plant wasn't far from the Euclid Hotel, and they soon approached a ten-foot tall chain-link fence surrounding a sizable complex of buildings. Grass, weeds, and shrubs encroached upon the fence and the edges of the property. A well-worn patch of pavement remained free of growth and the gate appeared as if it'd been used quite often.

Night had fallen on them faster than Jasper expected and with it came a sense of foreboding. He switched off the Charger.

"What if this isn't the right place?" he said. "What if we missed something and we're at the wrong building?"

Temple touched his arm again. "And what if this *is* the right building and we're sitting out here screwing around while Steve and Carlos are dying inside?"

He glimpsed movement on the other side of the fence. A man ducked down, but remained visible despite the dense foliage.

His mind was instantly made up. "Okay," Jasper said, "let's—"

A roar filled the Charger's interior from behind. Jasper whipped his head around and saw—

Steve's pickup truck sailing toward the fence. Penny was inside gripping the wheel with both hands, bracing for the impact.

"Oh, Christ. I hope she—"

The gate collapsed under the truck's weight and momentum, metal clanking and screeching amidst the roaring engine. So much for a stealthy approach. The man who'd tried hiding behind the fence popped up and ran toward the opening.

"I'm getting out and grabbing this clown—Temple, start the—"

But Temple leaped from the car before he finished the sentence, closed on the man within seconds, and drew down on him with her Glock.

Jasper started the Charger, and punched it for the gate. He exited and assisted Temple with the man she shoved down on his knees—his hands clasped together on top of his head. The man's appearance resembled other cult members they'd encountered so far. Plain in appearance and wearing variations on a white robe theme, but this man wore what amounted to a martial arts uniform, a gi of some sort. Hopefully he didn't fancy himself a real martial artist.

"You have cuffs?" Temple asked sheepishly.

"I'll cuff, you cover." Jasper grinned, then turned to the cultist. "Hey, asshole, spread those knees apart. Now, bring your hands to the small of your back, knuckle to knuckle, palms out." Jasper approached, cuffs in hand while Temple moved off to the side, triangulating on the man. At least her time at headquarters hadn't eradicated arrest procedures from her mind.

Jasper grabbed for the man's right hand with his left. As Jasper's fingers brushed the kneeling man's, his right shoulder dipped as if he was going to roll. Jasper drove his left leg forward and into the man's back, sending him face first into the dirt.

Drops of rain hit, a few here and there, creating divots in the soft dirt, rapidly followed up by a steadier fall.

"Don't move," Temple said. She moved to the man's right, but still at an angle to Jasper. "Put your hands at the small of your back. Do it, now!"

This actually made Jasper's handcuffing more difficult—when a subject was proned out, the usual procedure was to have them make like an airplane and raise the arms off the ground, palms up, and at the same time have them look away from the person handcuffing. Temple used the Bureau procedure for a standing or kneeling subject. Jasper would make do, but the last thing he wanted was for this man to go into ground fighting mode. They didn't have the time to waste on this lackey.

The man obeyed. Muddy water formed around his prone body. Jasper dropped to the mud and rammed his knees into the man's side. He grabbed the man's left hand and cuffed, and quickly cinched the free cuff down on the right wrist. He grabbed the man's left elbow and rolled the man toward him on his side and checked the waistband area for hidden keys, weapons, or contraband. He pushed the man back down into the mud and checked the waistband at the sides and back as he had for the front.

"Okay," Jasper rolled the man on his side once more, "now, I'm going to sit you up. When I do, you'll tuck a leg in and I'm going to push you forward and you'll stand up. Got it?"

Rain pelted the man's head and water dripped off Jasper's forehead and into his eyes. At least this was summer and not a late fall rain. Jasper sat him up, the man tucked a leg and Jasper pushed him forward, all the while maintaining a grip on the handcuff chain. If the man struggled, Jasper would simply either yank up on the chain or if he wanted the man back down in the mud, would—

The man tried to run. Jasper pushed down hard on the chain and drove his foot into the back of the man's right knee. "That's it. Get down on the ground and stay there."

"What are we going to do?" Temple asked. Her hair, usually so well-maintained, looked like a wet squid or octopus. Normally, Jasper would find the sight humorous, but not tonight. Not with this asshole being, well, an asshole.

"Keep him here." Jasper turned for the Charger. "Keep him proned out, but you're going to have to step away quick when I punch it."

"What?" Temple's voice screeched. "You can't—"

"Oh yeah? I'm tired of this and what's one less cult asshole, anyway? Who's gonna miss this jerkoff? You?"

Temple kneeled in the mud and grabbed the handcuff chain. The man squirmed, but didn't say anything.

"He's going to do it, you know," Temple said, in a conversational, almost cheerful, tone of voice. Jasper slammed the Charger's door and put down the window so he could hear the man and communicate with Temple. He revved the engine.

Jasper nodded at Temple, who said to the squirming man, "I can't stop him."

The sound of the Charger's tire grinding rock and mud gave way to rubber spinning in mud. The man attempted a roll, but Temple kept a firm grip on him, holding him in place. The Charger lurched, and Jasper thought for a second his foot might slip off the brake, and well—

"Oh, hell no," Temple released the handcuff chain.

"Wait!" the prone man yelled. "Wait."

"What?" Temple leaned forward.

Jasper grinned. When would criminals stop falling for the good cop, bad cop routine? Ever?

Temple stood on the left side of the muddied, prone man. Jasper released his foot from the brake and allowed the Charger another lurch, but far to the right of the man. The man curled into a ball as best as he could with his hands cuffed behind his back. Jasper laughed.

Rain dripped in through the open window. Temple's glare, normally of withering quality, looked downright silly with her soaked hair.

He put the window up and got out. Together, he and Temple got the man situated in the back seat, and she slid in beside him to ensure he wouldn't try anything else. Jasper glanced up the driveway, but didn't see any taillights. Penny had never even looked back after crashing through the gate.

As Jasper opened the Charger's driver's side door, three more trucks rumbled through the entrance and over the wreckage of the gate.

"We're of the Hammer!" one of the men yelled. "Where we headed?"

"Follow us!" Jasper climbed into the Charger. He turned around and stared at their prisoner. "Where we headed?"

Temple poked the cultist in the side with her Glock. "Well?"

"Follow this road, when you reach a fork, head right," the prisoner's voice was flat, as were his eyes. The man seemed dead despite being alive.

"You better not be misleading us."

The man chuckled, a hoarse staccato, chuckle. "You don't stand a chance inside the building. In fact, I'm happy to lead you there. More sacrifices for the nâga, and in turn, we'll be granted powers beyond your imagination." He closed his eyes and smiled.

"Whatever." Jasper punched the accelerator. A glance in the rear-view mirror confirmed the mini-convoy was in effect with the trucks following close.

Chapter 37

RAO WAS PLEASED—SO SMUG. LALI HAD NEVER SEEN A MAN SO pleased with himself. He was pleased with the quality of the evening's sacrifices. Pleased with the weather and the purple skies. Pleased with his discovery of the new sacrificial site. And this weird-ass place, so perfect, what with all the metal present and a portal greater than the one at the Euclid Hotel he'd once shown her.

The smug look hadn't left his face since the blow against Völundr's Hammer.

Perfect. Lali turned from him and rolled her eyes.

"Soon, Eulalia, soon," Rao said. "The time is nearly upon us for the sacrifices to begin."

Rao's khâu stood guard at the entrances to the building, as well as over the sacrifices—both part of a soon to be defunct Völundr's Hammer. Rao wouldn't have accomplished this without Lali. With members such as Carlos, she couldn't believe the group ever truly threatened the Câ Tsang.

"Tonight we'll see the end of Völundr's Hammer—the fools refuse to gorge on the power gifted by the nâga."

Lali bowed her head, but not far enough where she wouldn't be able to keep the vile man in her field of vision. "Yes, Rao. The nâga will be pleased."

"And what do you understand of the nâga, woman?" Rao arched an eyebrow.

"Nothing, I am yours, Rao."

Rain pelted the building's roof, pinging in a rhythmic and soothing manner.

"Rao must rest."

She straightened and watched as Rao eased on the bed and closed his eyes.

This was a rare moment—Rao rarely reined in any of his urges. Lali climbed into bed next to him. Even in his most vulnerable moments such as on the borderland of sleep this man's countenance remained menacing. And Lord knew sex never had a lasting effect on him.

As if on cue he opened his eyes and glanced at her. He licked his lips—"Tonight I will drown in the otherworldly nectar, and soon you will taste the infinite power."

She dared a faint smile and a slow blink, showing her appreciation.

The rain hit the metal roof harder, and with more urgent, rapid pings until the cacophony created steady white noise. Rao closed his eyes and in seconds his respiration slowed.

A distant rumble hit Lali's ears, but Rao's eyes remained shut. She sat up, rustling the sheets.

"Be still, woman," Rao said, but remained on his back with his eyes shut.

She said nothing, but a sense of foreboding crept along the edges of her thoughts.

Footfalls clambered against the metal steps, but she couldn't tell if they were far below, near the sacrifices, or coming up to his perch. Now, Rao sat up and kicked free of the satin sheets. Lali acted as if she were reacting to his stirring, and ran her hands down his back, tracing the lines and scars crisscrossing there.

"What is it?" Lali asked.

"Quiet. Rao is soon to be informed." Rao slid off the bed, pulling his robe with him. Rather than tie it, he let the garment hang open.

The footfalls grew louder and higher pitched. A gasping man, one of the heavier khâu, reached the top and waited at the edge of Rao's platform.

"Why are you up here?" Rao placed his hands on his hips.

"The gate—" the khâu heaved, bent over, and swallowed—"the front gate's been breached." The khâu addressed Rao while bent over and staring at the floor.

"You will stand upright when addressing Rao."

The khâu grabbed the nearest rail and pushed himself up

until his back nearly straightened, but not quite. He appeared on the verge of nausea and that, Lali had learned, would not do on Rao's personal platform.

"Pathetic." Rao strolled toward the khâu, who tried standing at attention. "How was the gate breached, and by what?" Rao stood a head taller than this tubby mess of a man. He stared down at him, as if daring the khâu to look him in the eye.

Lali slid off the satin sheets. Rao's head twitched, but he remained focused on the khâu, but the khâu's gaze followed Lali's movements.

Rao smacked the khâu on the cheek. The blow, though open-handed, was incredibly powerful. The man's head swiveled almost impossibly around. The khâu fell, head smashing against the railing with a dull clang. Lali blinked. Rao stood over the khâu, whose eyes remained open, and mouth agape, twisted awkwardly—the man's stupidity transcended death.

"What have you done?" Lali ran up behind Rao.

"Yes," Rao stared at the dead khâu, "we needed him. The nâga needed their honey."

"What?"

Rao spun on Lali, open hand raised—she flinched despite telling herself she wouldn't show this monster weakness. The khâu was dead before his head hit the railing. Rao's strength remained, even days after his last coupling with the other world, but it was obvious enough power still coursed through him.

Rao laughed. His laugh was very high-pitched, and one that Lali never got used to. He gazed at his hand. "If only Rao possessed this power during his days in the military, so long ago, when Rao was but a mercenary performing ill work in ill countries and conditions. Imagine power such as this, Eulalia," he clenched the open hand into a fist, "wreaking destruction upon the enemy."

"Rao, are you okay?"

He licked his lips, as if anticipating an enormous feast. "We must prepare for the ceremony. The sacrifices."

"Excuse me," Lali said and averted her gaze from his, remembering Rao's rules, "did the khâu say something about the gate being breached?"

"Yes," Rao said, "but the breach is of no consequence. Soon the nâga, the greatest of nâga, will roam free, collecting bjang from the Sha 'Lu provided. All of the Sha 'Lu."

Lali scrunched her nose, thinking of what the words bjang and Sha 'Lu meant—honey which the nâga draw from the people sacrificed.

Rao arched an eyebrow, and reached for the robe's belt as a noticeable shiver worked up his legs and into his torso.

"There are other sacrifices?" Lali backed away from him.

"Yes." Rao smiled, noticing the terror in her eyes, something she had hid from him for so long. "Good, everyone needs a dose of fear and terror from time to time. But not you, you are not to be sacrificed—you are khäp, an adept, and my second. You will share in the glory of the other side and understand what it is like to gä—cross over to the other side."

Lali licked her lips and swallowed with relief. She averted her gaze and turned her head as to not show him the shame replacing the terror of a moment earlier.

"I need to get ready then." She walked back toward the bed where her clothes lay in a pile at the foot and watched Rao as she dressed.

Rao picked up a handheld radio on the desk he maintained on the platform and keyed the mike. What he said now would be broadcast to all the khâu in the building:

"*Report any suspicious activity. Any. A failure will result in serious punishment.*" Rao tossed the radio on the desk and walked over to the recently deceased khâu.

He kneeled, scooped up the overweight khâu into his arms and lifted him over his head. Well below the right side of the platform, on the bottommost level of the plant was a large vat with a thin layer of a nebulous liquid coating the bottom. "Behold your destruction if you fail me." He heaved the khâu from the platform. The falling khâu's limbs flailed like a rag doll. The descent happened in slow motion, but the man hit the liquid with a heavy slap and thud.

"Prepare!" Rao's word echoed off the metal roof, filling the open areas of the building, "Prepare for the sacrifice. Prepare for the coming of the nâga. Prepare for glory." He spun back around, a wide smile spanned the width of his head. "Fear works well on the sheep of the world. You must accompany me as we tend to the Völundr's Hammer sacrifices, and if all goes well, the nâga will find quite a feeding frenzy waiting."

"Yes, Rao." Lali kept her gaze averted.

"You may look me in the eyes, my khäp." Rao stood before her and lifted her chin. "You are not simple. Not a mindless animal like most of my khâu." Rao pointed at the platform's decking, under which, and a few floors down, the khâu made the preparations and guarded for whatever penetrated the front gate.

The rumble grew louder. The radio crackled. *A truck has pulled up to the main entrance, a lone woman within.* It clicked off. The main entrance was completely sealed off and provided no means of entry. The building's true entrance lay cleverly concealed. Rao had overseen the construction when he bought the property after discovering the building rested on an ideal site for enticing the nâga through the membrane and allowing Rao entrance into their world.

Rao laughed. "Let her come. It's likely Stahlberg's daughter, and now we'll have both leaders of Völundr's Hammer. I think she should be made to watch her father's sacrifice. What do you think?"

Lali shrugged. "The end result will be the same, but if she is here, I see the logic."

Rao grinned. Rather than respond on the radio to the reporting khâu, he dropped the robe, and dressed himself in the ceremonial garb he had saved for this occasion. He pulled on tight black breeches, adorned with vertically running strips of metal, covering stitched seams along the sides. He slipped into a crimson sleeveless tunic ringed with stainless steel up and down both the front and back. He opened a metal case the size of a jewelry box resting on a chest of drawers, withdrew a heavy linked chain and fastened the piece about his neck.

"Why all the metal?" Lali approached him, her hand reaching for the chain. "What if the nâga confuse us for the sacrifices? The Sha 'Lu we've prepared?"

Though Rao had assured her she'd not be sacrificed, Lali wasn't sure if she believed him. What if the nâga went for her? Mangled her body as they'd mangled so many others?

Rao reached into the metal case and withdrew another chain, but with smaller links and much lighter than his. "The nâga only like certain types of metal. But"—he draped the necklace across her chest and fastened it at the back of her neck—"this type of metal confuses them, turns them from us and toward the right sorts."

"But why? How do we know?"

"You must have faith in Rao."

Which meant he didn't understand how these weird metal-adorned necklaces worked.

Metal on metal reverberated throughout the building.

Rao went to the railing and peered down to where the main entrance once allowed entry—nothing amiss. However, all along the main level, khâu ran about in a disorganized manner.

"It's time for Rao to descend," he said. "I trust you will use your newfound power for the good of the Câ Tsang."

Screeching metal, scraping and crunching filled the building, and withdrew. A long and loud rev caught Lali's attention—

A louder crunch and the crinkle of metal buckling drew her gaze to the site of the problem, which was not the fortified main entrance but one of the standard walls with little support.

Another crash and the metal buckled in, exposing the inside of the building to the outside air—but the opening created was not big enough for anyone to squeeze through.

"Silence!" Rao commanded.

An engine on the other side of the wall sputtered and knocked. White smoke, or steam, depending on what had gone wrong with the vehicle, poured through the sliver of an opening the truck created. So much for that strategy.

The rumble of other engines filled the night, taking the place of the lone truck's dead engine. This wasn't going to be quite as easy as Rao anticipated. Lali grinned.

Chapter 38

TEMPLE SQUINTED AGAINST THE RAIN PELTING THE CHARGER'S windshield, and Jasper did the same.

Lights flicked on—floodlights—from an enormous structure about a quarter mile ahead on the right. The sharp light reflected off the raindrops and despite Jasper setting the wipers on the highest speed, the weather impaired Temple's vision.

"That's the building, I'm guessing?" Jasper glanced back at their prisoner and then brought his gaze forward again and took another peek in the rear-view mirror.

"Yes. Head toward the light."

Temple poked the man hard in the gut—an oof puffed from him.

Jasper chuckled. "Fine."

"Why don't you watch where you're going and get us to the building in one piece—sound good?" Temple tried to keep the edge out of her voice.

"It won't matter," their prisoner said.

"Oh? And why is that—uh, you have a name?" Temple twisted in her seat and stared at the man. "You know, other than useless cult member number five? That's how you'd be listed in the movie credits when they make the film based on this shit."

Temple noticed Jasper's grin in the rear-view mirror.

"We'll have to discuss who'd we want to play us in this crazy film," Temple said.

"You won't be around to see this movie," the prisoner said. "You'll meet your doom tonight when the nâga is loosed upon you."

"Too bad they didn't have a gag for this clown," Jasper said. "Though a sock would do just fine, especially an old and smelly one."

"I don't know, you saying your socks are smelly?" Temple asked Jasper.

"No, but if this joker is wearing socks, I bet his smell," Jasper said.

"I guess we'll see about that, Bob. How does Bob work for you? Better than useless cult member number five?" Jasper grinned. "And don't you think, 'you'll meet your doom tonight' is a little over the top? Sounds like you've watched too many movies there, Bob."

The man closed his mouth and stared down into his own lap.

"We already know who should play Ed in the movie about all this." Temple played along.

"Heh. That'd be great—though Billy is getting a little old for the part."

The Charger slid in the mud, but righted itself with the all wheel drive the Bureau sprung for with the latest batch of cars. A few outbuildings covered their approach, but by now, with the floodlights flicking on and Penny's head start, the cult no doubt knew they were coming. They rounded a corner and before them, the industrial structure stood like a monolith against the purpled sky.

"Whoa—haven't been this close to a building that size since my Marine Corps days and the Navy's stateside hangars," Jasper said.

"You see Steve's truck yet?" Temple leaned forward, poking her head between the bucket seats.

"Not yet."

The overall condition of the building was fair, though there were visible rust and water stains running down the sides of the building. Blacked-out windows stood in rows, running horizontally along the sides about two-thirds to three quarters of the way up the building. Floodlights dotted the perimeter of the building at the highest points. A blank wall covered the spot where a main entrance should have been.

"That is an odd building. I wonder why I never noticed it before, since I'm in the area quite a bit," Jasper said.

"Why would you notice it?" Temple scanned the visible parts of the grounds surrounding the building for evidence of Penny and her father's pickup. "When Vance and I first arrived in the area, we were struck by all the rail and industrial buildings and complexes dotting the entire northwestern part of Indiana."

"Good point. Why would I care about this one in particular?" Jasper shrugged.

The Charger bogged down in a stretch of thick mud, now about a tenth of a mile from the building. The tires spun while the engine revved high, the rpms climbed—would a rev limiter kick in? The Charger slid sideways, but the AWD and traction control and all the other bells and whistles attempted to correct for the engineers' plans for lousy drivers behind the wheel.

Grinding sounds, of rubber on slick mud, filled the car, and smoke from the friction oozed inside.

"Shit. We're stuck." Jasper smacked the steering wheel.

The miniature convoy behind him stopped, but only because it had bogged down. "Looks like we're getting a ride in the back of one of those. Let's go." Jasper opened his door, and stepped into thick mud, his low-rise boots sinking deep. "Careful when you get out, it's deep." He shielded his eyes from the stinging rain and the headlights of the trucks behind them.

"What about Bob?" Temple yelled out to Jasper, who laughed and ducked his head back inside the Charger.

"Let's take Bob with us," Jasper said. "I don't trust he'll be a good little boy if left alone in my bucar—and I'm in enough trouble already."

Temple flung open her door, and she too stepped into the mud, sinking at least an inch and a half. "This is horrible."

"Not as horrible as what is about to happen inside, so we need to get going." Jasper motioned for the first truck to pull up beside them.

The rain softened, and with little indication, suddenly ceased. Temple took a deep breath of the suddenly cooled air. Steam rose from the ground against the chill—a strange, odd night.

"Let's get Bob into the pickup's bed, we'll ride with him back there, okay?" Jasper asked Temple. Since the rain stopped, their clothes clung tightly—uncomfortably so. The heavy wetness of the clothes bore down on Temple like she wore a weighted vest while doing pull-ups, and her boots might as well been made of cement the way the mud sucked down on them.

Jasper yanked Bob from the Charger. The man fell into the mud and lay there, a lame attempt at resistance. "Hey," Jasper rapped on the passenger window of the truck that pulled up beside the Charger, "give me a hand here?"

The door swung open and a burly man jumped down into the mud with a squish. Temple hopped into the back of the pickup while Jasper and the burly man lifted Bob, swung him a couple of times, and tossed him up and over the side of the pickup's bed. Bob screamed when he hit the metal.

"Something broke," Bob's words were punctuated with quick breaths and his voice a whine. "I—I heard something snap."

Temple winced. "Handcuffs. So sorry, Bob. My apologies."

Jasper turned to the burly man. "Thank you. Give me a minute. I have to grab a few items from the Charger." Jasper popped the trunk and unlocked the padlock linking two chains together serving as another theft deterrent—Bureau protocol for storing weapons in the trunk. He took out two Kevlar vests—presumably one was for Temple, but would be huge on her. At least he hadn't turned in his old one when his Firearms Instructor issued his new vest. Jasper also grabbed a case that appeared to contain an M4 and another case holding a pump action twelve gauge Remington shotgun. Temple reached over the side and grabbed the long guns from Jasper. He came back with another bag, this one heavy and likely filled with extra ammo, but Temple yanked it aboard the truck.

"What else is in this bag? Wow, it's heavy," Temple said.

"Ammo, a first-aid kit, tactical flashlights, and extra water bottles and granola," Jasper said. "You know, all the staples."

Temple laughed.

"All right," Jasper hopped into the bed of the pickup and through the pickup's tiny cab window said, "Let's head around the other side of the building, I don't see an obvious entrance. We need to find where Penny got to." Hopefully the brash woman hadn't already gotten herself hurt, or worse, killed by charging ahead and attempting to take on the cult solo.

The truck spun, but found purchase—the extra weight in the bed assisting—and off they went. Much better than driving, Temple kept an eye out for pitfalls. She realized no strategy was in place and they hadn't done any real planning. But most of the time, when the Bureau planned, Murphy visited and the plan fell apart immediately, and for many reasons: faulty intelligence, an unexpected number of people in a residence, animals, nosy neighbors. She loved being organized, but also enjoyed working problems out on the fly and she thought Jasper's adaptability matched her own.

She wasn't sure about the Völundr's Hammer folks, though. If Jasper was like most other former military types then his Marine Corps days taught him the concept of adapt and overcome. And her entire life had been one of adapt and overcome—all the usual nonsense such as prejudice and bigotry, with a healthy dose of sexism tossed into the mix. But she'd not be the person she was without going through some hard times. Being held back made her push back, and hard.

Fog pressed down as the short line of pickups closed on the building and proceeded to circle around, searching for Penny.

"It's cold." Temple hugged herself. "But not miserable—I've been colder."

"Probably the raid vest pressing on your wet shirt. I'm a little chilled myself. So, how's he doing?" Jasper nodded at Bob, who was stretched out in the bed, hands still cuffed behind his back. He was wincing and scrunching his eyes shut and pressing his lips together, but at least he had stopped whining and crying.

"Beats me," Temple said.

Through the thickening fog, Temple glimpsed movement, but not at ground level. A strong breeze whisked by. Ozone and copper touched her nose, taking her breath away for a second.

The gray fog turned orange before her. The back of the truck sagged, bogging down. Temple glimpsed over the side of the truck—they were on asphalt now, why had they stopped—

"Holy shit!" Jasper cried out.

At the rear of the truck stood a massive figure, deep orange against the fog. The wide snout of a beast opened wide as if yawning. Sinewy tendrils reached from the sides of the snout. The Nephilim stood on two hind legs rather than on all fours like a dragon—but the overall appearance remained similar to the one at the Euclid Hotel. But now, the longer Temple stared at the Nephilim, the less the form resembled a dragon. This could have been the devil for all Temple knew, Lucifer himself materializing on earth to take his due. Horn-like appendages swept backward from the top of the beast's head—its face was wide and its eyes were white without irises and pupils. Its eyeball bulged, as if volleyballs protruded from the sockets. Thick legs poked into the bed of the truck, blending with the metal, the orange merging with the gunmetal gray, becoming one. The creature grew in size as the pickup's bed dissolved.

The tiny hairs on Temple's arms stood straight up and a deep shiver wracked her body. She was aware of the men inside the cab pounding on the roof and knocking on the cab's back window, but Temple paid them no heed. Not now. This could be the end for them.

Arms, muscular arms, reached for Bob, whose eyes flicked open. His lips curled back and his eyes widened in horror.

"But I'm not Sha 'Lu. I'm khâu!" Bob said, half pleading, half in resignation. Then his eyes closed and a look of calm came over him.

Temple, sitting next to Bob, kicked and scrambled backward for the cab. Jasper, his back already next to the cab, pressed himself further against it.

"Roll over the side." Jasper waved at Temple. "Bail out of here, now! Grab one of the cases and go."

But she didn't. She remained in the bed next to him, wedged into the front passenger side corner.

The Nephilim's arms and tendrils reached Bob and tugged on him.

Jasper scrambled forward and grabbed Bob's shoulders. Cult asshole or not, the man didn't deserve that kind of death—nobody did. Jasper yanked hard, lost his grip, and fell backward on his rear end. He scuttled back and grabbed Bob's shoulders again.

The Nephilim pulled against him, the white eyes dead. The tendrils grasping Bob inched their way toward Jasper's hands, the black tips touching his finger's tips. This was one tug of war Jasper was bound to lose.

Jasper yanked free. The beast stood upright. A dent roughly the size and shape of the hammer Penny wielded earlier resting in the creature's torso. It must have been the one they encountered in the basement of the Euclid Hotel.

The Nephilim's arms and tendril's retracted; and Bob's body shot toward the beast.

Gunshots echoed from behind the pickup truck. The idiots in the trucks behind them were shooting.

"Hold your fire, damn it! We're still alive back here!" Jasper shook—the fear of gunshots and fear of the Nephilim was too much, almost overwhelming.

The shots stopped immediately. Thank goodness.

The Nephilim bored down on Bob, who hadn't screamed, until now, as he was devoured alive. Temple covered her ears. Jasper crawled across and shook her.

"We need to go. Now." Jasper stood and grabbed the M4 and shotgun cases. Temple nodded, sprung to her feet, and grabbed the bag full of the staples. Jasper hopped over the side. The Nephilim didn't appear to even notice.

Temple stood atop the bed of the truck and stared, her mouth hanging open—the foul air smacked her in the face and her eyes squinted involuntarily. The back of the truck reeked of road kill, as if the act of the Nephilim enveloping Bob sped the body's decay, only Bob still lived.

The Nephilim's form morphed—what once resembled a bipedal form, now dispersed into a thick orange shell draped over a body. The beast writhed and contracted and expanded and contracted. Beneath the form, Bob's body ripped and folded in on itself. Bones popped and protruded from the skin, breaking free of the muscles. At least he stopped screaming. The Nephilim's orange hue turned red, and settled into deep crimson.

Sweat poured from Temple's forehead, stinging her now wide-open eyes.

"Come on!" Jasper yelled from beside the truck. "That is what the sacrifices are, don't you see?"

Oh, God. Jasper was right. Of course, this was the sacrifice. They'd found the end product before; now, they were witnessing a sacrifice up close.

Bob wasn't Bob any longer, but a pile of meat and bones covered in a clear liquid with a hint of pink. The creature must have already extracted the iron content, the red blood cells. Apparently the creatures, the Nephilim, must be attracted to iron, but they couldn't eat it—absorb it, whatever the monster was doing—in solid form.

The creature's legs, however, were still melded with the truck's metal. Maybe it was able to siphon some solid iron from the truck, just not as easily as liquid or semi-solids?

Temple's head lightened and vertigo overcame her. The bag of gear grew heavy in her hands. She took a deep breath and tossed it over the side of the truck.

The Nephilim's form congealed, morphing back into the

bipedal form, but with wispy protuberances poking from the top of its back. Wings?

"Temple!"

Jasper's shout broke her reverie. She planted a hand on the side of the pickup and vaulted over.

Metal creaked and compressed. The Nephilim shot into the air, aimed at the building. The orange form disappeared into the fog.

The pickup's bed rested on the ground—the Nephilim had melted the vehicle into the asphalt. None of the Völundr's Hammer people were around them—they'd all run for the building, apparently.

"Trying to be a meal for that thing?" Jasper breathed hard and fast.

Temple realized she was doing the same. "We can't let Steve and Carlos succumb to that fate. I didn't like Bob, but he didn't deserve that. We have to find Penny and get inside that building. I wonder if the cult realizes a Nephilim roams loose out here?"

Chapter 39

JASPER AND TEMPLE REGROUPED BEFORE GIVING CHASE TO THE Völundr's Hammer people who had scattered after the Nephilim crushed the pickup.

"My clothes are so uncomfortable right now." Jasper opened the M4 and shotgun cases.

"Yeah, I'm miserable too," Temple said, "but once we get going, I doubt we'll notice."

"Which do you prefer?" Jasper held up the long guns, one in each hand. "M4 or shotgun?"

"The M4 have iron sights or laser?"

"Laser."

"Sold. If the lights go out in there, or there aren't any, iron sights won't do me much good, right?" Temple opened her hand.

Jasper handed her the M4 and three fully loaded magazines. "You remember how to use advanced weaponry?" He grinned. "I know you headquarters types don't often pull out the long guns."

She rolled her eyes. "I remember."

Jasper ensured the shotgun's safety was engaged then opened the action, rolled the gun on its side, dropped a rifled slug in and closed the action. He then pushed rifled slugs into the shotgun's tube. He grabbed his extra bag, the one containing extra rounds, first-aid kit, flashlights, and food and water, and slung it over his shoulder.

Temple slapped the M4's bolt and held the weapon slightly depressed, angled at forty-five degrees to the ground.

"All right, we'll head around the back side of the building, opposite the main entrance. Low and tactical, using cover as much as we can. I doubt these clowns have snipers."

"No, they have these Nephilim roaming about maiming and killing people," Temple said.

"I'm trying not to think about that part."

They stayed low, using random barrels and bushes as they came upon them. A muddy patch of asphalt displayed multiple sets of footprints heading in the direction they'd decided on.

"Must be the Hammer people."

The building's southeast corner poked out almost to the grassy and muddy area they traced. The floodlights high up on the building remained on, but they heard nothing coming from inside the building. However, voices echoed from around the corner they approached. Jasper and Temple paused for a breath.

"I'll take a peek." Jasper poked his head around and pulled it back. "All right. Steve's truck is jutting from the wall, the nose smashed and steam or smoke wafting from the mangled hood. Penny is slouched against the wall of the building beside the totaled truck. The men we came here with, the Völundr's Hammer people, are arguing with each other. I think I saw another mangled body off to the side of the truck. So, either the Nephilim who killed Bob did that, or there may be another Nephilim."

Temple's eyes widened. Jasper knew another Nephilim flying about was a stretch, but they should be prepared for all possibilities, right?

"We can't even deal with one," Temple said. "These weapons are likely to be useless against those things. You emptied your Glock's magazine on one and it never flinched, right?"

"Yeah. Steve's hammer when Penny swung had a noticeable effect, though. But let's hope Penny's okay."

They rounded the corner, making enough noise so they wouldn't startle the men arguing about fifty feet away from them. The men looked up, but didn't react.

"Penny, you okay?" Jasper walked up to the woman and barked, "Penny!"

The woman came to life, blinking. "The beast took us by surprise as we planned our entry. Billy got it bad." Penny's eyes drooped.

"I'm sorry, Penny. But we have to get inside—"

"We're too late. That thing must be in there now. My father—"

"We don't know that. We don't know that at all." Temple glared at her. "We need to rescue your father and Carlos."

Steve's hammer rested beside Penny, head down, handle up. One of her hands gripped the hammer's pommel and she pushed herself up. The energy she'd displayed earlier seemed to be gone. Had she artificially stimulated herself before coming over here and ramming through the gate? Or had the evening's events just been too much?

"You're right," Penny said at last. "I found the opening, the way in. By mistake."

"I'm guessing it isn't where you rammed the vehicle." Jasper pointed at the dented wall and demolished truck.

"No. Follow me. You men, fall in behind." Penny's voice assumed the air of authority Jasper remembered.

"Hold up a second," Jasper said. "We need to plan this. In my haste, I failed to develop any sort of mission plan."

"Well?" Penny raised the hammer and rested the haft on her shoulder.

"Right. Do we have any idea of the layout inside?" Jasper asked the group, who formed a semi-circle around him. No one said anything, but heads shook. "What sort of weaponry do we have? I count nine of us, including me, Temple, and Penny."

Penny piped up. "We have a mixture of high-speed steel hand weapons as well as conventional ones like the guns you carry. You'll be useless against the Nephilim, but deadly against the Câ Tsang. Let us handle the Nephilim and we'll back you up on any cult members we encounter. Sound good?"

"All right." Jasper scanned their faces, looking for hesitation or questions. "Penny located the entrance. Once inside we need to find the sacrificial altar. My guess is we'll find Steve and Carlos in the lower levels of the building, if they stick to the setup at the Euclid Hotel. We won't have group communications, so once inside you'll take your cues from the team leader. We have two Bureau-issued radios—we'll use the coded channel the radio is already switched to—each team will have one. Temple and I are going directly for the sacrificial altar, or altars if they have both Steve and Carlos. Let's divide the group roughly in half."

Penny coughed. "I need to go where you go then. Perhaps you and I, Jasper, should be paired. Temple and four of the others can go after the cultists and their leader."

"All right." Jasper glanced at Temple, eyebrows raised. She

dipped her head in acknowledgment of the plan and division of labor. "Get your shit together. We'll make entry in two minutes."

Temple approached. "That's it? That's your plan?"

"What other options do we have?" Jasper pulled out his phone and texted his friend, Pete, of the East Chicago Police. The text was simple, providing the address of the petrochemical plant and a time Pete should rally the police and come down hard on the building if he didn't hear from Jasper.

"What are you doing?"

"Arranging for the cavalry if our plan doesn't work out the way we think it will." Jasper smiled. "All right, saddle up, Partner."

Temple smirked.

"I was already talking cavalry." Jasper shrugged.

Penny pointed at a wall—a solid wall. "This is the entrance."

Jasper put his ear to the metal wall, but heard nothing within. Wait—chanting. Distant chanting. "The ritual or whatever they're doing started. Apparently they don't care what goes on out here."

"I'm not surprised." Temple and her team stood off to the right side of the section of wall Penny pointed out.

Jasper squinted. "I don't see anything."

"Down there. The drain—not a real drain." Penny pointed with the hammer. Her strength impressed him.

"No?"

"Look, a drain pipe for a gutter, but nothing coming out, not a drop. The pipe is plugged so it won't drain into here. So, my friend, this is the entrance. Trust me."

Jasper shrugged. "All right. So Temple's team will enter and clear the first room and move off. Then we'll make entry. Penny, show us the way in."

Penny rested the hammer against the wall and kneeled down. Her fingers poked into the holes of the grate and lifted. What appeared as only a small grate actually came free as a larger piece of metal, painted to resemble the surrounding asphalt.

A stairway descended into darkness.

Jasper opened his pack and tossed a blue chem light down the stairs. No obvious dangers. They could try a flare, but igniting one would be a little more dangerous if the place was wired.

"Never mind." Temple raised the M4 to low ready and switched on the mounted Surefire flashlight.

"And here I didn't think I changed out the battery in the M4 lately."

Temple cocked her head.

"Kidding. Kidding."

She sighed. "Jackass."

Temple's team descended the stairs with her leading the way. A minute later, Temple directed Jasper and his team to come down and join them.

Jasper scanned the room with his flashlight, as did the others creating a miniature light show. The chem light on the ground glowed blue, hardly competing with the bright white lights. No obvious exits presented themselves. "Has to be somewhere. Perhaps Penny will use her keen observation skills and locate a door. Penny?" She squinted against Jasper's light, and shrugged.

A bad situation. Nine people trapped in a room with no apparent exits, and an easy setup for a trap.

"Everyone," Jasper said. "Use your lights and search for anything odd or unusual. We need a way into the main part of the building or we have to get out of here fast." He refrained from using the word "trap." The last thing they needed was panic, and he had no idea of the backgrounds of the Völundr's Hammer people other than what Penny told him about herself.

Temple ran her light along one of the walls, frowning as she did so.

"You have something?" Jasper scanned the same wall, but saw nothing unusual.

"The edges, they don't marry up to the adjoining walls and the ceiling. See?"

"I think you're right—so, poor craftsmanship?"

"No. Remember the strange dividing wall at the Euclid Hotel, appearing as a complete wall but camouflaging another area beyond?"

"Of course," Jasper said.

"This is almost the same. I bet this thing moves." Temple allowed the M4 to hang at her midsection by the strap and walked toward the wall.

"Everyone, hold up a second. Get ready." Jasper motioned with his arms for them to quiet down, like a quarterback did for the home crowd when they got too excited.

Temple put her shoulder into the wall, but the structure didn't budge. Penny trotted over and rammed into the wall. The metal squealed, and moved. Tracks appeared on the floor and the wall rolled on tiny wheels for about five feet, revealing two doors, one on the left, the other on the right.

"Temple's team will go right, mine and Penny's left." Jasper stacked his team on the left door and Temple did the same on the right. He gripped the handle and pushed down. The door pulled free easily. He glanced over at Temple—her door did the same. So far, so good.

Temple poked her head inside the door. "Hallway over here, light at the end."

Jasper glanced inside his door. "Same here. They likely lead to the same place, don't you think?"

"Probably."

"All right, see you on the other side." Jasper led his team through the door and into the dimly lit hallway, the only light supplied by whatever was shining on the other end.

Thirty seconds later, Jasper peered through the opening and glanced to the right where Temple should be poking her head through. He waited a few more seconds. Nothing. He keyed the radio. "Temple, you read?" Nothing. Bad. "Temple." This time static answered him. She'd obviously heard him transmit, but had she heard the words or heard him simply keying the mike? Ugh. He took a deep breath and took another peek, this time for intelligence purposes.

He turned back to his team. "Large area. I believe we're already on the lowest level so I wouldn't be surprised if we find the sacrificial altar here. There is extensive scaffolding above us, a few platforms, as well as an entire level comprised of metal flooring, not solid, but like a grate."

He didn't know how to explain the layout. Once inside, the team would see and hopefully adjust. A few vats as well, decent cover if empty, but if full of flammables, they'd be screwed. The perfect setup for a trap or ambush.

Something was missing or amiss, but whatever it was eluded him. For such a large building the noise level was certainly low—the chanting ceased. More bad. The cultists probably laid in wait for them in elevated positions.

On second thought—maybe not—the elevated position was a military tactic, not a bunch of untrained goons who, so far, displayed zero fighting prowess. Their leader, however, might have military training of some sort, but again, the odds were against the notion based on the Câ Tsang's performance so far.

Jasper turned to Penny. "I don't see Temple's team. The hallway they entered must lead elsewhere."

Penny remained unfazed. The woman recovered, or hid pain well, and compartmentalized. Both FBI and military preached compartmenting problems—specifically in not allowing personal feelings to get in the way of the mission.

"We can't stand around here all day." Penny straightened. "Temple's team has their orders and so do we. Let's get going."

All right. Jasper led the team from the hallway into the greater hall of the building. From this position, much of the building's structure was visible—at least the upper levels. Down here, in what he believed was the lowest level, presented doors on both sides, more areas to clear. The last thing they needed was for the enemy to cut them off or come up on their rear.

"Before we go farther, we need to clear the rooms down here." Jasper directed his team to break into smaller units of two. Penny took one man, and Jasper the other. No knock and announce, but a decisive entry—there was simply no time to fool around.

"What's your name?" Jasper asked his new temporary partner.

"Ian."

"All right, you know what a button hook entry is?"

"I do."

"Former cop or military?" Jasper raised an eyebrow.

Ian blushed. "No. 'Fraid not. Video games."

"Ah. Works in a pinch, I suppose. I'll go right. You go left. No itchy trigger finger."

"Yes, sir." The man's finger crept toward the trigger of a Colt 1911.

"You've shot your Colt before, I hope?"

"At the range, yes." Ian grinned.

The grin was reassuring, anyway. Jasper took a deep breath. "Here we go." He flung the door open and ran in, shotgun ready below eye level, but easy enough to raise if need be. "Ian, do not even think about discharging your weapon in here."

"Huh?"

Shelves lined the room from floor to ceiling. Boxes and crates crowded the floor in the center. No cultists hid in the room and, thank goodness, no Nephilim. The room did contain, however, all the ingredients for thermite, save the catalyst. Ugly. This one room and the amounts of chemicals here were capable of bringing down the entire building. Jasper had witnessed the results of thermite on vehicles during his time in the Marine Corps.

"Thermite. What the hell is their obsession with thermite about?"

"What in the blazes is thermite?" Ian asked.

Jasper chuckled. "Are you English?"

"By origin, yes, but an ex-pat now. Been living in the States for years, ditched most of my accent."

"Well, blazes is about right with thermite. The cultists destroy themselves with the stuff when cornered."

"Will the stuff blow?"

"Not spontaneously, and thermite doesn't exactly blow up." Jasper examined the shelves for other chemicals, finding a few jars and bottles containing unidentifiable powders. Maybe the cult leader mixed his own vile concoctions. Something he hadn't thought of before popped into his mind: someone in the cult, probably the leader, was either a chemist or had been exposed to thermite via military duty. Other reasons existed, he supposed, for understanding and using thermite—Internet searches and so forth, chemistry forums, disgruntled-jackasses-who-want-to-burn-shit-to-the-ground forums. "Anyway, thermite creates an intense exothermic reaction, generating extreme heat. Enough to break a human body down into powder."

"Oh." Ian backed toward the door.

"Let's move on, we have other rooms to clear."

Ian was out the door before Jasper finished the sentence.

The other two rooms contained simple supplies, such as dried and canned foods, and water—survivalist type gear. Perhaps a bunker existed below the level they now stood, so the cult could wait out the Nephilim apocalypse they were trying to incite—if that was what they were doing in the first place. It was difficult to figure out the thinking of a cult.

Jasper shivered. Not a good thought—but anything was possible now.

Jasper and Ian met with Penny and her partner after clearing the rooms on their side. Penny had found a half empty weapons locker, but nothing else. The group concluded and assumed the cultists were armed with small arms and thermite for the purposes of suicide.

"What now?" Penny asked. "We're going up, right? I don't think the altar is down here."

Jasper's radio crackled.

"Jasper, this is Temple, do you read?" It was a weak signal and full of static, but the words came through.

"I read. Go ahead."

"We've located where the sacrifices are to take place. From our vantage point below the area, we believe two people are on the platform for sacrifice—but can't see if it's Steve and Carlos."

"Ten-four, are you moving to free them?"

"Heavily guarded. Wait. Someone is descending a long stair toward the area. We're pulling back."

Jasper's body tingled. The idea struck him hard, but this was the right thing to do.

"I have an idea. I'm going to create a distraction."

"How?"

"Fall back and meet up with Penny and her group. I'm off to gather materials for creating a ruckus."

"Wait—"

"Don't worry, I'll find you. I'm not trying to trade my life—I'm not desperate yet."

The radio keyed and Temple's sigh came through crackling. *"Roger."*

"Great, now get ready to free Steve. I haven't seen any Nephilim since we've been in here, have you?"

"No. And that worries me."

"Not much we can do about them, anyway. I'm sending Penny to you. Meet back where the two groups split up. Out."

Jasper turned to Penny, who simply nodded and waved the two men with her to follow. Ian went with them. They disappeared back down the hallway to the area they'd split from Temple. Jasper glanced at his watch—Pete and the cavalry would descend on the place in another thirty minutes or so and he didn't necessarily want the attention of the locals here.

He ran back to the room where the thermite materials were stored.

Chapter 40

LALI CREPT DOWN THE METAL STAIRS. SHE'D LEFT RAO, WHO HAD secreted himself in an antechamber off the sacrificial area. Directly below her was the platform upon which both Steve and Carlos were tied.

She stared down at them. Lali harbored no animosity toward the man named Steve, for he'd done nothing wrong other than belong to what Rao described as their mortal enemy—Völundr's Hammer. Carlos belonged to the Hammer too but he'd also hurt her, and proved to be a lying sack of shit. She bit her bottom lip; then, sucked in a deep breath through her nose and released it. Still, she thought killing Carlos or serving him up for lunch to whatever Rao was summoning was over the top. She wasn't *that* pissed at the bastard.

Calm.

Lali desired calm. She'd come to question Rao's sanity altogether by now. He was volatile and unpredictable. But the power drew her, seduced her—she was about to witness the power of the nâga. Rao's strength impressed her, but the same power in the hands of an intelligent and capable street-smart woman? Unstoppable. She grinned. Her grandmother would have told her not to break her arm patting herself on the back—and would have completely disapproved of what she was doing.

Carlos moaned. Her ex's drug-induced stupor would soon end, and Steve's would follow.

Khâu surrounded the two sacrifices, the two Sha 'Lu. Soon the nâga would drink of their honey, their bjang, and leave them as lifeless piles of meat and bones. Witnessing the feeding didn't interest or fascinate her, but Rao insisted. The sacrifice was inevitable, as was Rao's ascent, but Lali desired the power and would rob Rao of the glory at the first opportunity.

Creaking metal from high in the rafters caught her attention. The half dozen khâu standing guard over the sacrifices glanced up as well. Wispy remnants of smoke, left over from the idiot who had driven the truck into the side of the building no doubt, wafted throughout the ceiling's metal bracings and cross members, but the acrid stench hung in the still air.

Carlos moaned again, drawing her gaze back to the pathetic man. His eyes opened, he licked his lips, and his head lolled. His blinking eyes focused on her, and widened.

"What—what have you done?"

"Quiet. You will soon understand," one of the khâu replied in their creepy monotone way.

Lali hated the drugging—they'd drugged her as well when the cult kidnapped her. But she enjoyed most of the other duties she performed in the service of the Câ Tsang. It was certainly better than waitressing and better than finishing her education, even though she'd been close to a two-year degree.

"You, khâu," Lali said. "Gag him. I don't want to hear anything come out of his filthy mouth."

"With what?" the khâu asked. Most of the cult members often seemed half-mindless. Lali had wondered where they came from, with their weirdly similar appearance, but she'd never found out. That was another secret Rao kept to himself.

She rolled her eyes. "Use a sock. Rip or cut some of your clothing. I don't care. Gag him, now." Lali glared at the khâu, then at Carlos. "You're about to pay for your sins. The nâga will feast upon your honey."

Carlos's eyes filled with terror.

Lali smirked. To think, the FBI agents came so close to finding her in the apartment when they came looking for her. The stupid simpering neighbor of hers had unwittingly distracted them. She had Carlos stuffed into the hatchback of her Yaris—parked a block away in an underground garage of another apartment building.

"Lali." Rao emerged from his antechamber, his voice boomed from above her. She spun.

Rao stood above them all, resplendent in a lavish crimson robe. Under it he wore his leather with all the shiny metal. The chain about his neck gleamed. He spread his arms as if embracing the world.

"Khâu, attend to your duties. The enemy is near, but so is the nâga. We will soon witness the greatest portal ever opened and the greatest of nâga." Rao lowered his arms with a flourish.

The bright lights inside the building extinguished, replaced by soft red light from sporadically placed bulbs. Rao must be controlling the light show with a foot switch or some app on his smartphone. This likely impressed the khâu, but Lali thought the theatrics a little ho-hum.

The khâu chanted.

Rao tossed a sack from his perch, which burst upon smacking the sacrificial slab, scattering powder everywhere.

Lali had no idea what that was for, but—

Chapter 41

JASPER FRANTICALLY SEARCHED FOR A CATALYST—THE THERMITE wouldn't be thermite without it, just another pile of chemicals. He emptied a crate of its contents and layered the wooden container with the necessary components, save for the catalyst. He pushed the crate into the open area, narrowly escaping the gaze of a cultist above. He heard a woman's voice. It could have been that of the waitress, Lali, whom they'd searched for at the apartment earlier, but with the echoes it was hard to tell. Hopefully, her voice would distract the cultists from catching him roaming about.

The catalyst was not in the room with the rest of the components—the cult was that smart at least, so why was *he* still searching there?

The second room searched contained mainly survivalist gear, but he ransacked the room, and behold—a container typically used for cooking oil held the proper catalyst for kicking the thermite into gear.

Jasper attached the container to his extra gear pack, slung the shotgun over his other shoulder, and pushed the crate. The cultists above remained turned away from where he'd be moving the crate and faced inward—he guessed in the direction of Steve and Carlos, and the area of sacrifice.

He considered using his shotgun as a distraction. But one slug wouldn't cause enough damage. Thermite, however, would wreak destruction on the building, requiring the cult's attentions.

He put his back into pushing the crate toward one of the giant vats on this level of the building. If there were anything in the vat, it'd cause quite a mess when the thermite ate the metal.

A voice boomed from above: "Lali." A few seconds later the booming voice added: "Khâu, attend to your duties. The enemy is near, but so is the nâga. We will soon witness the greatest portal ever opened and the greatest of nâga."

Must be the cult's leader.

The bright lights dimmed, replaced by the glow of red. Perfect. The cult couldn't be making this easier for him. However, that also indicated the time was near and both Steve's and Carlos's minutes were numbered.

Chanting fired back up, and for a moment, he pictured the scene as a modern Temple of Doom. He grinned. Temple. She'd likely have a hand in making this a temple of destruction before the evening ended. Say whatever else you would about the woman, she could be tough as nails.

Humming. No, thrumming reverberated down through the metal as Jasper pushed the crate full of chemicals toward the vat. His breathing labored under the load of his pack, shotgun, and the effort of shoving the crate. At least the chanting and dim lights covered his approach—unless these cultists possessed cat vision or night vision goggles.

A few seconds later, the vat filled his vision, and up close, appeared much larger. He jammed the crate up against the vat, positioning the wood container so not only would the thermite eat the vat, but a support structure for some of the metal walkways surrounding the vat. Once ignited, the thermite's odds of pulling down a good part of the metal structures on this side of the building were excellent. The reaction was far enough away, if he'd gauged the volume of the cultists' conversations properly, that Steve and Carlos, as well as Temple and the team, wouldn't be affected. But the echoes and size of the building was deceptive. No time remained for anything else, any other plan.

He dropped the pack off his shoulder, removed the container with the catalyst and twisted off the cap. He grabbed his pack, put it back on his shoulder. Next, he pulled the lid off the crate and stepped back.

Jasper paused, and lifted the open container.

"Here goes—"

He tossed the open container into the crate.

The thermite reacted immediately as the catalyst sloshed

from the container and into the stratified layers of chemicals in the crate.

Intense heat radiated, pushing Jasper back, while he shielded his face and turned away, wincing—

—two cultists ran toward him.

The heat behind him intensified, hot against his back—even through the Kevlar vest and still-damp garments. Shouts and clamoring echoed from above, fighting with the sizzling and roar of the thermite consuming all the metal it contacted.

Jasper pulled the shotgun off his shoulder and aimed the barrel at the cultists closing on him. They showed no hint of hesitation or slowing.

No warning shots. He squeezed the trigger, but unlike the Glock trigger's slack, the Remington shotgun's trigger had none, and the bang surprised him—a good thing.

The midsection of the cultist on the left blossomed red from the slug. The man's eyes widened—

—Jasper racked the shotgun and loosed another shot.

The cultist fell, bleeding profusely from his ravaged midsection.

The second cultist skidded to a halt, but fell on his ass and scrambled backward, kicking his feet and flailing with his arms, attempting purchase on the cement flooring.

Jasper bit his lip. Was this man still a threat? Not by the standard Bureau deadly force policy. If the man were armed and scrambling for cover in order to kill, yes—Jasper closed on the man, getting within ten feet before—

—the cultist rolled over on his stomach, got his feet under him and attempted to run. Jasper leaped and grabbed the man by his legs, pulling him back down. He would have preferred cuffing, but he had no time. "Sorry about this—" Jasper rammed the man's head with the butt of the shotgun. The man went limp, but still breathed and had a pulse. At least he wasn't dead, unlike the other man who—

A wall of heat crushed Jasper. The metal support structure and walkways burned and melted from the thermite. Creaking metal, fatigued and failing, crashed to the floor. The vat, surprisingly, had not yet given way.

The thermite reaction plumed at an angle, like a tilted roman candle. The vat's side weakened and ruptured.

The vat's contents remained a mystery, but regardless, his proximity demanded a little more distance in case of a random explosion. He took small steps back, morbidly curious as to what results would come about from lighting off the thermite.

Liquid poured onto the thermite. A petrochemical like gasoline only added to the mess. The explosive capability rested in fumes if present, but he smelled no overwhelming gas vapors near the vat.

The thermite reaction brightened. The vat collapsed. Jasper backed away. His training hit him—training he'd received more than a decade earlier while in the Marine Corps.

He spun and ran for the hallway.

Not a lot of liquid spilled from the vat, but pipes—many pipes fed into the vat—and with little liquid fuel, vapors existed in the pipes—

Jasper dove for the doorway, with no idea what might occur—explosion or collapse or both.

Heat touched his back as he slid through the doorway. The angle at which he landed, coupled with the momentum, rolled him on his back.

The blast concussed—an ear-crushing but mercifully short-duration *wooooof*, as if all the air in the building had been sucked through a hole in the roof. The fireball puffed and expanded as it escaped the wrecked vat and filled the upper reaches of the hangar-height building.

"Holy shit." Jasper shielded his scrunched eyes reflexively and winced.

Screams cut through the din.

A deep *wooosh*, like wind through a pipe surrounded him and likely most of the pipes running through the plant.

"Oh my God, what I have done?" Jasper shielded himself completely in the room, shutting the door, but the sounds of destruction remained. He hoped he hadn't killed Temple and Penny and all the Völundr's Hammer folks.

The burning fluids and vapors within the pipes whooshed and when they ran out of room, no longer allowed expansion—

Twisting, crumpling metal crashed beyond the door he hid behind. High pitched whirs and thunks from bursting pipes flung debris—Jasper did not need to see the destruction to understand what happened out there. His eardrums rang and a high-pitched tone rang in both ears.

The red light in the room extinguished. He flicked on his Surefire flashlight. Metal clanks and groans pierced the crack beneath the door.

The wall before him buckled and gave way.

He rolled over and covered his head, attempting to gather himself into a ball.

Arms, legs, back, and head ached.

The building shuddered. Metal creaked and groaned. Heat filtered through the empty spaces. A fireball erupted, followed by an ear-shattering blast and a sucking *whooosh*.

Temple's knees buckled. Penny winced. The men with them covered their ears, pained expressions on their faces.

"What did Jasper do?" Temple hissed at Penny, who shrugged.

"He didn't tell me his plan, but wow, what a distraction."

There was no way Jasper had survived that, no way. Temple's body shook. Anger mixed with fear and sadness. "Should never have let him go off on his own," she muttered.

"You think words over a radio would have persuaded him?" Penny asked.

"No." Temple keyed the radio, "Jasper, you okay? Jasper, say something. Grunt. Anything." She released the key, and waited. Nothing. Nothing. *Damn. Damn. Damn.*

"Now is the time," Penny said. "We're all here—well, you know—"

"Yeah, I know." Temple took a deep breath. Her team had merged with Penny's, ready to surge forward when Jasper's distraction came through.

"I'm going to keep trying him," Temple said. "Penny, go to his last known position, please."

Penny sighed. "But what about my father? We know his condition and we don't have time for—"

"Please," Temple pleaded. She had thought Penny had shown more than a passing interest in Jasper, but who was she kidding—of course blood would be thicker in this case, right?

"I'll go," Penny said, "I just hope he hasn't brought down the entire building on us."

She glanced around, as did Temple, both assessing the damage, and possible future damage from the weakening metal surrounding them.

Temple keyed the radio once Penny had moved off from the main group. Nothing.

"All right," Temple addressed the group, "let's go. We have to hit these bastards hard."

She tried one more time to reach Jasper on the radio, but released the radio's mic key and stared upward, mouthing, "Oh, my God."

A Nephilim swirled about above them, and descended as a line of cultists armed with all manner of weapons had taken positions above them. A storm erupted, a storm of screams and the booms and crackles of firearms.

Drips smattered Jasper's face, lukewarm, but a steady tap, tap, tap.

He opened his eyes, red light oozed through, likely from somewhere beyond the room since the wall had collapsed. His arms were under him, so he pushed up—

—but couldn't. He twisted his head, but met resistance. Trapped. Beneath what? The thermite and mini-explosions from the fumes and vapors attempting to vent had brought down quite a bit of the metal scaffolding and platforms then. He moved his legs and arms. Relief. Nothing beyond simple aches. Lucky.

His radio crackled. *"Jasper. This is Temple. You okay?"*

The mike head was at his shoulder, but he couldn't reach the damn thing. His arms ached; everything ached. He couldn't answer Temple. Damn.

"Jasper, answer. Please." Temple's desperation came through in her transmission. *"Jasper. Whatever you did worked—but I think I see a Nephilim up above. The ritual—"*

The radio cut out.

Metal moved above him and to his left side.

He wriggled. The cultists must have come for him.

The red light brightened, but burning white light replaced the red. A flashlight bore down on him.

"Jasper," a gruff, but definitely feminine voice said.

Not cultists. Penny.

"How bad?" Jasper asked, unsure of how loud he'd asked the question. The ringing in his ears was maddening.

Another piece of metal or debris or whatever lifted off him, and his breaths grew easier.

"There you go. Can you move?" Penny reached for him with one of her strong hands.

"Yeah, but how bad is everything else?" Jasper grasped Penny's hand and the woman displayed her strength, yanking him free. Jasper winced and grabbed his side, hissing in a breath.

"Your side is scalded," Penny said, "ooh, and your face, well, let's just say one side resembles my father's." She shook her head. "I imagine yours'll heal."

"I don't care, did I kill any friendlies and how bad is the building?"

"Still standing, though you managed to take out a few of those cultists, but we need to go. Can you stand on your own?" Penny released him.

Jasper wobbled and staggered. He glanced about for his shotgun, but couldn't see where the weapon rested. His pack was crushed against him. It was wet—a water bottle had probably busted.

"Steve and Carlos?" Jasper staggered to a wall and propped himself up.

"Up there," Penny motioned with her head. "Temple, along with the others are engaging the remaining cultists, but having a hard time getting onto the platform where my father and Carlos are tied up."

"The sacrifice? I mean, the ritual?"

"You haven't been out of the action long, the fireball happened only a couple of minutes ago. Temple sent me back to help you when whatever damn thing you did flared. Did you expect the sort of reaction you got?" Penny stood in the doorway. "You've blocked that way quite well." The blonde woman pointed behind Jasper, where the thermite continued burning, despite bringing down half the building's interior.

"I didn't expect the fireball or the amount of destruction." Jasper took a deep breath, the air a sickly mixture of cordite, burnt flesh, copper, and the strange ozone. He glanced at the ceiling. Smoke roiled and turned along the ceiling, white and black and gray, but tinged with crimson. "Shit. I think one of the Nephilim is up there. We have to get to your father and Carlos. Now."

Penny grabbed his arm and pulled him through the doorway with him to rejoin Temple.

Chapter 42

LALI STRUGGLED TO HER FEET. THE BLAST HAD BLOWN HER sideways and against a rail. She touched her side and winced. She might have a broken rib or two.

The stench of burning flesh and chemicals brought the contents of her stomach into the back of her throat, hot and bitter.

Rao stood triumphant upon a raised metal dais standing between the opening portal and the two sacrifices. The explosion hadn't touched the area at all. Some of Rao's plan had gone sideways when half of the khâu perished in the blast. Bodies had flown. Metal crashed. The intense heat melted everything in close proximity. Lali had never witnessed such destruction before.

The portal flexed. Rao had constructed an iron pane atop where he believed the other world touched upon earth. The iron appeared to melt, but didn't run. Lines etched into the metal, as if an instant irising doorway appeared.

A head emerged, the metal stretched across the snout. The mouth opened, ingesting the iron sheet as if imbibing an iron milkshake until none remained. The nâga turned bright red, like that of the thick blood coming from an artery.

Rao stepped before the great beast, arms outstretched.

In response, the beast coiled, like a snake ready to strike, but instead reeled. Two thick legs staggered and the head waggled as if in pain. So, Rao had been correct about the metal he wore beneath the robes.

Rao shrugged off the robe and reached for the beast. He took one step and touched the nâga. A squeal further deafened Lali, as if the blast hadn't been enough.

The nâga leaped into the air. Lali glanced up. Another nâga swirled about, deep orange and a little smaller than the one just through the portal. They had similar appearances, but the smaller one's ragged appearance gave the impression it had been put through the wringer, while the bright red nâga grew in size.

Rao laughed and watched the two nâga above him. The smaller one reeled, as if confused or hurt. The two nâga were fully aware of each other, or so it appeared to Lali. Shrieks and squeals intertwined, piercing her eardrums. She glanced at Rao—he laughed, arms outstretched, facing the portal.

Lali held her side and moved for the portal. Rao couldn't handle the power. She ignored the nâga above, at least tried to, and descended the stairs toward Rao.

A shriek filled the air. Lali started and sucked in a quick breath. Directly overhead, the two nâga danced, as if two rhythmic gymnasts twirled their ribbons, one orange, one red, around one another in an intricate choreographed routine. The movements mesmerized her.

Booted feet clanking on metal drew her gaze down.

Rao stood before her. He grabbed her wrists.

"You were to remain in place." Rao's face filled with fury. His grip on her wrists was crushing her bones. She cried out in pain.

"Rao, stop. I beg—"

Rao lifted her over his head. She kicked and squirmed. Below her, she saw the slab upon which Steve and Carlos were lashed. Rao grunted and Lali fell through the air, rolling onto her back as she did so. Above, the nâga twisted.

The smaller, orange nâga broke free, retreating for the rafters. The bright red one chased after it.

Lali smacked against the slab. Her breath left her, back spasmed, and she gasped.

A gruff male voice asked, "Nasty fall. You okay?"

Lali's eyes widened as she fought for air. A deep, raspy breath caught hold, and then repeated over and over. She rolled on her side and coughed. Metallic liquid bathed her tongue. Blood drooled from her mouth, running off her chin, and puddling on the slab.

"Oh, my God," Carlos said, "the Nephilim, it's—"

Lali rolled over. Above her the bright red nâga descended toward them. Lali screamed.

Chapter 43

JASPER AND PENNY REACHED TEMPLE, BUT THE CULTISTS PRE-vented any of them from getting to the sacrificial platform.

"We can't rush through. They'll pick us off." Temple pointed at one of the Völundr's Hammer men slumped against the wall. "He's alive, but took a pretty good hit from a long gun." Temple had ripped the man's shirt and used it as a bandage for his wound. The round had taken him in the leg, luckily missing arteries, but the bandage was soaked through with red.

"I've sent three of the men off to find a way of flanking this mess. The fireball you conjured up created quite a distraction. You should be proud, but damn I thought you'd killed us all." Temple's hands rested on her hips.

"I assure you, it was unintentional on my part—I'm not a chemist or bomb maker, you know."

"Pfft. The Unabomber's got nothing on you," Temple said.

"Uh, thank you?" Jasper's forehead wrinkled. "All right then, so what's the plan?"

Squeals and shrieks erupted from above. All of them winced.

"This is going to end poorly if we don't take the bull by the horns here, the initiative. I already blew up a good number of these assholes," Jasper said.

"Unintentionally," Temple said.

"So what, let me have it, okay?" Jasper laughed. "Let's go. I'll run through first and see what happens." Jasper made for the opening and the metal-runged ladder ostensibly leading to the slab where Steve and Carlos were being held.

"I'm first. My father's up there," Penny pulled him back and went through the opening. Silence. No gunshots. Nothing. Only squealing and shrieking.

Madness. But this no longer fazed Temple, or perhaps that was the adrenaline taking over. Jasper, sturdy beyond what she had imagined, appeared energized. By all normal standards, he should have passed out from all that'd happened to him the past few days. All of them should have been dead on their feet by now.

"Come on!" Penny yelled through the doorway.

A loud thump caught Temple's attention as she went through the door.

"What was that? One of the Nephilim landing on the sacrificial slab?"

Penny climbed the ladder.

A woman screamed.

Another scream pierced the air, but from a different woman and more shrill.

Jasper hurried up the ladder after Penny, and Temple followed, almost grabbing Jasper's ankles rather than the rungs in her scramble.

She reached the top in time to see Penny standing between Steve and the waitress, Lali. Temple glanced up—Lali must have fallen. Motion above caught Temple's eye. A bright red flame shot down from the top of the building. Penny raised the hammer, pointing the head at the rapidly descending beast.

The Nephilim closed to within ten feet and Penny allowed the head of the hammer to drop and she crouched, getting under the swing, and drove her legs up and hips around. The head of the hammer whirred, a silver streak in the air, and connected with the beast, appearing to cleave the Nephilim in two. A two-toned, dissonant screech split Temple's skull. Her head felt as if it would explode if the sound level increased.

The hammer clanged against the slab and teetered on the edge, but didn't fall off. Penny collapsed, and held her arm, wincing, but moved toward her father, now groaning. Both Steve and Carlos wore only loincloths, their bodies bare and slick with oil and sweat. The large man's arms bulged and his chest was thick with striated muscle. White scars crisscrossed much of his torso. Steve could have been a Titan chained to the side of a mountain.

The red Nephilim crashed beyond the slab, a writhing mess,

flopping about. But soon it righted and coalesced back into its original form, that of a bipedal dragon-man. A beast.

"Jasper." Temple tugged his arm. "We need to free Steve and Carlos and get Penny out of here."

"The woman, Lali," Jasper said. "She's badly hurt."

"We'll get to her after we rescue the good guys, okay?"

"Yes."

"Come on!" Temple shoved him.

Jasper shook his head. "Okay. Okay."

A man stood on a metal dais above them, positioned in front of a ruined section of wall shot with lines, cracks, and raised scars—stone scars. The leader of the cult—even from this distance Temple recognized him from the photo that Mandy had sent on Jasper's smartphone.

"Ah, this is even better." The man's voice boomed with power. "More Sha 'Lu for the nâga, of which we have two here this evening. More honey for them. More power for me." He pounded his chest twice with his fist.

"I'm taking this asshole out," Temple said.

"Uh, okay—"

Temple ran for the ladder leading to the dais where the cult leader stood—

"—but you don't have any weapons, what happened to your Glock and the M4?"

Temple had no time to explain, but turned before hitting the first rung of the ladder: "Free Steve and Carlos. Get them off the platform before the Nephilim come for them."

Her words set Jasper into motion.

"Look out!" Temple ducked down at the base of the ladder.

The metal walkways and scaffolding supporting the dais Rao strutted upon moaned and creaked, and began toppling over. Rao leaped off the falling metal and slammed against the giant metal platform upon which the sacrificial slab rested. Temple closed on Rao and kicked him in the side.

Jasper turned his attention to Steve and Carlos. Both were awake—fear filled Carlos's eyes and hatred filled Steve's.

Lali's hand touched Jasper. "Get her." The waitress nodded at Penny.

A squeal and hiss hit him, followed by hot air—metallic

scented with traces of sulphur. The solidity of the platform beneath the stone slab became less certain. Steve struggled against his bindings, loosening them, but Carlos's ties remained taut. Jasper wanted to free Steve first, but—

The bright red Nephilim stood between Jasper and Steve, though the beast faced away from Jasper. Why did the creatures go for the people on the stone slab and not him? Was there something about how the sacrifices were prepared that made them more palatable to the Nephilim? Or was he less visible to them for some reason?

"Grab the hammer," Steve said, continuing his struggle against the ties. "Do it while you can."

Penny crawled for Steve, toward the Nephilim.

"No. Wait!" Jasper cried out. He slid across the platform and grabbed the hammer. The weapon weighed a ton. He jumped to his feet, dragging the hammer with him, conserving his strength for a swing at the Nephilim. Where had the other one gone? He scanned the rafters, but the thick smoke camouflaged the other, smaller Nephilim.

Penny reached the Nephilim faster than Jasper anticipated, but the creature, not fully recovered from the hammer's first blow, wobbled about—confused, as if drunk. Penny reached for Steve before the creature fully coalesced and sprang upon her father.

The older man sprang to his feet, but staggered and held his head for a moment. "The hammer," he waved for the weapon. "Now."

But the Nephilim blocked Jasper's path. He lifted the hammer—

The beast spun on him. Jasper's eyes widened and he backed away.

"No!" Penny shrieked.

Steve embraced the Nephilim from behind, wrapping his arms around the beast as best he could.

Penny turned her head away from the scene of her father engaging the Nephilim, staring at Jasper.

Shrieks shot through the air as the Nephilim's head shook back and forth, snout in the air.

Jasper stared, awestruck over Steve's bravery. His thick arms turned red as if badly burning, but Steve never faltered. If anything his size seemed to increase, if that were possible.

Penny grabbed the hammer from Jasper, and marched toward the Nephilim. "Father, release, you must!" She took up the hammer in both hands and lowered the head, allowing the weapon to drop behind her as she coiled her hips. "Release your hold, now!" Penny's torso twisted, her teeth gritted and her eyes scrunched against her sweat-drenched face.

Steve released his grip on the Nephilim, stumbled and dropped on one knee, panting.

"Get my daughter out of here," Steve pleaded.

Penny's knees bent as she twirled, and at once her knees elevated and her hips twisted, uncoiling and swinging the hammer, a silvery streak—

—the gleaming head shot up and through the Nephilim, not quite cleaving the beast in two, but severely damaging it.

Penny readied the hammer for another blow, but the Nephilim stumbled away, weakened.

Behind the Nephilim, Steve's chest heaved and his face whitened.

The hammer fell from Penny's hands, and her shoulders slumped.

The Nephilim staggered and balanced on the edge of the platform, wobbling.

Steve's arms flopped and the big man collapsed, appearing as only a shell of what he'd been just seconds before.

The Nephilim's cries ceased for the moment, and the beast reached for Penny with tendrils and arms.

Penny cried out, but Jasper pulled the struggling woman away.

A screech from above pulled the Nephilim's attention off them. The creature staggered about, confused.

Lali had reached Carlos, and for a moment, Jasper thought she might still try to kill him. But then he saw that she was trying to untie him.

Rao recovered from his fall and Temple's kick within seconds. Temple's eyes widened.

"Fool woman," Rao said, "you think a human as pitiful as you can harm Rao? You are but a gnat." He brushed himself off. What in Lord's name was the man wearing? He looked like a refugee from a 1980s metal video, like a demented Rob Halford of Judas Priest fame. She remembered laughing at those ridiculous images back then, and it was even funnier in person. Except she wasn't laughing—this was real and he was about to kick her ass.

"Well? What are you waiting for, Halford?"

A look of confusion suffused his face, but soon twisted with scorn and he closed on her with inhuman speed.

She bladed her body and feinted with a kick before delivering a backfist to the bridge of Rao's nose. Nothing. She followed up with a straight punch which he ducked. He somehow got behind her, snaking an arm across Temple's throat. Was he attempting to choke her out or use her as a shield? Temple kicked back and tried to wriggle her hands under his arm as she bit down on his arm, narrowly missing a band of metal biting into her skin. Rao edged backward, presumably toward the ladder leading to his dais.

Blood trickled down. Hers or Rao's? She had popped him good, but the blood had to be hers. She brought her heel down on his foot, but he didn't budge.

"Ah, they are coming," Rao said, his breath hot against her ear. She brought her head forward and back as hard as she could, connecting with something, hopefully the man's face, but still he did not budge, but laughed. "Watch what happens now as your friends flail about on the sacrificial slab." Rao's hold on her tightened.

Penny struggled against Jasper, and nearly got free, but he held her tight. "We can't help him now." He was sure Steve was dead although he didn't have the heart to say it out loud.

The platform shook—did thermite still burn through the metal? Or maybe whatever petrochemical fuels remained in the vat and the pipes had started to burn also, rupturing some more of the metal.

"Penny, climb down. Get off of the platform." Jasper's hold on her failed.

She dropped to her knees and scrambled over to her fallen father. Up close, he was clearly dead. His eyes were open, staring sightlessly. She pounded the metal next to him with her fist.

"There's no time." Jasper grabbed her by the arm, and pulled her away, trudging toward the ladder leading down.

"I have to help see this through," Penny insisted. But her eyes looked glazed.

Jasper turned his attention back to Lali, Carlos, and Temple, assessing where the greatest need lay. Lali was still trying to untie Carlos. For some crazy reason, Jasper felt a lot more sympathy toward the waitress than he did for Carlos himself. Jasper stared at the cult leader, Rao, made his decision, and ran for him. The man's eyes widened and he released Temple, pushing her at Jasper as he closed on them. She collided with Jasper with an *oof*, and she sagged in his arms. Rao limped, clearly favoring his left leg, and tried climbing up the ladder.

"I'm going after him, I owe him," Temple said, wiping blood from her lip with the back of her hand.

"Wait, he can't hurt us while he's up there. We need to get Carlos and Lali off the platform."

Temple's expression was furious. "The man needs a beatdown, dammit!"

"Agreed, but let's get everyone off this platform and to safety, wherever that is. Rao isn't going anywhere."

Squeals and screeches ricocheted off the metal walls. Jasper spun around and saw that the Nephilim Penny had struck with the hammer, the bright red one, stood not more than twenty feet away. And whatever Steve had done during the embrace had taken its toll on the beast. It was still formidable, but not as menacing, even with the awful ear-rending dissonance spewing out of its maw.

A deeper, guttural roar drowned out the bright red Nephilim's screeches. Jasper and Temple's heads snapped back, and they gazed at the smoke in the rafters of the building. An orange shape uncoiled in the gray smoke, and shot toward them, or maybe the other Nephilim—

"Go," a female voice said beside them.

Jasper and Temple both started. Turning, they saw Lali standing behind them. She was holding up Carlos, who now seemed only half-conscious.

She pushed him toward them. "Take Carlos. Get him out of here." Lali looked up at the platform where Rao stood, his back to them, gazing into a swirling and pulsing portal of stone.

"We can get him together," Jasper said.

Lali shook her head. "Go, before these nâga tear the entire place apart."

Jasper and Temple saw orange reflected in Lali's eyes. The woman spun and grabbed the ladder leading to the platform.

Chapter 44

CARLOS MOANED—THE CULTISTS MUST HAVE DRUGGED HIM HEAV-
ily. For a second, Jasper wondered if any more Câ Tsang roamed
about. The strange absence of the cultists bothered Jasper. Where
had they all gone? Had they succumbed to fear of the Nephilim
or the actions of Völundr's Hammer folks and fled? He had no
idea. Only Rao and Lali remained, as far as he could tell.

Jasper dragged Carlos toward the ladder, but made Temple
descend first. Jasper stooped, grabbed Carlos in a fireman's carry,
and started down the ladder.

The bright red Nephilim came toward them but suddenly
stopped, reaching with tendrils and arms up above.

Jasper glanced up. The orange Nephilim plummeted like a
meteor from the rafters, the creature's rear quarters a wispy,
orange contrail in its wake.

Jasper hurried his descent, feet slipping on the slick rungs.
At the bottom, he eased Carlos off his shoulder, and collapsed.
He took deep breaths and rested his back against the wall for a
moment. Sweat stung his eyes.

"We need to get out of here." He glanced at Penny and Carlos.
Carlos's drugged state didn't help matters, and Penny, despite her
ruggedness, seemed to be in shock.

But a glance at Temple, combined with the way he felt right
now, made him doubt they'd be any use helping Carlos and
Penny out of the building.

The wall Jasper rested against shook.

"We have to try."

Temple touched Penny's shoulder. Her blank face and dead

eyes at were at odds with her heaving chest. A tear fell from one of her eyes, carving a trail down her dirtied cheek. Her chin wrinkled and lips quivered. The loss of her father seemed to have paralyzed her.

Carlos wasn't any better. He resembled a marionette with cut strings sitting against a wall.

Footsteps cut through the racket taking place on the platform. Jasper glanced about for a weapon. Nothing.

"Where are all the guns?" He asked Temple.

"The Völundr's Hammer men—they had a need—they had our back while we screwed around up there." Temple's smile was weak.

Three men burst into the area—three of the Völundr's Hammer men. The man who'd been with Jasper earlier, Ian, was with them.

"Ian," Jasper said. "Will you please assist with Penny? She's in shock."

"Where is Steve?" Ian asked, and the other two men stepped forward, their faces heavy with concern.

Jasper shook his head. "He's dead. We have to get out of here. Quick. I'm afraid we'll be trapped in here, or worse—" He glanced up to where the Nephilim were struggling with one another. He wondered what Lali was up to, how she was going to deal with Rao.

"All of you have to leave before the police get here," Jasper said. "I bet they're on their way by now." Had to be, more than thirty minutes had passed since he texted Pete to bring in the cavalry.

"Take Carlos too," Temple directed the two other men. Ian pulled Penny up and supported her weight, forcing her to put one foot in front of the other. The other two men got Carlos up, propped him up between them and dragged him off.

Temple hit the ladder, and got about halfway up before Jasper grabbed her leg. "No, don't."

She looked down. "But what if Lali isn't successful in resolving this?—and I'm not about to trust her. This all has to end tonight."

"But how are we going to be sure of anything?" Jasper sighed.

"Hey, at least we'll have a ringside seat for Armageddon."

"That's kind of melodramatic, don't you think?"

Temple stared at him.

"Fine," he said. "Let's get up there—maybe you can wield the hammer."

✧　　　✧　　　✧

A crack bisected the giant stone slab. Jasper realized the metal platform supporting the slab from beneath must have been weakened.

The two Nephilim fought about twenty feet above the platform, an orange and red writhing mess. Now they appeared as two giant snakes twisting about in a body of water.

Jasper and Temple stared straight up at the beasts as they twisted and jockeying for the kill, mesmerized.

Lali shouted something unintelligible.

Jasper shook from his reverie. "We have to move."

"Right." Temple ran for the ladder leading up one more level to Rao, where Lali stood at the base.

Jasper started after her, but a gleam caught his eye—Steve's hammer. He glanced between the fighting Nephilim above, the hammer, and the ladder Temple raced for.

He chose to go after the hammer, diving for the weapon teetering on the edge of the compromised platform.

"Jasper!"

He rolled over on his back in time to see Temple's face twisted with concern. What had happened? Jasper looked up. The two Nephilim spun in the air in a flat spin just above him. The two forms appeared welded together. The two large creatures maybe twelve feet tall were whirling about—and their fall would end near to him, or right on top of him.

His fingers closed around the hammer. He scrambled for the extreme edge of the platform, taking him as far away from the center as possible, but also as far away as possible from where Temple and Lali stood.

The Nephilim's crash split the platform in two, the weakened halves sinking in the middle. Steve's body slid and fell through the crack. Jasper winced.

The hammer dropped from Jasper's grasp, hitting the floor beneath the platform with a clang. Jasper threw his arms out for balance, and teetered on the edge, but balanced himself, at least for the time being. His eyes locked on Temple's. She nodded. Lali began climbing up the platform's ladder where Rao stood.

Rao was watching the Nephilim. He hadn't seen Lali and Temple. Good. Hopefully he'd remain distracted by the colossal struggle.

Behind Rao, the stone wall—well, another free-floating wall, a false wall—appeared like the one at the Euclid. Rao used the wall as an artificial barrier to the other world, what Ed White and Vance and the other physicist, Greg, called brane cosmology. Funny how the unimportant piece of information, the thing unable to save you at the moment, popped into one's mind. The stone wall shifted and pulsed and for a moment, Jasper caught a glimpse of another world—odd hues and strange swelling landscapes. He blinked a few times—at this distance, the shapes could have been anything. An alien forest or field, a city, or a wasteland even—or maybe just cloud tops.

Lali reached the top of the platform. Rao's eyes widened when he spotted her. Apparently, he hadn't expected her to still be alive.

Temple crept up the ladder, but remained below the lip, out of sight.

The Nephilim writhed before Jasper's eyes. The bright red one broke free from the orange, visibly shaken, visibly hurt. The orange Nephilim appeared trapped in the split platform, and struggled to free itself. Jasper couldn't grasp how these creatures functioned on earth, in this atmosphere. What was their world like? How did these things change their shapes and fly and—

Jasper turned his attention back on the platform: Rao's hands wrapped around Lali's neck, forcing her down on her knees as if she were nothing. The man was powerful, unnaturally so.

"Temple, don't climb any more!" Jasper shouted across the platform.

The bright red Nephilim shot toward Rao and Lali. Rao backed away, shoving Lali forward.

"For you, the greatest of the nâga!" Rao shouted, arms spread wide.

The beast landed atop the metal dais.

Temple dropped from the ladder, back to the bottom.

Rao stepped to the side. The Nephilim had a clear path to Lali and the portal leading back to its own universe.

In front of Jasper, the orange Nephilim fought for freedom from the metal crack, the platform acted like a giant pair of scissors attempting to cut the alien in half. The alien's body shifted, becoming less substantial for a second—then the metal immediately surrounding the alien liquefied and the beast shot into the air. There was an orange trail where the Nephilim's legs should have been, like a genie coming out of a bottle, the bottom still mist or smoke.

The orange Nephilim growled, and the sound shook the building.

The red Nephilim craned its neck, peering back up at its adversary. It made a squealing noise, its tendrils extended from the snout, waving.

Lali scrambled for Rao. He sneered at the woman, but she got on her feet and swung at him, connecting over and over, but he only laughed. He shoved her aside and stepped before the stony membrane, which was pulsing and stretching, as if the other world was attempting a breach, attempting to become a part of earth, and this universe.

The orange Nephilim coiled up and sprung before Jasper could think about what was happening, or what would happen.

Rao opened his mouth, words spilled out: "And now for glory. Glory and power!" He stretched his arms out to the side, wide open.

The orange Nephilim crashed into the red one.

Lali flung herself at Rao, knocking him into the path of both Nephilim.

The four bodies—the two Nephilim, Rao, and Lali—all slammed into the membrane as one. The stone bulged and stretched forward into the room, contracted, and fell into the other world. Lali's face poked from the membrane, her mouth wide but uttering no scream; her face sucked into the membrane. Part of Rao stretched from the elastic material, followed by orange and red tendrils and limbs.

The swirls and scars on the stone solidified and the building quieted.

Eerie quiet.

Soon though, trickling water or petrochemicals along with creaking and groaning metal reached Temple's ears. She wondered if her hearing might be permanently damaged.

"Hear that?" Jasper asked.

"What?"

"Sirens. I hope the Völundr's Hammer people got out of here."

"Yeah, but what are we going to do about all the dead Câ Tsang here? Won't it be obvious some of them were shot?"

Temple glanced about for an easy way off the platform. They could either slide down to where the orange Nephilim had been stuck, or hang off the side where Jasper was and drop.

Jasper shrugged. "Figure that out once we're down from here. Plus, we've got to get Steve's body out of here."

"What? Why?" Temple grimaced slightly. For the two of them to haul the big man's corpse outside was going to be a real effort.

"He's one of us."

"No, he isn't."

"Look, I'm a Marine. We don't leave anyone behind, even the dead. As long as the building doesn't come down on us, we're taking him out."

"If you say so." Temple studied the situation for a moment and opted for the drop—she had no desire to touch where the Nephilim had been stuck between two pieces of metal.

Jasper, however, didn't drop down, but instead climbed the ladder to the dais where the Nephilim, Lali, and the cult leader, Rao had been seconds earlier.

"Get down here, we need to get outside before the police arrive!" Temple sniffed. She had seen pipes running from the vats, but the scent of gasoline or some kind of petrochemical threatened to overpower her. A weak sizzle cut through the high-pitched whir still present in her ears.

"This is incredible," Jasper said from his position on the dais. "You ought to see this."

"Jasper, we need to get out of here, I have a feeling the destruction isn't over."

"What do you mean?"

"Fuel—unexpended fuel. And I think the thermite is still sizzling and if it reaches any fumes inside pipes not affected by the other explosions and fires, well—"

"You had me at 'unexpended fuel.'" Jasper slid down the ladder and dropped from the platform.

They found Steve and began carrying him out. Before long, though, they were mostly dragging his corpse.

Thermite burned indeed—seared flesh and acrid smoke gagged Jasper, and Temple coughed. Stone basins smoldered, containing apile of ash remains. Apparently the Câ Tsang survivors had committed suicide. Jasper wondered if Rao had ordered them to do so when the fight went south on the cultists.

Fresh air guided them toward an exit of opportunity where some of the falling metal scaffolding had torn a gash in the building's metal siding.

Sirens grew louder and louder—apparently the police were having trouble getting to the petrochemical plant. The blanketing fog thinned and lifted its veil, as if exposing the horrid face of the building behind Jasper and Temple. She didn't want to think about how close they'd come to dying at the hands of the cult—or, worse, the Nephilim. Lali called them nâga—perhaps Vance would understand the reference. Temple sure as hell didn't. Poor Vance, in the hospital, but hopefully pulling through.

Jasper turned to her. "Wow. No offense, but you look like you've just been kicked around by a demon-worshipping cult. Something right out of Revelations."

"Ha ha ha."

Deep bruises covered half of Jasper's face. She was pretty sure she didn't look much better. Bruises ringed her wrists and forearms, as if she had been gripped by a gorilla. Blood caked the corners of her mouth and a faint trail running from her nose had dried. Her nose felt swollen. It might be broken.

Temple shook her head. "All right, so the Vin Diesel–looking bastard put me through the wringer. Like you'd have done any better. You should be thanking me." She looked him up and down. "I thought you were pink before—but now you look like a hot dog that's been on the grill a bit too long."

They walked away from the building, dragging Steve toward the sounds and lights of the sirens.

Chapter 45

THE EAST CHICAGO POLICE ARRIVED IN FORCE, COMING UPON Jasper and Temple about one hundred yards from the smoldering and unstable petrochemical plant. Two unmarked cars behind the row of obvious police vehicles stood out.

Bucars. *Shit.*

Pete Hernandez reached Jasper and Temple first, with two other ECPD officers coming with him.

"Jasper, quick," the older cop said, "what happened—"

"—are there any *bodies* in there—"

"—you okay—"

"The man we're dragging is named Steve," Jasper said. "He died during the incident."

Pete nodded gravely and had Steve taken away by the two cops.

Jasper hurriedly relayed as much as he could before ASAC Masters and SSA Johnson got to him. Luckily, a mass of police blocked their approach quite well, but they pushed past people. The expressions on their faces were concern mixed with anger on Johnson's—mostly concern, being fair to the man—and unalloyed anger on Master's.

"The dead man was Steve Stahlberg, owner of Wayland Precision. He was abducted by those bastards. He died saving his daughter and another one of his people, Carlos, also an abductee."

"Our source," Pete said. "All right, here's the explanation: a kidnapping investigation worked jointly with East Chicago Police with possible human trafficking and drugs and a freak industrial accident." Pete took a deep breath after spitting out the interesting variation on the true events.

"You summed up the evening perfectly." Jasper started to grin, but the action hurt his face.

"You two look horrible," Pete said.

Silence.

Pete coughed. "What a mess—you're lucky you walked out—"

"Special Agent Wilde!" ASAC Masters pushed through and stood face to face with Jasper, but didn't say anything.

Jasper shot him a look.

Masters flushed. "What in the hell happened here and how can you explain your actions of the past few days? Agent Ravel is in the hospital, he's going to make it, but what in the hell were you thinking? And you, Agent Black..."

"That's Supervisory Special Agent Black," Temple responded forcefully. She pursed her lips, obviously ready for a fight if Masters wanted it.

Masters looked away from her and took a deep breath. Behind him, SSA Johnson grimaced.

Pete stepped between Jasper and his bosses. "Both of your agents need medical attention—"

"I'm—" Jasper started.

"You're in no condition for an inquisition right now, and neither is your partner," Pete said, very firmly.

Masters pointed to the building. "Does the building need clearing by SWAT or Hazmat? The special agent bomb techs?"

"There was a thermite reaction that got into some of the petrochemicals—there were also some gunshots and some deaths, I'm afraid." Jasper looked down at the ground.

"This is a disaster." Masters looked up at the sky.

"Yeah, it is," Temple stepped forward and got in the man's face. "People died. There were victims. We did the best we could. But yeah, it's a disaster—for them. But I know that you're really worried about whether it's a disaster for your career."

Masters took a step back. "No. That's not what I—"

Pete held up his hands. "Enough. This was a joint investigation culminating in the apprehension of the people perpetrating heinous acts after kidnapping innocents. Now I'm taking these agents to the hospital."

Masters stormed off, Johnson trailing after him.

"So," Pete said, once they were out of ear shot, "that was Masters and Johnson, eh?"

"Great pair, huh?"

"Well, they can go eff themselves," Pete said.

Jasper bent over and laughed so hard he thought he might retch. Temple's laugh, something he'd hardly heard since she'd arrived in Indiana was infectious and endearing.

Pete's was nonplussed. "What? Was that really so funny?"

"I am in so much trouble," Jasper said.

Chapter 46

THE EVENT, AS JASPER TOOK TO CALLING THE WEEK OF TEMPLE and Vance and cults and aliens/monsters/demons/take-your-pick, had occurred two months ago. The oppressive heat of summer gave way to a welcoming, comfortable fall. He'd been pulled back from the Scientific Anomalies Group by his field office's Special Agent in Charge and forced to work applicant matters.

"I was surprised when your name popped up on my cell phone this morning." Jasper stood and greeted Temple and Vance as they walked into the bar and strolled up to the table where he, Ed White, and Pete Hernandez sat sipping libations of varying stripes.

Ed jumped out of his chair and smiled broadly at Temple. "Looking fine, lady." She gave Ed a hug that seemed quite enthusiastic.

"All right, Billy Dee," Jasper said. "Give her a chance to ease into this, for crying out loud."

Temple laughed. "Still making stupid jokes, I see."

"Am I missing something here?" Pete asked.

Jasper shook his head. "Nothing important, Pete. I believe everyone here knows everyone else, so let's get down to the drinking and gossiping."

More drinks were sloshed on the table. Even Vance partook, sipping on a light beer. The little man had mostly recovered from his wounds, but favored his left side. The Nephilim hitting him really did a number on him. Jasper clenched his right hand, aching still from when he'd touched what he now believed was the edge of an alien world back at the Euclid Hotel.

355

Temple scanned the group. "You all don't look any worse for wear. We've been through a lot. How is Penny?"

Jasper blew out a long breath. "She's a mess. Steve's funeral—well, it was melancholy." Jasper studied the beer in front of him, the bubbles ascending within the pilsner glass. "I try getting together with her once in a while, but she spends almost all of her time over at Wayland Precision."

"Sorry to hear she's still torn up. Give her time," Temple said. "Anything else?"

Jasper chuckled. "Oh, yeah." He pulled a piece of paper from his jacket pocket and smoothed it out on the table.

"What's that?" Temple arched an eyebrow.

"My OPR adjudication paperwork."

"What's OPR?" Ed asked.

"Office of Professional Responsibility," Temple said. "Those jackasses ended up OPR'ing you, after all?"

"Yep. Here, I'll give you the highlights," Jasper cleared his throat. "Employee willfully disobeyed his supervisor and Assistant Special Agent in Charge, utilized resources, both FBI, state, and local during the course of an unauthorized investigation where he acted as a rogue agent."

"Whaaat?" Temple's eyes were wide.

"Yeah," Jasper said. "In mitigation, employee was under severe emotional distress from his recent divorce."

"But the divorce is so last year," Pete said. Everyone laughed.

Jasper took a deep breath. "In further mitigation, the employee saved lives and prevented further kidnappings." He grinned. "Now we get to the fun part. In aggravation, employee showed no remorse for his actions, circumvented FBI procedures, and caused damage to private property. Penalty: thirty-day suspension."

Vance whistled. "They didn't ding you on my hospitalization, at least."

"Oh, you're in here, but lumped in with the 'not following FBI procedures' part."

Temple shook head and took a sip of her beer.

"All right, so enough about me," Jasper said. "What brings you two out here? Following up on the event?"

"We were pretty much told by your Special Agent in Charge to get out of Indiana." Temple shrugged. "But I wanted to come here personally to discuss an important matter with you."

"Here?" Jasper spread his arms. "And with this sort of company?" His spread arms allowed him to pat both Pete and Ed on their backs.

"This'll work. I have a proposition for you—"

"No more Nephilim or brane worlds or whatever the hell we dealt with." Jasper took a sip of beer and wiped his mouth with the back of his hand. "No way."

"What a shame," Temple said. "Because I have orders here, if you choose to accept them—"

"How Mission Impossible of you—"

"Oh, shut up with the pop culture quotes for once and listen!" Temple smiled. "There is a spot for you with the Scientific Anomalies Group, if you like. I've talked my boss into funding another slot based on the anomalies we discovered in this area."

Jasper stared at her. "Wow. Okay, I wasn't expecting that."

"The job's a fourteen slot," Temple added.

"What's a fourteen slot?" Ed asked.

"Supervisory Special Agent slot, but this is the best kind—he gets supervisor pay without having to supervise. It's an FBI head-quarters–funded slot but one which allows him the freedom of continuing in an investigative capacity—but no more straight-up gang, drugs, or violent crime work."

"You need to take this job offer," Pete said forcefully. "You can't do what I did for twenty more years—it'll make you a zombie."

"Anyway, what about my management here in Indiana?" Jasper asked.

"My boss spoke with Masters and Johnson," Temple said, grinning, "and I know this will be hard to believe, but they're happy." She pursed her lips. "No, I take that back, they're ecstatic to be getting rid of you."

"They already know and they think they're getting rid of me? What made you so sure I would accept?" Jasper sat back in his chair.

Temple cocked her head.

"Fine. Looks like I'm gonna be part of the Scientific Anomalies Group. I assume we'll be based in DC, so when do I need to move?"

Temple shook her head. "No, we're all moving out here. Well, me and Vance, anyway. Speaking of whom, he's decided to step out of agent work due in part to his injuries."

Vance raised his beer bottle by way of acknowledgment. "But I'll be on the books as an Intelligence Analyst—more of a scientist, really, but we couldn't finagle that sort of slot for the group."

His change of status meant a slight cut in pay, but Jasper figured the man would probably be happier in his new job, given his interests and temperament.

"I've got a couple of other agents in SAG who'll stay behind in Washington," Temple continued. "They can shuffle around the paperwork well enough."

"You don't want them out here? Not even one of them?"

Temple got a slightly sour look on her face. "The reason the two of them got assigned to me is because both of them retired on the job quite a while ago. They aren't much good for anything besides pencil-pushing."

Jasper nodded. He knew the type. "Out of curiosity, why base ourselves in Chicago?"

"Chicago area, I should have said," Temple replied. "We'll have to figure out where the best place would be to set ourselves. It might well be here in northwest Indiana. That'll be your first assignment, in fact—find us a good HQ. As for the rest of your question, which I won't come right out and label as 'silly' although..."

Jasper grinned. "Yeah, I got it. This is the one place in the country where we *know* there are no-fooling scientific anomalies which could pose a threat to national security. Plus, we now have a pretty solid liaison with a civilian outfit that knows a lot about the danger, the Völundr's Hammer people."

"How solid it is, really?" Temple asked.

"Pretty damn solid, I think. I've spent a fair amount of time over there, getting to know them better. And, of course, it helps a lot that we have the bond of having fought the Nephilim and the Câ Tsang together."

"Good. I think we're going to find that liaison quite valuable." Temple nodded at Ed, sitting next to her. "The other big advantage of being situated here in Chicago is that we've already begun assembling a top-flight group of expert consultants."

Ed grinned. "Top-flight. I like that."

Temple brought her attention back to Jasper. "Can you report in a month?"

"Month? How about two weeks, the beginning of the next pay period?"

"Good. Accepting these orders officially makes you my—"

"Your what?" Jasper tried suppressing a smile, with only minimal success.

"Bitch," Ed White said, "of course."

"Ed." Temple waggled her finger at him. "Makes Jasper my responsibility." She snorted; another thing Jasper had never witnessed her do. "Oh who am I kidding? I'm sorry, Lord," she glanced at the ceiling, and back at Jasper—"yeah, Wilde, you're my bitch now."

Epilogue

AT FIRST, LALI COULDN'T SEE ANYTHING—OR RATHER, SHE COULDN'T *interpret what she was seeing. The new universe she'd entered was just too different from her own.*

Her first clear sensation was that she was floating in...something. There was no ground beneath her feet. In fact, looking down, she saw—or could not interpret what she saw—the same...whatever it was. A void, except it was filled with swelling and swirling currents.

Currents, though, which seemed to have no effect on her. And what was she floating in? It was neither water nor air.

For a few seconds, a terror of suffocating seized her. She wasn't breathing! But then she realized that didn't seemed to be bothering her.

How long had she been here? She had a sense that quite a bit of time had gone by compared to its passage in the universe she'd come from. She had no idea why she thought that, but she did.

So what—?

A mighty surge suddenly flung her forward. A moment later, she emerged from the formless existence into clarity.

And immediately wished she hadn't. Right in front of her—how far away? she had no idea how to gauge distance but she knew it was close—two hideous things were locked in a struggle. It took her a while to recognize them as the same nâgas *who'd been fighting in the petrochemical plant.*

They looked completely different. These were not dragons; their appearance was not even close to that of dragons. Instead, they looked like horrible gigantic insects with far too many limbs. Squat centipedes with huge mandibles.

Then, to the side, she spotted Rao. The cult leader seemed completely oblivious to the struggle of the nâgas taking place... very near to him, so far as Lali could gauge distance. Instead, he was gazing with ecstasy and wonder at a sight much farther away, his arms and legs spread wide as if he wanted to embrace the vision.

Which was...

More hideous, even, than the nâgas. Far in the distance—Lali had no idea how far but she sensed that the thing was at the limit of perception—there heaved and roiled a creature that was vast and mighty beyond her comprehension—and filled with rage. As if a multicolored amoeba the size of a star was both intelligent and furious.

Furious at what or whom? She had no idea—and didn't want to find out. She just wanted to flee the thing.

Suddenly, the battle between the two nâgas—she knew their names, somehow—called Samyaza and Armaros came to an end in a ghastly manner. The larger monster did something with the many legs it had buried in Armaros that caused the smaller one to burst into several pieces. But the effort caused Samyaza's own body to collapse inward, as if it were a deflated balloon.

Both Nephilim shrieked. In its agony, Samyaza lashed out with its hind limbs, which seemed to be relatively intact. Three of them struck Rao, ripping his own body into shreds. He had no time to scream. One moment he existed; the next, he did not.

Lali felt no grief or sorrow for his passing. Even if she had, she wouldn't have had time to think about it, because a piece of Armaros was coming right at her—the piece which had the mandibles and what she thought might be eyes.

Frantically, she tried to evade the horror, but she had no sense of how to move in this universe she was in, so she just floundered and thrashed about.

The Armaros piece swept by her. One of the mandibles pierced her in the torso, just below her ribcage.

Deeply, deeply. The agony was indescribable. Yet, bizarrely, knowledge surged into her as well. By the time Armaros passed away, the mandible withdrawing from her body, she knew many things she had not known. She understood almost none of it, though. It was not the sort of organized and coherent knowledge passed along by a teacher; it was more as if someone had just filled her with disorganized and incoherent data.

As soon as the mandible tip left her body, the torment ceased. Looking down, terrified at what she would see, but the wound was already closing up. She felt a vast sigh of relief.

A very short one. Three more nâgas *were coming toward her—racing toward her. These were much, much smaller than either Samyaza or Armaros, however. And they seemed in some indefinable way to be... undefined themselves.*

A sliver of the new knowledge took form and substance; became clear.

These were passagers. Akin to children in that they were newly come into existence, small, and still taking shape. They were spewed into existence by the gigantic, roiling monster at the horizon. One or another grown Nephilim would take charge of some of them, not to nurture them in any way, but in the hopes they might shape them in a manner that would prove useful.

These three had been among Armaros' crèche. Loosed, now, both from Armaros' rule as well as Armaros' knowledge. They were half-mindless; filled with appetites and desires but knowing little or nothing of the attendant dangers.

Two of them began fighting with each other. They were trying to place themselves...

They wanted her, *she suddenly realized. For what purpose? She had no idea—and didn't want to find out.*

The third and smallest of the passagers passed by its two companions—no, not that, for these creatures had no companions; they spent their entire existence in spiritual solitude—and came swarming down upon her, its multiple limbs spread wide to grasp her.

Grasp her it did; she had no way to move, no way to save herself.

TAKE ME TO THE HELL WORLD! The creature's thought passed into Lali's brain in a manner she didn't understand, but the meaning was clear enough.

TAKE ME! TAKE ME NOW!

She realized that the monster hadn't simply seized her, but was now plunging at what seemed an incredible speed toward a brilliantly colored fissure below them. At least, she thought it was below them.

Looking behind, she saw that the two larger passagers had broken off their struggle and were now racing after Lali and her captor.

They would not arrive in time. An instant late, Lali was deep into the fissure.

All she could see clearly was color—in this case, a violent crimson.

GIVE ME A NAME, LORRAINE! shrieked the passager. GIVE ME A GENDER! I WOULD BE MIGHTY, MIGHTY!

She had no idea what it was talking about. What was a "Lorraine"? And how could it—much less she herself—give such a creature a gender as well as a name?

Her ignorance seemed to penetrate the passager like a spear. NO, NO! it shrieked.

An instant later, the thing started coming apart. Its mandibles flew off; its limbs flew off; what might have been its eyes collapsed; not long afterward, its whole body started disintegrating.

But Lali was paying no attention to that. She knew she was plunging down into . . . something. But what was it? And was it dangerous?

A terrible impact answered that question. She lost all sense and consciousness.

A jagged line, like a lightning bolt, remained etched in Lali's mind. No. More like a permanent shadow across her vision. A scar. Her side ached, as did her entire body for that matter. She smacked her lips and licked them. The odor emanating from her mouth almost overwhelmed her, as if she'd eaten rotten meat with a lingering metallic aftertaste, not quite blood, though—

Her eyes opened. She hadn't even realized they were closed. The scar across her vision remained. She still couldn't see anything.

Hot. So very hot. She sucked in a deep breath.

"Hey."

She snapped her attention to the sound of the voice. Not Rao's. No. He'd been torn apart right in front of her. She shivered despite the heat emanating off her. She hugged herself, and discovered bare skin.

"Hey, what you doin' here?" a young man's voice asked. Not anyone she knew.

Lali stood and glanced around, blinking rapidly and taking in the environment. A haze surrounded her, but that was likely her vision attempting to adapt back to her own universe, and not that crazy place she'd been swept into with Rao, the hell universe; the nâga universe.

The haze cleared rapidly. Her back was near to a wall covered in peeling wallpaper that had once been white with tiny green designs, flowers perhaps, but the white had long turned yellow and brown. Her bare feet pressed against threadbare carpet, gray, or perhaps simply dirt and ash coated, gritty against her skin.

"How you get in here, anyway?" the same voice asked.

She focused in the direction of the voice and saw a young black man wearing a wifebeater and displaying muscular arms. He wasn't more than average in size, but toned and sinewy. He was leering at her, as if he hadn't noticed she wore no clothing until that moment.

She glanced beyond him and saw that the only apparent exit was a door against the far wall that had several locks and bolts on it. Clearly, the young fellow wanted no chance of being surprised by anyone breaking in quickly.

The table he'd been sitting at was littered with paper, plastic bags, a scale, and two stacks of money. The stacks weren't all that thick, but if those bills were any sort of larger denominations— even just twenties—they represented quite a bit of money.

Maybe this was a drug house. Hopefully not a meth lab, though. She'd been in one of those once and had only wanted to get out of there before the entire place went up in a fiery ball of death.

She laughed. Why? She had no idea. Nothing around her seemed the least amusing.

"What's so funny, bitch?" the man asked.

"You wouldn't understand." She coughed, and the man took a quick step back as if she might have the plague.

Maybe she did. For all she knew she had caught something while in the nightmare world.

"I can't explain. You wouldn't understand," she repeated. More coughs came, and a metallic taste flooded her mouth.

She laughed again, this time a deep and throaty laugh. She swallowed the metallic substances coating her tongue and the entire inside of her mouth.

"Here, let me help you," he said. But it was obvious from his expression what sort of help he had in mind.

"No, thanks," Lali said. "If you would kindly allow me to leave, you'll never see me again."

"Oh, hell no. I've seen enough of you to put me in the mood for getting to know you a whole lot better."

The young man—he was barely more than a boy—took confident, aggressive strides toward her. As he closed the distance,

Lali covered herself as best as she could with her arms, conscious of her naked body and the leering look. She glanced about for a weapon, but where she stood now there was nothing for her. No window to break, no lamp, nothing to grab. Not even an ashtray or glass or bottle.

"Please, let me go. I've been through a lot and I'm not in the mood."

"Oh, you will be," the man said. "I'll see to that."

He clasped his fingers around one of her arms, a solid grip like a vise clamping down on her. He pulled her close to him, but Lali's strength returned and she pushed the man's chest with her free hand. He frowned and his eyes squinted, pulling his cheeks up as his forehead wrinkled—pain. She wasn't sure if she'd hurt the man, but she'd certainly surprised him.

"You're a tough little bitch, aren't you?" He yanked her into him and embraced her. Her breasts pressed into the man's chest and his hands lowered to her bare bottom, squeezing. "You're on fire," the man said.

She squirmed and wriggled. Heat flowed through her and the metallic taste returned, resting on her tongue. The scar across her vision returned as well, blinding her. But she and her would-be assailant were pressed so closely together that she really didn't need to see. The man had left her arms free during the embrace. Lali reached behind her back, grabbed the man's wrists and pulled the man's hands away.

It wasn't any harder than removing a child's grip. Pushing him away from her completely was also no harder than pushing away a child. The man stumbled back, ran into one of the chairs at the table, and fell back into it.

"What the hell—" The man's voice was shaky. "You some kind of weirdo female body builder?"

"Something like that," she said, wondering at the answer herself. "Now just open that door and I'll be on my way."

"Fuck that," he said. "I want pussy and I'm gonna get it."

He snatched something from the cluttered table that she hadn't noticed before. Now he had a gun in his hand; some kind of pistol.

"I'm done playin' wit' you." He rose from the chair and pointed the pistol at her. "Just do like I tell you."

The metallic taste flooded her mouth again and heat washed over her entire body. She'd had enough of this insignificant beast.

She'd just break the damn door down. She was quite sure she had the strength to do it.

She headed for the door. "Stop, bitch!" he shouted.

She ignored him.

A loud crack filled the room. He'd fired the gun, she realized. Into the couch against the wall. She could see where it had punctured one of the seats, It was just a warning shot.

For the first time, she got really angry. She turned to face the young man and took a couple of steps toward him.

"Don't come no closer!" His voice was high-pitched and the gun shook in his hand. Another loud crack filled the room.

That shot had been fired by accident. But she saw the look of determination that now crossed his face and realized that he was going to shoot again, and this time he would be trying to kill her. Partly driven by fury, partly by fear—as much as anything, by the fact that he couldn't be more than nineteen or twenty years old.

She lunged toward him. Her best hope was to knock him down. She extended both hands to do that.

Too late. He had the gun aimed and was about to pull the trigger.

Bright orange plumes with streaks of blue shot from her palms. They slammed into the man's head. The plume coming from her left hand was off a bit—not that she'd been *trying* to aim it—and blasted the skin and hair off the right side of the man's face. It removed his ear, too.

But the one coming from her right hand struck him squarely in the face. It disintegrated most of his features—everything below the eyebrows and above the chin—and then bored a hole through the rest of his skull before exiting through the bone and spraying the ruins of his head against the wall behind.

The man—just a corpse, now—dropped to his knees. His hand released the gun which clanked on the wood. A second later he fell forward on what was left of his face amidst a pool of deep red blood.

Lali examined her hands, and noticed she no longer wore any of the rings she'd taken to the other world. Thankfully, though, her hands were unharmed. She touched her ears, and discovered the earrings had vanished as well.

The heat in her subsided, and the scar that had marred her vision faded, though she could sense it remained in the background.

"Well, that's interesting," she said.

Glossary

AD—Assistant Director, a top position in the FBI and the head of FBI Headquarters Divisions such as Cyber, Counterterrorism, Counterintelligence, Criminal. Assistant Directors in the field are known as ADICs (Assistant Director in Charge) and head up the Bureau's largest field offices: Washington Field Office, New York, and Los Angeles.

AOR—Area of responsibility. Field offices have specific regions they cover and are often quite territorial, especially with headquarters elements.

ASAC—Assistant Special Agent in Charge. ASACs report directly to the SAC, the Special Agent in Charge of a field office.

Baby Glock—smaller, more concealable, but smaller capacity versions of the Bureau-issued Glock service weapons carried by agents. As of this writing, most agents who carry the baby Glock carry the .40 caliber Glock 27, the smaller version of the .40 caliber Glock 22 and Glock 23.

Bucar, buride, busteed, or g-ride—slang terms for an agent's assigned Bureau vehicle.

CHS—Confidential Human Source. The FBI's version of informant or asset.

CIRG—Critical Incident Response Group. An FBI Headquarters Division responsible for providing expertise in crisis management.

ERT—Evidence Response Team. Highly trained and equipped teams ensuring evidence is collected and preserved for use in investigations and the court room. ERT is responsible for crime scene processing.

FBIHQ—FBI Headquarters is located in Washington, D.C. at the Hoover Building on Pennsylvania Avenue. Headquarters elements are located not only in D.C., but across the country.

IA—Intelligence Analyst. At the squad level, IAs analyze information, provide judgments and make recommendations to mitigate and exploit threats.

OPR—Office of Professional Responsibility. The FBI's disciplinary system, responsible for identifying and investigating internal misconduct.

SAG—Scientific Anomalies Group. A special project currently under CIRG, and specifically reports to the Assistant Director of CIRG.

SA—Special Agent.

SAC—Special Agent in Charge. The SAC is the leader of a field office. The only exceptions are Washington Field Office, New York, and Los Angeles where there is an Assistant Director in Charge (ADIC).

SOS—Staff Operations Specialist. Provides Special Agents and Intelligence Analysts direct support on case management and tactical intelligence products.

SSA—Supervisory Special Agent. An agent in charge of a squad of Special Agents. A typical squad may number anywhere from six to twelve agents.

CULT TERMINOLOGY

bjang—the honey extracted by the nâga or Nephilim from their sacrifice or prey.

Câ Tsang—also known as the Iron Thorn, a cultish offshoot of the ancient animistic/shamanistic Bon religion of Bhutan.

gä—to touch or cross over to the nâgas'/Nephilims' universe.

khäp—the rank of adept in the Câ Tsang.

khâu—the rank of acolyte in the Câ Tsang, also known as sticks.

nâga—the creatures of the other universe, also known as Nephilim, creatures described as half-dragon, half-man.

Rao—leader of the Câ Tsang, also known as the Tip of the Horn and the First to Glory.

Sha 'Lu—those who are sacrificed to the nâga/Nephilim.